For the Winner

Also by Emily Hauser

FOR THE MOST BEAUTIFUL

For more information on Emily Hauser and her books,
see her website at www.emilyhauser.com

For the Winner

Emily Hauser

Doubleday

LONDON · TORONTO · SYDNEY · AUCKLAND · JOHANNESBURG

TRANSWORLD PUBLISHERS
61–63 Uxbridge Road, London W5 5SA
www.penguin.co.uk

Transworld is part of the Penguin Random House group of companies
whose addresses can be found at global.penguinrandomhouse.com

Penguin
Random House
UK

First published in Great Britain in 2017 by Doubleday
an imprint of Transworld Publishers

ISBNs 9780857523174 (cased)
9780857523181 (tpb)

Typeset in 11/14.5pt Adobe Caslon by Falcon Oast Graphic Art Ltd.
Printed and bound by Clays Ltd, Bungay, Suffolk.

Penguin Random House is committed to a sustainable
future for our business, our readers and our planet. This book
is made from Forest Stewardship Council® certified paper.

For my parents
and for Oliver, always

Contents

Acknowledgements   ix
Map   xi
Prologue   1

PART I: GREECE
The Hunt   7
To the City   23
Loved by the Gods   49
The Heir Returns   57
The Killing of the Boar   79
The Quest Begins   99

PART II: OCEAN
On the *Argo*   107
All at Sea   127
Winds of Change   143
Hera's Revenge   159
Betrayal   169
In Exile   187
Poseidon Awakes   211

PART III: ANATOLIA
Defeat   223
The Return   235
Golden Apple   249
Before Greece   261

PART IV: GREECE

Farewells and Greetings   279

Iris's Last Message   293

Return to the Palace   303

The Race   315

Epilogue   325

Author's Note   329

Suggestions for Further Reading   335

Bronze Age Calendar   337

Glossary of Characters   339

Glossary of Places   343

Acknowledgements

There are so many wonderful people who go into the making of a book, and it is one of the real joys of writing to be able to work with and benefit from them all. First and foremost, of course, I am so grateful to my publishers, Transworld: I couldn't imagine a better home for my books, and I benefit every day from the team's endless enthusiasm and expertise. Among many, I would like to thank my fabulous editor Simon Taylor, whose shared passion for the ancient world makes working together a true pleasure, as well as Tash Barsby, whose fantastic assistance made everything run more smoothly; many thanks also to Hannah Bright and Patsy Irwin, Viv Thompson, Becky Glibbery, Phil Lord and Candy Ikwuwunna. Beyond Transworld, my sincere thanks go to my agent Roger Field for his advice on everything from books to boar-hunting, and my copy-editor Hazel Orme. I'm so grateful for all you do to help in making these ancient myths a reality.

I am also greatly indebted to many scholars and resources in my research for this book. My thanks go in particular to Professor Vakhtang Licheli at the Tbilisi State University, Georgia, for his assistance in explaining the Bronze Age history of Colchis and its relations with the Greeks, and to Professor Richard Hunter, who first introduced me to Apollonius' *Argonautica* at Cambridge. Otar Lordkipanidse's important *Archäologie in Georgien: Von der Altsteinzeit zum Mittelalter* (1991) was an invaluable resource on the archaeology of ancient Colchis, and Georgij A. Klimov's *Etymological Dictionary of the Kartvelian Languages* (1998) was particularly helpful in elucidating the Kartvelian/ Zan language. The *Routledge Handbook of the Peoples and Places of Ancient Western Asia* (2009) was a useful resource for understanding the geography and ethnicities of ancient Anatolia, and Hara Georgiou's 'Bronze Age Ships and Rigging' (1991) was extremely helpful in reimagining the ancient *Argo* – as, of course, was our visit to the reconstructed *Argo* at Volos. In this regard I would also like to thank our wonderful host Nasia Chatson for her hospitality during our visit to Mount Pelion, when I was lucky enough to explore the ancient Bronze Age sites of Iolcos, Pagasae, and the slopes of the mountain on which Atalanta grew up. My thanks also go to the Harvard Archery club, especially Natalie Chew, for bearing with me as I got to grips with a bow and learned how to (almost) hit a target like Atalanta.

A writer is only as good as the colleagues, friends and family who support her and make the process of writing not only possible but enjoyable. My colleagues, friends and mentors at Yale and at Harvard – Emily Greenwood, Irene Peirano-Garrison, Diana Kleiner, Linda Dickey-Saucier, and all my colleagues at Phelps; Greg Nagy, Ivy Livingston, Teresa Wu, Alyson Lynch, my Boylston friends and my Latin 1 students – have supported me in my creative endeavours far beyond the call of duty. I am so grateful to all the wonderful people at The Biscuit in Somerville – Hannah, Ryan, Bryan, Ilona, Emmy, Emily, Greta and all the others – whose smiles, conversation and encouragement (as well as their almond chais) powered the writing of this book. My friends – too many to mention them all – in the US, the UK and Austria, have been a constant source of support and inspiration: I am so grateful to Farzana, Athina, Natalia, Bells, Alice and all the others who are always cheering me on from the sidelines.

This book is dedicated to my parents, Andrew and Jenny, whose love and support have managed to reach across the Atlantic and five time zones over the past six years. I am so grateful to you for the important lessons you taught me in life and the encouragement you give me, now that my ship has sailed from the harbour. And I also dedicate it to my wonderful husband, Oliver, whose love and unfailing support along the journey makes living every day and writing every line a joy.

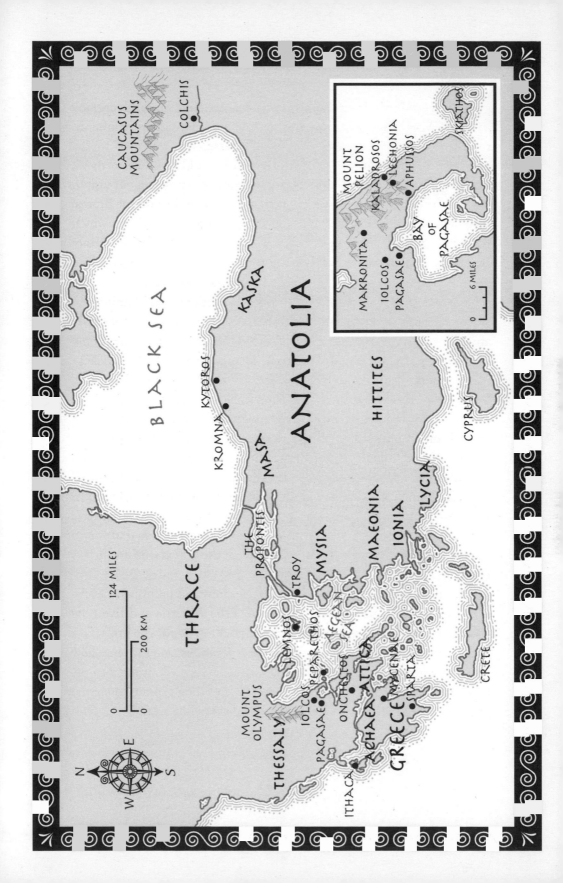

Inset map:

MOUNT PELION
MAKRONITA
KALADROSOS
LECHONIA
APHUSOS
SKIATHOS
IOLCOS
PAGASAE
BAY OF PAGASAE
0 6 MILES

Main map:

CAUCASUS MOUNTAINS
COLCHIS
BLACK SEA
KASKA
KYTOROS
KROMNA
MASA
ANATOLIA
HITTITES
THE PROPONTIS
TROY
MYSIA
MAEONIA
IONIA
LYCIA
CYPRUS
THRACE
124 MILES
200 KM
MOUNT OLYMPUS
THESSALY
LEMNOS
PEPARETHOS
AEGEAN SEA
IOLCOS
PAGASAE
ONCHESTOS
ATTICA
MYCENAE
ACHAEA
SPARTA
GREECE
ITHACA
CRETE

N
W   E
S

Prologue

The king's adviser trudges up the side of the mountain. Snow whirls around him, blistering his skin with cold. He clutches the precious bundle he is carrying closer to his chest, as if he could protect it from what is to come. Wind lashes the pine trees, bending them like blades of grass, and the snow swirls across his vision through the darkness, the cold biting at his fingertips through his boar-hide gloves. This is no night to be out on the slopes of Mount Pelion, alone, exposed to the fury of the storms of Zeus, with flakes of snow frosting your eyes and bitter ice crystals forming upon your beard. This is no night to be doing such a deed.

But the king has been firm, and he can only obey. He is a mere adviser, after all, and newly raised to the position. If he denies the king's orders, what will become of his family? He has his wife to think of, his children, his own little daughter.

He shudders.

Yet he wishes he did not have to do what he must tonight.

The trees are clearing now. He will soon reach the mountain peak where the bare rock reaches up into the sky. A flash of lightning illuminates the path, a steep curving trail up sheer rocks, the only handholds the roots of young trees, the stone slippery with new-fallen snow. It is as if the swirling squalls of wind are pressing him on, on, like the hand of a divine being at his back. The rumble of thunder seems to shake his very bones and sets him mumbling prayers for deliverance as he climbs the treacherous rocks, the bundle clasped to his chest in the howling wind, prayers to gods in which he can hardly believe any more — for what gods could look on and allow King Iasus to order such a thing? What gods could allow him, the powers forgive him, to do what he is doing now?

And then he thinks: it is not himself he should be praying for.

1

The top of the mountain is bare, whipped clear by winds that blow hard across the sea from Troy to the east, and shaped into jagged peaks of stone, like waves upon the ocean. He searches for shelter, somewhere that the pounding of the wind and the sweeping snow will not reach, then curses himself for a fool. As if it will make any difference.

But he finds a small cleft within the rocks, and tries to sweep a few dead leaves into a pile to create some warmth. He bends down and places his burden carefully upon the bed of leaves. It is no larger than his two palms placed together, a little bundle of fine-spun cloth and wool. The baby stirs in her sleep, clenching and unclenching her tiny fists.

He stands up. His fingers are trembling as he turns back towards the path, back into the dark, cold night.

'Farewell, daughter of Iasus,' he says.

Back on Olympus, the home of the gods where eternal beings live in endless time, a goddess is hurrying through the empty halls of Hera's palace. The only light comes from beneath the door of the chamber at the far end of the hall: Hera's bedroom, her refuge when she is plotting against Zeus or too furious to sleep beside him. Iris knows that Hera, queen of the gods, will be awake at this midnight hour, pacing up and down the cool marble floors, awaiting her return.

The messenger goddess pushes the door open softly.

Hera is standing at the centre of the chamber, as Iris had known she would be, back turned, curling dark hair knotted beneath a golden wreath of oak leaves, determined to the last, it seems, not to show how much she wants to hear this news. Hera turns slowly.

'Well?' she asks.

Iris bows her head. 'It is done.' Her face is blank, expressionless, except for a tiny crease in the centre of her forehead where her brows are drawn together. As she tilts her head up to look at Hera her tunic ripples slightly, iridescent in the lamplight.

Hera lets out a breath. 'It is done, then,' she repeats, in a whisper. She moves to her bed and sits upon it, gazing at her hands, thinking. Then she looks up. 'And no one saw you go? Hermes?'

'Welcoming Dionysus and the maenads to his palace as I left.'

Hera nods. 'Good. And Zeus?'

'Watching the Battle of Qadesh.'

Hera laughs, and the sound echoes off the marble walls. 'You have done well, Iris – very well. Not even Hermes could have done such a good job.'

'I'm sure he couldn't,' Iris says. She glances at the ceiling, which opens to the night sky and shows a velvet-black darkness dotted with a veil of stars.

Hera blows out one of the guttering oil-lamps, and the silvery stars become a little brighter. 'Indeed,' she says. 'So the girl will die.'

'Yes,' says Iris. 'She will.'

There is a pause, and it is as if, for a moment, Iris and Hera can see the three Fates seated together in the gaping chasms of darkest Hades, slowly unwinding the golden thread of Atalanta's life from their spinning wheel and slicing it through with their teeth, until only an inch of thread remains; as if they see one take it between her ancient, time-weathered fingers and flick it over the cavern's edge, floating down to the infinite depths of the Underworld, to be piled with all the other remnants of mortal lives that were never lived. The two goddesses move softly around the room, extinguishing the remaining oil-lamps hanging on their bronze stands and sending wafts of smoke drifting through the darkness.

'Did you require anything else?' Iris asks, as the last of the lamps goes out and the goddesses are left shining in the moonlight, slim and pale as two columns of Parian marble.

'No,' Hera says. 'It is done. I can sleep in peace at last. I have won.'

'Then I will leave you.'

But as Iris closes the door behind her and makes her way through the silent sleep-filled palaces of Olympus, she cannot help but wonder whether the Fates, and the snip of their teeth against the thread of mortal life, are always where the story ends.

Whether it might be possible to defeat destiny itself.

PART I

Eighteen years later

GREECE

1260 BC

There grows corn without measure, and grapes
for the wine: rain-showers are there always and sweet dew;
it is a land good for pasturing goats and oxen, and upon it grow trees
of every kind, and pools that never dry.

Homer

The Hunt

Mount Pelion

The Hour of Offerings
The Fourth Day of the Month of Sailing

I was running, beating away thorny brambles and ferns, trampling the shoots of saplings. Thighs tensed, breath coming hard, soles of my feet arched, arms pumping by my sides. The path was barely there, a hunter's trail criss-crossed with overgrown wild grasses and tree heather, but I knew my way through the mountain forest as well as any seasoned huntsman. My eyes were stinging with sweat, a few strands of chestnut hair stuck to my forehead, but still I ran, determined not to stop until I had put as much distance between myself and Kaladrosos as I could. I skirted a low-hanging branch and jumped a fallen tree trunk, moss-covered and damp, landing sure-footed.

'Aura – faster!'

Aura, my father's hunting dog, increased her pace to match mine, panting, her ears flat against her head as she ran. The oaks were packed close here, twisting grey-green trunks ploughing into the earth on every side, roots snarling across the path. The afternoon sun was a faint disc above, flashing through the canopy. I ran faster, heart pounding, my aching thighs shining with sweat, my leather quiver – one half lidded for my arrows, the other open for my bow – bouncing on my back. A waterfall flew by, tumbling over rocks into a green-blue pool, and then I was leaping through the stream of the Kissos, Aura splashing through the shallows, and up, up through the oak forests to the spreading beeches that climbed the flanks of the mountain towards the peak.

The light was filtering through the dense branches more insistently now, brighter, pooling over the leaves in puddles of gold. A clearing was opening between the trees, and I paused, hands resting on my thighs, breathing hard. Aura stopped too, flanks heaving, as I looked around me. Bare outcrops of rock alternated with low buckthorn shrubs and yellow-flowering broom, surrounded by a circle of pale-trunked trees, and there was the scent of fresh growth and the iron tang of water from the Kissos nearby. I took a deep breath. My anger was beginning to ebb, rinsed out of my body by the blood pumping through my veins, though I could still feel the frustration smouldering in the pit of my belly. *She does not understand*, a voice in my head said. *She thinks her life in Kaladrosos is all there is, spinning wool to thread, weaving it to cloth all year long, seeing the same people, staying always within the village.*

I snorted and flicked my dagger out of my belt.

And then I stopped.

There was a rustling in a thicket of wiry hawthorn on the other side of the clearing. I turned, listening. Aura started to growl, her hackles raised.

'Quiet, Aura,' I whispered, putting my finger to my lips, and she stopped immediately with a whimper. I laid my hand on the scruff of her neck and held her, tightening my hold on the dagger in my other hand. She was straining to move forwards, her black nose sniffing at the trees. The undergrowth rustled again, louder this time. A twig snapped as it was crushed under a heavy weight, the sharp crack echoing around the forest glade.

My hand tensed on Aura's neck.

Without a sound, I sheathed my blade, reached back to the quiver behind me and slid out my bow with practised ease, looped the bowstring over the peg and pulled it taut. Kneeling behind a broom shrub, I took an arrow, nocked it and stretched its feathered fletching back to my ear, feeling the familiar bite of the string against my fingers. My blood was pounding in my ears, the mixed thrill and terror of imminent danger pulsing in my veins as I peered through the branches, trying to get a glimpse of the animal.

I aimed the tip of the arrow towards the lowest of the boughs in the thicket opposite, a little above the ground. I could sense where the creature's movement was coming from. I felt its heavy body prowling across the forest floor; I could almost hear paws padding over the moss and the guttural throb of a growl. I drew the arrow back to its fullest extent, the edge of its flint head biting into my thumb, and aimed. *Remember, Atalanta*, I thought. *You do not miss.*

You never miss.

But before I could let the arrow fly, there was the sound of cracking branches from my left. I swivelled around. Another beast was charging towards me from the other side of the clearing a hundred paces distant, roaring, teeth bared, its paws thudding against the earth. My heart leapt to my throat as I turned back towards the thicket where I had heard the first beast, and saw another wall of muscle tearing through the undergrowth the same distance away. Aura was barking again, and the two beasts flashed gold, their jaws full of white teeth, claws ripping at the ground.

Lions.

With a roar that seemed to shake the trees to their roots, one leapt forwards, charging towards me faster than the torrent of a river pouring over rocks, huge muscles heaving, a bronze blur against yellow flowers and dark leaves. My fingers shook on the bowstring, the twisted ox-gut cutting into my skin, but I was ready. I narrowed my eyes until only the very tip of the arrow existed in my vision and, beyond it, the target of moving muscle. I held my arm steady as the curve of the bow moved to follow the lion's progress. As if time had slowed to an infinite pro-gression of moments I saw the tightening of the beast's haunches as it prepared to spring over a fallen tree, heard the crunch of the dried leaves beneath its paws as it leapt, and in that instant I let the arrow fly. It whistled through the clearing, spinning unwavering around its point. I did not stop to hear the bellow of pain from the animal as the arrow met its mark, tearing through the thick muscles of the chest to the unprotected heart, but pulled the dagger from my belt once more and flung it after the arrow to lodge deep in the animal's chest. It gave a terrifying roar of pain, the life force wrested from it in that final blow.

Whirling on my heel, I pulled another arrow from the quiver and fitted it to my bow, pulled it to my ear and faced the second beast. It had stopped its charge, amber eyes wary. It started to circle me at a distance, prowling swiftly and silently, choosing the best angle from which to pounce. Aura raised her hackles, a growl escaping her throat.

'Aura, *no!*'

The lioness had bounded forwards and was launching herself towards Aura. With one movement I kicked Aura aside, ignoring her yelp, then, with the speed born of years spent upon the mountain slopes, knowing I had only a single moment before those razor-sharp teeth ripped into my flesh, I turned and pulled the arrow off the string, tossing the bow clattering to the ground. The beast was almost upon me, so close that I could see the drool flying from its maw. With a single swift movement I vaulted to the right, stretching out my arm to lay the arrow I was clutching flat against the ground as I somersaulted. The lion skidded around, its huge weight sending it onwards, clawing at the rocks for purchase as I crouched, eye to eye with the beast, both hands gripped around the shaft of the arrow. There was a moment of silence, and then it leapt, uttering a low, throbbing growl from the back of its throat, claws unfurled, teeth bared. In the space of a heartbeat I brought the arrow around and then up, driving the sharp, cold flint tip straight into its belly and heart, fingers pressing it deeper, deeper . . . In an instant I rolled to the side, feeling rather than seeing my way to safety, fingertips scrabbling at the dark earth. It was barely half a moment later, when I heard the deafening roar of agony and the thud of a gigantic carcass falling to the earth behind me, that I knew I was safe. I stood up, panting hard, gazing down at the huge head lolling, limbs collapsed beneath, blood pooling around the broken arrow shaft into the earth and eddying among the dry leaves. I could hear the sound of something else in the distance, crashing through the undergrowth and coming closer. *There is a third*, I thought, my heart beating faster. I bent to pick up my bow and nocked another arrow.

'*Atalanta!*'

I turned to the place the voice had come from. Aura wheeled around, her black-tipped ears drawn back, tail straight and alert.

'Daughter!'

The voice came again. I lowered my bow. Through the trees I could make out a stooping, brown-skinned figure, a straw hat upon his head, beating aside the brambles with a wooden stick.

'Father . . .' I let out my breath. 'What are you doing here?'

He approached slowly, one hand on the small of his back. I waited for him, crouched to the ground, my fingers clutching the scruff of Aura's neck once more as she tugged against me, desperate to greet him.

'Atalanta,' he panted, as he sat down on the stump of a lichen-covered tree trunk, wiping his brow, 'you must not . . .' he took a breath '. . . run away like that.'

I let Aura go. She bounded forwards and began to lick my father's hand, but he ignored her. His gaze had fallen upon the carcasses of the two lions several feet away. I watched his face blanch. 'What, by all the gods . . .'

Slowly his eyes roved over the arrows sticking from the lions' bellies, the crusted rim of blood around the edges of the wounds and the dark, spreading stain upon the leaves, then to the quiver on my back and the bow lying at my feet.

'By all the gods on Olympus,' he said, 'did you do this, Atalanta?'

I nodded.

'But . . .' he swallowed '. . . but *how?*'

I raised my bow and set the arrow back upon the string, kept my gaze steady as I aimed across the clearing, then released my fingers and let the arrow fly. There was a rustle, and then a faint clatter, as a cluster of pine cones dropped to the forest floor, pinned by my arrow. 'With the bow and arrows that you gave me, Father.' I turned to him. 'Do you see now that I am capable of defending myself? That I am capable of more than –' I kicked at a stone upon the ground '– women's work?'

He did not reply, but took off his straw hat and wiped his forehead again. At length he stood and clasped my face in his hands. 'Do you have any idea what might have happened?' he said, and I heard the low thread of fear in his voice. His eyes flicked once again to the still masses of the lions' bodies, surrounded by growing pools of thick, trickling blood. 'Why must you always put yourself in such danger? Bands of thirty huntsmen armed with spears and nets have failed to kill a lion before!'

'But nothing happened, did it, Father? I defeated them!'

'This time, Atalanta, but what about the next? And the one after that? You are too young to think of such things, but we are worried for you, your mother and I. You cannot always win, and when you do not . . .'

He bent to pick up his hat and put it on his head, tying the cord in a knot. He beckoned to me. 'Come, Atalanta. We must go home. Your mother wishes to speak with you.'

I said nothing. I tried to turn aside but he took my chin and turned my face up to his. I met his gaze and saw that his forehead was creased with worry. 'Ah, my daughter,' he said. 'You always knew your mind, even as a child.' He smiled a little, and I saw the memories flit across his eyes. 'But there is more to this than simply a quarrel over women's work. There is something I must tell you.'

I ducked as I entered the mud-brick house in Kaladrosos, my eyes adjusting to the smoky darkness. The wooden ladle flew over my head and clattered into the wall behind me, then dropped to the floor with a hollow sound.

'What by all the gods did you think you were doing?'

My mother picked up a second ladle and stood pointing it at me accusingly, like a warrior holding a bronze sword on the field of battle. She was standing by the hearth at the centre of the room, her apron smoke-stained, her hands covered with ash from the burning logs beneath the meat roasting over the fire. I took the bow and quiver from my back and set them against the wall.

'Atalanta! Answer me!'

'Peace, Tyro,' my father said, stooping to enter behind me. He took off his hat, hung it on a wooden peg on the wall and propped his walking stick beneath it.

'And what of the goat left untied, which I had to chase over the fields in the heat of the day?' she demanded, hands on hips. Irritation bubbled up inside me. 'What of the stew I told her to watch – burnt?' She gestured towards the fire, where a clay cauldron had been set to one side, its contents blackened. 'Why is it that you cannot simply *stay*,' she shook the ladle emphatically in my direction, 'and *do* as you are *bid*?'

14

I sat down upon a stool, pulled my bow, a wool cloth and some bees-wax from the kit-pack in my quiver – dagger, linen strips for bandaging, a whetstone and a few squares of oil-cloth – and started polishing the ash-wood handle, determined not to meet her eye. 'Perhaps it is because I desire more,' I rubbed harder than I usually would, feeling the smooth wood beneath my fingers, 'than to sit by the hearth in the same place I have always been,' I found a mark upon the upper limb and burnished it, 'doing the same things I have always done.'

'Come, wife,' my father interjected. He laid a hand upon her arm, and although his face was grave, his mouth was twitching into a smile. 'There will be time enough for reckoning Atalanta's errors later. I would speak with you a moment.' He glanced towards me. 'Atalanta, watch over your brother and sisters while I talk to your mother.'

I nodded, looking at little Corycia in her cot, swaddled in a patched and frayed woollen cloth, then at Maia and Leon, chattering as they played with a wooden doll in the corner by the family shrine, where a simple wood statuette of Artemis, goddess of the mountain, watched over us all. My father pulled aside the curtain leading into the room where we all slept, and followed my mother in, letting the thick material fall behind him.

I tapped my foot against the tiles in frustration, running the cloth up and down, up and down the length of the bow's limbs. Nothing here had changed, in all the eighteen years of my life: the bricks surround-ing the hearth, slightly charred from the flames; the cot in the corner, made from planks of pinewood; the bleating of the goat outside the window. How could they not understand that I wanted more – that I was capable of more? My father had sat me upon his knee beside the fire in the long winter nights when I was young, and told me tales of the greatest heroes the Greeks had ever known: Hercules, slayer of the man-killing Amazons; Perseus, who destroyed the Gorgon Medusa; Bellerophon, rider of the winged horse Pegasus. I had dreamt of being such a hero, with all the single-mindedness of a child. Each night I had placed beneath my pillow a dagger the fishermen had crafted for me from a sharpened conch shell; each day, when my mother's back was turned, I slipped out into the woods to race the hares along the rocky trails. As I grew older I taught myself to aim arrows at the trunks of the pine trees, to fight the branches with sword and spear, to hunt deer, foxes and wild birds, and to run faster than any of the farmers upon the slopes of Mount Pelion. Yet all they wished was to see me inside, sitting upon a stool with my spindle and distaff, cramping my limbs into the postures proper for a woman.

I sat for a moment, thinking.

Then quickly, quietly as I could, I set my bow upon the floor and pushed the cloth back into the quiver. Corycia was sleeping, one fat thumb pressed into her mouth, and Aura had lain down in a patch of sunlight upon the stone flags, her snout quivering as she snored. Maia and Leon, now occupied with building a house for their doll from wood shavings and straw, noticed nothing as I crept across the room, avoiding the spitting fat from the meat upon the hearth, towards the opposite wall.

I pressed myself flat against it, feeling the coolness of the stone against the bare skin of my arm, my ear as close to the gap between curtain and wall as I could keep it without being seen.

'. . . time that she was told,' I heard my father saying, in a low voice, barely audible over the hiss of the meat upon the fire and Leon's delighted giggles.

There was a silence, in which the fire upon the hearth crackled.

'But now, Eurymedon?' came my mother's voice, a little higher than usual, though muted in a whisper. 'I thought we had said when she reached twenty years of age . . .'

There was a pause.

'We always said, my dear, that the time would be hard enough when it came.'

'But—'

'We have held it from her long enough.' My father's voice was calm, but firm. 'She deserves to know the truth.'

'And how will you tell her?' My mother lowered her voice until it was the merest murmur of breath. I pressed harder against the wall, listening. 'How can any child be told that she is not her parents' daughter?'

My father said something in return – I could hear that he was speaking – but what he said, I did not know. A shocked buzzing had filled my ears, as of a thousand angry bees, growing louder, louder . . .

How can any child be told that she is not her parents' daughter?

The words echoed in my head as I struggled to take in their meaning. My eyes were fixed upon the flagstones as if I would memorize every ridge, every crack, and I could feel the grainy roughness of the carved limestone against my fingertips, as though my senses were sharpened by shock.

Not her parents' daughter.

My heart thudded against my ribs, as fast and hard as if I were in the midst of the chase.

Not her parents' —

A loud wail split the air. I whirled around, blinking. Corycia was crying, flailing her fists, her eyes pressed shut, tears squeezing out. Maia was prodding her sister with the wooden doll, gurgling with laughter, and Leon was jumping about, crying, 'Again, again!'

'Gods be damned!' I hissed, under my breath. Quick as a snake slithering through the undergrowth, I darted across the room, waving the smoke of the fire from my eyes. Leaping past Maia and Leon, I had just scooped Corycia from the cot when the curtain drew aside.

I busied myself hushing the baby, rocking her back and forth in my arms, avoiding my father's gaze as he approached me. I hummed an old lullaby under my breath, and her crying eased a little.

'*Sleep, my child, sleep sweet and light—*'

'Atalanta.'

'*Sleep, my love, my little child—*'

'Atalanta.'

I turned my back to him, moving towards the cot as I finished the last line of the song: '*Gods send you sleep, and may you wake again tomorrow.*'

I bent and tucked Corycia back beneath the covers, my heart still racing, the words I had overheard thrumming a beat in my head as if they, too, were part of the song I had sung.

Not her parents' daughter . . .

I straightened at last and faced my father. The tips of my fingers were tingling and warm, a sensation of dread for what was to come, or perhaps anticipation that something, at last, was happening – which, I could not tell. 'Yes, Father?'

He gestured to the stool where I had polished my bow.

'Sit,' he said, his face grave, and drew up another stool beside me, carved from green oak on three sturdy legs. I had watched him make that stool, when I was barely twelve years old. I remembered the rustling of the leaves on the summer breeze as I traipsed after him, wanting to watch the tree felled upon the slopes of Pelion, the sound of the sharpened blade of the axe biting into it, the men from the village – how tall they had seemed to me then! – who had helped my father to carry it down, and the warm, comforting smell of the wood as he sawed it and chiselled it, polished it with beeswax, drilled holes in the seat for the legs and bound them with twine. I smiled a little at the memory, and my father's lips turned up too.

At another corner of the room, my mother's hand slipped on a clay pot as she lifted it to the cupboard. It fell to the floor and shattered. 'Oh, by the god of mischief! Not the stewpot . . .' She dropped to her knees and gathered the sherds into her apron, muttering.

My father laid a hand upon my knee. 'Even the greatest trees upon the mountain grow from a seed,' he said. 'An oak from a small acorn, a beech from a soft brown nut. What you are born determines who you will grow to be. My daughter . . .' he swallowed, and continued, his eyes unusually bright '. . . this you must know, because I see the world calling to you, and I know your spirit.' He took a breath. 'I always said you were a gift to us from the gods, but I did not tell you all. I—' He stopped and swallowed again, the skin around his throat constricting.

I rested a hand on his arm, my heart leaping wildly in my chest. 'I already know, Father.'

He stared at me. 'You know? How – how can you know?'

'I heard you talking with my mother, just now, in the bedchamber. I am no daughter of yours.' The words sounded so strange upon my lips. *Eighteen years in Kaladrosos . . . eighteen years, knowing where I came from, who I was, who I was meant to be . . . and now . . . what?* I felt the same inexplicable surge of mingled fear and excitement. 'Truly, Father, I have had the best parents in you.' Stinging tears welled in my eyes. I took his hand in mine and pressed his fingers tight.

'You are not – you are not surprised?'

'I was shocked, of course,' I said, swallowing hard. 'I still can hardly believe it. And yet, in truth, I have always been different from you, and Mother, Maia and Leon, have I not?' I looked aside at Maia as my mother scooped her into her arms, her cloud of golden hair the exact colour of my mother's plait, at Leon and baby Corycia, both with my father's grey-blue eyes. How had I not seen it before? 'It feels more as if – as if I always knew, but did not know it.'

Silence fell between us, broken by the spitting fire and the soft bleating of the goat outside. I sat beside my father, my hand clasped around his, and listened to my mother cooing to Maia as she turned the meat upon the spit.

I could pretend it never happened, I thought blankly. *I could pretend I never knew, and all would be as it was. I would hunt upon Mount Pelion, my mother would scold me, my father would chide me with a weary smile, then let me off again to the mountain slopes to run and chase the deer in the shade of the forest.*

Except that everything would be different.

'I found you upon Mount Pelion.'

I started, my mouth suddenly very dry. 'You – you found me?' I repeated.

He nodded and closed his eyes. 'I was gathering firewood upon the mountain, in winter – our stores were low and the damp had reached the last logs in the outhouse, else I should never have ventured out so late in the season, and so near to dark.

'I was just turning for home when one of the winter storms came down upon the mountain – so sudden I scarce had time to run for cover before the thick clouds rolled down the slopes and I was enveloped in howling winds and snow.'

I opened my mouth, not sure if I wanted to stop him speaking or beg him to go on. He seemed to know, and placed his other hand over mine, patting it gently. It was a gesture of such familiarity, and I felt a sudden rush of affection, warm in the pit of my stomach. I dug my fingernails into the palms of my hands to distract myself: I would not let him see me cry. I turned away and shut my eyes, and as I did so it was as if I could see before me the scene he described: the ice hanging in stiff crystals from the branches of the trees, the snow crunching beneath his boots.

'Zeus' thunder was raging around me,' he went on, his voice all I could hear. 'The wind whipped me so hard and cold that I almost turned back home, though I had collected barely enough dry wood to last us a few days . . . and then a gyrfalcon, pure white, swooped out of the air before me. Though it was madness, I felt in my heart that it was leading me, and I followed it. Up and up we climbed, following the most perilous paths to the very peak of the mountain where there is nothing but rock and a few bare pines. The wind was lashing my cheeks, and the gyrfalcon soared above me and away into the snow-clouds – and then I saw you. A tiny bundle of white, like new-fallen snow. You were left there upon the rocks to die, barely a day old, your little eyes still closed . . . I could not bear to leave you. I brought you with me, to Kaladrosos, bundled with the firewood on my back.'

He was silent once more.

I opened my eyes. It felt strange to see the sunshine pouring in through the open windows, to smell the familiar warm scent of Aura upon the air, mixed with the roasting meat and the straw from the goatshed, when a moment ago I had been there upon the mountain with my father, the snow swirling around us, the wind bitter. I looked down at my bow in its slot within the quiver, the arrows I had sharpened upon this very stool, the fletching feathers I had plucked from a tufted duck we had caught together upon the lake in the woods.

'I was not wanted,' I said. 'They left me on the mountain to die. Is that it?' I turned to my father. 'They did not want me?'

I had grown up in Kaladrosos, raised to think I was cared for, that I was loved – too much at times, perhaps, too close, yet as constant and steady as the mountain rocks. And now to find out I had been consigned to death, that the mother who had borne me had given me up to the snows and the winds in the dead of winter. That I had been saved only by chance . . . that my fate had been to die . . .

A sob caught in my throat, and I banished it with difficulty. The tears were threatening to spill down my cheeks as a yawning emptiness filled me, terrible, desolate, and every certainty I had ever known fell away.

I was not wanted.
Why?

Why did they not want me?

My father said nothing in reply but stood, went over to the wooden chest by the wall where he and my mother kept their few precious things, unlocked it and brought out a small square of linen wrapped around an object I could not see. 'You had this around your neck,' he said, pressing it into my hands, 'when I found you. The workmanship looks Pagasean to me – they have more goldsmiths than Iolcos, at any rate.' He sighed. 'If I had to make a guess, I would say you came from a family in the city, though whether this belonged to a wealthy noble or was a gift to his slave, I cannot tell.'

Fingers trembling, I lifted back the edges of the cloth. Inside was a golden medallion on a long leather cord, beaten thin into a circle, an image of two huntsmen chasing a stag hammered into it. I lifted the medallion and felt the cord slide over my hand, saw the disc sparkling in the light cast by the fire. The loss I was feeling inside was changing slowly, growing, kindling into a burning desire – and with it, a question: *who am I?*

Why was I left to die?

I looked up into my father's face, seeing the hesitation in his eyes as he watched me, waiting for a reaction. I wrapped it back in its cloth, feeling the thin edge of the medallion with my thumb, and bent to place it in my quiver. The burning in my chest was flaming, leaping higher and higher – whether it was shock or anger or excitement I could not tell: all I knew was that I had to do something. To do nothing would be unbearable.

'I could not have asked the gods for a better father,' I said, my throat tight. 'But, Father, would you understand if I said I wished to go to Pagasae? To find my parents – to prove to them they were wrong to abandon me to die?'

My father let out a long sigh and gave me a faint smile.

'You do understand?' I pressed him.

He squeezed my hand. 'I would have expected nothing less of you, Atalanta, my dear.'

There was a sound from beside me, and I turned. My mother had approached, unnoticed, and stood beside me, Maia still on her hip. She reached to her girdle and untied a leather pouch that hung from it, then handed it to me. It chinked softly as I opened it and looked inside to see a handful of silver and bronze coins. 'We do not have much, Zeus knows,' she said, her expression fierce, as if challenging me to say otherwise, though her cheeks were glimmering with the tracks of tears, 'but I put this aside knowing that this day would come, sooner or later. It is enough to keep you in the city for a month or so, maybe more.'

I gazed at her, unable to speak.

My father reached up and patted her hand. 'You are a good woman, Tyro.'

I nodded, swallowing hard. 'My thanks to you – to you both. I shall return – I promise you.'

And in my thoughts, that flickering, spreading, burning desire: *I have to know who I am.*

To the City

Kaladrosos

The Hour of the Middle of the Day
The Thirteenth Day of the Month of Sailing

I left Kaladrosos nine days later when the sun was halfway to the arch
of the sky, my father standing by the door in the porch watching me go,
my mother inside with the smoke and the children. I looked back down
the slope of the hill. He was leaning on his wooden walking stick, his
hat askew upon his head, one hand on the scruff of Aura's neck as she
strained against the rope tethering her to the doorpost, her ears flapping
as she leapt and barked and tried to follow me. I nodded to my father,
tears at the corners of my eyes, trying, with one gesture, to tell him why
I had to leave. I saw him smile a little and wave me on. I hesitated,
looked back one last time, a lump rising in my throat as I thought of my
mother within, fighting an urge to turn back and allow myself to be
held once more in her arms, to inhale the scent of soot on her tunic, to
kiss Corycia a last time on her plump pink cheek and to tell Leon
to remember to practise with his little wooden bow while I was gone.

Then I turned and began to run.

I had fastened the medallion my father had given me around my
neck, and the disc leapt against my chest beneath my tunic as I went.
For the first part I was pounding along paths I knew, following the
steep flank of the mountain south and west through the woods,
the dappled shade cooling my limbs and the scent of the pines on the
breeze. I stopped now and then to drink and splash water upon my face
at the streams along the way. The path wound back and forth,

25

following the contours of the foothills, and to my right the towering rocks shrouded in olive shrubs traced the route north towards the mountain's peak. Those first steps from Kaladrosos were harder than I could ever have thought, each bend in the track filled with memories – the carpenter's hut in the village of Lechonia, where my father had had my first bow made; the glade where I had picked branches of silver fir sacred to the goddess Artemis to cover our door when my mother was lying in with Maia; the mountain lake where Aura and I used to swim together, with its veil-like waters and pine-edged sandy banks. But as the sky above became more expansive, and the ground fell away at my feet, revealing a vista over the rolling olive-clad slopes towards the vast blue bay and the distant mountains on the other side, my excitement mounted, as my thoughts turned from what I had left to what I might find ahead.

Pagasae lies furthest to the west of the cities of the bay beneath Mount Pelion, past the citadel of Iolcos at the place where the land curves back towards the sea. My father's words echoed in my head as I ran, each word beating with the slap of my sandals against the rocks. I had never been so far from Kaladrosos – we had never needed to venture further, exchanging the wood my father cut from the forests for fish at Kaladrosos harbour and spices from the merchants that sailed the open sea – yet already I was savouring the new sights and sounds: the warmth of the sun sinking over the mountains to the west upon my face, the burning golden disc turning the sky to orange and pink, then to a pale purple, a myriad of colours. Cicadas were chirping gently in the boughs of the pines, calling to and answering each other, while swifts circled overhead, shrieking and swooping towards the bay. I felt myself thrill with anticipation, and ran on down the winding path.

I spent the night at a woodcutter's hut set just above the harbour of the little village of Aphussos, and ate companionably outside with his family around a small fire built up from dry underbrush. The stars began to glimmer overhead, and I sat tearing bread, cutting the skewered meat from the spit and talking with the man's wife, all the while gazing towards the dotted torchlights of the towns to the north and west of the bay, wondering which was Pagasae and what I might find there.

I left early the next morning as the sun's rays broke through the mists rising from the water, and turned to run north as the sun climbed towards its peak, following the sandy shores of the bay, fording rivers running down from the mountain to the sea, passing olive orchards and small clusters of dwellings surrounded by cypress trees, the many-ridged slopes of Mount Pelion rising green-clad on my right. As I rounded the north of the bay, away from the mountain, the ground became drier, dustier, swallows swooping overhead, the grass a paler green and tufted beneath my feet. The path forked to the right, leading up the plain towards a distant hilltop fortress set back from the sea, but I followed the track on, running past fishermen, tradesmen and pedlars with trays slung around their necks, keeping close to the bay as my father had said. I was aiming towards a headland curving back into the ocean. Above it, a long, low hill was coming into view upon which another city was built, its fortified limestone walls tracing the contour of the rocks, the rooftops of the buildings behind just visible, the path winding up the slope to a pair of wide gates and a tower. My stomach churned and I slowed to a walk, breathing hard, brushing my fingertips through the marram grass and rushes growing nearby.

Pagasae.

I swallowed, doubt and fear leaping in my chest like cold flames as I contemplated the enormity of what lay before me.

Lady Artemis, I thought, turning my eyes to a nearby pine, willing the goddess to speak to me from its branches. *Tell me, was I a fool to leave Kaladrosos?*

Was I a fool to think I could come to the city, and be welcomed there?

I was deserted upon the mountain, left to die . . . What if I find my family, and am told they do not want me?

I bit my lip, glancing back over my shoulder towards the mist-tinged outline of Mount Pelion on the other side of the bay. I had left my family behind, my whole way of life: the familiar crowing of the cockerels in the village at dawn, the smell of hay, smoke and burnt wood in our house, the breeze through the olive leaves in the yard just before the sun dropped behind the mountain, and the evening light that tinged the leaves with gold, like first-pressed oil. My heart tugged as I remembered Aura, barking and straining at her leash to follow me as I ran away, as I thought of the tear-tracks on my mother's cheeks, and my father waving farewell. Had I done wrong? Should I, perhaps, have stayed, pretended I had never known, as my parents had done all my life?

I shook myself. *You have to be strong*, I thought, clenching my fists. *Free from fear, as your father and mother taught you, as you taught yourself upon the mountain slopes.*

I drew myself up straight and tall, chin raised.

You have come this far.

With that, I took a deep breath and started to run up the hill towards the gates of the city ahead.

As I neared them I saw two guards stationed on top of the gate-tower, clothed in tunics and cloaks, carrying bronze shields and long, horn-tipped bows with quivers upon their backs. A small bronze bell hung beside them on a wooden frame, a rope dangling from its clapper. They watched, hands resting on the curved ends of their bows, as I approached.

'I wish to enter the city!' I called to them, shading my eyes against the bright rays of the sun. An olive tree nearby, its trunk twisted and knotted with age, offered some shade and I moved towards it.

'What is your name, and where do you come from?' the guard on the right called down, a swarthy, bearded man. I could see him taking in my short wool tunic, leather sandals, and the quiver hanging at my back.

'I am Atalanta of Kaladrosos.'

'An inhabitant of the city?'

I hesitated. I had no idea who my family might be: as my father had said, they might be nobles or slaves. Who could tell whether my medallion had been owned, given or even stolen? 'No.'

The other guard, shorter, broader, with curling red hair, frowned. 'You are a slave from the hunt, run from your master, then? It is a strange man who keeps a woman to do his hunting for him.' They laughed.

'Surely it would not matter if I were a slave, for all, free born or not, should be given entry to your city,' I asked, attempting to keep my voice even.

'Not during a festival,' said the first guard. 'The rites of Zeus forbid it. The feast of the god lasts from the waxing of the moon to its waning, and in that time no one is allowed into the city who has not been properly cleansed.'

I stared at him. At our shrine upon Mount Pelion, the sanctuary had always been open to anyone who wished to lay an olive branch or a cluster of black grapes upon the altar. The priests – though in truth they were more fishermen than priests: they came in from the harbour and donned the white robes of the priesthood for the festival days – had always said that there were more gods in the blue of the sea, the sky and the dark clods of the earth than in the temples built by men. When I ran through the glades of the mountain, surrounded by the shimmering needles of Artemis' pines, I had always thought I agreed.

'Our Lord Zeus,' the guard repeated, as if I were a halfwit who did not know the name of the king of the gods. 'The patron of our city.'

'Yes,' I said. 'Yes, of course. Where may I cleanse myself to appease our lord god?'

The guard shook his head at my ignorance. 'All worshippers at the festival bathe in the mountain spring at Makronita.'

I was growing impatient. 'Then I shall go there.'

'Wait!' he called, as I made to walk back down the slope. 'I have not yet told you all. Two days ago, at the hottest hour of the day, the fountain disappeared, dried up, the water draining into the earth. The king's priest read the signs: it is an omen from the gods. Zeus has decreed that no one who has not already been cleansed at Makronita shall enter Pagasae. The bell has not been rung to open the gates of the city since.'

'Yes, indeed,' the other guard said. 'Not until the festival ends.'

I frowned. 'How long? Until the festival is finished?'

'Ten days.'

'But—' My thoughts flew to Kaladrosos, and how hard it would be to leave my father – my family – a second time. And, besides, there was something tantalizing about the unknown city that lay ahead, filled with strange new possibilities. 'Please! I beg you!'

The red-haired guard laughed. 'You had best be on your way, little

29

slave,' he said, and he lifted his bow, drew an arrow from his back and fitted it to the string. 'The king does not want stragglers around the walls disturbing the peace of the festival, and it would be only too easy for my hand to slip . . .' He let the arrow slide a little forward, the bronze tip glittering in the sunlight.

My temper was rising. 'I am a guest at your gates! You dare to threaten to kill an innocent stranger when you claim piety to the festival of the gods?'

He lowered the bow to his side. He had stopped laughing now. 'Why, you impudent—'

But the second guard laid a hand on his arm. 'I could have you strung up and fed to the crows for your insolence, girl. Go back to where you came from, and cease wasting our time with your foolishness.'

Before either of them had time to raise their weapons, I drew my bow from my back, nocked an arrow and pointed it directly between the eyes of the guard who had just spoken. 'I would like to see you attempt it.'

There was a pause, as the two guards stared at the arrow tip. Then, as one, they burst into laughter.

One nodded towards me. 'Where did you steal that from, then, peasant?'

I saw their hands move towards their bows. Before they could so much as lift them, I aimed my arrow, drawing my right hand towards my ear till the arrow tip grazed my thumb. I saw their eyes widen, saw them scramble for their shields. I swivelled to the side, took aim, and let loose. The arrow sprang from the string, flying through the air around its point, up, up, up – and then it hit its target. The bronze bell rocked to the side, once, twice, clanging loudly over the city.

There were a few moments in which nothing happened, and all I could hear was the ringing of the bell and the thumping of my heart.

Then there was a creaking sound from beneath as the bolt was drawn away from the gates and first one gate, then the other, was pulled slowly back upon its hinges.

'No, wait—' One of the guards rushed to the edge of the gate-tower and called down to the slaves below. 'She has not been cleansed, she cannot enter! Close the gates! *Close the gates!*'

But they were already swinging back. I nodded to the guards. 'My thanks to you!' I called up to them, then ran forwards, slipping into the city.

'*Stop!*' I heard the guards clattering down the tower steps; the slaves who were pulling the gates open with long ropes, knotted around bronze rings upon the doors, turned in surprise as I dashed past them.

'*Catch her!*' the guards roared.

But I was already gone, disappeared into the crowds of people swarming up the street and into Pagasae.

I was hurrying down the wide, stone-paved street, my head turning to the wooden carts trundling past me, the fishermen, with nets of silver fish upon their backs, and the blacksmiths, faces darkened by soot. I had never in all my life seen such confusion – so many people crammed together, all pushing past each other, talking, crying out their wares or shouting after thieves: cloaked merchants and swearing traders, priests robed in white, mules dragging carts, and as far as my eyes could see, an array of different hues – red-patterned tunics, brown-and-green tunics, blue woollen cloaks, red-and-yellow skirts, cloth of purple, and clay pots of ochre and black.

I felt a little dizzy from the deluge of sound and colour. How was I to know where to even begin to look?

A hand touched upon my shoulder. 'You had better come with me.'

A young woman, slightly older than I, was standing before me, her curling black hair done up loosely on her head, her eyes dark and her mouth curved into a half-smile. Her simple tunic clung to her hips, and over the coarse material a girdle was fastened, crossed over her chest and knotted at the back, framing her breasts. As she tucked a strand of hair behind her ear, I noticed a brand in the sign of a cross, bordered by a circle, burnt onto the inside of her wrist, marking her a slave. We had no slaves in Kaladrosos, for all of us worked the land and sea to earn our living; I had heard tell of slaves in cities, where warring lords took the freedom of others to buy themselves a life of luxury.

'Why? Who are you?' I could not stop staring at her: there was something about her expression – guarded. I saw self-possession in the set of her mouth, and yet a hint of vulnerability in her eyes.

31

'My name is Myrtessa,' she said. 'Come. Quickly.'

She hurried away through the crowds, the hem of her tunic swaying around her sandalled feet. I hesitated, wondering whether to trust her – who knew what she might be planning, or whom she worked for? Perhaps she was trying to rob me of my purse – or worse . . .

But as she glanced over her shoulder and beckoned, smiling – as if she knew what I was thinking – I made up my mind and followed her, unable to resist my curiosity, though I kept my hands at my sides, ready to draw my dagger. She moved before me, ankles flashing beneath her robes, tracing the main street up the hill towards the crowned battlements of the upper city. As I followed her I took in the small mud-brick dwellings with shops opening onto the road, their rickety wooden tables laden with olives, fruit, fish and large clay jars. Shopkeepers cried their wares, and lines of buyers eager to quench their thirst huddled around the stalls. We pushed through the crowds on the main road for several hundred paces until we were directly beneath the walls of the upper city. I was still wondering whether this had not been a trick to rob me of my coins when I saw her dart aside and turn into a narrow side street. I hesitated, then went after her, and found myself in a quiet road before the facade of a square yellow-stone house, the dwelling of a wealthy lord, constructed of hewn blocks and built on two floors against the upper city's battlements. It had narrow windows set between the stones and was roofed with wooden timbers that stuck out over the eaves. I glimpsed a colonnaded garden to one side, covered with trellised vines and circled by fruit trees, and from the windows on the upper storey, gauzy curtains billowed in the breeze. She turned, gestured to me, slipped down a narrow alley to its side, then through a door into the darkness.

I followed, mystified and wary, my right hand on the hilt of my dagger. An overwhelming scent of fish and fresh-pressed cheese assailed me as I pushed through the door and blinked, adjusting to the darkness. To my surprise, we had entered what appeared to be a kitchen – a large hall that seemed to run the length of the house, its walls unplastered, the air thick with smoke, filled with sweaty-faced slaves. Some were carrying bundles of wood for the fires, others bringing buckets of water from the well outside, scouring dirty cups, scooping fish bowels for paste or peeling barley husks into bowls. Three long trestle tables ran the length of the room, laden with lemon-stuffed fish, jars of pickled black olives, large round cheeses and bread – and slaves were tipping more loaves, warm from the oven, onto the table with wooden bread-peels. Two young women and a man by the ovens looked up as we entered, their tunics ash-smeared and hands blackened with soot, expressions alight with interest. As I walked, rushes strewn over the floor crackled beneath my feet, sending up their clean, sweet scent, mixing with the heady smoke from the fire.

'Sit,' Myrtessa said, guiding me to a stool, which was placed near the ovens. 'Mead?'

'Who is she, Myrtessa?' a redhead asked. Her tunic slipped off one shoulder as she bent to slide a loaf into the oven and she pulled it up. 'A new slave for Lord Corythus? Does he not have enough as it is?'

Myrtessa shook her head as she picked up a jug, poured some mead into a clay cup and handed it to me.

'What am I doing here?' I asked, taking it from her and setting it upon a nearby table.

Myrtessa settled herself next to me, the two of us squeezed onto the single stool. 'I saw you outside the gates. I was walking on the walls.' She leant over and tapped my quiver, which I had slung off my shoulders and set down beside me. 'Where did you learn to use a bow like that?'

She was grinning at me, her head cocked to one side. In spite of my qualms I sensed, in the frankness of her gaze, that I could trust her.

'A bow?' the man said, looking up from the dough he was kneading and raising one eyebrow. 'This girl can aim an arrow?'

I slid the bow one-handed from its compartment within the quiver, my fingers wrapped around the ash handle, and they all stared. 'I learnt it as a young girl. I grew up in Kaladrosos, on the other side of the mountain,' I told them. 'My mother always said it was not proper for a woman, but . . .'

'Your mother had it right,' an older matron remarked as she passed, a linen scarf tied around her head. She was carrying a basket of mint leaves. 'Besides, weapons ain't supposed to be in the kitchens. This is woman's work 'ere, not a hunt.'

The redhead shrugged. 'Never mind Hora – she'll be able to find fault in anyone, even if the gods can't.'

A loud blast of what sounded like hunting horns halted the conversation, and I heard the clip-clopping of several horses' hoofs outside. Myrtessa darted to the window and stood on tiptoe to look out. She turned back to me, her face alight with excitement. 'Come here,' she called, pointing. 'Over there . . .'

I peered through the small, square window. It looked down over the main street and, as my eyes adjusted to the brightness of the light reflected from the stones outside, I saw a short procession of several men on horseback. The corpse of a lion was slung over two long wooden poles, held upon their shoulders, a retinue of slaves and wine-bearers trailing behind. A tall, slender young man, with red-gold hair that hung to his shoulders, caught my eye. He sat upon a bay mount, and as he passed I saw he had the clearest hazel eyes and the merest hint of a beard. His skin was olive-brown, and the sweat on his arms made him shine like a god in the sun. He flashed me a smile, tilted his head and bowed to me. I felt my heart thud a little faster in my chest.

'Who is he?' I asked, pointing through the window.

Myrtessa laughed, one cheek dimpling. 'Taken by the lord Meleager, are you? You would be one of many, believe me. Neda likes to watch him as he passes sometimes, don't you, Neda?'

Neda tossed her auburn hair and pointed a loaf at Myrtessa, like a sword, though she flashed a smile. 'I enjoy what little I can.'

'Meleager is son of Oeneus,' Myrtessa continued to me, her voice low, confiding, 'lord of Calydon in Aetolia, one of the most eligible young men in the land and a libertine if ever there was one. They say he takes his pleasures where he likes – pretty boys on the verge of manhood, handsome courtesans, slender young girls like you.' She shrugged. 'They say he has had them all, and left them besotted. And they say worse, too.' She lowered her voice. 'That he is vicious in his very heart – that he has men and women when he wants them, that he relishes the violence, that though he may seem lordly on the surface he is hot-blooded and savage in his desires. I'd advise you to keep well away from him.'

I grinned at her. 'I'm not one to lose my wits over a man, though I thank you for the warning. In any case, I doubt a girl of no family would be the lord of Calydon's first choice, however hot-blooded he may be.'

Neda nodded with a half-shrug and the male slave pummelled a fistful of dough, saying, 'True enough.'

'So,' I turned back to the window, 'the procession – for the festival, is it?'

Myrtessa shook her head. 'A hunt, to welcome Prince Jason – the king's nephew,' she added, seeing my blank look. 'He is taking refuge in the city, since Pelias drove him from the throne of Iolcos. Though I've heard it said that the people of Iolcos are glad to be rid of him.'

She indicated a man, smaller than the others, with grey eyes, a straight nose set in a narrow face and slim, sloping shoulders. He wore a cloak embroidered in blue and green, secured with a golden clasp. He had pulled his horse aside and was crooking his finger at one of the slaves to bring him wine. The boy ran to his side, untied the thong around the pouch and lifted it to Jason. As he did so, a drop of wine spilt upon Jason's cloak. His roar of rage echoed down the street, followed by a sharp *thwack* as the back of his hand hit the slave's head with such force that the boy reeled, tripped and smashed upon the stones of the street, sending the wine pouch flying. The wine pooled upon the flagstones with the blood from his jaw, where several teeth were broken. I gasped and started, as if to run to his aid, but Myrtessa laid a hand on my arm.

'Leave him be.'

'But – but how can he do such a thing? I would not treat a wild animal with such cruelty – and for such a slight offence!' My pulse was racing in indignation. 'Can one of the nobles not inform the king of his nephew's misconduct?'

Myrtessa did not reply, but pointed at a figure near the head of the party, just past Meleager, a tall man with a stubbled grey beard who sat astride a chestnut horse. He was watching the slave, upon all fours on the street now and gasping with pain, a curious, twisted expression upon his face. 'That's the king,' she said. 'You can see he has the report of Jason's deed, and thinks nothing of it. And the prince's treatment of his slave is nothing to what the king will do to you if the guards tell him you entered the city without cleansing. He'll have you imprisoned, I should wager.'

'Thrown to the dogs, more likely,' the old woman Hora muttered, as she stuffed mint leaves into the fish carcasses.

Myrtessa nodded. 'Neither Jason nor his uncle is well known for a sense of justice.'

I took a sip of mead, wondering at how commonly the vices of these nobles were known within the city, and thinking how little I knew of kings and princes from my sheltered life upon Mount Pelion. 'And you do not mind,' I asked, raising my eyebrows and looking at the four of them, 'that I have not been cleansed, according to the laws of the gods?'

The sandy-haired man snorted. 'The gods care only for our deeds,' he said, pounding at the stiff dough. He gave me a wink. 'To believe they take offence if we do not bathe ourselves – well, Neda for one would be in trouble.' He elbowed the red-haired girl, who laughed and slapped him playfully on the shoulder.

'Oh, and you wouldn't, Philoetius? You haven't bathed since the winter solstice, at least.' She pretended to sniff his hair and wrinkled her nose. 'Or before, by the smell of it.'

As Philoetius pushed her away, grinning, I turned to Myrtessa, who was laughing along with her fellow slaves. 'So is that why you brought me here?' I asked. 'To keep me safe from the vengeance of the king?'

She smiled. 'I thought a girl who can use a bow as well as you was worth talking to.'

I bowed my head, gratitude for her act of kindness sweeping through me. 'Then I hope to live up to your expectations.' I hesitated. 'Perhaps you can tell me . . . The lions,' I said, pointing again out of the window. 'Were they part of a royal hunt? A hunt led by the king?'

Myrtessa frowned. 'Lions? There was only one.'

'Yes, but were there more?'

Myrtessa looked me up and down. 'Yes,' she said at last. 'Three, in fact, captured from the wilds of Thrace and released on the mountain in honour of the prince. I heard Lord Corythus telling one of his companions last night, at the evening meal. How did you know that?'

I shrugged again. 'A guess.'

She stepped back. 'By Hermes, god of tricks and thieves, don't tell me . . .'

I tried to look modest, but I couldn't help grinning. 'Would you believe me if I said I killed two myself?'

Neda gasped and covered her mouth with her hand, Philoetius dropped the bowl of flour he was holding upon the floor, and even Hora had stopped stuffing fish with herbs to listen. The other slaves, who were near enough to hear, were laughing, half in horror, half in disbelief, and I heard snatches of their whispers to each other – 'Not possible . . .' and 'A woman cannot!'

Myrtessa chuckled. 'You were well worth the effort of your rescue, hunter-girl.'

'Atalanta,' I said, and held out my hand to grasp hers in a gesture of friendship.

'Atalanta,' she said, taking it. 'The equal of all others – isn't that what it means?'

I nodded.

'I think I'm going to like you, Atalanta. Now, I reckon you haven't spent much time in a city?'

I set my cup down. 'What would make you think that?'

'Oh, I don't know,' she said, her eyes gleaming. 'Why don't you change into this,' she reached down to rummage in a chest beneath the window and pulled out an old slave's tunic, 'and I can show you our city properly. I'll wager you'll get a warmer welcome than you did at the gates, if you'll only make sure to leave that bow of yours behind.'

We wound our way back down the street from Corythus' house towards the gates, Myrtessa talking all the while and pointing things out.

'That's Actor's bar,' she said, indicating a house with an open front and a dark-red awning stretched across it for shade. Large clay jars with ladles hanging over the edges stood beneath it. 'Neda, Philoetius, Opis and I sometimes go there in the evenings, when the master allows it. And that's the marketplace, over there.' She pointed to a small open square at the junction between two streets, where makeshift wooden stalls – barely more than planks propped on legs – covered with cloths were scattered about, laden with everything from cherries, peaches, purple vetch and red meat to close-woven sacking, painted pots, barrels and even slaves. The cries of merchants filled my ears as we approached, along with the clanging sounds of the blacksmiths' hammers on anvils, children laughing, bells ringing on carts, horses whinnying. I felt a shiver of excitement. I wanted to run everywhere at once, to see everything, to taste all the delicacies that were on offer, to drink in all the sights and smells of this new, colourful, bustling town. There was more danger and adventure here than I would encounter in a year in Kaladrosos, and I was thrilling to the newness of it all.

'Wait here,' Myrtessa said, leaving me beside a stand selling painted bead necklaces, and she moved ahead through the crowds. When she returned, she held a basket of apricots covered with honey. 'I know the stallholder,' she said, pointing to a large man with black hair and beard. 'His son is a carpenter and occasionally comes to the slaves' quarters at Lord Corythus' house. I give him bread from the ovens in exchange for such small jobs as he can help us with – mending broken stools, fixing shelves and such. Sagaris there always gives me something to eat, when I come by.' She popped an apricot into her mouth and sucked her fingers with relish.

At the south-western end of the city, when we reached the walls, Myrtessa led me up a stone staircase onto the ramparts, yellow-painted crenellations fencing us in on either side. The view was towards the harbour, not five hundred paces distant, pale sea rippling around a rocky shore lined by olive trees, then over the bay to Mount Pelion opposite, with its sloping green flanks, small villages and towns dotting its foot along the wide, sweeping crescent of the shore. I looked away quickly: Kaladrosos was behind the ridges of the mountain, and with it my father, my mother, Maia, Leon and Corycia. I would not allow myself to think of them, not yet. There would be time enough to return, and I did not want, just now, to lose the delicious sense I felt in the city that anything might happen – that, at any moment, something unexpected might spring upon me, like an antlered stag charging from the trees in the hunt.

'Where now?' I asked Myrtessa, turning to look down over the city, its streets filled with crowds and carts and flat-roofed houses.

She pointed. 'The upper city,' she said, directing my gaze to the hill at the other end, ringed with a lower wall, where I could see a red-columned palace fringed by pine trees and what seemed to be a temple to the gods, though it was larger than any I had ever seen. She began to walk, passing a group of female slaves approaching us from the opposite direction, along the flat rampart of the wall towards the gates.

I caught her arm. 'The gates!' I hissed, moving aside to let a woman pass. 'If the guards see me . . .'

Myrtessa gave me an appraising look. 'Come here,' she said. Deftly, she untied one of the long white bands from her hair, wrapped it three times around my forehead, then pulled up my hair and tucked it in. She pulled a few stray curls out at either side of my face. 'There,' she said, cocking her head to look at me. 'Though it hardly matters. They will never think to connect the girl who outwitted them with a woman dressed in a slave's tunic.'

I patted my head, a strange urge to grin almost overwhelming me. It was odd to feel the cool breeze on the back of my neck.

'Come,' she said, and pulled me along the wall. Other slaves who were using the ramparts to circumvent the crowded main road pushed past us as we went, bustling along the narrow stone walkway holding stacks of clay tablets or jars of water that spilt as they walked, and snagging the hem of my tunic in their hurry. I kept my eyes down, but none seemed to notice me.

As we approached the tower I saw the two guards who had tried to prevent me entering the city leaning on their bows and talking to each other, gazing out over the bay. They turned to us as we came nearer, and I felt a little shiver of apprehension as one leered at me, moistening his lips with the tip of his tongue. Myrtessa gave them a smile and walked on, hips swaying. I hurried after her, feeling their eyes following us.

What if they recognize me?

'Do you think they noticed?' I asked, as we walked away, my voice a whisper.

'The only thing they noticed was our backsides, I assure you,' Myrtessa said. She exchanged a glance with me, and I smiled at the pure mischief dancing in her eyes; then the two of us were laughing together. As Myrtessa walked on, she tossed me an apricot over her shoulder and I caught it. As I bit into it, I thought the gods had truly blessed me to send me such a friend upon my arrival to Pagasae. The fruit was juicy and sweet, the honey sticky on my lips and fingers.

There was a silence, as we walked along the wall, looking out to our right over the white-plastered houses, then to the left over the boats bobbing in the bay and the distant outline of the mountain.

'Why did you come to Pagasae?' Myrtessa asked, trailing her fingertips along the side of the wall.

I was caught off guard. 'I – I wanted to see the city.'

She turned aside, eyebrows raised. 'Ah. I see. And it was to see the city that you demanded entry at arrow point, was it?'

I wondered how much to tell her. I finished the rest of my apricot and threw away the stone to give myself a moment's pause. It flew through the air and disappeared into a clump of bushes on the other side of the wall.

'I was abandoned upon Mount Pelion as a child,' I said at last. It felt strange to say it aloud – to acknowledge that I had not been wanted.

She sucked in a short, sharp breath and, for a moment, her face twisted in an expression of pain. I blinked, and it was gone. She stopped and placed a hand upon the rampart to steady herself, and when she spoke, her voice was even. 'On Mount Pelion,' she said. 'And you came to Pagasae . . . ?'

Instinctively, I reached out a hand to her, my voice filled with concern. 'Myrtessa, are you well?'

She shrugged me off and glanced away. 'You came to Pagasae?' she repeated, her tone firm and unyielding. It was clear she would talk no further.

'I came for my family,' I said, and untucked the medallion on its leather cord from the neck of my tunic as I spoke. 'I came to find out – to find out who I am, to be recognized for who I am.' I could not hide the yearning in my voice. *All those years on the mountain, searching for more . . . And now . . . what?*

She reached out for it, holding it in her fingertips and shifting it from side to side so that it glinted in the sunlight. Then she looked up at me. 'It is well made, and worth a good amount, I should think – but I do not know it,' she said. 'There are at least a dozen families in this city wealthy enough to commission such finery, and each has its own private sign upon its seal-rings. It could have come from anywhere. But,' she said, beginning to walk again, 'I am sure I can ask the master tonight.' There was an odd tightness in her voice. 'He is certain to know which family it belongs to when I describe it, for he does business with almost all the nobles and merchants of the town.'

'You would do that?'

She laughed. 'It requires little effort, Atalanta. You need not look so surprised. Now, see over there,' she said, directing my attention through a gap between the high crenellations. We had reached the upper city now, past the second, inner circle of wall, which surrounded the citadel, and were climbing up steps as the hill rose higher. I peered through the embrasure, my fingers gripping the rough stone.

I was looking down upon a city in miniature. Below, a temple loomed up towards the walls, its flat roof jutting against the ramparts, lined with red-painted columns thick as tree trunks and gilded along the frieze, two budding oaks – sacred to Zeus, father of the gods – planted either side of the temple entrance ahead. The precinct was thronged with brightly dressed people just as I had seen in the streets below, and in front of the temple, on a square stone altar, a young slave was pressing gilt onto the curving horns of an enormous snorting bull, chained to a ring set in the stone flags of the precinct. Nearby, a priest was sharpening the sacrificial knife upon a whetting stone. The cloying incense streaming up from the bronze braziers made my eyes smart, and my ears rang with the sounds of deep bells clanging and the chanting of hymns as choirs of girls, dressed all in white with gilded oak leaves on their heads, circled the altar, singing to the god.

'The festival?' I guessed, and Myrtessa nodded.

'And that – over there – that's the palace,' she said, pointing.

We climbed up the steps two at a time until we reached the highest point of the wall. There was a ledge protruding from the ramparts, and we sat, gazing down at the palace. It was larger than any building I had ever seen, with the same red-painted columns as the temple, rising three, four storeys high, coloured curtains billowing from the windows, and a paved courtyard in the centre filled with trees and sparkling fountains.

'The king lives there, with his son, Prince Lycon,' she gestured to the highest tower of the palace, crowned with battlements, 'but they say Lycon will never be king of Pagasae.'

'Why?' I asked, crossing my legs beneath me and taking the apricot Myrtessa was offering.

She picked up another for herself and bit into it. 'The king desires an heir worthy of succeeding him,' she said, her mouth full. She wiped her lips on her sleeve, and continued, 'They say Prince Lycon is not the heir the king would have hoped for . . . He writes poetry,' she said, in answer to my unspoken question. 'Composes lyric love songs. Faints at the sight of blood, and would prefer to be in the palace library, reading clay tablets about wars long gone, than fighting and hunting as his father wishes. Which is why Prince Jason's return to Iolcos was so well timed.'

'Iolcos? What does Iolcos have to do with it?'

She laughed. 'You don't get much news in the country, do you? Though in truth it is a long tale, and much of it not worth the telling.' She wrinkled her nose in distaste.

'Still, I should like to hear it, if you can tell me,' I prompted her.

She finished the fruit, then tossed the stone aside. 'I know only half of it,' she began, 'and what little I know comes from the rumours that blow around the markets and taverns.' She sighed. 'It starts, I suppose, with three sons, born to King Cretheus, sovereign of all Thessaly – our own king, Pelias and Aeson, father of Jason.

'When Cretheus died, he wished to divide his lands between his three heirs. To our king, the eldest of his sons, he gave the city of Pagasae, close to the sea and with a calm harbour, good for trading. To Aeson, the youngest, he gave Iolcos, a fortress further inland where the fertile slopes of Mount Pelion meet the plain. But there was no third city to give to Pelias, the middle child, so the king granted to him the pastures and fields of Thessaly, rich in wheat. Yet Pelias desired more. He longed for a city over which to exercise his rule. And so, when Jason was barely more than a child, Pelias overran his younger brother Aeson's city, taking back what he felt was rightfully his. He killed Aeson, took

Jason's mother as his consort and threw the rest of the family in chains.

'Somehow, Jason managed to escape, fleeing to the woods and caves of the mountain. What he did there, how he lived, no one knows. But many years later – a few weeks ago – Jason reappeared from the mountain slopes at the palace of Iolcos, a man grown, with the beard upon his chin, demanding that he be restored to the throne as its rightful heir and in reparation for his father's death.'

I was staring at Myrtessa, absorbed in her tale. 'What did Pelias do?'

She snorted. 'Sent an armed guard to welcome him and threw him from the city, with the promise that he would be king as soon as he recovered the Golden Fleece of the gods from the ends of the earth,' she said. 'Or, in other words, never. The prince fled here, to Pagasae, to his other uncle, looking for sanctuary. And, perhaps . . .' she lowered her voice '. . . they say that, perhaps, in his determination to win Iolcos' throne, he is taking Pelias at his word. That he is, indeed, planning a quest for the Golden Fleece of legend.'

'A quest?' I repeated, my breath catching in my throat, my pulse quickening. *A quest . . . Just as I always imagined – like the quests of the heroes Hercules, Bellerophon and Perseus . . .* 'But the Golden Fleece?'

Myrtessa's eyes were alight with excitement. 'The mythical fleece of the golden ram that flew across the sea to the ends of the earth.' She spread her hands before her, like a poet telling his tale. 'The bards, and those few who have travelled beyond the Bosphorus to the open sea, say that it lies in the lands of Colchis, at the very edge of the world, that it is guarded by bulls with hoofs of bronze and breath of fire, and a serpent that never sleeps. It would be no journey for the faint of heart.'

I frowned. 'But what has this to do with Pagasae or Prince Lycon? Surely, whether Jason recovers his kingdom or dies in the attempt, it will have no effect upon the king of Pagasae, and his succession.'

She waved a hand. 'Except that Jason may not only be proving his worth for Iolcos alone. Jason is the king's nephew, after all, as well as Pelias.' She lowered her voice. 'And he knows about the prophecy.'

'Prophecy?'

'Two years ago, the king journeyed to the sacred oracle of Hera at Perachora, near Argos, to ask for the goddess's counsel upon the succession to his throne. The oracle of the goddess gave him a prophecy, and everything changed.'

'What did the prophecy say?' I asked, my voice hushed.

Myrtessa took a deep breath and recited:

> *'Bring back the treasure gold in legends twin,*
> *That's at the black earth's furthest ends concealed;*
> *Or else hope not the city's crown to win,*
> *And see your city to destruction yield.'*

She pointed towards a column of stone I had not noticed before, rising up in the very centre of the temple forecourt in the city below, engraved with words I could not read. 'The king inscribed the words of the oracle upon a pillar for all to see. It tells of a golden treasure, spoken of in myth, lying at the ends of the earth.'

She stood and began to pace. 'The heralds declared it in the market and meeting places of the city on the day the king returned from Argos. They say there are only two treasures of legend to which the prophecy could refer – the Golden Fleece of Colchis, in the lands furthest to the east where the sun rises, or the apples of the Hesperides, at the very edge of the world where the summer sun never sets.'

The Golden Fleece . . .

'Jason wishes to fulfil the prophecy,' I said. 'He wants to succeed in retrieving the Fleece, as Pelias ordered, so that he can rule Iolcos and Pagasae together – the heir to both thrones.'

'Precisely,' Myrtessa said, seating herself again beside me. 'I have heard more than one rumour speculating that, if Jason is successful in recovering the Fleece, he will be offered the crown as heir to Pagasae instead of Prince Lycon. They say that Jason hopes to unite the kingdoms of Pagasae and Iolcos as one, so that Thessaly is once more joined beneath a single ruler. There are even whispers that he will move the crown and the palace to Iolcos, and leave Pagasae a backwater, needed by none, subservient to the Iolcian king.' She spat an apricot stone into her hand, stood up and threw it over the wall.

There was a long silence as I thought of all she had said, in which the sounds of the bells and choral hymns to Zeus floated up from the city below. *Pagasae and Iolcos . . . the three kings of Thessaly . . . the death of King Aeson, and Jason's quest for the Golden Fleece . . . the prophecy from the gods . . .* I rubbed my forehead. It seemed a wholly different and far more complicated world after the quiet, steady rhythms of Kaladrosos.

I turned to look at my companion beside me – her pale skin, her rich dark hair, the fine lines of her brow and cheekbones. It seemed strange to me that someone who could speak so eloquently, who knew so much about the affairs of the city, could have been born a slave. Then I thought back to her reaction earlier, when I had talked of my abandonment upon the mountain. 'Myrtessa,' I said, into the silence, 'how – how is it that you came to be a slave?'

A shadow flitted over Myrtessa's face, but only for a moment. 'Shall we go down to the gardens?' she said, getting to her feet. 'They're beautiful at this time of year.'

A week passed in Corythus' house without incident. As Corythus had sworn he did not recognize the symbol on my medallion when Myrtessa had described it to him, she had invited me to remain disguised as a slave within the kitchen quarters where I could plan my next step unnoticed. There were so many slaves in Corythus' house, she told me, most of them unknown to their lord, that my presence was certain not to be remarked upon. I did not mention Myrtessa's enslavement again. Indeed, there was so much to do in the kitchens with their constant hustle – the clanking of bronze cauldrons, the shouts of slaves preparing the master's meals, heating the water for his bath, pounding herbs, gutting fish, kneading bread – that I barely had time even to think of my search for the family who had abandoned me all those years ago, let alone to ask questions of Myrtessa. She was in the thick of it as always, all energy and business.

'Where's the fruit knife, Philoetius?' she asked, over her shoulder, one afternoon. We had just returned from the market, where she had bargained hard and filled her basket with chicory leaves and leeks in return for a jar of honey from the beehives in the master's gardens.

Philoetius handed her the knife, his face shiny with sweat from the heat of the ovens.

'Did the master send for me while I was out?' Myrtessa called to Neda, who was peeling and chopping onions opposite her, pervading the air with their sharp, tangy scent.

Neda shook her head. 'No,' she said, briefly brushing an arm across her smarting eyes, then sweeping aside a pile of prepared onions. 'He asked for Opis.'

Myrtessa let out a long breath. She pulled a leek towards her and started slicing it. 'Another day's reprieve,' was all she said, and she tipped the chopped vegetable into a bowl.

Neda rolled up the sleeves of her tunic and began to skin a haunch of venison with a knife, pulling the skin from the meat in swift strokes. 'Atalanta, pass me the salt, will you?'

I leant across the table for the jar. As I did so, the medallion fell from between my breasts, the leather thong tightening around my neck, the disc clattering on the table.

I straightened up, fumbling to push it back beneath my tunic, but Neda, quicker than me, tossed her knife onto the table, and snatched me by the wrist. 'What are you *doing*?' I exclaimed.

'What's that?' Neda's eyes were wide, her tone urgent. She shook my arm. 'What is it?'

Slowly, the clatter and talk in the kitchen died as, one by one, the slaves turned to stare at Neda, her hand tight around my forearm, and at me, my fingers clutched around the leather thong at my neck. I saw a couple lean together and whisper something, their eyes upon me.

Slowly, I opened my fist from around the medallion, and it tumbled into view, glinting gold.

Without invitation, Neda took the medallion between two fingers and peered at it closely. Then she dropped it and looked up at me. 'Do you have any idea what you have here?' she said, her low voice carrying across the sudden hush.

I shook my head, feeling mounting apprehension. 'Why? Do you know what it is?'

Neda said nothing.

A slave at the other end of the room called, 'What is it, Neda?'

Neda was staring at me, and I felt my heart beat faster under the intensity of her gaze. *What does she know that I do not?*

'Out with it!' Myrtessa said, wiping her hands on her tunic.

'Yes, come, Neda,' Philoetius interjected, from where he was standing by the bread ovens. 'It's not like you to have nothing to say.'

Neda cleared her throat, and when she spoke it was in no more than a whisper. 'That emblem,' she said, her eyes still on me, 'is the personal seal of the king.'

Loved by the Gods

Mount Olympus

Somewhere, on the very highest peak of Olympus, there is a small pool surrounded by lilies and lotus blossoms, its waters clear as crystal and the rocks around its edges touching the clouds. It is turning towards evening, and the sun is sinking behind the mountains to the west, creating a warm orange glow on the horizon. A nightingale pours music into the air, heralding the night, and cicadas are humming in the cypress trees. It's very beautiful, the mortal poets say, but then, they can only imagine what it looks like. No mortal has ever seen it.

Because this pool belongs to the gods.

'This was never meant to happen!'

Hera's cry rends the evening air, like a stone dropped into still water. She is storming up and down the pool's banks, her white robes billowing behind her, the gold oak circlet on her hair slipping down over her forehead, her eyes flashing and her cheeks pink with temper. She pulls the wreath up and rams it back into place. 'The sheer audacity of it!'

'What's happened now?' *Aphrodite's voice floats up from below. She is seated on a rock submerged within the water, eyes closed, a faint smile upon her lips, twirling a lock of golden hair around one finger and sinking deeper into the depths so that the waters swirl about her shoulders.*

'She shouldn't be alive!' *Hera explodes.* 'She was meant to have died eighteen years ago – under your direction, Iris, I might add!'

Iris, Hera's messenger, does not reply. She is sitting by the pool's edge, dipping her toes in, apparently lost in thought.

'It's enough to make me want to destroy the mortals once and for all,' *Hera goes on, striding back and forth.* 'I prepared everything, made things easy for the Fates. The child was left on the peak of Mount Pelion in a storm in*

51

the dead of winter, for Zeus' sake! How, by all the gods, did she survive?'

'You did not see that she was alive?' Artemis, goddess of the hunt, asks, with a frown, from the brink of the pool beside Aphrodite, her pale ankles dangling demurely in the water. 'I thought we were all-seeing?'

Hera snorts. 'All-seeing, yes, but it depends on where we're looking, doesn't it? I was busy watching the kingdoms of Pagasae and Iolcos. I never thought to look at a carpenter's shack on the slopes of Mount Pelion.'

Aphrodite unties a band from around her hair and lets both fall into the water, shrugging. 'Perhaps the Fates intervened to save her.' She glances over her shoulder, shivering a little in the evening breeze. 'It's getting cold. I wish I had my shawl.' She pouts, thinking of the gorgeous golden cloak the cupids had made her, with its thousand shimmering threads. 'You're sure you haven't seen it anywhere, Iris?'

As Iris shakes her head for the hundredth time, Artemis shoots Aphrodite a quizzical look. 'I've never heard of the Fates troubling themselves for a woman before. The prophecies have always concerned men, have they not? Who will get the kingdom next. Who will kill the king . . .' Artemis counts them off on her fingers. 'Who will destroy the kingdom—'

'I care nothing for the Fates!' Hera interrupts, bringing her fist down upon a nearby rock, which shakes with the force of the blow. 'What I want to know is, how am I to be rid of her?' She flicks aside her robes and seats herself upon the rock. 'I already have Mycenae, Sparta and Argos,' she says, still breathing rather hard, her eyes turned to the south-western horizon and the high walls of Mycenae, the palace of Sparta and the broad green plains of Argos.

'A worthy crowd of cities for any goddess.' Artemis nods. 'I myself—'

'Atreus of Mycenae sacrifices to me three times daily. Tyndareus of Sparta has set up a temple in my honour, and Diomedes of Argos leads festivals every month in my name,' Hera continues, ignoring Artemis. 'But it is not enough.'

Aphrodite raises her eyebrows. 'You would want more cities as your own?'

Hera shrugs. 'Of course,' she says. 'You have often heard me say that Zeus neglects his cities. He leaves the mortals completely to their own devices, as if they were capable of looking after themselves! But I care for them. I watch over the kingdoms of Mycenae and Sparta and Argos as a benevolent goddess, *in return for their worship of me. All I want is for Iolcos and Pagasae to have a patron deity who cares for them, too.'*

'And I suppose you don't mind their pretty princes, either,' Aphrodite interjects, sliding her eyes sideways in Hera's direction.

Artemis coughs. 'And all the sacrifices – the smoke sent up to heaven in your name.'

Hera gives her a dignified smile. 'I suppose I wouldn't.'

A silence comes over the four goddesses, broken only by the soft slapping of water against the pool's edges and the gentle chirping of the cicadas in the pines.

'And Atalanta comes into this how?' Iris asks at last, speaking for the first time.

Hera shrugs. 'Atalanta is the daughter of the king, his first-born before Prince Lycon, and as such would be the rightful heir to Pagasae.'

'Ah,' Artemis says, her expression clearing, as if she has just understood something. She presses her fingertips to her temples and glances up at Hera. 'Ah. Jason. That's the connection, isn't it?'

Hera nods once. 'The connection between the cities of Pelion, yes.' She pauses, as if weighing up how much to tell them. Then she leans towards Artemis, her tone confiding, eyes bright: 'Who was it, do you think, who made sure that Jason was driven from Iolcos and commanded by Pelias to bring back the Golden Fleece to recover his kingdom? Which, with my help, he will achieve. Who was it who ensured that, ousted from Iolcos, he is forced to stay with his uncle in Pagasae, thus proving to him – and the people – what an able king he will be? And finally,' her mouth curls into a smile, 'who was it who gave the priests in my sanctuary in Perachora a prophecy, commanding that the heir to the king of Pagasae will bring back a mythical treasure of gold from the very ends of the earth?' She takes a deep breath. 'Which means—'

'Which means,' Artemis finishes for her, 'that when Jason retrieves the Fleece, he will have won not only the kingdom of Iolcos but that of Pagasae too.' She shoots Hera a look of grudging admiration, as at a player at dice who has just cast the winning throw. 'You will unite the cities of Pelion once again under Jason, and bind him to you at a single stroke.'

Hera glimmers a smile at her stepdaughter. 'Yes,' she says. 'I will. The citadels of Mycenae, Sparta, Argos, Iolcos and Pagasae – the foremost kingdoms of Greece – all under my care, making sacrifices to me.' The look of contentment slips from her features. 'And I swear by the waters of the Styx, I shall be rid of Atalanta.'

'Peace, Hera,' Iris interjects softly. 'You forget, you are a goddess and she is but human.'

Another smile curls Hera's lips, and her shoulders relax. 'Yes,' she says. 'Yes, that is true. You are right, Iris.'

'Does Zeus know?' Artemis asks, swirling her feet so that the water eddies around her ankles.

'Know what?'

Artemis rolls her eyes. 'Does my father know you're favouring Jason?'

Hera reaches up to the orange-gold clouds that are floating just above the peak and makes herself a soft golden towel, which she lays at the water's edge.

'No,' she says at last. 'No, he doesn't.' She settles herself beside Iris and Artemis, one foot dangling in the water. 'But what Zeus doesn't know would fill a library, and,' she glances archly at Artemis, 'it hasn't hurt him yet, has it?'

'Is she there?'

Zeus is hiding behind a rock nearby, his hair tousled, his robe creased and scented with the unmistakable lingering perfume of a woman. Hermes peeks out from behind an olive tree.

'Yes,' he hisses at Zeus. 'Her and the whole gang – Artemis, Aphrodite and, of course, Iris.' He rolls his eyes.

Zeus glares at his messenger, then glances up to his palace. The winding path to the entrance passes directly beside the pool where his wife is bathing, and there is no chance that he can creep past unnoticed.

'Why did we have to land here?' he hisses at Hermes. 'Why didn't we go further up?'

'I didn't know they were here, did I?' Hermes replies, peering around the tree again. 'Oh, wait!'

'What?' Zeus asks urgently.

'Aphrodite just got out of the pool . . . Yes . . . Oh, my! Will you look at that!'

There is a pause as the two gods tilt their heads to one side and stare at the figure of Aphrodite in admiration. Then Zeus shakes his head, like a dog trying to get water out of its ears. 'Hermes!' he whispers. 'I haven't got time for this! I must get back into the palace before Hera comes home!'

'Right-oh,' Hermes says, but he takes a moment longer, his eyes still lingering, before he tears himself away and looks at Zeus. 'What was that? Oh, yes. The palace. I think this is a back-entrance situation, yes?'

'Anything! Just get me in!'

Hermes nods. 'Very well. This way . . .' He leads Zeus out from the rock and down onto a narrow, stony path, lined with prickly thorn bushes, that circles beneath the pool and skirts the mountain peak.

'You're sure she can't see me?' Zeus hisses, clutching at his robes and shuffling along the narrow path. 'Ow!' He winces as a thorn pricks his shin. 'I think I prefer the normal way in!'

'Yes, well,' Hermes says, his voice a remarkable imitation of Athena's when she is at her primmest and most proper. 'You shouldn't have secret assignations, then, should you?'

Zeus snorts. 'You're one to preach. In any case, you know what would happen if I told her. The last time she found me sneaking out on her she destroyed the city of Ur. What am I supposed to do?'

Hermes considers. 'Well,' he says, in the tone of a judge balancing the verdict, 'I suppose the safest route, all things considered, would be not to cheat on her at all.' He flashes a wicked grin at his father and winks.

'And what else are we supposed to do to keep ourselves entertained for all eternity than set the mortals to fight with each other, to watch over those we favour –'

'Atalanta, apparently, in your case,' Hermes interrupts him, 'although I still don't see why.'

'– and to lie with them when we can?'

Hermes cocks his head to one side, then grins and gives Zeus an elaborate bow, as if conceding the point. And with this irrefutable show of logic, the father of the gods and his messenger set off again, back towards the palace.

The Heir Returns

Pagasae

The Hour of the Setting Sun
The Twentieth Day of the Month of Sailing

'But I don't understand,' I said, looking from Neda to Myrtessa, then to Philoetius, my thoughts a whirl of confusion. 'The symbol of the *king*?'

'*Hush!* Not in here!'

Myrtessa and Neda laid their hands on my arms and half pushed, half dragged me through the open door of the kitchen into a smaller side room that adjoined it. It was a pantry, built of mud bricks with a small window at one end that let in a little light. Wooden shelves were stacked against the walls, heaped with dried herbs and salted meats wrapped in linen. Strings of onions and garlic hung from the ceiling, and rushes were strewn underfoot to keep the air cool and dry. Myrtessa pushed me down onto a stool, and they all three stood in front of me, Philoetius looking between Neda and Myrtessa, clearly sharing my bewilderment.

'What is it, by all the gods?' I said angrily, attempting to stand up, but Neda pushed me down again, both hands on my shoulders.

'Listen,' she said, and at the tone of her voice I stopped struggling. 'I was a slave in the palace before I came to Lord Corythus', wasn't I? I was a handmaid in the royal chambers. I lay with the king when he wanted me. He sold me when he took no more interest in me – and I came here.' She shrugged, as if this were a normal way of life. 'But I've seen that sign before.' She took a deep breath. 'On King Iasus' seal-ring.'

I stared at their pale faces. 'What of it? So I was born to a slave of the king's, just like you—'

'No, you were not,' she interrupted me. 'This is the king's personal emblem – the symbol of his family. He would give it to none other than his kin. There is only one other medallion like it, and I have seen it around the neck of Prince Lycon – the king's son.'

I paused to take in the full absurdity of what she had said. Then I let out a laugh. 'You cannot be serious!'

'I assure you she is,' Myrtessa said.

I looked from Myrtessa to Neda, then to Philoetius, who was staring at Neda as if he had just realized something. 'You are playing with me!' I said. 'It is not possible! How could I—'

'Listen to me,' Myrtessa said, kneeling upon the rushes next to me and taking my hand, her eyes fixed upon mine. 'Were you ever told, in that faraway village of yours, that Prince Lycon once had a sister?'

I shook my head slowly.

There was a pause, as the three slaves exchanged looks.

'What of it?'

Neda settled down upon the floor beside Myrtessa, knees tucked into her chest. 'Eighteen years ago, the queen was about to give birth.' Neda was speaking steadily, clearly, her brown eyes boring into mine as if willing me to memorize every word. Myrtessa and Philoetius were silent, barely breathing, the atmosphere in the room tense as a taut bowstring. 'I remember the swell of my mistress's belly, though I was only a child-slave in the queen's chambers, the pride and excitement of the kingdom of Pagasae as they awaited an heir to the throne at last. And the look on the king's face when the messenger came to him and told him that there were two children and the first-born was a girl.' She took a deep breath. 'None of the priests had predicted such a thing. They had all prophesied a single heir, a prince fit to rule the kingdom. Declaring that all he needed was a son to continue his line, the king acknowledged Lycon and ordered the girl banished, exposed upon the peak of Mount Pelion, in the middle of winter.'

I was staring at her now, my eyes never leaving hers.

'Queen Clymene died shortly after giving birth, and the prince remained in the palace with his father but grew up sickly and small,

60

choosing to read poetry rather than to fight in battle. When Jason returned to the city, what other solution could there be? There was no other heir to be had, for Prince Lycon would never have been able to retrieve the Fleece, and the king's only other child had been exposed upon the rocks as a child and left to perish. Everyone thought she had died.'

Myrtessa nodded. 'Until now.'

Something very painful was happening inside my chest. I felt as if I had been hammering all my life against a bolted door, and now someone had slid aside the bar and I had tumbled into the darkened passageway beyond. I did not know what lay ahead – only that there was no way of turning back.

'My father,' I swallowed, 'told me that he came upon me on the mountain.' I paused, remembering the image of swirling snow and ice hanging from the trees. 'In winter.'

Myrtessa stood up and stepped back. 'Atalanta,' she said, her expression serious. 'You are the daughter of the king.'

My heart was beating so hard that my chest could barely contain it. I was taking fast, shallow breaths as if I were running from a wild beast through the forests. What had I expected? I had thought perhaps to be the child of a noble, fathered upon a slave, or a merchant's daughter, the youngest of the children and too costly to be kept. But the daughter of a king – a king who had abandoned me to die for the crime of not being the son he had wished for? I felt the same chasm of loneliness as I had in Kaladrosos, a gaping hole in my stomach gnawing at my flesh. *Declaring that all he needed was a son to continue his line, the king acknowledged Lycon and ordered the girl banished . . .*

Tears sprang to my eyes but I forced them back. *He did not want me. My own father ordered me to die simply because I was not a man.*

I looked up at the three of them. 'I am the king's daughter . . .' I said, my voice faltering. 'The king's . . .'

Can it really be true?

A light began to flicker, slowly, in the darkness of my mind.

The true heir to the kingdom of Pagasae will bring to the city a treasure of gold, spoken of in myth, hidden at the very ends of the earth.

Slowly, all I had heard these past few days in Pagasae began to come together in my head, as if it were a pattern set for me by the gods, a twisted labyrinth through which I had been stumbling and had suddenly come upon the key . . .

The search for the heir to Pagasae . . . the quest for the Golden Fleece . . .

The king's own daughter . . .

I am the king's own daughter . . .

The light was growing stronger, bolder, glowing, lighting the way ahead, like a guttering lamp upon a stone-flagged path in the dark.

'Atalanta?' Neda said, stepping forwards hesitantly. 'Are – are you well?'

Suddenly, I stood up.

Neda and Philoetius backed away.

'Atalanta . . .' Myrtessa began.

But I ignored her. I strode past all three back into the kitchen, pulling at the band that Myrtessa had wrapped around my hair to keep it in its elegant style and shaking my head, letting my hair fall down over my shoulders. I reached down beside the ovens and lifted up my bow and quiver.

'Atalanta, what are you doing?'

Myrtessa, Neda and Philoetius had come after me. They were staring at me, eyes round as clay drinking cups.

I took the quiver by its strap and slung it over my shoulder, the bow stave tapping the back of my head. 'What do you think I am doing? I am going to prove I am as worthy to be the king's child and heir as any son.' I turned to the three of them, breathing hard, every nerve in my body trembling with determination for what I was about to do, determination to show them all what I was capable of – what a mistake they had made in believing I was anything less than a man.

'I am going on the quest for the Golden Fleece.'

Myrtessa caught up with me in the corridor leading away from the kitchens. 'Wait – *Atalanta*!' she called, laying a hand on my arm. 'Think for a moment!' She lowered her voice to a clipped whisper. 'Do you not think you are being hasty? Why do you not go to the king, now, show him your medallion, and tell him who you are?'

I glanced up and down the corridor. Slaves were pushing past us, running to and from the kitchens, their arms filled with pots and linens; at the other end, I spotted Corythus' steward, conspicuous with his dark-red tunic and staff, reprimanding a slave who had smashed a pitcher of oil, the golden liquid spreading over the tiles between the sherds.

'In here!' I pulled Myrtessa into a small alcove set into the wall, where the dark leaves of a laurel shrub afforded some shelter from prying eyes. I slid behind it, pressing myself against the cool plaster of the wall, and felt Myrtessa creep in beside me, the sleeves of her tunic brushing my skin, her breath warm upon my face. 'You ask why I do not go to the king,' I whispered. 'Have you forgotten the prophecy from the gods which you yourself told me? King Iasus clearly attaches a high importance to the oracle, for why else would he have inscribed it upon stone? If I do not fulfil it, will he not have yet another reason to disbelieve me? And,' I pressed on, as Myrtessa opened her mouth to interrupt me, 'even if the king accepted my claim to be his child without the Fleece, why would he wish for a daughter now, any more than before? How can I know he would not hound me from the city once more for being a woman? No.' I shook my head, still peering warily through the leaves for any sign that we might have been seen. 'I must prove my worth.'

Myrtessa hesitated, and I could see that she was struggling to find some other reason to persuade me to stay. I pursed my lips, leaving unspoken perhaps the greatest reason of all to go after the Golden Fleece, a silent, desperate desire: to fight, to journey to uncharted lands, to sail far beyond Greece and use my hard-won skills with the bow to survive every passing danger. To show what I was capable of. *To excel upon a quest, and prove that I am worthy.*

There was a long pause as Myrtessa eyed me and I stared back at her, jaw set with determination. I could be as stubborn as an ox when I wanted to be, a quality that I knew had tested my mother's patience.

'Oh, very *well*,' Myrtessa snapped, crossing her arms over her chest and setting the leaves of the laurel tree quivering, as if in a slight breeze. 'Very well! But you cannot go after the Fleece as you are!' Her eyes swept over the rough tunic she had lent me, the gentle curve of my breasts rising beneath the material, my slender arms, my long chestnut hair sweeping my waist. She snorted quietly. 'Do you truly think that Jason will allow you to join his voyage as a woman?'

I hesitated. In truth I had hardly thought beyond my thrilling realization that I was meant to go upon the quest; that perhaps, even, it had been a path laid out for me by the gods. I shivered. 'I had thought to go alone . . .'

Myrtessa batted away the idea as if it were an irritating fly. 'Impossible,' she said. 'The Fleece is said to lie at the very ends of the earth. Do you think you can sail the most dangerous waters of the Ocean alone? Do you have sufficient gold to charter a ship from a merchant?' she continued, ignoring my attempts to interrupt her. 'No. You will join Jason's voyage – though how you will wrest the Fleece from him the gods only know. I can say with some certainty that there will be two conditions for getting aboard his ship. One, being a warrior, good with a weapon, which you are; and two, being a man, which you are not.'

'Very well,' I said, half irritated, half amused. 'So what would you have me do, then?'

Myrtessa gave me a sidelong smile. 'I think I know just the thing.'

An hour later, we were standing, breathless, in front of a pair of cedar double doors, Myrtessa fumbling with an ornate bronze key in the lock.

'Quick!' I hissed. The corridor was deserted, yet still I took each flickering shadow cast by the torches upon the walls for the silhouette of an approaching slave or, worse, Myrtessa's master. My shoulders were taut, every muscle tensed at the risk Myrtessa was taking.

What will he do to her if he discovers she has stolen the keys to his store-room? What will he do to her, a slave, when he finds that she knows where they are hidden, concealed in a chest beneath the bed within his very chamber?

'Quick!' I muttered again.

'I'm trying!' Myrtessa shot back, pulling out the key and trying a smaller one, its handle inlaid with ivory, shaking it in the lock with both hands so that the leather thong tying the keys together flapped against her skin, like a whip. 'It just – won't—'

She took another key at random and pushed all her weight against the lock. With a sudden *clunk* it sprang back and the doors swung silently inwards, revealing a dark, cavernous room that smelt strongly of cedar oil and lavender.

'*In!*'

Myrtessa slid in behind me, pulling the key from the lock and closing the doors after her. We were plunged instantly into darkness, and I could hear her kneeling and fumbling beside me to light the small terracotta oil-lamp she had brought, striking a flint against the rough stones of the wall. 'There.' She was holding a glimmering taper, which she placed at the lamp's wick. The light flared, glowing orange-gold in the engulfing darkness, like a firefly in the olive groves of Kaladrosos at night.

I looked around, my mouth slightly open. Corythus' storeroom was built high with a vaulted ceiling, strips of polished oak laid upon the floor. Precious objects lay piled around the walls, some in chests, others leaning against the stone. The lamp's light flashed from vases fashioned from clay, painted with delicate patterns; bronze shields and spears; curved bows the size of a grown man; many-coloured tapestries, draped across the shelves; cedarwood chests with large bronze locks. I took a deep breath. Here was more wealth than I could ever have imagined, more than I could ever have dreamt one person owned.

Myrtessa crept over towards a chest at the back of the room, its lock fogged with cobwebs but just visible, shimmering palely in the lamplight. 'Here!' she whispered, and pointed at the chest. 'They're in here!'

She pulled out the collection of keys she had stolen from Corythus' chambers, took the ivory-handled key and pushed it into the lock, which clicked and then released. She lifted the lid.

A waft of lavender, crushed rose petals and sage gusted into the air. Several tunics lay inside, folded neatly, one upon another, embroidered with red, gold and blue threads. I picked one up and let it fall out of its folded shape, a little creased from the years. It was a boy's tunic, about my size, and I held it up to my body, the soft wool warm against my thighs. There was a pattern of golden laurel leaves stitched on a red border along the neckline and down the long sleeves, while tasselled fringes lined the front and back of the hem. A belt, also embroidered in gold, lay rolled neatly beneath it, along with a dark-brown cloak and a pair of leather greaves.

'It's perfect,' I breathed.

Myrtessa nodded. 'It was Corythus' own, when he was a boy,' she whispered, picking up the belt, cloak and greaves, pressing the lid of the chest down again and locking it, making a faint rattling noise as bronze tapped against bronze in the echoing silence. 'He kept them all, in case—' Her voice faltered.

'In case?' I prompted her.

But she shook her head. 'We don't have time, and you need a sword,' she said. She pressed past me and reached for a long slim weapon of hammered bronze, with an embossed golden hilt, decorated with a scene of a bull-leaping contest spiralling around the grip.

I hesitated. 'It has to be one no one will recognize.'

She nodded once and brushed her fingers along the swords stacked against the wall, finally selecting a sturdy mid-length blade with a plain wooden hilt. 'Now give me the tunic,' she whispered, swiftly bundling the woollen cloak and belt around the sword blade and folding them into a rough blanket she had brought up from the slaves' quarters. 'Take this,' she thrust the lamp into my hand, 'and *go*! If we're caught the lord will flay me alive.'

We slipped back through the doors, Myrtessa closing and locking them behind us, trying hard not to let the soles of our sandals flap against the stone-flagged floors as we ran, hearts thudding, along the corridor. I followed her down the steps, along a series of passages and back to the slaves' quarters, which lay just behind the kitchens; a large, low-roofed room with straw pallets lined in rows on the floor. A slave girl was in there with a young man – whether noble or a slave I could not tell – and as we pushed our way in she leapt up from one of the pallets, panting, her tunic slipping from her shoulders, her face eloquent with guilt. She was trying to shield the man, who was still lying prone on the pallet, the thin woollen blankets tumbled over his legs.

'Oh, it's just you, Myrtessa,' she said, letting out a sigh of relief. 'I thought it might be Hora . . .'

Myrtessa tossed the bundle she was holding upon a nearby bed, sending the sweet scent of hay wafting up into the air. The girl grinned, bent in one swift motion to help her lover to his feet, wrapped them both in the blankets from the bed, then pulled him away from the slaves' quarters to a more private spot.

As she left, Neda and Philoetius pushed their way in from the kitchen, Neda still holding a wooden bread-peel in one hand. 'Did you do it?' she asked, her face pale.

Myrtessa nodded, breathing hard. Philoetius' jaw was set, and he seemed to be struggling to stop himself speaking.

'You have my gratitude, Myrtessa,' I said, clasping her hand in mine. 'I know the risks you took for me. If there is ever anything I can do for you—'

Myrtessa cut me short. 'That is all very well, Atalanta, but we do not have time. If we are found with these,' she gestured to the bundle lying upon the pallet bed, 'it will be both our necks upon the line. You need to transform yourself into a lord of standing,' she gave me a wry smile, 'and I need to return these keys to Lord Corythus' chamber before he notices they are gone. Come.'

She gathered up the tunic and sword, plucked my bow and quiver from where they lay beside my pallet, and led Neda, Philoetius and me through a doorway in the back wall, across a small dust-covered yard filled with chickens, and to a wooden shed at the opposite side, where the barley for the hens and the firewood were stored. An open window in the hayloft above let in the last rays of the setting sun. As Myrtessa closed the door and drew the bolt behind us, she seemed to breathe easy again.

'Very well,' she said, unrolling the blanket upon the straw-covered earthen floor. 'Tunic,' she held it up, 'cloak, belt, sword.'

I reached for the sword, but another hand grasped it – a broad hand with short, square-tipped fingers. I looked up, startled, to see Philoetius holding it, his face tight, his eyes slightly narrowed.

'You will get yourself killed.'

I stared at him in disbelief. 'I— What?'

'No woman can wield a sword as well as a man,' he went on, in a tone which suggested that what he was saying was a well-acknowledged truth. 'It's unnatural. It's against the laws of the gods. You should be ashamed of yourself, Myrtessa, for encouraging her.'

My mouth fell open. 'Does anyone else believe this?' I asked at last, my voice bitter.

Neda hesitated, then shrugged her shoulders, avoiding my eye. 'The Fleece is said to be guarded by a fire-breathing bull and a hundred deathless warriors. A woman cannot – that is to say,' she said, colouring, 'can you not stay here in Pagasae, and tell the king that you are his?'

'Well,' I said, my temper rising, 'I, for one, do not give credence to myths and legends composed by bards too deep in their cups. A fleece of gold, shorn from a flying ram? Bulls with hoofs of bronze?' I was so infuriated by their caution that I ignored Neda as she opened her mouth to speak, and carried on: 'There is something in it, no doubt, but more likely it is a store of treasure in Colchis' palace that lords and princes had been trying to steal until the king of Colchis spread such stories to scare them from his shores.' Neda bit her lip. 'And what do you think would happen to me if I went to the king who left me on the mountain to die as a girl? Will he welcome me back with open arms, now that I am a woman grown?'

I took a deep breath, calming myself, then continued steadily: 'The gods know I hate a boastful person as much as any other, but trust me when I say: I can handle myself with a bow and arrow.' I looked Philoetius in the eye, willing him to believe me. 'I can wield a sword with skill. I am fleet of foot, the fastest runner of all those I have met, and I can hit a moving target with an arrow at a hundred paces. As a warrior, Jason will, I am sure, have no objections to my joining him. And as a woman?' I pushed the hair back from my brow with my forearm. 'He will not have to know.'

Philoetius was silent for a long while. Then, at last, his face still registering doubt, he handed the sword back to me, hilt first. 'If you wish to be killed,' was all he said.

Myrtessa clapped her hands together, breaking the tension between us. 'Now that that's resolved,' she said, 'come.' She led me behind a partition in the store-shed where the firewood was piled and moved around me to help me out of my clothes. I laid the sword upon the ground and lifted my arms as she slipped the slave's tunic over my head, then pulled on Corythus'. The soft threads brushed against my bare skin, and I felt strange in its odd cut, with broad shoulders and sleeves so long they went past my wrists. I plucked at the neckline so it lay properly, rolled the sleeves back a little, then took the war-belt from Myrtessa and tied it loosely around my waist.

As I stepped out to show Neda and Philoetius, turning from side to side so that my empty sword sheath tapped against my thighs, Myrtessa followed me, carrying the sword balanced upon her palms. 'We should thank the gods you have a flat chest,' she said, with a half-smile. 'You look like a man, Atalanta. I'm sorry to say it but . . .' She took the sword by the hilt and lifted it, holding the blade to my throat.

'What?' I stared at her in confusion, my pulse racing.

Surely she wouldn't. I scanned the ground, saw my bow and arrows lying several feet away. 'Myrtessa, what are you *doing*?'

With a single swift movement she bunched my hair into her fist and twisted it around her palm, then sliced through it with the blade. I winced at the curious sensation, then reached up to feel the coarse ends, newly cut. I turned my head, and my hair grazed the tops of my shoulders, as the nobles of the city wore it. It felt oddly light.

'There,' Myrtessa said. I glared at her, and she grinned defiantly back. 'She looks the part now, does she not, Philoetius?'

Philoetius grunted and said nothing.

I bent down to pick up my bow and arrows from the pile Myrtessa had set upon the dusty floor, squatting to check that my dagger and the rest of my effects were still secure in my quiver, then stood and turned. '*Myrtessa!* What have you done?'

Myrtessa's glossy locks were lying on the floor beside mine. The sword was still in her hand.

'You – your *hair*!'

She had cut hers at her ears, a little rough, perhaps, but unmistakably the style in which all the male slaves had their hair – short, like a barbarian's. Neda gasped and covered her mouth with her hand. Philoetius started forwards. 'What are you *doing*?' he shot at her.

'I'm going with her,' she said.

'Myrtessa, no!' I exclaimed. 'You cannot leave—'

She raised her hands to the roof, to the gaps between the rafters that opened on to the darkening sky, the bird droppings upon the cross-beams. 'Leave what, Atalanta? What do I have that I cannot leave behind?' she said, and I noticed a hard glint in her eyes I had not seen before.

'Do you have any idea what this means?' I hissed. 'You cannot defend yourself! You will be killed the very instant you step outside the gates of Pagasae!'

She bent down and unrolled the blanket a little further. Hidden inside it was a second tunic – a male slave's, short around the thighs with a plain cloth belt. 'I will be your slave,' she said, and as she spoke she slipped out of her tunic, tore a panel from the front and started to bind her breasts with the strip of linen, occasionally wincing. 'No one ever notices a slave – I know that much at least.'

'You don't have to do this,' Philoetius said angrily, stepping forwards and placing a hand upon her arm.

'Yes, I do,' she replied, shaking him off, gasping as she twisted the material round a last time, then knotted it at the back. She looked up at me, her eyes gleaming with tears. 'I have nothing to lose. I am a slave.' She slipped the rough-spun tunic over her head and fastened the belt at the back. It was a little large for her, but, as she straightened and stood beside Philoetius, imitating his stance – legs slightly apart, arms crossed over his chest – I had the strange sensation that I was gazing at a beautiful young man with dark eyes and soft skin, just about to ripen into the brawn of manhood. 'And, besides,' she added, 'you swore to me that I could have whatever I wished from you. Well, this is it. This is what I want.'

She was staring me out, challenging me, though her eyes were still glistening with tears.

I made a last effort. 'But when you come back to Pagasae, Corythus will have you killed for deserting him.'

She turned away, but not before I had seen a shadow flicker across her eyes. 'There are worse things than death. And Neda will ensure that Corythus does not find out I am gone for as long as she can. I know it will not be for ever.'

I looked at Philoetius, who scowled, then to Neda, who nodded at Myrtessa's words and, I felt, was avoiding my eye.

'Then I suppose – you may come,' I said, giving up, and Myrtessa's face glowed; yet for some reason I could not explain, I felt a twinge of unease in the pit of my belly.

Myrtessa and I spent the next week in the city, staying in a tavern paid for with a few of the coins my mother had given me, where our windows were shaded by cypress trees and clean linen coverlets were spread upon our beds – for I would not hear of Myrtessa sleeping in the slaves' quarters. During the days we sat hidden in the small garden behind the house, rehearsing my name, birthplace and upbringing as a man – Myrtessa had embellished it from a tale she had heard a Cretan visitor relate to Corythus – until I had memorized it. More difficult was the effort to adopt the bearing and demeanour of a nobleman. We practised over and over again, observing the men who visited the tavern, follow-ing and imitating the lords who walked the streets, often beginning before the sky lightened and ending long after the sun had set. Some days we laughed together till we cried. On others Myrtessa became so frustrated with my slow progress she would hardly speak to me. As the days went on, though, there was no doubting that my voice, my mannerisms, even my walk, were beginning to pass adequately for those of a man.

The freedom we had as men was more liberating than I could have imagined. As I grew more confident in my disguise, I began to talk politics and gamble at dice with the blacksmiths, bakers and merchants passing through the tavern while Myrtessa – now a male slave by the name of Dolius – poured us honeyed wine, staying up late into the night until the lamps guttered and went out with no one to reprove us. I heard many things during my time in the city. I heard of King Iasus' dislike of Prince Lycon. I heard of his hopes that Jason might one day become the heir of Pagasae, uniting the two cities of the bay. And I heard much of the Golden Fleece, hidden far away in the kingdom of Colchis past the empire of the Hittites, far beyond the wealthy city of Troy. I heard how a winged ram with a fleece of gold, offspring of the god Poseidon, was said to have appeared to the children of the king of Orchomenos in Greece, Helle and Phrixus, when their stepmother Ino was plotting their deaths. It was flying them to safety across the sea

– or so it was told – when Helle fell and drowned in the strait that later was given her name; but Phrixus came to Colchis at the very furthest lands on the edge of the circling Ocean. He sacrificed the ram, they told me, and placed the mythical fleece there, guarded by the bronze-hoofed bulls and serpent of legend.

Most importantly of all, however, we learnt that Jason was still with his uncle in the palace – and that he had gathered there twelve of the finest heroes in the land to join him in his quest. I still thrilled with excitement at the thought of it – the greatest heroes of Greece, all gathered in the palace not a thousand paces distant!

And soon, if the gods are looking favourably upon me, I might even be among them . . .

'Are you certain this will work, Atalanta?' Myrtessa asked, for the hundredth time, that evening as we climbed the steps to the gate in the walls of the upper city, seven nights after we had left Corythus' house. The torches in the walls flared orange in the darkness to either side of us, as her fingers brushed the rough edges of her short hair. She turned, her anxious face outlined sharply in the light thrown by the flickering flames. 'I am not one to be cautious, but I know some of the slaves at the palace. They may recognize me. And Lord Corythus – if my lord is there he may know me, and even if he does not, he may know the clothing you have on, his tunic, his sword.'

'We need to be invited on the quest for the Golden Fleece. For that, we need Jason. And for Jason, we need—'

'The palace,' she finished. 'I know. But there are worse punishments awaiting me than for you, if I am caught.'

'If you want to go back now, you may,' I said. 'Remember, it was not I who forced you to come.'

She shook her head. 'No, no, I'm staying. And, besides, if you attempt to enter the palace without a slave, how will they ever take you for a true-born noble?'

We passed through the gates by two guards standing sentry either side, who nodded at me, clearly thinking I was a well-born lord come to pay his respects to the king. I shivered a little and, taking in my surroundings, tried to remember to stand straight and tall, to look as if I bowed to no one, as if I were indeed a lord who owned a hundred slaves and thought nobody but a noble was his equal. At the palace entrance, a squire with a short, pointed beard stood to attention by the doorpost and bent low as we approached.

'Your name, my lord?' he asked, looking past Myrtessa at me, taking in my embroidered belted tunic and the long sword that hung at my waist.

A wave of sickness washed over me, and I was overtaken by an overwhelming urge to flee. *How did I ever imagine I might do this?* I thought frantically. *I will be recognized for who I am, I am sure of it. He must know I am a woman . . .*

'Your name?' he repeated, a slight crease appearing between his fine eyebrows.

I forced myself to square my shoulders, as Myrtessa and I had practised, my heart pounding in my chest. 'Of course,' I said, realizing at once that in my fear my voice was far too high. I cleared my throat and lowered it as deep as it would go. 'Of – of course,' I spluttered. 'I am Lord Telamon of Crete, son of the lord Deucalion.'

The squire paused, then bowed again.

'Follow me, my lord,' he said. He glanced at Myrtessa, and his nose wrinkled a little as he surveyed her threadbare tunic. 'He may go to the servants' quarters.' He snapped his fingers and a second slave stepped out of the shadows. 'Take the slave to the kitchens. Make sure he has something to eat, and find him a pallet to sleep on.'

'Yes, Phocus.'

I caught Myrtessa's eye as she moved to follow him, and I could almost hear her thoughts, a mixture of excitement and barely concealed panic: *there is no turning back now.*

'This way, Lord Telamon,' the squire said, and marched off down a corridor, its tiled floors gleaming in the light of lamps burning on the walls. I could hear men talking and laughing, the smell of roasting ox wafting towards me on the breeze as we walked through room after room, all darkened, with the soft, whispering quality of a busy chamber deserted for the night, until we reached a pair of double doors, which the squire pushed open ahead of me.

'The Lord Telamon,' he bellowed, bowing me through.

Apprehensive, I looked around as I entered, trying my hardest not to stare. I had never seen anything so magnificent. This hall was four, five times larger than the one in Corythus' house, with several large, red-painted pillars carved like tree trunks with palm fronds at the top set around a circular hearth, where an entire ox was roasting on a spit. Slave-girls walked to and fro with silver platters in their hands, loaded with bread and slices of dark meat decorated with sprigs of rosemary, or carrying golden ewers filled with wine. Wooden chairs covered with cushions and fleeces were scattered about the hall, and everywhere men dressed in embroidered tunics were talking to each other in low voices or laughing at some shared joke, double-handled golden cups in their hands. I could feel the eyes of all upon me, a stranger to the king's court. *How very much I stand to lose if I am caught*, I thought, and felt my legs weaken and tremble so that I could barely go on. Then I spotted Meleager, a long cloak of dark-blue wool draped over him, whispering in the ear of a slave-girl, who laughed, throwing her head back so that her dark curls rippled.

'Lord Telamon,' I heard a voice say. 'You are welcome to our halls.'

I turned. King Iasus was sitting on a painted throne, a brown cloak falling from his shoulders. His face was sharply outlined, as if the gods had drawn it with a stylus upon clay, the nose defined, his eyes piercing, the stubble of a greying beard traced upon his chin.

My father.

I felt a curious sensation of panic, and a rush of unexpected anger tighten around my chest, like a girdle, and I stared at him, unable to think of anything to say. He leant forwards.

'Telamon,' he said, and narrowed his eyes. 'You cannot be Telamon of Aegina, for he must be older than you – why, he has two infant sons, and you look as if the down has barely begun growing upon your chin.'

I recovered myself. 'I – I am Telamon of Crete,' I said, my voice wavering slightly. 'My family comes from—'

He waved his hand and leant back on his throne with a thin smile. 'That is enough. Why, you will think we have no manners here in Pagasae, asking our guests to reveal themselves before they have had a slice of meat and a draught of good wine.' He gestured to one of the empty chairs near him. 'Please, sit. I will ask of your family once you have eaten, though I hardly think I need to,' he swept his eyes over my richly embroidered tunic and the bow hanging on my back, 'since your father's lineage is evident in you.' He looked around at the gathered lords. 'You are clearly of the race of sceptred kings favoured by Zeus.'

I bowed, trying not to show a flicker of expression, aware that the eyes of all those within the hall were upon me. *He does not know the extent of the truth he speaks.*

'You are very gracious, my king,' I said aloud, avoiding his eye, and I moved to sit on the chair he had indicated.

King Iasus waved his hand to one of the cupbearers, who stepped forwards, dipped a golden cup into a large vase filled with wine and handed it to me, his head bowed.

'Stranger,' the king said, 'pray to Lord Zeus, whose feast you have happened upon in our halls. When you have poured libations and prayed to the deathless gods, as is right, pass the cup of honeyed wine to the man beside you so that he may do the same.'

I accepted the vessel with both hands and tilted it forwards slightly, so that a few drops of sweet wine fell to the tiled floor, as we used to do with our clay cups in Kaladrosos before every meal.

'Wait,' King Iasus said, holding out his arm as I opened my mouth to make a prayer. 'I presume the guards at my gates told you to go to the spring at Makronita to purify yourself before you came?'

'Yes.'

'And you went?'

'Yes, indeed, my king.'

He looked at me for a long time, and I held his gaze. 'Good, good,' he said, and he smiled slowly. 'We could not do with angering the gods, could we?'

I bowed my head. 'Indeed not. Lord Zeus,' I said, holding the cup to the sky and trying to stop my hands trembling as I recited the words Myrtessa and I had practised, 'I pray you fulfil what I ask: may you grant fame to King Iasus and all his heirs, and grant that I accomplish the task that has brought me to this city, then let me reach my home again.'

The tension in the air had increased at the mention of Iasus' heirs, and I saw a few of the lords glancing at a thin, sallow-faced young man with straw-blond hair on the king's left side.

That must be Lycon – my brother, I realized with a jolt.

'A good prayer,' the king said, turning deliberately away from his son and towards a young man who sat to his right. I immediately recognized Jason, the noble I had seen in the hunting procession, with his grey eyes and sloping build. He was wearing the same blue-and-green cloak I had seen before, draped over one shoulder in a careless gesture of self-assurance. I noticed the small red stain upon the hem. 'What say you, Jason?'

'May the gods fulfil our friend Telamon's words,' Jason said, bowing, though his grey eyes never left mine as he, too, tipped a little of the wine from his goblet onto the floor. I felt uneasy under his clear, sharp, calculating gaze – as though he were looking directly through me. I glanced away, biting my lip.

The tension in the hall broke at Jason's words, and he stood up and knelt by the hearth to carve the roasted ox himself, as a formal mark of honour. He placed the choicest cuts from the inner, tender part of the ox's chine on a plate and handed it to me. 'For our guest,' he said. I accepted it, my head inclined, and a slave came with a woven basket piled high with bread and placed two round rolls, still warm from the oven, upon my platter.

I barely ate, looking around me as the rest laughed and drank and crammed their mouths with meat, going over and over in my mind the story Myrtessa and I had rehearsed – the names of my ancestors, the palace in which I had been born, the journey I had made to reach Pagasae . . .

When all had eaten and drunk their fill, the king leant back in his throne. 'So. Telamon.'

The hall went quiet, and I felt my stomach clench in anticipation. Even the bard ceased strumming upon his lyre and laid it across his lap.

'Tell us, who are your parents?'

Everyone in the hall turned to me and the king's dark eyes bored into mine.

What if he knows?

What if he finds out who I am?

I forced myself to think back to the many nights Myrtessa and I had spent in the tavern in the city, and felt a little calmer. We had chosen the story of a Cretan lord since Crete was far enough from Pagasae that – we hoped – no one would know Telamon and recognize me for an impostor.

I cleared my throat. 'I will tell you who I am, my king, and proudly. I am the son of a wealthy man, Deucalion, whose father was the great Minos who ruled over mighty Knossos in Crete's rich and fertile land. Deucalion had two sons, Idomeneus and I. I killed Orsilochus, son of Aethon, with my arrows when I heard he was plotting to steal my great bow from my treasure-room. Then, having killed him and fearing the wrath of brave Aethon, I fled in a ship bound for Athens. The winds blew us off course round Cape Sounion, where Poseidon's temple gleams out from the clifftop to sea, and I landed here, troubled at heart, to beg your hospitality.'

The king leant forwards. 'Deucalion,' he said, his tone thoughtful. 'We exchanged gifts twenty years ago, I believe, when I visited Crete on my return from Sparta.' I touched my thumb and forefinger briefly together in the sign of luck as the king turned to his squire, my heart beating rather fast.

'As I recall, he gave your lordship a golden vase inlaid with silver in return for a sword from our forges, encased in the finest bronze sheath,' the squire said, bowing.

King Iasus turned back to me. 'You will pass on my prayers to the gods for your father's health, whenever you return. In the meantime, you are welcome to stay within our halls for as long as you require.'

'My thanks to you, my king,' I said, and inclined my head, feeling the tension in my belly slowly release. Around the hall, the conversation began again, lords turning to each other to talk or calling to slaves who ran across the tiled floor, sandals slapping, to serve their masters.

'Polycaste,' the king said, snapping his fingers, and a slave came up to his side, her long black hair braided down her back and her eyes lined with black kohl, in the Hittite style. 'You will bathe the Lord Telamon, anoint him with scented oil and do anything else he asks of you.' He gave me a wry smile. 'He must be fatigued from his journey. I am sure some company will be welcome in his bed tonight.'

I felt my cheeks grow warm. 'No indeed, my king,' I said quickly, then reddened further, realizing my mistake. 'I – I prefer not to bathe this night, for I fear I am too tired. I have travelled long and far these past days.'

'Too tired to bed a slave?' the king said, and raised one thin eyebrow. 'The lords of Crete are very different from the lords of Pagasae. Very well, Polycaste – make him up a bed in the colonnade, by the fountain. You will find it pleasantly cool there at night.'

'I thank you,' I said, my shoulders relaxing as I bowed to the king, and then to Jason at his side. I stood to leave, but as I did so I felt a hand upon my arm, and flinched instinctively.

'You have a fine weapon,' Jason said, his eyes upon the curved bow on my back. His fingers ran lightly over the smooth wood and the strong sinew bindings, and I had a sudden, strong urge to knock his hand away from it. 'You can handle it well?'

'Better than any other man in the land, I'll wager.'

He considered me, his expression revealing nothing, and I felt again that he was testing me, like an eagle eyeing its prey. 'I am leading a hunt in three days' time, once the festival is over,' he said. 'I would be honoured if you would join me there.'

I bowed my head. 'It would be my pleasure to accompany you, my lord.'

'Very well. We meet in three days by the gates of the palace at dawn.'

The Killing of the Boar

Mount Pelion

The Hour of Daybreak
The Thirtieth Day of the Month of Sailing

Three days later I was climbing the western flanks of Mount Pelion as
the first rays of the sun glowed in the sky, the birds twittering on the
branches, the tips of the trees still clinging to the last shreds of the
night's mist. I had left Myrtessa – or Dolius, as I now had to remind
myself to call her – with the palace slaves, and had met Prince Jason as
he had asked by the gates. I was greeted there by the other nobles whom
he had chosen to accompany him on the hunt, all carrying polished
shields, short stabbing spears and thick-shafted javelins with saw-
toothed, viciously pointed blades. They bowed to me, one by one, and
murmured their names: Jason, prince of Iolcos, and Lycon, prince of
Pagasae; Nestor, lord of Pylos; Castor and Pollux, twin sons of
Tyndareus of Sparta; Laertes of Ithaca; Meleager of Calydon; Orpheus
of Thrace; Bellerophon of Corinth; Theseus of Athens; Peleus of
Phthia; and Hippomenes, son of Megareus of Onchestos. Twelve
heroes in all.

I had felt a quiver in the pit of my stomach as I recognized many
from the tales my father had told me during the winter nights in
Kaladrosos. Theseus, king of Athens, who was now striding ahead up
the forest slopes with his hand upon his sword-hilt, had slain the
Minotaur in Crete. Bellerophon, munching on wild berries and laughing with Meleager, his bare arms criss-crossed with the scars of battle,
had killed the legendary Chimera, part-lion, part-snake. Nestor, who

walked only a few paces distant, grey-bearded and with lowering eye-brows, had defeated the centaurs many years ago in the fabled battle with the Lapiths.

What by all the gods am I doing in their midst?

My legs weakened and I stopped to lean against a tree, breathing hard.

'You have hunted boar before, Telamon?' Meleager asked, moving back beside me, his footsteps crunching on the dried leaves of the forest floor, breaking into my reverie.

I began to walk, pretending to look away over my shoulder and search the darkened undergrowth lest he recognize me from the day the hunt returned to Pagasae. 'Many times.'

'I did not know you had wild boar on Crete.' Hippomenes was frowning at me, a broad-shouldered man who carried his six-foot cornel-wood javelin as if it were light as a walking stick.

'We do not,' I said quickly, my throat drying as I searched for some-thing to say. 'I – I hunted boar when I visited my cousins, in the mountains near Parnassus.'

Laertes nodded to my left. 'I have hunted there myself,' he said, rubbing at the bristles on his chin. 'With my wife's father, Autolycus. They have good game there. Where exactly—'

But Jason held up a hand to silence him, his eyes darting left and right. 'Quiet!'

I tensed, my hand upon my sword. One of the dogs, a lean hound with sand-coloured fur, had halted, ears pricked, its nose quivering a few finger-lengths above the forest floor. Then, tail beating at the air, it moved forwards swiftly, tracking an unseen trace over the earth.

'That way,' Jason ordered, pointing after the hound through the dense wood. We followed, beating our way through low-hanging branches and treading aside prickly brambles and woodberries. I fitted an arrow to my bowstring, all thoughts of doubt stifled in the thrill of the chase, and the others drew their swords or held their spears by their sides as the rest of the hounds ran ahead, sniffing the ground. My heart was lighter than it had been in days at being back upon the mountain, surrounded by my familiar oaks, maples and pines, the scent of damp earth and the sound of trickling springs I knew so well. Soon I was spotting the marks of the boar's passage: broad hoofprints upon the black earth, thick-trunked saplings crushed to the ground by the weight of our quarry as it moved through the forest.

'This is a wide trail, my prince,' I said, in a low voice, as I moved to walk beside him at the head of the group, marking the width of the path trodden by the animal. 'The nets,' I gestured towards the coils of rope carried by two slaves, 'may not be the wisest way to capture such a large animal. He may be strong enough to break them.'

Jason considered me with a curious veiled expression – as if he were attempting to mask some irritation.

'Hippomenes,' he said at last, over his shoulder, 'what do you think?'

There was a pause as Hippomenes thought it over, and our sandals crunched upon the twigs and last year's leaves as we walked.

'The nets should keep him,' he said at last. 'We should abide by the plans we made before we set out from Pagasae. And if the nets do not hold, we still have our javelins and spears.'

'Laertes?' Jason turned to him. The sun caught his angular face and accented the slope of his jaw and straight nose.

'I am inclined to agree with Telamon,' Laertes said, gesturing towards the swathe of the path ahead. 'I would counsel ambushing the beast and bringing him down with our spears as he charges, rather than risk losing the advantage of surprise.'

The early-morning light filtered down through the trees and dappled the rocks protruding from amid the ferns of the forest floor, and set the coats of the hounds ahead shining russet and gold. Jason glanced at the nets, then at the sharp point of the ash-handled spear he was weighing in his hand, and shook his head. 'No,' he ruled. 'We set the nets. As Hippomenes said – we have our spears.'

I bowed my head. 'Very well, my lord.'

We slowed to a halt, the men around me breathing hard from the climb, the dogs skittering ahead, barking loudly and baring their teeth. We had reached a wooded glade, more thickly seeded with beech than the clearing where I had killed the lions, covered with a sprawl of rock brambles and with a dense thicket of willow scrub at the centre. The branches bent over and twisted together to make such a thick covering that I doubted any rain would penetrate it. The tension in the air doubled, and I checked my grip upon my bow.

'In there,' Laertes said quietly, pointing towards the thicket.

'You.' Jason indicated the slaves. 'The nets. Between those trees.' He pointed to a beech and a chestnut with blossoms rising in pale columns. The slaves separated, stepping quietly over the white-flowering brambles, each holding an end of the net and looping it deftly around the trunks, securing it top and bottom with thick knots. One of the slaves tested it with his hand, then nodded once towards his master, eyes downcast, before slipping away into the shadows once more.

There was a moment of silence, penetrated only by the chattering of the birds in the branches overhead, and the sound of my own uneven breath in my ears.

Then Jason raised his arm and cried, *'Forward!'* Hippomenes, as the tallest and strongest of the lords, lifted his javelin to his shoulder at the signal and approached the thicket with the dogs beside him, urging them on. They bayed and howled, skirting the edge of the covering. I followed with the rest, keeping a wide space between Castor to my left and Bellerophon to my right in case the boar broke and charged our line.

And then, at last, a loud, roaring grunt pierced the air. I saw Castor to my left tighten his grip upon his spear, and the familiar excitement coursed through me that only a hunt could bring. I raised and drew my bow. The shrill grunt grew louder, and then the thicket exploded and the boar charged out fifty paces distant, baited by the sounds of the dogs. Its hide was bristling, its small dark eyes gleaming as it shrieked and grunted, and at once I saw that in one respect at least I had been right: it must have equalled the weight of several large men, huge muscles tightening and loosening down its sides as it charged, hoofs thundering upon the rocks, its gaping maw open as it roared, long white tusks slashing from side to side. My hands were slippery upon my bow with fear, but I doubled my grip and blinked, pulling my fingers more firmly against the string and refusing to allow myself to listen to the thundering of my heart. Three of the dogs fell to the ground howling as their flanks were slashed by its tusks, white ivory now stained dark red with blood, and still it charged, closer, closer, twenty paces from the net, ten . . . And then it barrelled into the rope mesh, and the cords around the two trees pulled tight, showering leaves upon my head.

The boar was trapped.

Jason shouted with triumph and lifted his spear, aiming at the struggling animal. The boar was bellowing, twisting its head this way and that, fierce tusks of hollow ivory swiping through the air, caught in one of the net's meshes.

I drew my hand back to my ear, and released the arrow, sending its glistening, spinning point towards the throat of the trapped beast and hitting home with a splatter of blood and a shriek from the wounded animal. But as I drew and nocked a second arrow, one of the boar's tusks snagged on the net. A ripping, tearing, splitting sound rent the still air of the clearing, and the boar barrelled forwards, my arrow spiralling past its mark and into one of the trees behind.

'Round! Get *around*!' Hippomenes shouted, gesturing to the men to make a semicircle to entrap the boar, and I ran with them, the blades of our weapons glinting in the early light.

'Now – *run it to ground*!' he cried.

The boar was shaking its great tusks back and forth, working itself into a frenzy as it tried to loosen the deadly arrowhead buried in its throat, its tiny eyes darting from side to side, grunting. It lowered its enormous skull and began to charge through the ruined net towards us, flanks heaving, hoofs pounding. In one movement I sheathed my bow in the quiver on my back and, catching a spear Hippomenes threw me and following the lead of the other lords, planted it firmly in the ground, blade upwards, making a barbed fence around the beast, breathing hard, my face flushed with sweat.

Then the boar broke and swerved aside. There was a shrill cry from my right and the clatter of a spear upon the earth. I turned to see Lycon fling himself aside, just in time to avoid the boar's assault. The edge of one razor-sharp tusk grazed his arm, leaving a deep gash. The prince held it to his chest, spluttering as blood dripped to the ground, then pushed himself to stand one-handed and retreated, his face pale, breathing ragged.

'Orpheus, take care of Lycon!' Jason snarled. A man left the circle and ran towards the prince, catching him by his good arm, then half supporting, half dragging him away beneath the cover of the trees, trailing blood. The boar was skidding around to make a second charge, hoofs digging into the earth, and we moved closer together to fill the gaps left by Lycon and Orpheus, forming a line across the clearing. I could feel the warmth of Meleager's body pressing against mine to my right, Hippomenes' spear-arm, tensed and ridged with muscle, on my left.

I am doing it! I thought. I almost wanted to slap myself across the face, to prove it was no dream, but knew better than to do so in the midst of the hunt. *I am here, fighting side by side with the heroes of Greece – the greatest warriors the land has ever known!*

I felt a sudden thrill as the boar squealed again and charged towards us, a blur of deadly bloodied tusks and bristles, hoofs flying, and tightened my grip upon my spear shaft, filled with determination. Two men, who had scrambled higher up a bank to one side, hurled their javelins down at the animal but missed, the wooden shafts clattering over the forest floor, and still it was charging, screeching and snorting, aiming directly for Jason at the centre of the line . . . Moments were slowing to half their usual pace as I watched Jason square his shoulders and plant his feet firm upon the ground, bronze sword held steady before him, though he must have known that there was no fighting such a brute coming towards him at full charge.

Quick as I could, I tossed my spear aside, pulled my bow from its quiver, lowered myself to kneel on the forest floor and drew the string tight to my jaw. I squinted down the arrow shaft, moving the arrow tip in a line, sighting the boar's movement, knowing, feeling where it would be, as if the heart beating in my chest was the boar's own.

I let the arrow fly. It whistled ahead, and I felt as if I were with it, spinning round and round, following the movement of the boar. Then there was an unearthly shriek of agony as the sharp flint tip made contact, burying itself deep in the beast's eye. Dark-red blood was spurting from its head as the boar skidded to one side.

'Corner it! Corner it *now*!'

Jason's face was red with anger as he hurled the command, swishing his sword from side to side, cutting through the air as he ran.

'You cost me my glory!' he roared at me.

I ignored him, my whole being focused on the task ahead. We ran around to encircle the beast as it thrashed from side to side, leaving a trail of blood, bellowing.

'Now!' I yelled at him. 'Take it now!'

Jason raised his arm above his head, holding his sword in both hands so that the tip glittered. Then, sprinting forwards, he brought his arms down, throwing his whole body into the thrust, burying the sword point first through the boar's side, cracking the ribs with a splitting crash and piercing the heart. The boar shrieked and fell to the ground with a shudder that set the earth beneath my feet quivering. I aimed again and heard the *thwack* as my arrow severed the beast's windpipe, and its squeals became a guttering, gasping sob of blood and air through its neck. Hippomenes, then Meleager, then Theseus sent their javelins flying through the air to transfix the dying animal, each determined to fell the quarry and win their glory. Blood was now pooling freely from its side as it gasped and convulsed with pain. I ran forwards.

'Spear!' I called, and someone, I did not know who, placed a shaft in my hand. I reached the fallen corpse of the boar, swung the weapon upwards, up towards the sky where the sun was now shining like a beacon, white against the canopy of the leaves, then plunged it down beside the glimmering blade of Jason's sword, between the ribs of the beast and deep into its heart. There was a final shriek of pain, and then nothing.

We had killed the boar.

We bound the boar's legs together on the mountain, strung it up in the nets that should have caught it, lashed four thick poles together with rope, and tied the net bearing the corpse to the poles feet first. The slaves carried it over their shoulders down the mountain, while the dogs leapt and barked at it. The rest of us laughed and drank wine from leather pouches, at our ease. I had never, in all my life, felt such companionship – the sensation of being surrounded by warriors as determined as myself, hunters who knew the joys and dangers of the chase – and I was revelling in it.

That night a feast was held in the palace to celebrate our hunt. I was almost dizzy with our success, my senses still heightened, everything brighter and more colourful than it had been before. Myrtessa was allowed to attend me – I had told Jason that evening that I required my slave for personal matters, for many a lord kept a squire beside him at all times – so she was sitting on the floor at the feet of my cushioned chair, chewing the mouthfuls of meat and black olives I surreptitiously passed her in my napkin.

I was leaning forward now, talking to her in a low voice, relating the events of the day's hunt as the nobles around us laughed – Corythus was not there, I was relieved to see – and slaves swept past us serving meat and pouring wine. She had been wryly amused by my excitement as I described each twist and turn in the killing of the boar, and was now slipping a slice of meat into her mouth, licking her fingers to catch the red-wine sauce.

'I look forward to seeing how you fare against the serpent that guards the Fleece,' she said. 'I hear its teeth are as sharp as the points of whetted swords, but I suppose that will be as nothing to our Atalanta.'

'Not so loud,' I said through gritted teeth, though in truth no one could have heard her but I through the scraping of platters and cups, the spitting of the boar's carcass upon the fire, and the loud talk as the lords played at dice upon small cedarwood tables. 'Do you want us to be found out?'

But Myrtessa did not reply. She had lowered her eyes in the submissive stance of a slave, and I saw that my napkin had disappeared from her hands into the folds of her tunic.

I felt a wave of apprehension.

Jason had approached while we were talking, and was standing before me now, holding a two-handled gold cup. He had taken off his cloak in the heat of the Great Hall and was wearing a tunic of bright blue, stitched with a pattern of gold spirals upon the edges and fringed with tassels of red. A dagger, inlaid with gold and silver, gleamed at his waist. I stood to acknowledge him, Myrtessa crawling out of my way, and bowed my head.

'My lord Jason.'

What can he want with me now?

He cannot have discovered me – can he? Not so soon?

'You hunted well today,' he said, a muscle twitching in his jaw, and I wondered whether he was remembering how I had kept the boar from him earlier that day. The babble and chatter in the hall died as the other lords stopped to listen. 'You were the first to hit the boar and to draw blood. Your skill with a bow is such that I have not seen it in men twice your age.'

I felt as if I had grown taller as I looked up at him. 'It was my honour to hunt alongside you and the other lords,' I replied, my voice steady, though inside my heart was dancing and I was longing to break into a grin.

'A libation to the gods in the honour of the first to wound the boar,' King Iasus called across the hall, and the many nobles gathered there, along with the lords who had accompanied Jason on the hunt, nodded their assent. Jason tipped the goblet forwards a little and a drop of wine, red as fresh-spilt blood, dripped to the floor.

'May the lord Zeus, whose festival we here hold, look favourably upon my prayer,' he said. 'May you, lord god, bring it to pass that Telamon, son of Deucalion, continues to surpass his equals with as much courage as he has shown today.' He raised his cup.

The lords roared their approval, and the sound of clattering metal filled the air as they banged their goblets upon the tables. I felt the colour rising to my face, and inclined my head so that the lords would notice nothing.

Jason held up his hands, and the shouting and banging died down.

'There is something else I would say,' he said, and his grey eyes moved from mine and swept from the crowds of nobles spread throughout the banqueting hall to the ten lords seated closest to the throne, then to the straw-haired Prince Lycon and finally to the king. King Iasus nodded once.

'My prince Lycon. My lords Meleager, Theseus, Nestor, Bellerophon, Orpheus, Peleus, Hippomenes, Castor, Pollux, Laertes,' Jason said, turning and addressing each by name. A shiver ran down my spine as I realized what was about to happen. The atmosphere in the hall seemed to tauten like a tensed bowstring. 'I have spoken with Argus, the ship-builder, this day after we returned from the hunt, and I have seen our ship with my own eyes, gleaming upon the sand of the harbour, every plank honed to perfection, every stitch in the sail pulled tight. Argus assures me that he has checked over the ship once and once again, and that nothing remains to be done but to set upon our voyage.' He placed his goblet down upon the table in a deliberate manner. 'I believe the day has come when we may sail upon our quest.'

The gathered nobles had begun to talk in loud, excited whispers. I swallowed and kept my gaze upon him, heart beating fast. *He must be about to ask me upon the quest for the Golden Fleece! Why else would he have singled me out, before all the others?*

He must be about to ask me now!

Jason turned to the ten heroes and the prince. 'Twelve of us, my lords, the twelve finest men in Greece,' he said, picking up his goblet and raising it to them. 'May the gods look favourably upon each one of you, and may they bring us safely back again to our women and our beds! We meet at the harbour in the morning.'

He turned and bowed to me.

I held my breath.

Now – it has to be now!

'I look forward to hunting with you again on our return,' he said.

And then he walked away.

That night, as the moonlight filtered through the branches of the cypress trees in the courtyard and cicadas hummed in the darkness, I lay fully dressed and awake upon the layers of fleeces and blankets that had been laid out for me. Anger coursed through me and I was unable to sleep. Myrtessa was snoring gently upon the floor, one arm flung out over the tiles of the colonnade.

I pummelled the cushion that served as a pillow and turned over to face the courtyard, where a fountain was tinkling into a basin of stone surrounded by fragrant box hedges.

Why had Jason not asked me to accompany him on the voyage for the Golden Fleece? I had proven my valour, had I not? I was dressed as a man, was I not, with a man's strength and speed, a man's skill at arms? He had said as much himself! What more did he require?

I twisted onto my side, rage thumping through my veins. To have come so close – so close! – yet be thwarted at this final moment! It was not simply my desire to prove my worth to the king. It was more than that . . . I rolled onto my back and stared up at the dark ceiling, biting back tears. I had felt, even if only for a moment, that I belonged. That I had found my purpose. That I was, at last, upon a quest with comrades at my side who held me as an equal. And my failure to be summoned to the voyage had taken all that away as, next day, Jason's ship would slide over the waters to the east . . .

I sat bolt upright in the moonlight. 'Myrtessa!' I hissed. 'Myrtessa!'

'Hmm . . . what?'

'You have to wake up *now*!'

'I don't . . . Let me sleep, Atalanta . . .'

But I had already got up and was pulling her upright. She looked sleepily into my face and rubbed her eyes. 'What is it?'

'We're going to the harbour,' I said, picking up my quiver. 'We're going to join the quest, whether they want us to or not.'

We crept through the western edge of the city towards the gates, staying in the shadows and treading lightly down the side streets past the silent, looming facades of the houses, their shutters closed against the night's chill, with the city wall to our right. My bow and arrows were bouncing upon my back, Corythus' sword at my belt, his cloak swirling behind me in the faint breeze. I was looking right and left as we half ran, half walked through the darkness, alert for any movement, any sign that we might have been seen, my thoughts whirling. If we waited hidden beside the gates until Jason and his lords arrived to pass through them, we might be able to slip through behind – but there was hardly a chance that neither they nor the guards would notice us in the full light of day.

And if they saw us, we would likely be sent back to the palace – perhaps thrown from the city. From what I had heard, we might even be put to death for our insubordination.

No: there had to be another way.

We turned onto the stone-paved main street and I pressed myself flat against a column cornering a shuttered shopfront. At least three pairs of guards were patrolling the ramparts around the city – I could see their helmeted silhouettes and the tall, dark shafts of their spears outlined against the silver-blue sky.

'What now?' Myrtessa asked, shivering.

'Hush! In here!'

I pulled her into the shadows of a low-hanging archway to a stable, the earthy smell of hay and horse dung filling the air. Myrtessa was rubbing her arms and her teeth were chattering: her slave's tunic was thin and she had no cloak. I passed her mine without a word, and she clasped it around her neck with a brief murmur of gratitude.

I peered out from the archway to look more closely towards the looming wooden gates at the street's end. I could hear the faint sound of the guards talking to each other up above and the clanking of their bronze armour, audible over the snuffling and snoring of the horses in their sleep. The gates stretched fifteen cubits high into the night sky, solidly built and secured by a heavy wooden bolt, just visible through the darkness, which I judged would require the strength of more than five men to lift. The battlements soaring above were topped with the same stone crenellations I had seen before, gently curving stone protrusions from which archers would aim their arrows upon attackers, if the city ever had to defend itself. And then I noticed something I had not seen before: a small side door beside the gate, barely a man's height and hidden in the shadows, closed with a plank slotted through a couple of sockets.

Pray the gods it is not locked.

It was our only chance.

I took Myrtessa's hand and slipped out onto the street. I glanced up to the walls: two guards had just walked past the fortifications above the gates, their figures dark against the moonlit sky. The next pair could not be far away. We did not have much time.

I ran down the street, keeping to the darkness beneath the eaves of the houses, treading softly and skirting dogs lying sleeping on the paving stones and merchants' stalls standing empty before the shops. I could hear Myrtessa behind me, her breath coming short and fast with fear; my whole being was alert, every stone upon the street sharp in my vision, every flickering shadow drawing my attention. As we reached the walls we were enveloped in darkness, and I blinked, my eyes adjusting. I stretched my hands before me and let my fingertips graze the rough stone of the walls, feeling along the blocks of limestone until—

'Here,' I hissed at Myrtessa, as my fingers slid onto grainy wood and followed the veins of the door down until I reached the bolt. I pulled it sideways, trying to slide it noiselessly through the sockets while Myrtessa held her breath. As I urged it through the last there was a soft scrape of wood on wood, and a dog nearby, sheltering in a shop doorway, raised its head, eyes gleaming in the darkness.

Hermes, god of travellers and mischief, let it not give us away, I thought, standing motionless, holding the bolt in both hands, eyes fixed upon the animal. Myrtessa clutched at my tunic, her breathing shallow.

Please, gods – let it be silent!

There was a moment, in which the dog blinked at us. Then it laid its head down again upon its paws.

I let out a shaking breath and bent to prop the bolt against the wall. I pulled at the door's handle, hoping against hope it was not locked as well, but it swung silently open at my touch, sending a stream of silvery moonlight pooling over the flagstones at my feet.

'Quick!'

Myrtessa slipped through, and I followed her, pulling the door closed behind me. I could hear the voices of the next pair of sentries on the wall above us now, their words growing ever clearer. They could be no more than a few paces away. I moved swiftly aside and pressed myself flat against the rough stones beside Myrtessa, trying to silence my ragged breath.

'Stay where you are,' I mouthed to her.

We stood side by side, hearts thudding, waiting. Artemis' moon shone brightly in the sky before us in a curving sickle, vanishing the stars.

It seemed like an eternity before the guards passed. Quick as I could, I nodded to Myrtessa, then began to run across the plain over the silver-tipped grass towards a large maple tree that stood a hundred paces from the walls.

I turned and held out a hand to Myrtessa as she arrived behind me to pull her into the shadows of the tree.

'That was well done,' she said, panting hard, her eyes bright. 'Now – to the harbour?'

I looked over to the wooded olive groves that lined the cliffs above the shore, the sparkling sea two hundred paces distant.

'Yes. To the harbour.'

*

I woke a few hours later, hidden in the boughs of an olive tree, my neck aching, joints stiff from the cold. Myrtessa was still asleep, her forehead resting against the tree's trunk. It was just after dawn, and the rays of a young sun were skimming the horizon to the east, tinging the sky with pink and gold. Sounds were coming from the bay below.

Voices.

I sat upright, trying not to set the tree's branches quivering, and peered through the slim, grey-green leaves. Now that it was light, I could see at least twenty ships moored in the bay, the waves slapping against their hulls mingling in my ears with the piping songs of the birds in the trees around me. Most were tethered to posts along a pier that stretched out to the sea, floating on the waves stirred by the early-morning breeze. Some were small fishing skiffs, others heavy merchants' galleys with deep rounded hulls, but it was clear at once which was Jason's ship. I took a deep breath, marvelling at its beauty and splendour. It must have been at least forty-five paces from prow to stern and was drawn up directly upon the shore nearest to where we lay hidden, held up on wooden props. Its keel cut into the fine white sand of the beach, its long narrow hull tarred black. I could make out the figures of twenty or thirty slaves already bustling around it along the shore, the sounds of the commotion floating towards me on the air as they climbed the landing plank and loaded supplies into the storage holds at stern and bow. Here and there I caught sight of some lords from the hunt: Laertes, with his dark-stubbled beard; grey-haired Nestor leaning upon his staff; Theseus, with his barrel chest and rolling gait. I let my eyes rove from the small raised platform at the stern, with two black-painted steering oars, to the prow in front, where a golden figurine of an eagle crouched, symbol of Zeus, its wings gathered in by its sides, its beak curved. The sail was furled along the lowered yardarm beneath a mast planted at the ship's centre, secured by tight forestays tied to the bow. Twenty-five pinewood thwarts, six or seven cubits long, crossed it: rowing benches wide enough to seat two men, each matched by oars tied to the ship's sides with leather thongs. Polished wooden railings surrounded the raised decks at bow and stern, and the glittering letters, *Argo*, shimmered gold on the hull in the sun. Though I had often sailed

94

the waters of the open sea with the fishermen of Kaladrosos, and knew my way around the skiffs that had moored in our harbour – the rigging and brails to reef the sail, the loops on the masthead for attaching the sheet, the steering oar and the pole for punting in shallow water – I could not have imagined such a glorious ship, as graceful and slender as a bird.

I elbowed Myrtessa awake. She grunted, started, then squinted in the light.

'You have to join the slaves,' I whispered, a raw excitement tingling in my belly as I pointed down to them. Their arms were filled with weaponry as they approached the ship – beaten bronze shields, breast-plates, helmets, greaves; others carried fat leather pouches, large orange-red clay pots brimming with grain, nuts, olives, and meat wrapped in linen. I spotted Jason striding among them, his cloak swirl-ing as he shouted orders and sent goods in all directions. 'They'll never notice another slave join them,' I continued, 'and if you bear yourself with enough confidence I'm sure they'll not question you. Mingle among them; carry what you can up into the ship, as if you are another of their slaves.'

Myrtessa yawned and stretched. I saw her eyes sweep the harbour, then narrow as she caught sight of the *Argo* and remembered why we had come, what we were about to do.

'And you?' she murmured, straightening herself on the bough with a small grimace. 'What will you do?'

I tapped my fingers upon the bark beside me. 'Jason at least is sure to recognize me before I have a chance to board the ship. I'll have to find another way.' I bit my lip, thinking hard. I had to make sure that he did not simply turn me away . . . that I did something daring enough to impress them with my worth . . .

Myrtessa grinned. 'Then I shall see you on the *Argo*.' She hoisted up her tunic and prepared to slip to the ground, then turned and laid a hand upon my arm. 'This plan of yours, make sure it works. I don't want to find myself sailing to the ends of the earth without you.'

As Myrtessa leapt down and pushed her way quietly through the olive trees that lined the slope towards the harbour, I turned my atten-tion towards the group of lords upon the beach. They were there, all

95

twelve of them. I sat for a while, wondering again, with a shiver of fear, at the sheer strangeness of it, that I, Atalanta, should be attempting to join the warriors of Greece – Bellerophon, Castor and Pollux, Peleus – of whom I had only heard tell in stories . . . That there, just before me, busying themselves on the shore below with their preparations for the voyage, walked the greatest heroes of the age – perhaps the greatest there had ever been . . .

Then I shook my head, trying to bring myself back to my senses. *There will be time for that later*, I told myself. *For now, you still have the hardest part to do.*

Jason was still pacing up and down the beach, ordering the slaves to work faster, shouting more commands. I thought I could make out Lycon, too, standing close by the ship's keel, deep in conversation with the lord Orpheus, and Argus, the ship-builder and steersman, at the stern leaning over the railings and directing the storage of grain to the hold below the steering deck. Hippomenes and Meleager were standing upon the beach beside a pile of weapons, weighing spears in their hands before the slaves carried them to the ship, testing them for balance. I smiled slightly, remembering how it had felt to stand between them at the hunt, side by side, their spear-arms beside mine. The desire to join them burnt within me, like a kindled flame, more fiercely than I had ever felt it before. I adjusted my position so that I could see more of the bay, careful not to let the leaves rustle or the branches crack as I moved.

I cannot afford to be seen.

Yet.

I watched as, one by one, the slaves, including Myrtessa now, carrying sacks of grain, began to climb up the plank onto the ship. Once all the slaves had boarded, followed by the lords' stewards, then the nobles themselves, I saw Jason step back to let Prince Lycon climb on, then turn and scan the olive trees around the edge of the harbour and the city walls, as if to say farewell. For a single moment my breath caught in the back of my throat. I thought he had seen me, that his gaze was resting directly upon me; but then he turned and followed Lycon onto the ship. My stomach contracted.

It was nearly time.

Almost all, lords and slaves alike, were now seated at the thwarts, two to a bench with an oar drawn across their laps – though I noticed the lords were clustered at the stern, where the wind would blow freshest on the open sea. A group of broad-shouldered slaves were left upon the shore, and as I watched, I saw them set their shoulders to the hull of the ship; then they leant forwards and pushed, heels digging into the sand. At first nothing happened. Then, slowly, very slowly, with a creaking sound that rent the still morning air and set several gulls flapping from the calm surface of the sea, the boat began to move from its props, wood scraping against the sand as it shuddered down the beach. The men were leaning close to the ground now, pushing, like oxen guiding a plough across the dark furrows of a field. The ship was gathering speed, slipping slowly but surely into the shallows. There were only moments before it was entirely seaborne.

As the first wave lapped around the prow and the rowers banked their oars, I made my decision. Jumping from the olive tree I landed on the rocks below, my bow and quiver rattling at my back, and was running as soon as I hit the ground. I sprinted towards the sea and across the bay, every muscle of my body alive with excitement, my entire mind charged with a single thought: *get aboard the ship*.

In one leap I knocked aside two fishermen who were gathering their nets around a fishing boat upon the shore, then continued on, racing faster than I ever had before, towards the pier jutting out to sea. I scaled the steps in three leaps and then I was on the wooden landing stage, running full tilt across the planks towards the open ocean. I knocked aside a merchant carrying a crate and he dropped it in a cloud of colour, cursing me as red, gold and brown spices filled the air. Still I ran on, leaping over nets and the unloaded cargo of a trader's galley. The *Argo* was already floating on the water, and the slaves who had pushed it off-shore were splashing through the shallows, then climbing a rope up the rounded sides onto the thwarts. The sail was flapping in the breeze as the yardarm was hoisted to catch the wind, like the huge white wing of a bird. The rowers dipped their oars into the shallows, moving slowly as I had guessed they would as they navigated past the ships clustered at the jetty. I could hear the sound of the drum beat, keeping time for the rowers, and the oars splashing the water in response – they were already beginning to move more quickly. There were only moments left. With a last burst of speed, I flew across the wooden planks, vaulting the posts jutting out from the pier's end, and then I was flying through the air, over the sparkling blue waters of the sea and—

I hit the side of the *Argo* with a loud smack of bone on wood that knocked the air from my lungs and sent a bruising shock of pain shooting through my ribs. At once, I firmed my grip, trying to get a purchase with my fingers on the thick ridged beam that topped the ship's side, clinging to the edge of the hull, my sandalled feet dangling over the two-fathom drop to the sea where weed swayed and silver fish glittered. I took a deep breath, summoning my strength, and clung tighter as the ship rocked and swayed to the beat of the oars.

'What was that?'

I heard the voice from the deck above, then feet coming towards me over the drummer's beat. I pulled with one hand and raised one elbow, then another flat against the beam of the ship's side, gasping for breath, sweat trickling down the sides of my forehead. Pushing down into the palms of my hands I straightened my arms, pulling myself up, one knee onto the side, then swinging the other around and over to jump down into the boat.

I was standing face to face with Hippomenes.

The Quest Begins

Mount Olympus

Iris is seated on a jutting crag just below Olympus' peak. She is surrounded by pale wild flowers and swifts that spiral through the clear air, away from the palaces, the gardens and the fountains of the gods. Her chin rests on her hand.

She has just come from Hera's chambers, the room filled with the peach light of dawn from the east, the white curtains at the windows rippling in the breeze. Hera — as she always does, as if Iris were her servant, not an immortal goddess born of an old sea god — has ordered her, with a chilly half-smile and a patronizing pat on the shoulder, upon a task to which Hera has been building up for days, weeks even: the granting of the favour of the gods to the sailors of the Argo, or Argonauts, as generations to come will know them.

She looks towards the distant outline of the citadel of Pagasae far to the south, and a memory flits into her mind, distracting her from her task. She almost smiles as she remembers Hera's rage a few days before when she discovered that Atalanta was still alive. How she would have loved to tell Hera then that it was she, Iris, who was responsible for Atalanta's continued existence — she, who had flown ahead of the mortal Eurymedon eighteen years before in the guise of a snow falcon and led him to the place where the child had been left to die. But it is in her disguise as Hera's loyal messenger, the self-sufficient, constant goddess, that Iris's freedom lies. That, she thinks, is the privilege of the messenger: to watch from the sidelines as the rest of the world meddles in its own affairs, then to deliver the message that changes everything.

Although Hermes, she has noticed, seems to use it mainly to find mortal women to seduce.

She stands up, stretching her arms to the sky. Her iridescent robes billow behind her, glowing pink, green and blue in the morning light, fluttering like a butterfly's wings. She feels purposeful, powerful: like a dark, slim-feathered hawk eyeing its prey. In a single, graceful gesture she dives from the rocky outcrop, her robes feathering the air behind her into strips of crimson, gold, emerald and aquamarine. She soars down the side of the mountain, following the ridges of the sun-sharpened hills, barely brushing the tips of the feathery pines. She passes Mount Ossa on her left, a lump of a mountain that the giants once tried to heap upon Mount Pelion to reach the sky. She flies over the strong walls of Meliboea, and the glittering line of the coast curving out towards the island of Skiathos. There is Thessaly, with its broad plains full of wheat, and Iolcos, the kingdom of Pelias, set like a golden jewel in the crown of Thessaly's cornfields, its turreted palace shimmering pale pink in the light of dawn. She follows the distant glimmer of the sea, the small villages dotting the bay, until at last she sees it: the rocky, wooded promontory of Mount Pelion and, on the bay's other side, Pagasae, perched above its harbour, its walls ringed with ramparts like a coronet.

She lands on the tip of Mount Pelion as effortlessly as an eagle returning to its nest, and gazes down at the curving white sickle of Pagasae's harbour, then turns to see the creamy furrow upon the sea that marks the passage of the Argo, *a black-hulled ship bearing a white sail as frail as the petal of a flower.*

It is time to give the favour of the gods to the greatest crew that has ever sailed the Ocean.

Or the favour of Hera, at least, she thinks wryly. Which often amounts to the same thing.

'Jason,' she says. As she does so, she touches the trunk of an old oak nearby, and a single golden leaf floats off the branches and drifts on the wind towards the ship and the glittering dark-blue sea beneath the mountain.

'Theseus.' A larger leaf falls from the tree and spirals towards the ocean.

'Meleager. Peleus. Lycon.'

For each hero she names, another golden leaf makes its way slowly on the breeze towards the ocean waves, binding the heroes to the quest for the Golden Fleece.

Iris pauses, as she thinks what each hero Hera has chosen will bring to the quest. For command, Jason, and for skill in arms, Theseus and Bellerophon, of course. For counsel, Nestor and Laertes. For strength, Pollux, and for insight, Castor. For courage, Hippomenes. And Orpheus, the lyre-player, for music. The gods know as well as mortals that a long voyage needs music to lighten the heart.

She gazes down at each in turn as she names them and admits them to the quest. Suddenly, her eye falls upon another figure, standing upon the ship: a woman to the eyes of any but a mortal, though she wears a man's tunic, a quiver of arrows upon her back, her face set in determination and with long, slim legs, good for running.

Iris catches her breath. Slowly, she begins to smile. Why not? Why should Atalanta not join the quest? By the time Hera discovers she is aboard the Argo it will be too late. Destiny be damned, she thinks, and then she catches herself and almost laughs aloud: for who would understand better than the Fates that a woman can excel as well as a man?

'Atalanta,' she breathes.

The final leaf spins gently down the side of the cliff, then, softly, settles on the dark surface of the water.

The oath has been made.

The greatest journey the world has ever seen has begun.

PART II

OCEAN
1260 BC

. . . the quick swift ships
Poseidon gave to sail the great ocean expanse –
swift, like a light feather or a thought.

Homer

On the *Argo*

The Ocean

The Hour of the Rising Sun
The First Day of the Month of the Harvest

A body fell upon mine with the force of a stampeding bull. A shoulder rammed into my chest and I was flung backwards over one of the thwarts, knocking aside several of the rowers, my head slamming into the wooden planks. Hippomenes slid past me, thrown by the force of his assault, and as I scrambled to get to my feet I squinted upwards, saw him regain his footing and raise his fist against the bright sunlight. Fast as I could, I rolled to one side over the bench as he brought it down, hammering his knuckles against the wood, then grunting with pain. I darted to my feet beside a startled slave, who was trying, amid the confusion, to keep to his oar. As my attacker turned to face me, I balled my fist and drove a sharp blow into Hippomenes' right shoulder. The slave beside me gave a cry and abandoned his seat, kneeling in the gap between the thwarts with his hands over his head. Without pause, Hippomenes swung his fist back to return the blow and, though I leapt over another bench to avoid it, I was too late and his knuckles caught me beneath the ear. I staggered a little and put my fingers to my neck, feeling the impression of the blow lingering upon the skin in an exquisite mesh of pain, the beginnings of a bruise swelling beneath my fingertips. I twisted to reach into my belt for my dagger, fury pounding in my ears, when—

'Cease fighting, both of you!'

Peleus, tall, with flecks of grey in his hair and a mild-mannered expression, had signalled to the rest to stop rowing and was striding towards us, climbing over the thwarts from where he had been sitting near the mast. He turned to Jason, who was seated nearby, his eyes flicking from Hippomenes to me and back again.

'My lord, unless I am very much mistaken this is the young man who so excelled in the hunt. Lord Telamon, son of Deucalion, is it not?' he asked, bowing to me.

I inclined my head. 'Indeed,' I said, still breathing rather heavily. 'I am glad to see you again, my lord Peleus.'

The other nobles, all of whom were still seated at their benches, drew their oars over their laps at Peleus' signal, and the slaves followed suit – Myrtessa among them, in her slave's tunic. She gave me a half-smile as I caught her eye. The *Argo* rocked gently on the waves, the blades of the oars dripping into the sea. I turned to my attacker, my fingers on the bruise at my neck. He was panting slightly a few benches away, his dark-brown hair sticking to the sweat shining on his cheek-bones, his gold-embroidered cloak thrown over one shoulder. He had dark eyebrows and a strong aquiline nose that had clearly been broken at least once, and his eyes registered nothing but dislike.

'What in the names of all the gods are you doing here, Telamon?' Laertes asked, leaning forwards over his oar.

'What do you think, my lord?' I said, daring to hold his gaze, exhilar-ated but also wary: there was still much that could go wrong, as Hippomenes' reaction had shown. 'I have come to join your expedition.'

Some of the men laughed. The beat of the drum faltered and stopped, and everyone was staring at us as the ship floated peacefully on the water, the sea lapping at its hull.

'You were not invited to join the quest,' Jason said, his voice cold and distant.

'No, my lord. But the Fates favour those who make their own paths, do they not?'

Meleager, seated two benches away, let out a bark of laughter, his clear hazel eyes gleaming, the soft dark hair upon his chin shining in the sunlight with a sheen of sweat. 'He has you there, Jason.'

Hippomenes gave a grunt of impatience and waved a hand in the air.

'He has nothing. He was not invited to join us, and then he leapt aboard our ship like a common thief. This is no qualification for joining our quest. And besides,' his eyes skimmed over me, 'he is too young. Why, the beard is not yet growing upon his chin – and he thinks he can equal proven fighters twice his age?'

Jason stood and surveyed us both, his expression calculating. 'Telamon, perhaps you have not been introduced to Hippomenes, son of Megareus,' he said. 'There is no finer wrestler in all of Greece, is there, Hippomenes?'

Hippomenes snorted.

'Yet Telamon is our guest, and the guest of King Iasus, too,' Jason said. He was gazing at me, sizing me up with cold reckoning, as if I were a calf to be bought at the market. 'And he did not dishonour himself in the hunt.'

'He certainly knows how to handle himself with his bow,' put in Meleager, his arm resting upon the ship's side, his eyes upon me.

Jason nodded, lips pursed. Hippomenes spat over the side of the ship.

'That is enough, Hippomenes,' Jason said. He turned to me. 'Very well, Telamon, you may join our quest, and lend your bow to our cause but,' he held up a hand to forestall me, 'this is no easy voyage we embark upon. There are trials ahead – dangerous, deadly even – that will put all of us, experienced warriors as we are, in mortal peril. Your youth will afford you no protection from us.' His eyes hardened. 'Ensure you have thought over your choice carefully before you decide.'

'I have, my lord.'

'And next time,' his voice took on the hint of a threat, 'you will discuss the matter with me beforehand, rather than attempting to commandeer my ship, like a brigand.'

I bowed my head, though it was all I could do not to leap into the air in triumph. 'As you say, my lord.'

That night, as the evening star appeared on the horizon, we put in at the island of Peparethos. The *Argo* was built without a large hold and the thwarts were too hard to sleep upon, so Jason had ruled that we would draw the ship up to land and sleep upon the shore. We had come into a sheltered harbour with steep rocky promontories at either side where the waves lapped softly upon the sand. Once the *Argo* was beached and we had hunted and roasted a pair of wild goats, the slaves unloaded woollen blankets from the storage beneath the stern deck and laid them out upon the ground for us to sleep.

But as the stars shimmered in the sky above, the waters of the bay reflecting them in flashes of silver, and Myrtessa's breathing beside me grew soft and steady, I could not sleep. Thoughts and images were whirling through my mind – the hero Bellerophon striding up the flanks of Pelion, his arms crossed with scars, my first sight of the *Argo* that morning, the letters on her prow gleaming gold, the sparkling water beneath me as I leapt aboard the ship, the low threat in Jason's voice as he had warned me not to disobey him – and I grinned, propping myself up on my elbows, reliving it all. I could never, in all my daydreams at Kaladrosos, have conceived of such an adventure.

An hour later, my mind still filled with the day's memories, I pushed myself to stand. Quiet as I could so as not to wake Myrtessa, I fastened my cloak and sword-belt, picked up my quiver, slotted my bow into its compartment, and swung it over one shoulder. My sandals crunched a little on the sand as I walked across the beach, the faint silvery moonlight guiding my path towards the grove of olive and pine trees that stretched up the hill behind. The sound of the cicadas grew louder as I approached, a soft murmur to match the whispering of the leaves. Dried pine needles crunched softly underfoot as I ducked to make my way into the trees, the moonlight casting shifting shadows over the grass.

And then I spotted a figure kneeling upon the ground, twenty paces ahead in an open clearing, lit silver by the rays of the moon. His pale face was gleaming, his eyes closed, arms outstretched to the sky, yet even at that distance, there was no mistaking those sloping shoulders, the jutting jaw and the tilt of the head, or the glittering clasp of his cloak and sword, fitted with princely jewels.

Jason.

He was speaking aloud, his palms upturned in prayer – it was only the sound of his voice that had prevented him hearing my approach. I slipped without a sound into the shade of a pine, pressing my palms into the bark and peering around, alive with curiosity, straining to hear.

Jason's voice emerged through the whispering of the leaves: '. . . Lady of Iolcos, hear me, hear my prayer. If you answer me, I vow to sacrifice to you twenty white heifers, not yet mothers of calves, so that you will hear their bellowing and see their blood upon your altar and receive the smoke from their burning on Olympus. Grant that I fulfil my destiny as Aeson's son . . .'

A breeze through the trees shook the pine needles overhead. I frowned, leaning forwards, trying to catch the words. I could see Jason gesturing to the heavens, heard a few phrases, 'Grant . . . revenge . . .' and then his voice grew louder: '. . . those who stood by as I watched my father killed by my uncle, who did nothing as he twisted my mother's hair in his fist and beat her with my father's sceptre and raped her upon the king's throne, again – and again – and again . . . And left me to crawl through my father's blood to escape the palace . . .' Jason's voice was harsh and ragged now, a high wavering note of uncontrolled anger and torment.

I saw him stretch his hands higher towards the dark vault of the sky. 'Kingship is my right – it runs in my very veins! Your lord, Zeus—'

An owl hooted in a nearby tree and I almost cried out with shock. Cursing under my breath, I tried to steady myself, leaning closer – for surely this was the very moment where he would reveal what Myrtessa had guessed . . .

'I *am* a king,' I heard him say, his voice rising, his words broken as though by sobs. 'And not only king of Iolcos! I will rule Pagasae, Makronita and Kaladrosos, Lechonia and Aphussos. Help me, lady, queen of the gods, to burn all the towns of Pelion, to raze them to the ground, and torture anyone who dares to challenge me, man, woman or child, till they wish they had never been born, until everyone cries out my name in joy and recognizes me as their one true king!'

He was panting, his eyes open now, and the air around me was still, the leaves of the trees motionless.

I felt my blood chill as an image of my home flashed before my eyes – Kaladrosos – burnt to ashes, flames leaping to the sky, the houses sending up columns of smoke, my mother and father lying hurt in the ruins, my little sisters and brother crying for help . . . My stomach churned with fear and my heart was hammering, making me want to gasp aloud with pain. *So this is what he intends . . .*

Jason's voice floated across to me: 'Hera, grant me this prayer, as I pray to you every night and have done since my father's murder. Give me revenge, and kingship of all the towns of Pelion, as is my birthright and my due. Then you will be honoured in Iolcos as no goddess has ever been honoured before . . .'

Bile was rising within my belly. I could not bear it – I had to do something. With one swift movement I reached for the sword at my waist, unthinking, started to stride out of the shadows towards Jason, unsure whether I wanted to fight him or to reason with him, knowing only that his words were madness, that he must be stopped . . .

Swifter than I could have thought, Jason turned and saw me approaching, his eyes like dark shadows meeting mine. He leapt to his feet, and the slender, gleaming blade of a sword appeared from nowhere before I had the chance to block it, the point digging into my neck. Slowly, barely moving, I followed the blade with my eyes, to the hilt, then the hand, the arm holding it, to the shoulder, draped in a dark cloak . . .

'What are you doing here, Telamon?'

'I – I wanted to walk,' I spluttered, dropping my sword upon the grass and raising my hands, feeling them shaking slightly. 'Nothing more, I swear it.'

'You were not trying to eavesdrop?' he asked. 'Or perhaps to meet with someone?'

'W-what?' Fear was coursing through me, and I wiped my clammy palms against my tunic. *How can he possibly know? Did someone tell him? But how could they know?*

Was he going to kill me for disguising myself as a man, here, upon the shores of Peparethos, before I had even sailed a day upon the *Argo*?

He lowered the blade a little and circled me, pointing the tip directly at my heart. 'You heard nothing that I care about. But I do not trust you, Telamon. Why did you follow me tonight? Why did you force your way onto the *Argo*? Are you a spy of Pelias? Tell me the truth!' The words had a ring of command to them, as of one who was used to giving orders.

'I speak nothing but the truth!' I stammered, raising my hands to the sky so he could see I was not going for my sword. 'I was unable to sleep upon the shore, so I came here to walk. As for boarding the *Argo*,' I continued, my voice unsteady, 'perhaps I should have asked for your consent; but after the feast, when I considered your choice of the men you would take with you . . . I felt I could not lose such an opportunity. I can think of no greater honour than fighting alongside the heroes gathered upon this ship. I swear to you by all the gods, and Zeus, lord of Pagasae, I speak the truth.'

Or at least a part of it.

'You call it honourable to thrust your way onto a ship unasked?'

'You accepted me,' I retaliated, my courage returning. 'Why? If you are so distrustful of my presence?'

Jason took a while to answer. At last, he sheathed his sword and took a step backwards, eyeing me up and down, his lips tight. 'Because I prefer to have one I do not trust under my gaze than out of it,' he said.

Silence fell between us. I was breathing hard, the remembrance of Jason's words – *I will burn all the towns of Pelion, raze them to the ground* – still drumming through my mind, mingling in my ears with the screams I had heard of Maia, Leon and Corycia when he had spoken of Kaladrosos until it was almost unbearable. In a sudden, wild moment I bent swiftly and reached to pick up my sword, but Jason saw me and lashed out, catching my wrist before I had even grasped the hilt, his fingers digging into my skin with unexpected strength. My eyes watered with the pain.

Jason took a deep, shuddering breath and jerked my chin up close to his face with his other hand, a muscle in his jaw twitching. 'As you see, Telamon,' he said, and though his voice had returned to its usual tone, his breathing was shallow, his fingers still gouging my flesh, 'I will brook no opposition to my throne. If you do anything to stand against me – if you set one foot outside this camp again – I shall have you speared through and slung over the ship's side to be eaten by the fish. Do you understand me?'

His teeth glittered in the moonlight.

'Oh, yes,' I said, looking him squarely in the eye, though my voice shook a little. 'Oh, yes. I understand you.'

115

*

Over the next two weeks, Jason and I did not speak again, and though I avoided him as much as I could, I had the impression that he was keeping a careful eye upon me, watching me closely as I pulled at the oar, adjusted the rigging or hunted for the evening's meal. I told Myrtessa of my meeting with Jason the very next evening, when we drew the ship up on the shore and laid our blankets side by side, at a little distance from the other lords, to share food and stories of the day's adventures in muted whispers. She had gasped, as I described to her the full extent of what I had overheard of Jason's ambitions for Pelion.

'But what are we to do?' she had asked, her eyes round with fear, hand over her mouth.

I shook my head in the darkness, kneading my forehead with my knuckles. The same question had been echoing in my mind ever since, plaguing my dreams with nightmares of towering flames, the smoking ruins of my home, and my family, their voices growing weaker and weaker, calling to me for help. I felt a twist of guilt in the pit of my stomach: *I should never have left them* . . .

'I do not know,' I said aloud. 'But there must be something.'

After six days of good winds, with the breeze blowing into the belly of the sail and sending us speeding over the whipping waves of the sea, past the isle of Lemnos, through the narrow strait of the Hellespont where the proud city of Troy, with its high walls, looked out over the plain and into the sea of the Propontis, our luck turned. The winds changed, blowing hard and strong from the north-east, springing up in the mornings and dying away with the setting of the sun, so that there was nothing to be done but set all hands upon the oars and row throughout the day, with no rest until we stopped to sleep at night. Myrtessa was seated at the thwarts near the bow with the slaves, her tunic stained with sweat as she pulled at the oar. I had my seat beside Peleus, and my palms were blistered, chafing against the smooth wood of the oar so that the skin was rubbed raw and it was all I could do not to cry out in pain each time I made a stroke.

Despair, guilt and frustration coursed through me in turns, sometimes filling me with an irritation so great it was all I could do not to throw down my oar; at other times, I was consumed by a desperate fear that perhaps they had all been right – that I was not good or strong enough to accompany the heroes on their voyage, that I should have stayed at home in Kaladrosos, where I could at least have known that my family was safe. The calm swell of the waves, the white seagulls bobbing on the water of the ocean, the sound of the ropes slapping in the wind, the sea salt on the air and on my tongue, all of which had seemed exhilarating, a portent of the adventure to be had, were subsumed now in the rasping pain in my hands, my aching temples as the sun beat down upon my bare head, the sweat that trickled down my face and back, making my tunic cling to my skin, the tearing, seizing pain in the muscles of my arms, which begged me to stop, and through it all, the ever-present knot of fear in my belly. Yet I had to go on. I could not stop, I could not . . .

'Telamon.'

I pushed my sweaty hair out of my eyes with my forearm and squinted up into the sunlight. Hippomenes was standing before me. He was not wearing his cloak, merely a simple blue tunic threaded with purple and a belt around his waist. His arms were bare, well-muscled, like the arms of the woodsmen who had lived in Kaladrosos: knotted and crossed with veins that pressed up against the skin, sinews hardened by many hours spent with the axe or the sword. He held out a hand, and I noticed the coarse skin beneath the fingers, clear and unbroken.

'Hippomenes,' I panted, making another stroke to the beat of the drum, trying to mask my grimace of pain. 'What brings you here?'

Without a word, he stepped over the bench and pulled the oar from my hands, sat down beside me and made the next stroke with powerful ease, the muscles of his arms tensing beside me, the rhythm of his body sturdy and swift.

'What—?'

'Go,' he said, shrugging me off as if I were a slave.

'But I—'

'Go,' he repeated.

I looked down at my hands. One of the blisters had opened and was bleeding, and I could feel my arms trembling. I glanced towards the hold beneath the raised deck at the back of the ship, thinking of bandages dipped in salt water to ease my wounds and wine for my parched throat. I stood up and climbed, legs shaking, over my thwart, back to the bench behind, making my way towards the stern. Then I turned, determined to make sure he knew I was not a weakling, that I was capable of this. 'I did not—'

But Hippomenes was not listening. He was already pulling the oar with swift, steady strokes, his arms moving to the rhythm of the drum.

As I walked away, squeezing through the rowers and stepping over benches, I heard him say, 'He should be at home tending his fields in Crete.'

The voice of Peleus answered him, 'We may have overestimated him, Hippomenes – that much I will grant you. Though I do not understand your unfounded dislike of the boy.'

'He is swift with a bow, true, but he has not the strength of a man,' Nestor added from behind.

I turned aside, the corners of my eyes burning with tears of shame. I almost wanted to answer back to them, but I was so exhausted, and my hands were riddled with pain – so, head bowed, filled with anger and humiliation, I made my way instead to the stern of the *Argo* to bandage my bleeding wounds.

'Wait, Telamon.'

I turned, my hands shaking, vision blurred with tears. I felt a hand – cool and gentle – upon my arm. I wiped my eyes upon the shoulder of my tunic. 'Meleager?'

He drew in his oar, leaving only the blade projecting, and got to his feet to stand beside me. His eyes were gazing down into mine, his brows drawn together in concern. 'They should not have said such things.'

I shook my head. 'No, no, they were right. I cannot do it. I should never have—'

He raised his hand and stroked my cheek with a finger, very lightly. I looked up at him, the blood rushing to my cheeks, an unexpected, irresistible pulse of desire flooding me at his touch. His lips were so close I could see the sweat glistening in the fine brown hair of his beard, and I found myself wondering what it would feel like to be caressed by those lips, to have his hands in my hair, his fingertips tracing the curves of my back down, down and then further . . .

I looked away.

Do not be a fool, Atalanta. Remember why you are here – on a hero's quest, not to fall for the first man who looks at you with lust in his eyes.

Remember – he thinks you are a man.

I felt the heat in my cheeks subside, but his finger lingered, cool, pressed against my skin, his eyes bearing down upon mine.

And if he desires you – as a man? a voice within my head whispered. *What then?*

Meleager placed both his hands on either side of my temples and leant forwards and kissed me, very lightly, upon the top of my head. I felt my whole body thrill, impossibly, irresistibly, at the brush of his lips upon my hair. The lord Pollux, who was seated on the thwart to Meleager's left, let out a whistle, and a couple of the nobles laughed and catcalled from behind. I looked away quickly, filled with confusion and embarrassment, but Meleager's expression did not falter.

'Take care of yourself, Telamon,' he said, and though I knew we were being watched I could not help it: I felt my gaze drawn back to him. His eyes flickered down to my blistered hands and lingered there, making my heart thud so hard that I could feel the leather cord of the medallion quivering upon my collarbone beneath my tunic. 'You have such beautiful hands. It would be a shame to see them harmed.'

And with a smile and a slight bow, he turned on his heel and walked away.

Later that day I was seated at the ship's stern with the others who were taking rests from rowing. A few days before, Argus had persuaded Jason to reduce our crew so that we might alternate on and off the benches, to allow us to recover a little of our strength for the journey ahead. Hippomenes had refused to allow me to return to my oar, however much I protested: he himself worked through the day, not stopping for rest at all, and I was left to huddle by the stern brooding upon my shame. By good fortune, however, Myrtessa and an older slave, Phorbas, whom she had befriended, were also allotted a rest not long after I left my bench, so we were conversing together, crouched just beneath the stern deck beside the stowage, out of sight and sharing a pouch of wine to quench our thirst. I had bound Phorbas' hands, which were pockmarked with blisters and bleeding freely; he was a steward, charged with managing his master's slaves and balancing his accounts, and was unused to much physical exertion.

The conversation reached a lull, and I stretched up to peer over the edge of the raised deck above. Jason was there, pacing the boards above us, restless and irritable, striding past Argus where he stood guiding the steering oar, his eyes upon a cluster of storm clouds gathering upon the horizon, trailing a veil of rain in their wake and growing larger as they blew across the sky, billowing, darkening.

'My lord Jason,' I heard Argus say. 'I know you do not approve of letting the men rest—'

'It is not about approving, Argus,' Jason said, in clipped tones. 'It is about the storm you see approaching. If we do not make time, we shall be out on the open sea before it hits. I do not want the *Argo* harmed – nothing that will slow my progress to the Fleece.'

'What are you doing?' Myrtessa whispered, but I hushed her and cast a significant look up to the deck above us.

'That is all very well,' I heard Argus respond, 'but if the men's hands are so sore that they cannot row, it will do us little good, no matter how soon we make harbour, for we shall not be able to leave again tomorrow. I saw Phorbas' hands – he's Peleus' steward, you know – and they were quite raw with blisters all over the palms and—'

'What do I care for slaves?' Jason's voice was growing louder. I shrank back, gesturing to Phorbas to duck his head.

'But if they cannot row any longer—'

'If they cannot row, we shall toss them overboard to see if they can swim.'

Argus hesitated. 'But, my lord—'

'No, Argus. I have had enough of your attempts to overrule me. The slaves will go back to work. You!' To my horror, I heard the sound of his sandals approaching closer across the deck, then felt his shadow fall across the three of us, where we sat huddled together. I struggled to my feet. He was pointing at Phorbas, his grey eyes cold with malice. 'Get up and row.'

Phorbas was almost forty years of age, slightly rotund in the belly and with the hair greying at his temples. He took hold of the railing to pull himself to stand. I saw him wince with pain. 'My lord, please,' he said, his eyes filling with tears. 'A little more rest, I beg you.'

Jason's eyes hardened. 'To work, slave.'

'But—'

'Silence! I will not be defied!' Jason's face was reddening, a vein pulsing upon his temple.

Phorbas held up his damaged hands in a gesture of supplication. 'I beg of you, my lord . . .'

'What are those?'

His eyes were upon the linen bandages, taken from the supplies we had loaded upon the ship when we left Pagasae.

'I can explain,' I said, moving forwards.

'Quiet,' Jason said, his eyes darting towards me, then back to Phorbas. His voice grew quiet with menace. 'Did you steal those, slave?'

Phorbas shook his head, muttering, 'No, my lord, I—'

'You dared to take what was not rightfully yours from your betters?'

I stared at Jason. 'Those supplies were brought for all the crew, nobles and slaves alike!'

'Take them off,' he said, ignoring me. The sky was darkening above us with a deep layer of grey clouds. The wind was whipping the waves into momentary peaks, then calm again. I could feel the breeze blowing sea spray against my cheeks, and the taste of salt was growing stronger in my mouth.

'W-what?'

'Take them off!'

Cringing, Phorbas obeyed, unravelling the strips of linen to reveal his bloodied hands. There was another blast of wind, stronger now, and the sail filled, making the ropes creak, pulling the boat into the waves and sending spray shooting up the ship's sides.

'Hold out your hands.'

Phorbas extended them forwards. Jason loosened his leather belt, then untied it, bringing it slithering through one hand, his mouth slightly parted, his breathing ragged. He raised the belt above his head, and Phorbas squeezed his eyes shut—

'No!'

I pushed Phorbas aside. 'No, Prince Jason,' I said, breathing hard. I held my hands forwards, palms up, feeling the blisters stretch. 'I wish to be punished in his place. I took the bandages. It was my fault. Beat me instead.'

Jason's lip curled in contempt. 'You are an even greater fool than I thought, Telamon.'

I met his gaze and held it, challenging him. It was the first time I had spoken to him directly since our meeting on the shores of Peparethos, and I felt myself shudder to look again into those wintry grey eyes, and remember how they had shone in the darkness as he had described burning my home, torturing my family. 'Do it.'

The waves were peaking into rolling hills of water so that the ship's prow dipped and fell, dipped and fell, like a child's cot, rocked by the fingers of the gods. Phorbas, his face crumpled with relief, mouthed to me, *My thanks to you, Telamon*, and fell to clutch at the ship's side with Myrtessa.

'My lord Jason . . .' Argus called out in a warning tone, both hands tugging upon the steering oar, which was beginning to veer out of control.

But Jason was bringing the leather strap up, up above his head, and in the *crack* that followed, as it met my bare skin with a stinging, resounding slap, Argus' words were drowned. I sucked in my cheeks and bit them, determined not to cry as Jason hit me, again, and again, and again, his eyes alight with a strange, fierce joy, and my hands were glowing with pain, the blisters cracked and bleeding down my wrists and forearms . . .

'That is enough!'

I felt someone wrest me aside. I looked up, dazed with pain, and saw Argus – pointing not at me but at the clouds covering the sky, blotting out the sun and pounded by the wind into a furling mass. 'Will you put this whole ship and its crew at risk for your pride?'

Jason paused, panting. He looked overboard towards the waves, which were working themselves up into dark, roiling walls of water. A low rumble of thunder shivered through the air and the ship pitched forwards, setting the boards of the hull creaking.

The storm was coming.

*

Jason tossed aside his belt and strode down the ship, shouting orders. 'Bank your oars,' he bellowed at the rowers. I ran from the stern deck towards the mast, cradling my burning hands, and slipped slightly on the wood, wet from the light rain that was already falling in a sheer mist from the sky. I reached out for the rope of the backstay to steady myself.

'Telamon,' Myrtessa gasped, making her way unsteadily towards me, clutching at the leather tholes that held the oars for support as her feet slid beneath her. 'What – what should I do?'

'Keep close by me,' I said, and fumbled to untie the sheets, twin ropes that attached the mainsail to the side of the ship, smearing the rush-woven cords with blood from my hands. I looked around. Myrtessa was crouching there, clinging to the leather loop of one of the oars as the swell of the waves carried us up, up, then plunged us down into the raging sea, her eyes tight shut.

'I am afraid,' she said, her voice very thin.

'Then do something!' I called. I threw her one of the sheets and started trying to coil it around my elbow, slipping and sliding on the wet planks as the ship pitched from side to side and clutching at the beams for support. Several of the slaves were hanging onto the ship's side, crying out prayers to Poseidon, and Phorbas was vomiting into the sea.

'Argus – can you steer her into the waves?' I heard Nestor shout, bending low to hold onto the thwarts as he fought his way towards the steering deck. The wind was howling around the ship now in tearing, screaming blasts, the sky darkened to the indiscriminate blackness of deepest night. A fork of lightning split the air ahead, blinding white, followed instantly by a rumbling growl of thunder, and then the rain was falling hard, so dense it was like a wall of water pouring upon us.

'I am doing all I can!' I heard Argus call back from the stern. He had both arms wrapped around the steering oar and was clearly fighting with all his might to keep the prow pointing forwards into the storm. A massive wave curled and crashed over the bow, drenching us in salt water. 'Poseidon has cursed us!'

'We have to – reef the sail!' I gasped to the men around me, and saw

Hippomenes nod, his hair plastered to his head in the torrent pouring from the heavens. He ran to the backstay, slipping and sliding, and started to try to undo it. I saw the muscles of his forearms straining as he pulled at the knot.

'It's no use!' he called after a moment. 'The rope is soaked through – I can't untie it!'

I squinted upwards as a flash of lightning tore through the air, illuminating the yardarm fixed high up the mast, the sail flapping wildly in the howling winds.

'There's no time!' I shouted back. 'If we cannot lower the yard we will have to climb the mast and reef the sail – any longer and the ship will heel!'

He nodded, rain dripping from his nose as he ran back towards us. I gestured to Myrtessa and, one after another, Hippomenes, then Myrtessa and I climbed the slippery wooden pegs fixed into the mast up towards the yardarm, water streaming into our eyes, my lacerated hands screaming in pain, the ship creaking as she rocked back and forth on the plunging waves, the wind whistling in our ears. We had reached the yard now, and as the prow dipped up again Myrtessa reached out to me, trembling, and I grasped her hand briefly, trying with all my might to maintain my grip upon the slimy wood. I checked my foothold upon the mast, firmed my grip with my elbow around the yardarm, then reached with my free hand and began to pull the sail up by handfuls. Hippomenes on the other side was doing the same, and Myrtessa beside me was fumbling at the sheets, her face pale, wiping her wet hair out of her eyes, then throwing the ropes across to me and Hippomenes to secure the canvas. The sky split open again above us and another foaming white wave crashed overboard. There was a groan from the *Argo* as she plunged downwards and then, as she broke into another wave, a colossal snapping noise. A rope flew towards us from the prow, flying loose through the wind, whipping back and forth, and the mast rocked dangerously. One of the cables that supported it had snapped.

'One of the forestays has broken!' I bellowed to Myrtessa and Hippomenes. 'We have to get down!'

Myrtessa's eyes were wide and the corner of her mouth was

trembling. The mast swayed again, and I redoubled my hold on the yardarm. 'Dolius – get *down*!'

Myrtessa clung to the linen of the sail as she sought with her toes for the footholds down the mast. Then, at last, she was out of sight in the rain-drenched darkness.

'Hippomenes – you next!'

He had climbed so far out along the yardarm that he was over the roiling, foaming sea, clutching at the last of the sail, which was flapping wildly out of his reach, one of the sheet-ropes Myrtessa and I had untied whistling back and forth through the air.

'Hippomenes!'

I squinted through the curtain of rain. There was a sudden terrible tearing sound from the prow, a creaking of wood and rope. The second forestay was breaking. With one last, desperate look at Hippomenes I swung myself onto the mast and shimmied down it – and not a moment too soon. With a dreadful *crack* the second forestay, the last of the ropes supporting the mast, whipped up from the prow. I leapt the last few paces as the mast shuddered in the mast-box and then, with an awful, final inevitability, Hippomenes still clinging to the yardarm, like a limpet to a rock, it wavered and fell sideways, keeling over the ship's side into the sea with a terrible, reverberating thud of breaking wood, and a final crash of sea spray.

All at Sea

The Ocean

The Hour of the Stars

The Fourteenth Day of the Month of the Harvest

'*Hippomenes!*'

I clung to the ship's edge as we pitched and tossed, desperately scanning the leaden surface of the sea for a head bobbing on the surface. At last I saw him.

'There!' I shouted, pointing through the blackness. 'There!'

Peleus, beside me, had already gathered up a coil of rope and was knotting a fragment of wood to the end. As I pointed, finger trembling, he whirled the rope tight around his head and then let it out, slithering over the surface of the sea – but as it shot forwards it was lifted by the wind and whipped to the side. He reeled it in and tried again, but the rope was lashed once more by the raging winds and hit the waves far to the stern of the ship – and, though Peleus had gathered it in and was about to try a third time, the waves were carrying Hippomenes further away into the darkness of the storm. Soon he would be too far even for the rope to reach . . .

Jason appeared behind us and laid a hand on Peleus' shoulder. 'There is nothing you can do,' he shouted, over the fury of the storm. 'The man is lost.'

I turned to stare at him, and Jason looked back at me, eyes cold as the sheets of rain pouring overhead.

'There is always something you can do.' I pushed the wet hair back from my forehead, scanning the heaving sea, keeping my eyes fixed upon the figure of Hippomenes dwindling ever further into the blackness.

Jason scowled as the ship pitched, sending us staggering forwards. 'I am here to recover the Fleece, not to waste my time on men who are already dead,' he bellowed.

I was outraged. 'Hippomenes gave his life to aid you on your quest – and this is how you repay him?'

'He has done nothing more than his duty to his king,' he roared. 'I *command* you to leave him.'

I did not even pause to think. I tore off my belt, my bow and quiver and my dagger and thrust them into Myrtessa's arms. 'You take these,' I said, my voice shaking with anger. I turned to Peleus. 'Hold fast to the rope,' I said, 'and when I tug three times, pull me in.' Then, before Jason could do anything to stop me, I slid to the end of the bench, snatched one end of the rope from Peleus' hands, climbed onto the edge of the hull and dived over the side into the churning ocean.

Cold enveloped me as I hit the water, and as I surfaced and took a huge, deep lungful of air a wave crashed over me and pushed me under again, swirling, foam and bubbles obscuring my vision, the taste of salt sharp in my mouth, my throat and nose filled with water, the palms of my hands stinging almost beyond endurance. I surfaced again into the blackness and heaved a cough, blinking my streaming eyes, tightening my grip around the bit of driftwood I was holding and the rope tied to it.

'*Hippomenes!*' I twisted round, searching through the heaving mass of water for a face, a body . . .

And then a wave lifted me high and I saw him. At least twenty paces away, clinging to the wreckage of the mast, his hair plastered to his head and his mouth open, gasping, as wave after wave crashed over him. Summoning my strength I struck out towards him, pulling against the water, kicking my legs with all my might, trailing the rope after me, my eyes focused upon the wet mass of sail and broken wood floating on the surface of the sea ahead . . .

Ten paces to go . . .

Five . . .

And then I was there, panting and choking, the rope still clenched in my hand, clutching the mast for support.

'Y-you!' Hippomenes gasped. There was a deep bleeding gash in his shoulder from where a piece of falling timber had struck him, the flesh lacerated and torn at the edges. His face was deathly pale. He was gritting his teeth, trying to prevent himself passing out.

'Can you swim?' I shouted, spluttering as salt water filled my mouth, straining as hard as I could to keep myself afloat. I tried to stretch towards him, but the rope was pulling me backwards as the ship pitched and swayed over the waves. 'You have to swim towards me, Hippomenes!'

Hippomenes let go of the mast, slipped, and his head submerged under the water. As another wave surged over him he came up, choking, kicking his legs.

'I cannot – I cannot move – my arm,' he stuttered, and again he went under the water, the foam swirling around him.

I turned my head this way and that, looking desperately for anything that might help us. Another wave enveloped me and I emerged, coughing, eyes streaming. At last I spotted it: an oar, floating upon the sea a few paces distant. Striking out towards it, forcing myself to fight against the surge of the sea, I pulled it towards me, looped the rope around the handle and knotted it twice. Then, taking a deep breath I dived. I kicked once, twice, and there ahead of me was Hippomenes, sinking down into the blue-green depths of the ocean, head nodding, a few last air bubbles escaping from his lips. I put both arms around his waist and pulled with all my strength, kicking against the water harder than I had ever done, and after a breathless, head-splitting moment we emerged above the surface, gasping for air, the water pouring from our faces.

'Hold on!' I called to him. 'Hold onto me!' Kicking with my legs, one arm around him and the other pulling at the water, I dragged him over, almost senseless, towards the floating oar and tugged three times at the rope.

After what felt like an eternity I felt it pull taut; then, slowly, very slowly, it began to reel in. I started to kick again, one arm around Hippomenes, the other clinging to the rope, and I felt the current beside me stir as he started feebly to tread water. Though it felt as if we were hardly moving, I could see the dark outline of the *Argo* coming closer . . . closer . . . My calf muscles were straining so hard I felt as if they would tear, my breath coming in huge gasps. Hippomenes' eyes were half closed in the darkness, and his legs were failing . . .

And then, at last, the shadow of the boat's huge, tar-black side rose above us. I pulled Hippomenes' semi-conscious form towards me and tied the rope around his waist, knotting it twice, swallowing several mouthfuls of water as waves engulfed us and I fought to keep him afloat. I tugged again, saw the rope tighten and then, slowly, Hippomenes was drawn up the boat's hull and over the side. I trod water, fighting with all my strength to resist the urge simply to stop moving, to succumb to blissful oblivion and to sink deep into the embrace of the blackness of the water beneath . . .

When the rope came down a second time I was barely conscious of taking hold of it, and it was all I could do to prevent myself passing out as I swung like a caught fish over the ship's hull, clutching at the slippery rope with all my remaining strength. As I reached the beam of the ship's side I felt warm hands grasping me, pulling me over and onto the sopping-wet bench, saw Myrtessa's white face and Hippomenes lying on one of the thwarts nearby, surrounded by slaves, his rasping breathing audible even over the sounds of the storm.

'He – he is alive,' I muttered. 'Thank the gods.'

Then everything went black, and I saw no more.

I awoke the next morning to a splitting headache and a pain in my arms and thighs such as I had never felt before. I blinked my eyes open and found myself blinded by a bright white light. I squinted and tried to hold my hand to my eyes, but it would not move. I blinked again.

The open blue sky, spotted with spider's-web clouds, swam into view above me. The sun was shining on the horizon, a burning disc of white light. The brightness made the backs of my eyes ache. I groaned and tried to sit up. The wounds on the palms of my hands seared and I let out a cry of pain.

'Wait, master – you shouldn't move.'

Myrtessa was at my side at once. My vision was clearing now, and I saw that I had been laid upon one of the empty rowing benches at the stern and wrapped in several thick woollen blankets. The air smelt fresh and clear with a slight tang of rain upon it after the storm and, now that I focused my attention upon it, I could hear the rhythmic beat of the rowers' drum from the bow and the faint *splash*, *splash* of the oars upon the water. I swayed with the movement of the ship and Myrtessa put a hand upon my shoulder to stop me falling.

I propped myself up gingerly and the blankets fell off me. A sharp breeze caught my bare skin, making the hairs prickle with cold, and as I felt the dampness clinging to my arms and chest I realized I was still wearing my sodden tunic.

'I dared not take it off,' Myrtessa whispered, so quietly that only I could hear. 'Not with everyone watching me.'

'You did well. Hold these.'

I pushed the blankets into her arms and swung myself up to sit, steadying myself as the world whirled in front of me. As my sight cleared, I took in the scene before me: the men sitting on thwarts still slippery with water and seaweed, snapped ropes trailing into the water, several of the oars lost, the broken stump of the mast in the mast-box, splintered wood scattered around it.

'We were blown back towards the isle of Prokonnesos,' Myrtessa explained, in a low voice, as she folded the blankets. 'Jason wanted to run you through for your disobedience in going after Hippomenes, but Peleus and Laertes stopped him . . . You should have seen the look on his face.' She shuddered. 'We did not lose too much distance, all things considered, and it was a blessing that we were not blown upon the rocks of the island, though the loss of the sail will cost us some— What are you doing?'

I had stood up and was climbing towards the storage beneath the deck at the stern. I turned to face her. 'I am going to row.'

'But you cannot! You were unconscious all night, you barely even—'

I ignored her. Did she think, after what Hippomenes, Nestor and Peleus had said the day before, that I was going to languish wrapped in blankets all day? The very thought of their taunting voices, the words Peleus had said – 'we may have overestimated him' – made me burn with shame so that I wished for nothing more than simply to *do* something. I moved away.

'My lord!' she called.

'I must do this. I thank you for your care of me.'

The storage chamber, hidden beneath the raised deck at the stern, was dry when I reached it. The doors, locked by a wooden bolt from the outside, seemed to have held fast against the storm. I reached inside to a pile of tunics near the front and drew out the smallest, a simple, plain tunic of dark-green wool. It was nothing near as fine as Corythus', for it had no embroidery in gold and no tassels around the skirt, but it was dry. I pulled it over my head and slipped my sodden tunic out underneath, then picked up Corythus' old leather sword-belt and fastened it around my waist. Some clean linen bandages lay in a heap to one side and I unravelled a couple and, wincing in pain, bound my hands.

As I stepped back out into the bright sunshine I spotted a bench free not too far away, beside the broad-backed figure of Theseus, and I sat down and took the banked oar in my hands, the handle still slimy. The warmth of the sun beat down on my face as I waited for the next stroke, then, as the rest of the crew buried their blades in the sea, dropped mine and fell in with them, following the rhythm of the drum, my body rocking to the movement of the oar and the salt spray flying up into my face. Though the wounds on my hands burnt and my arms were still straining from the night before, it felt good to be pulling on the oar alongside the heroes, to be showing Peleus and the others that I was not the weakling they had taken me to be. I redoubled my efforts, and as the oars stroked the surface of the sea the *Argo* flew forwards, skimming the Propontis like a bird in flight.

'Lord Telamon.'

I started. I had been so engrossed in the rhythm of the drum and the sway of the ship to the oars that I had not noticed the approach of footsteps. Beside me stood Hippomenes, wearing a dry tunic also, the wound on his arm bandaged, his shoulder-length hair encrusted with salt.

'You saved my life, last night,' he said, his voice low.

'I would have done it for anyone,' I said, continuing to row with strong, even strokes, my eyes upon the distant land to the east, rising and falling in curving hills down to the sea. A small inlet caught my eye, where the sea was palest blue. A tiny fishing boat was moored there, the anchor thrown down into the shallows, and a single figure leant over the side, catching fish.

'And yet you did it. No one else on this ship thought to do so, though they call themselves heroes of Greece,' he said. 'I am for ever in your debt. I – I apologize for what I said before.' His voice was stiff, and now it was he who was avoiding my eye.

'I bear you no grudge,' I said, and as I lifted the oar through the air to begin another stroke I knew I had spoken nothing but the truth. 'You were right to distrust a newcomer, and a young one at that – untested by the trials of war. I should have done the same.'

He nodded, his shoulders relaxing a little. There was a pause. Then: 'We are eating, up at the ship's bow. Prince Lycon, the lords Meleager, Castor, Peleus, those of us not tasked with rowing for the hour . . . Perhaps you would . . .'

I dipped the blade back into the sea. 'It would be a pleasure, my lord,' I said. 'I shall join you in a moment, but . . .' I leant back and pulled the blade through the water, then cast him a quick smile '. . . I should like to row some more first.'

It was the first time I had eaten with the lords since I had joined the *Argo*, for with Hippomenes' dislike pouring down upon me like a storm cloud and the chill spreading through the other lords – even those who had been favourably disposed towards me after my performance in the hunt – I had taken to breaking my fast with Myrtessa, huddled together on an empty rowing bench at the stern and talking together in low voices. As Hippomenes led me now to the group seated upon the raised platform at the prow, they moved aside to allow me space to join them. Meleager – who was sitting nearby – winked as he handed me a cut of meat wrapped in linen, with a handful of pickled olives and some dried figs. Most of the gathered lords were regarding me in silence, though a couple were nodding, and I saw Peleus flash me a swift smile. I felt my pulse quicken. Perhaps I had been accepted among the heroes at last . . .

'My thanks to you,' I said, bowing my head and keeping my eyes downcast as I accepted the food from Meleager, then settled myself to eat, trying not to grin like a fool at the fact that I was dining alongside Nestor, and Theseus, and Peleus, at their invitation – as an equal, almost! The meat was chewy and tough and tasted mainly of salt, but I was hungry enough not to care. By the time I had finished the last fig, covered with sticky honey and filled with summer-sweet seeds, I felt full for the first time in days.

'Here,' Castor said, passing me a leather pouch, and I smiled at him, took a swig of the watered wine and wiped my mouth on the back of my hand.

The lords seemed to be watching me, as if they did not wish to be the first to speak, and at last it was Hippomenes who broke the silence.

'You see that slave over there?' he said, pointing to a young woman with auburn hair and a slight figure, who was bent over holding a bucket, her face flushed, emptying the water that lay ankle-deep in the bilges after the storm. She had been captured a few days before during a raid on the island of Imbros – I had refused to join and had remained upon the ship, for I abhorred the ways of war that made a slave of a free woman – taken with a few others to sluice the thwarts and mend the ropes by day, and to pleasure the heroes at night. The skirmish on the island had been easy for a group of such battle-hardened warriors, and they had returned with barely any cuts or wounds, though – as I had heard Jason boast, to my disgust – they had left many of the husbands and fathers of the women they had captured slain in the fields, blood staining the long grass, their goats and sheep untended now. I had noticed her a couple of times since, throwing slops over the ship's side or scrubbing dirt from the hull when it was drawn up on the shore for the night, and had passed her some of my bread and olives in secret when I could, for I knew that she was not being well fed.

I took a fresh swig of wine. 'What of her?'

'I believe she has taken a liking to you. Talks about you. She was mine from the raid, but you're welcome to her, if you wish it.'

I stared at him, the pouch of wine halfway to my mouth. 'You are offering me a slave-girl?'

He shrugged. 'There will be few opportunities for wenching over the next few weeks. I should take the chance while you can, if I were you.' He leant towards me and lowered his voice. 'And I will tell you this. She is well worth the effort.'

I searched for some excuse, some reason, but my mind was as empty as the skies in summer. 'My lord, I— You are too generous.'

'I have not known Hippomenes to be so generous with his slaves,' Peleus said, joining in. 'I'm sure there are several men upon this ship who would leap at the chance for a night with – Thalia, did you say her name was, Hippomenes?'

Hippomenes nodded.

Castor was staring at the girl, grinning. 'I, for one—'

'I thank you again for your generosity,' I said, standing up rather suddenly and knocking the wine pouch to the floor in my confusion. Red liquid spilt out onto the deck, glugging onto the floor and filling the air with the warm, sweet smell of wine. I ducked to pick it up. 'But I do not – I cannot – I must go,' I said, and pushed my way out of the circle and back down the ship towards Myrtessa.

'Telamon,' Hippomenes called after me, but I ignored him. I climbed over a few more thwarts, attempting to put as much distance between myself and the talk of Thalia as I could – but it was impossible to block out Peleus' next words, for they rang clear over the ship.

'Poor Thalia.' He chuckled. 'But it looks as if young Dolius there has captured Telamon's heart. You must have noticed how much time they spend in each other's company. Why, they are hardly ever parted.'

I glanced back to see the assembled nobles laughing together, and Meleager beside them, his chin propped upon his elbow, his brows contracted in a slight frown as he watched me. I hurried away, cursing under my breath at my stupidity.

We put in that night at a stone-strewn bay as the sun dipped into the waters of the sea, rippling the waves with gold. We had made good time, though we had had to row all day now that the sail was lost. I could just make out the narrow strait of the Bosphorus in the distance to the north, the land sloping down either side of it to channel the waters of the Propontis through to the great expanse of the encircling Ocean beyond.

I looked over the beach, at the slaves and nobles scattered around, some lying upon their backs, looking up at the pink-orange sky and the clouds, edged with gold. Others were tending the fire that had been lit partway up the beach. A young deer, caught in the woods with Laertes' spear, was now roasting over the flames, spitted upon a pine branch. The smell of roasting meat drifted towards me on the breeze, sweet and juicy, mixing with the scent of wild rosemary and thyme upon the air. I closed my eyes, remembering Kaladrosos where the rosemary had grown upon the southern side of the house, a feathery silver-green bush, which my mother had plucked every day to season the evening meal. Every night, before we slept, she had laid a branch upon our family's shrine to honour Artemis. And then the nightmare vision surfaced again, clear as it did at night until I woke, sweating and panting with fear: *flames, burning high, licking the house and sending a pillar of black smoke to the sky . . . The voices of my father, my mother, calling out to me, Maia, Leon and Corycia wailing, their voices growing weaker, asking why I was not there . . .*

I forced myself to open my eyes and pushed myself up to stand, heart pounding, throat constricted. *There is nothing you can do now. You cannot leave, or Jason will have you killed, and that will benefit no one, your family least of all.*

I clenched my fists at my sides, trying to prevent the tears rolling down my cheeks. *You will simply have to find a way to return to Kaladrosos before Jason gets there, to return to protect your home.* I shook my head, willing myself to regain self-control, and was just about to force myself to join Theseus, Laertes, Hippomenes and the other lords gathered around the fire when I noticed someone else.

Prince Lycon, who was usually so inseparable from the Thracian noble Orpheus, was sitting alone further along the shore, a few paces from the waves, his lyre held cradled in his arms, plucking at the strings as he gazed out to sea. I hesitated, glancing around for Myrtessa, but she was laughing with the slaves, sharing bread and olives and wine. She would not miss me. I started out over the shore, the flat pebbles smooth beneath my sandals.

'My prince,' I said, as I approached him, 'I hope I am not disturbing you.'

His eyes had a distant, unfocused look, as if he had been

immeasurably far away and was only now recalled to his surroundings. After a while he said, 'Lord Telamon, is it not?' He gestured to the shore beside him.

I seated myself, removing my cloak and spreading it over the stones, my hands still shaking a little. Prince Lycon continued to strum at the strings of the lyre. It was a haunting tune, sweet but with an ineffable sadness. It had something of an Anatolian strain. I took his distraction as an excuse to look him over properly for the first time.

I felt a wave of disappointment as I realized that, close to, my brother was nothing like me. His straw-blond hair was dishevelled, curling at the ends. He had a full, soft mouth, his jaw jutting slightly forwards, and dark eyes with the same distant melancholy I had heard in the song. His fingers were long, delicate as he plucked at the strings. I looked away, a shiver shooting down my spine.

What if Neda and Myrtessa were wrong? How can this fair-haired, soft-skinned young man be my brother?

Have I made a terrible mistake?

'What can you tell me of your father?'

The question was out of my mouth before I had even properly considered it. He looked at me, startled.

I cleared my throat and lowered my voice, hastening to correct my mistake. 'That is to say, my prince, I meant – what is there that I should know of the king of Pagasae? I am new to the lands of Thessaly, and I would know all I can of my benefactors.'

His expression softened. He inclined his head and plucked again at the strings, with gentle, caressing strokes. 'What is it you would know?' he asked.

I paused, wondering if I dared say it. 'I heard tell,' I said, my voice a little unsteady, 'from the other lords that you once had a sister. That your father left her on the mountain to die.' I pressed my hands tight together in my lap, knuckles white, trying not to hold my breath, to look as if I were merely a young lord from Crete with no interest in the affairs of Pagasae.

Lycon nodded. 'What you heard is true. I never knew her.'

'Do you . . .' I gazed down at my fingers '. . . do you think that what he did was right?'

'No,' Lycon said, with something of a sigh. 'But my father is the king, and what he commands is law. A sceptred ruler is granted his kingdom by the favour of the gods. It is for us to obey him.'

Indignation rose within me, and my gaze snapped up to confront his. 'A king is a mortal like any other – it does not exempt him from committing unjust deeds!' I picked up a stone and threw it over the water. 'For King Iasus, and for Jason – both of them – kingship is merely an excuse to exercise cruelty. I do not believe the gods wish for such things. I think the gods love every mortal who walks upon the earth, noble or slave, man or woman, king or poet, for our deeds, not our wealth, or our occupations.'

I paused, breathing hard, wondering whether I had gone too far, but Lycon smiled faintly.

'Those in the palace who knew my mother say that she, too, was ever arguing with my father, begging more justice for his people, until she died. Indeed,' he took me by the chin and bent close to gaze at me, 'I see something of her portraits in you – the set of your mouth and,' he turned my face up, 'the colour of your eyes is just the same.'

I bit my lip, hanging on his every word, terrified that I might be discovered and yet longing for him to go on. *Perhaps it is true after all . . .* Unconsciously, I moved my fingers to my chest, felt the thin round circle of the golden medallion hanging at my collarbone, the leather thong around my neck.

Lycon looked away. 'Forgive me, Telamon, I am unused to being so far from home. And not a day goes by that I do not think of my mother, and wish I could have known her.'

I let out my breath slowly. 'I miss my mother and my home too,' I said, and I meant both of them: my family in Kaladrosos, and in Pagasae – my friends Neda, Philoetius and Hora – and perhaps now, my brother, too. Warmth for him kindled in my breast as I picked up another pebble and skimmed it over the surface of the sea. It leapt a few times across the silken water, then plunged into the waves with a faint splash.

'You are an unusual man, Telamon.'

I nodded, half wanting to smile at the irony of his words, half saddened by how little he knew. I wished I could confide in someone, but knew how much I risked if I did.

Lycon bent forwards to lay the lyre across his knees, and as he did so, I noticed something I had not seen before: a leather cord around his neck and, just visible above his tunic, a sliver of something round – something gold . . .

The medallion . . . The one Neda said she had seen . . .

My heart began to race, my mind filled suddenly with a whirl of thoughts. *It is true, then!*

He is my brother!

And then, with another jolt of terror and excitement: *I am, indeed, the daughter of the king!*

My pulse pounded in my throat at this final proof – at last! – after all the doubt of the days before, and I was about to open my mouth to say something, though what, I hardly knew, when—

'Who did you say your father was?'

I stared at him, appalled. I could not remember the name Myrtessa and I had practised . . .

What was it?

'Deucalion,' I said, relief flooding through me. 'Deucalion, son of Minos of Knossos, in Crete.'

'Well, son of Deucalion,' Lycon said, and he smiled properly for the first time, 'I would welcome more of your company. It is not often that I meet men like you in my father's court.'

Winds of Change

Kytoros, Anatolia

The Hour of Offerings
The Twenty-seventh Day of the Month of the Harvest

After two weeks' slow progress – for the winds were slack and we had lost many oars in the storm on the Propontis – we at last put into the port of Kytoros on the northern shores of Anatolia, in the territory of the Kaskaeans. Jason, determined to reach the Fleece at any cost, had refused to put in at the harbour towns of Sesamos and Aigialos to re-equip the *Argo* and mend her broken mast. But Argus had now demanded in no uncertain terms that we put in at port and barter some of our wine in return for wood, rope and canvas to repair the ship – or else, as he put it, we would all soon be sailing with the Nereids at the bottom of the ocean.

Jason had, at last, agreed.

The harbour of Kytoros was ringed by sheer wooded cliffs and a looming mountain on one side, from which we later learnt the port town took its name. The sea eddied around the twin headlands that enclosed the mouth of the bay, but within the harbour the water was calm and still, moving glassily over the stones beneath, and the warm breeze carried to us the scent of boxwood. Several fishing skiffs were bobbing upon the shallow waters, and a couple of low-bellied merchants' vessels were drawn up on land. To sailors who had been sitting at their benches for several weeks, hands blistered, backs sore, tunics drenched with sweat and legs cramped from days at sea, it was as good as the Isles of the Blessed.

145

I leapt down into the sea and splashed to shore, throwing the cool water over my head and shoulders, hearing the cheers and splashes behind me as the other lords and their slaves followed suit. I collapsed, panting, upon the sand, my tunic damp around my thighs and clinging to the skin, my chest rising and falling as I regained my breath. I felt a movement beside me and saw Meleager drop to the ground, his gold-brown hair crusted with salt, the smooth lines of his jaw and collarbone outlined in the sun. He turned to me and smiled, intimate as a lover. His eyes flickered over my face to rest upon my lips. My skin tingled in answer to his unspoken question, and his brief half-smile as if he knew what I was thinking, and all the while I was lost in those clear hazel eyes, almost gold in the sunlight . . .

'Meleager?'

Hippomenes was standing over us, broad shoulders blocking out the sun. I gasped at his sudden appearance and pushed myself up to sit, my hand shielding my eyes. Meleager did the same.

'What do you want, Hippomenes?'

Hippomenes jerked a thumb over his shoulder. 'It's not what I want, it's what he wants,' he said, and I assumed by 'he' that he meant Jason. 'We're to go up to the town and scout out where we might find materials for the ship's repairs, while the others remain here and assess the damage. They'll send a couple of slaves behind us bearing a message with what they need.'

'Is there such a hurry?' Meleager asked, lying down again upon the sand and squinting up at Hippomenes. 'We have only just arrived.'

Hippomenes shrugged. 'It's Jason's orders,' was all he said.

'And who else is to go?'

'You, me, Peleus and, if he will consent to come,' he added, rather awkwardly, 'I thought I might ask Telamon to accompany us, too.'

I hid my smile at his gesture of friendship, extended rather hesitantly after what must have seemed my ill-mannered rejection of his offer of the slave-girl, Thalia. 'With pleasure,' I said. He extended his hand to help me to my feet, but I pushed myself up without his aid and cocked my head at him with a grin. He raised his eyebrows and gave his hand instead to Meleager, who took it and stood with a groan.

'By the gods, I am sore,' Meleager complained, rubbing at the taut, slim muscles from his neck down to his shoulders, then the muscles of his upper arm, kneading the skin.

'We are all sore, Meleager,' Peleus said, striding up towards us and clapping Meleager upon the back. 'You had better become accustomed to it, for we have many weeks ahead of us yet, and more, if we do not get the ship mended soon. Hippomenes, Telamon,' he said, bowing to each of us. 'I have brought a couple of slaves to carry some samples of the wine for bartering.'

I looked over his shoulder and saw Myrtessa approaching, with several others, each carrying a pouch filled with wine. I exchanged a smile with her.

'Shall we be on our way, then?' Peleus said, glancing up at the sun.

The town of Kytoros was a little way up from the harbour, set upon a small hill that overlooked the bay. We climbed the winding path that scaled the steep cliffs ringing the harbour and crossed a plateau edged by scrubby, boxwood-covered hills. The afternoon sun beat down upon the backs of our necks and we were sweating by the time we passed through the gates into the small, winding streets of the town, the stench of straw and horse droppings in our noses, the clatter of pots and pans and the laughter of children in our ears. There were so many merchants and traders bustling around the alleys that we were barely noticed: hawkers from Masa with dark olive skin, local fishermen carrying trays around their necks filled with fish, Egyptian slaves bearing two-handled jars of wine on their heads, and priests dressed all in white. Myrtessa was struggling to keep hold of the heavy leather pouch in the bustle of the streets, her hands slippery with sweat from the climb, and I moved over to take it from her. She flashed me a grateful smile.

'What are we looking for?' I asked, falling in step with Hippomenes.

He gestured to a slave, Hantawa, a tall, imposing man with curling dark hair, an Anatolian by birth who had been sold into slavery and had risen through Bellerophon's household to become his steward. He was striding ahead, leading the way through the narrow alleys and pushing past merchants dangling golden chains from their fingers or foisting painted clay cups upon us. 'Hantawa has spoken with a local trades-man, who tells us there is a carpenter's workshop not far from here. Wood we can forage from the forests, but drills and saws, mallets and pegs for fitting the planks together – not to mention the canvas required for the sail – well, that we must barter for.' He motioned towards the pouch of wine I was carrying. 'That was kind of you,' he said, 'to take it from the slave.'

I said nothing, but I smiled up at him and, after a moment, he returned it.

'You come from Boeotia, do you not?' I asked him.

He nodded and bent beneath a sign hanging over the street above a baker's shop. 'From Onchestos – yes. My father rules the city.'

'And what do you do, then, in Onchestos?' I asked. 'If you are a lord, but do not rule.'

He shrugged his shoulders. 'Visit the farms on the plain, along the fertile valley that leads from Lake Copais down to the city of Thebes. I help them with the ploughing, drive the oxen along the furrows, or take the rods to the olive groves to beat down the fruit.'

I looked over his broad frame, his sturdy, wide palms. 'I could see you as a farmer,' I said, tilting my head to one side. 'In a straw hat and with a stick in one hand, you would look quite the part.'

He nodded, quite serious. 'I enjoy it. Being upon the fields. Putting my strength to the spade or the plough, then resting quiet at night beneath the stars after some good wine.' He caught my eye and laughed. 'I must sound like a regular Boeotian country lad to you, coming from Crete, with your palaces and your dances and your bullfights.'

I stared at him for a moment, then looked quickly away. In truth I had been thinking not of Crete, but of my father's house – the apple trees in our orchard, the goat tied to his pole, the comforting smell of the chopped woodpiles in autumn and the sweet scent of the blossoms in spring. I felt a tug of terrible sadness mixed with fear, remembering Jason's words: *And not only king of Iolcos! I will rule Pagasae, Makronita and Kaladrosos, Lechonia and Aphussos. I will burn all the towns of Pelion, raze them to the ground . . .*

'Oh, yes,' I said, but I did not return his smile. 'Yes. Quite.'

I was saved any more discussion in this vein, for at that very moment

Peleus, who was walking before us, called back, 'Hippomenes! Telamon! We've found the place.' We followed him around a corner and down an even smaller alleyway, if that were possible. The air was clouded at once with sawdust and the dry, sweet smell of wood shavings. The shop was small but with a wide open front that led directly onto the street, and the carpenter within, though he spoke no Greek, was soon conversing rapidly with Hantawa, gesturing with open hands. Peleus stepped inside and began bargaining through Hantawa for the tools and materials we would need to repair the *Argo*, while Hippomenes, Meleager, Myrtessa, the other slaves and I hung back by the entrance to the shop.

'I am parched with thirst,' Meleager announced, after an hour or so of such bargaining, loosening the tie of the tunic around his neck. 'Telamon, what say you and I go in search of a fountain?'

Peleus turned. 'You should all go,' he said. 'This will take a while longer, and Jason should be told that we have a man to supply us. Tell my lord,' Peleus looked at Hantawa, who nodded, 'that he will send the tools we ask for, with several slaves and axes to fell the trees, upon his ox cart in return for ten jars of the wine we offered him. The cart should be at the harbour by dawn tomorrow.' Peleus stepped further into the little shop, and began pointing to various hammers, chisels and saws, bartering with Hantawa in rapid Greek.

Hippomenes nodded. 'Our thanks to you, Peleus.'

We took a different way back to the city gates, through the marketplace. It was a broad open space covered with cobblestones, hawkers displaying their wares on wooden stands shaded from the sun with linen, or spread out on cloths upon the ground. I lingered a little over the wares, fingering the smooth clay cups painted black and red with exquisite scenes of lion hunts, handling daggers with weighted bronze handles incised with circular patterns, eyeing plump cherries displayed in woven baskets. At the opposite end of the market, closest to the street that would take us back to the gate where we had entered, there was a small fountain carved from limestone with a jet of water gushing from the spout. After Meleager and Hippomenes had drunk their fill I leant forwards and took several draughts, feeling it burn my dry throat, splashing a little on the front of my tunic and wetting my eyelashes and hair. I hardly cared: the cool, free-running water was delightful after several weeks of wine.

When at last I was done I turned to find Meleager standing behind me.

In his hands he was holding a delicate one-handled cup, one of those I had seen earlier upon the stalls, a scene of a dog chasing a young stag painted upon it in bright red, surrounded by spirals, as if the hunt were taking place in an undergrowth filled with curling leaves.

His eyes were boring into mine with an intensity that almost frightened me, a mixture of greed and desire, and for a moment I thought I saw the sensual mouth curl up in a triumphant sneer – as if the huntsman had cornered his prey at last. But then it was gone, and he extended the cup to me, all smiles and courtesy. I took it from him, my fingertips brushing against his and sending a charge shivering through my body. I looked up into his eyes, my lips parting with a mixed rush of confusion and, to my intense embarrassment, a flush rising to my cheeks.

'A ritual gift,' Hippomenes said, from somewhere beside us. I blinked and looked at him. His voice was clipped. 'An offering of love, made formal in the petition of three gifts. Is that not the way of things, in Crete? A triad of offerings from the lover to his beloved: a breastplate, an ox and a drinking cup?'

I stared at him. I could feel Myrtessa's eyes upon me, sense her sudden stillness.

'Y-yes. Yes, indeed, it is,' I said. I glanced up at Meleager, my thoughts a whirl of fear and confusion, and felt my heart skip a little at the intensity of his gaze, like heat upon my face.

If Meleager finds out who I am, what will he say?

I lowered my eyes.

But he desires me, a fiercer voice said. *He desires me. Perhaps he would not care. Perhaps he would want me for who I am.*

'Master?' Myrtessa's voice cut across my thoughts like a whip. 'May I speak with you a moment? There is an urgent matter of business I would ask your opinion of – something that cannot wait.'

I hesitated, still holding the cup cradled in my hands.

'Yes – yes, very well, Dolius,' I said at last, and pushed the cup back into Meleager's hands. 'Please carry it back to the *Argo* for me. I will see you both at the ship,' I said, nodding to Hippomenes and Meleager.

Then I left, without looking at either of them.

'What by all the gods do you think you are doing?'

Myrtessa slammed the door of the chamber behind her and faced me. She had led me into a tavern beside the marketplace. It was respectable enough, fronted with a long countertop serving ale and honeyed sesame buns to passers-by, leading behind into a low-ceilinged bar scattered with stools and, at the back, a few private chambers for the wealthier customers. Myrtessa had made me toss one of my bronze coins to the barman, then pulled me into the room: a small, shabby chamber with a low couch with a few tasselled cushions and a couple of rickety chairs. From the smell of the room, a faint mixture of cheap perfume and sweat, it was clear that at night it served as a place for the merchants of the town who could afford a private rendezvous to take their pleasure with the girls of Kytoros.

She was standing before me, glaring. 'Well?'

I stood my ground. 'I have done nothing.'

She threw her hands to the ceiling. 'You swore to me you would not fall for him! You said to me that you were not one to lose your wits over a man! Is this nothing? A cup – then a touch upon the hand, a kiss behind the rocks upon the shore and then he will have you and we will both be ruined!'

'I have not fallen for him,' I said calmly. 'There were a few moments, I admit, where I felt a desire for his touch, but you know as well as I that I would never let him take me if I did not think he could be trusted with our secret. There is a difference,' I glanced around the room in which we stood, thinking of all the men and women who had lain together there, 'between feeling the pulse of desire and acting upon it.'

'Yet you accepted his gift.'

'What else could I do?' I spread my hands wide. 'I did not know as well as you that it was a lover's gift till Hippomenes said so, and I could hardly pretend to ignorance, could I, when the custom itself is supposed to come from Crete?'

'I warned you against him,' she said. 'I told you he is violent in his desires and a libertine, for all that he looks like a young and careless god.'

'And I am grateful for your warning. Yet have I not said already I will be careful?'

She paused, clearly searching for some other criticism to level at me. Her eyes swivelled towards me, and I could see the glimmer of a laugh in her face, suppressed with difficulty. 'You were blushing as red as a milkmaid.'

I raised my eyebrows and surveyed her coolly. 'A milkmaid, you say?'

With a single flick of my wrist I drew the dagger from my belt and flung it across the room, my whole body behind it, the bronze blade sharp as a razor. It flew in a blur, missing Myrtessa's right ear by a hair's breadth, and buried itself, handle quivering, in the wooden planks of the wall.

Myrtessa raised a hand to her ear to check she was unscathed, then turned on me. 'You could have killed me!'

I grinned at her. 'But I did not.'

She glared at me, eyebrows contracted, mouth tight. I held her gaze, unflinching.

'Oh, very well,' she said at last, giving up and waving a hand towards me. 'I will not call you a milkmaid again. But I *will* say that you blushed.' She slid her eyes sideways at me again and her mouth twitched. 'It is as well you have not fallen for him, as you say,' she arched an eyebrow, 'for if you had, you should remember that if he tries to have his way with you – which, knowing Meleager, he *will* do, whether you be maid or man – then,' her expression became graver, 'we will both be discovered, and we know that there is only one penalty for lying to the king, deceiving the prince, and joining the expedition in the guise of a man. Death.'

There was a pause as we weighed each other up.

'Do you swear you will take this no further?' she asked.

I nodded. 'Unless I have good reason – I swear.'

'Unless you have good reason?' Her voice was wry again. 'You sound like one of the king's heralds – always covering himself at the end of each treaty and summons in case one day the king chooses to disobey his own laws.'

I laid a hand upon her arm. 'I do not know what the future holds, Myrtessa,' I said. 'It may be that Meleager may be of use to us,' she rolled her eyes, 'but I shall always be your friend and your ally, and I would never – *never* – willingly do anything to put you in danger.'

At last she subsided. She sank down onto the thin couch, making the cushions bounce up and down a little. 'Very well,' she said, changing tack as fast as a skiff in a storm. 'Very well. What about it, then?'

'What about what?'

She snorted. 'The future. We have made it this far but,' she tossed her head, 'what of when we get to Colchis? What . . .' she said, then lowered her voice to the merest thread of sound '. . . of the Fleece? Have you thought any more about how you plan to take it before Jason and his men – let alone how we shall return to Greece?'

I had, in fact, been thinking of little else the past few weeks – ever since Jason had revealed his terrible ambitions against my home – since the nightmares of Kaladrosos burning and my family's pleading to me had begun.

I cleared my throat and looked down at my hands. 'I came on this voyage to prove my worth to the king,' I said. 'To fulfil the prophecy, and to prove that he should not have abandoned me upon the mountain. That I was worth more than that. If I am truly honest,' I saw my smile reflected upon her lips, 'and I do want to be honest with you, Myrtessa, I came, too, to engage in a heroic quest, to have an adventure. I wished for more than the quiet life I had been given in Kaladrosos. But I have seen for myself Jason's cruelty – I have felt it,' I said, and I extended the palms of my hands towards her, where the stretched red marks of Jason's strap could still be seen. 'I heard his plans to ravage the towns and villages of the bay in war. I cannot let people like you, Neda, Philoetius and Lycon fall under his cruel rule – for what might he do to you and all the others? If Jason's ambitions truly extend to all the cities of Mount Pelion, then who can say that my family in Kaladrosos will be safe?' I swallowed, thinking of my father splitting logs with his axe beside the house, my mother gathering apples from the orchards into her apron. I imagined the cloud of dust rising to the skies and the shuddering of the earth as Jason's army descended the flanks of the mountain, their bronze weapons rattling and their war cries

153

drowning the pounding of the sea. I saw the terror on my mother's face as she gathered Maia and Corycia in her arms and fled to the shelter of the house . . . 'Perhaps I am meant to capture the Golden Fleece, not to prove to the king that I am his daughter but to save the kingdoms of Pelion from Jason.'

I turned to Myrtessa, breathing hard. Her whole face was alight, her eyes burning with pride.

'It truly was a day blessed by Zeus when you broke through the gates of Pagasae, Atalanta,' she said, with a laugh, and sprang to her feet. 'I am with you! We shall recover Pagasae from Jason and free Neda and Philoetius, Hora, Opis and your family, from his rule!' She hesitated. 'And yet, still, there is one thing remaining . . .'

'The Golden Fleece,' I said. 'Exactly.'

There was a pause, in which the faint sounds of the marketplace beyond floated to us through the high narrow window above. I felt strangely calm and filled with purpose, my mind clearer than it had been in weeks. It was as if I had been pursuing a path, imagining it would take me towards what I thought I desired, and now I had discovered that in fact it ended elsewhere – and that that was precisely where I was meant to go.

I frowned, leaning forwards. 'I have been considering it,' I said at last. 'And I believe I cannot plan more until I know for sure where the Fleece is hidden.'

'It is said that the Fleece is guarded by—'

'I know what the legends say,' I interrupted. I stood and began to pace up and down the small chamber, kicking up small clouds of dust from the floor that sparkled in the light slanting down from the window. 'I told you before that the legends are fabrications, told for children. When have you ever seen a serpent that never sleeps? Or a bull with hoofs of bronze? Or a flying ram?'

'But—'

'No,' I continued, filled with a new determination. My heart felt light as a sycamore seed upon the summer wind: there might be something I could do for Kaladrosos, for the cities of Pelion, after all, and it was driving me on, filling me with renewed energy. 'We need to think where the king of Colchis would hide something as valuable to him as

154

– whatever the fleece of gold is,' I said, stalling Myrtessa's interruption. 'A ram's wool cloak, perhaps, dyed gold. Or a golden breastplate emblazoned with Poseidon's ram. If I were king,' I said, continuing to pace, biting my lip as I thought, 'I would hide it either in a treasury, deep within the palace, guarded by sentries, most likely, or in a place that was unreachable – the top of a cliff that cannot be climbed or – or the depths of a lake. The guards I could deal with – but if it is hidden too well . . .' I shook my head.

'I cannot plan until I know for sure where the Fleece is located. As for the return, now that is easier,' I said, turning to face her. 'We cannot go back by ship with the rest of the lords if I succeed in stealing the Fleece – that much is certain. The only option remaining to us, then, is to travel on horseback, riding by day and resting at night. I have been following the coastline as we have sailed the Ocean beyond the Bosphorus – we have never been too far from the shore – and it is good terrain for riding. I have heard the Anatolian horses are swift and strong. If we change mounts at towns like this one we should be able to make good speed.'

Myrtessa grinned. 'I suppose it would be foolish of me to ask if there is anything I can do to help, since you have everything already planned.'

I shrugged. 'I work better alone,' I said.

She flopped back upon the cushions, picking at one of the tassels.

'One thing, though, I have noticed – during our journey,' I continued.

Myrtessa raised her eyebrows. 'Oh, yes?'

I considered carefully. 'There seem to be two factions among the lords,' I said. 'Nothing open – nothing that could be observed without several weeks spent at their side. But there seem to be some who are entirely for Jason, who respect his authority and his orders, and then there are others who, though on the surface they appear to respect him, beneath I sense that they baulk at his command . . . That, perhaps, they, too, have come to know him as I have.'

'Who? Which of the lords?'

'Hippomenes,' I said. 'The tone of his voice earlier, upon the beach . . . And Peleus. I swear there was just a moment, upon the *Argo* in the

155

storm, when Jason ordered him to desist in reaching out to Hippomenes as he drowned that Peleus' eyes registered his contempt. And Lycon is no willing participant on the journey – he told me so himself.'

'And how does this help us?'

I rubbed my knuckles on my forehead and sat down beside her, elbows on my knees. 'I don't know,' I said, thinking hard. 'But I cannot help but feel it may be of use to us.'

There was a sudden knock upon the door – three loud raps, followed by silence.

I started up, exchanging a nervous look with Myrtessa, and saw my panic reflected upon her own pale face.

'I— Enter,' I said, my throat suddenly dry.

The door was pushed open and, to my horror, Jason himself stepped over the threshold. His grey eyes swept the dim, threadbare room, and came to rest upon Myrtessa and me, seated side by side upon the couch.

'Well, well, Telamon,' he said, with a glimmer of a smile, though there was no warmth to it. 'It seems that Peleus was right. You and Dolius are hardly ever to be parted, and hiding away together in such a room . . .' he paused to inhale the scent of desire that hung around the pillows and the curtain upon the door '. . . well . . .'

I stood and bowed. 'My lord Jason. You find Dolius and myself discussing matters relating to the running of my estate in Crete. Nothing else, I assure you.'

Jason eyed me, his lip curling in a sneer.

'Is there something you wanted from me, my lord?' I did my best to appear calm, though my palms were cold with sweat.

'You are needed back at the ship,' he replied, his tone pleasant but his eyes as hard as a pond under the grey skies of winter. 'I came to the city with a band of men to oversee Peleus' negotiations, and Hippomenes told me he had last seen both of you disappear in here. And we would not wish to lose you – would we?'

I inclined my head. 'Of course, my lord. I will come, if that is what you wish. Dolius,' I said, gesturing towards Myrtessa. She leapt to her feet at once and stood behind me, hands clasped before her, eyes downcast.

Jason's lips curved into a smile as he looked between us, his expression inscrutable. 'Good,' he said, his eyes lingering upon my face. 'Obedience – that is what we like, eh, Telamon?'

Then he turned and pushed open the door.

As I followed him, head bowed beneath the low lintel of the door, I could feel the fear throbbing in my veins and knew that, behind me, Myrtessa was thinking the same as I.

How much had Jason heard?

And what would he do to us if he knew?

Hera's Revenge

Mount Olympus

It is the twilight moment between day and night, when the lamps in the palaces of Mount Olympus are being lit and the mortals below gaze up at the first of the twinkling stars. A soft hush has fallen over heaven, and all that can be heard is the tinkling of fountains and the piercing song of a nightingale perched upon an oak tree in the garden of Zeus' palace. It is a perfect evening, mellow and sweet with the scent of the spring irises, the grass just tinted with drops of dew.

Hera, however, is oblivious to the peaceful scene. She has placed herself behind one of the marble columns outside the entrance to Zeus' chambers, her robes held in one hand so that they do not show around the column's sides, casting furtive looks towards the double cedar doors. To a casual observer it would seem for all the world as if she were – well – hiding. Hera knows that this is not the case, for the queen of the gods does not hide in shadows, like a common thief. She is . . . She hesitates for a moment, searching for the right word.

Ah, yes. Redressing things. That is what she is doing.

Rectifying the balance of the universe.

Getting her revenge.

'Aha!'

The double doors to Zeus' rooms have opened a crack, and Hera pounces. Zeus is halfway through the doors when his wife leaps upon him, and it is all he can manage not to shout aloud.

'Hera! What are you doing here?' he hisses, in a voice that is both defensive and a little sheepish, holding onto the door for support. 'If it were possible, I would say you had frightened me almost to death.'

'Yes,' she says, crossing her arms and glaring at him. 'Well, you can't have everything, can you?'

Zeus recognizes an oncoming storm when he sees one – he is the god of thunder, after all – and backs into his chambers resignedly, pulling off the travelling cloak he is wearing and tossing it under the bed. 'To what do I owe the —'

Hera cuts him off. 'Let's get straight to the point, Zeus,' she says.

'Oh dear,' he says. 'The point. I'd better get myself a drink.' He moves over to an inlaid table upon which a silver jug and two goblets are standing beside a bowl filled with ambrosia.

'Nectar?' he asks, pouring a glass and offering it to her.

'No, thank you,' she says.

Zeus takes a sip, closes his eyes for a moment as if relishing the silence, then turns with an air of inevitability to face his wife. 'So, what is this about, Hera?'

The wife of the king of the gods eyes her husband beadily. 'Atalanta,' she says. 'You've been favouring her. Why?'

Zeus raises his eyebrows and takes another sip with apparent enjoyment. 'Hm. I didn't expect that.'

'How long have you been watching over her, Zeus?' Hera demands, one foot tapping upon the marble floor. 'How long have you been keeping her safe, when my back was turned?'

Zeus swirls the contents of the goblet. 'I think she may be my offspring.'

Now it is Hera's turn to look stunned. She stares at her husband, mouth opening and closing. After a while, however, she seems to regain control of herself. 'And why exactly,' her voice takes on a tone of menace, 'would you think that?'

'Because I lay with her mother Clymene, nineteen years ago.'

Hera looks set to explode with anger. Her eyes are flashing like twin fires of black flame. 'You lay with —'

'Yes, Hera dear, I lay with her – nineteen years ago,' Zeus repeats, a little impatiently. 'Can we put things in perspective, please? If you must know, I was as surprised as you when I found out she was still alive. I never intended to favour the child. But as she has survived, perhaps the Fates wished it . . . And she is mine, after all.'

There is a pause as the two gods survey each other across the chamber, and the curtains at the window billow softly.

'So,' Hera says, exhaling, trying to force herself to focus on the matter at

162

hand. 'So. She is your daughter. That changes things, I suppose. And the boy? Lycon?'

'Not mine,' Zeus says. 'Fathered by the king on the same night. I mean, look at him – he's a poet. Hardly the son of a god, I'm sure you agree.'

She nods. 'And the storm?' She tosses the next question at him, like a huntsman throwing a dart – precise, targeted, arrow-sharp.

Zeus' expression registers his surprise. 'I thought that was you.'

She raises her eyebrows. 'Why would I set a storm upon the Argo?'

'Well,' Zeus says, setting down his goblet and spreading his hands wide, 'to hazard a guess, you seem to have been favouring Jason lately. Perhaps you were trying to get rid of Atalanta . . . Am I close?'

Her tone is distinctly cold as she says, 'If by that you mean to suggest that I have any desires for the mortal . . .'

Zeus shrugs. 'You said it, not me.'

Hera glares at him. 'I feel protective of him. That is all.'

'And you are not, by any chance, attempting to sway him to your side and to claim the cities of Iolcos and Pagasae as your own?'

'Now, why would I do that?' she asks, her eyes widening in a look of wounded innocence. 'You know I respect your rule over your cities, as my husband and my lord.'

'Why indeed?' Zeus replies.

He moves to the four-poster bed, carved from four oaks and laden with soft woollen blankets. He seats himself upon the edge and stretches. The piles of cushions and blankets sag a little beneath his weight. 'Well, I can put your mind at rest. I did not set the storm.'

'And I assure you I did not either.' Hera taps her fingers against her thighs in irritation.

'Then who did?'

'I have no idea.'

She moves over to sit beside him upon the bed, chin on her hands, thinking.

There is a pause, each god wondering who will break the silence first, where to turn next in the stalemate between them.

'Very well,' Zeus says at last, twisting to face her and steepling his fingers. 'I take it that you have come here tonight for my word that Atalanta will not get her kingdom.'

Hera is caught off guard. 'Well – yes.'

Zeus presses his fingertips together, then looks up at his wife. 'Agreed.' He holds a hand out, palm up, towards her. 'You have my word.'

She looks at him for a moment, measuring him, as if uncertain how to respond to this unexpected move.

Zeus slides over towards her, puts his hands on her shoulders and kisses her neck. 'Oh, come to bed, Hera,' he says, fumbling through her hair and drawing out the ivory pins that hold it, one by one, so that it falls lock by dark lock over her shoulders. 'You look so beautiful when you're angry,' he says, planting a kiss on her wrist. 'And I love it when your hair's down.'

She lets herself be pulled slightly towards him, though her body is still stiff and her lips pursed. 'I have your word?'

Zeus is tugging down the shoulder of Hera's robe with his teeth. 'Absolutely,' he croons, into the soft skin of her arm.

She doesn't relent. 'And you promise you will stop favouring the girl?'

'Promise,' he says, unfastening the golden brooch holding her robe together.

'And that, in future, you'll listen to what I tell you, and not go off favouring mortals behind my back?'

Zeus has managed to draw her onto her back and is slowly pulling her towards him across the blankets, his lips pressing upon her cheeks, her neck, her collarbone. 'I always listen,' he says. 'But now, wife, it is time for bed.'

And with that, he pulls Hera under the covers.

An hour or so later, Hera is easing herself from where she is lying entangled in her husband's arms and climbs softly out of the bed, her bare feet making no noise as she stands, dresses herself, then begins to walk, her robes whispering around her ankles. The lamps on their golden stands have guttered to a dim, flickering light, and there is no movement from the bed as she looks back over her shoulder, opens the doors and slips outside.

Now that Zeus is taken care of, she is turning her attention to his brother.

Iris is waiting outside the chambers as she bade her, leaning against one of the columns, tossing a glimmering golden apple up into the air and catching it. As Hera appears she straightens and swiftly pockets the apple. 'He's in the library,' she says, without preamble. 'With Hermes.'

Hera raises her eyebrows. 'The library? He never took an interest in reading before.'

'I imagine he is searching for Jason's fate among the scrolls.'

'Then we have not a moment to lose.'

The two goddesses hurry along the colonnades that lead onto the path, bathed in moonlight, away from Zeus' palace, lit by stars on either side, like clusters of shining lamps — the ones that mortals call the Milky Way. The Library of the Muses is not far, and soon the goddesses are entering the gardens, skirting the edge of the oblong pool, the blackness of the sky reflected in its still surface, the whispering of the pines upon the slight breeze and the sweet scent of the trees welcoming them into a still, silent world. They ascend the marble steps swiftly and pass through the doors into the small entrance chamber, its walls glinting with inlaid gold and the green marble tiles upon the floor cool beneath their feet. Hera crosses it in a few steps, Iris following, then hurries across the inner courtyard and through the bronze double doors opposite.

A vast room opens before them, the ceiling so high that it is shrouded in darkness, the walls lined with endless shelves of papyrus scrolls, tables loaded, with more scattered across the marble floor. Here and there, the white-robed, slender figures of the Muses move between the shelves holding flickering lamps or are seated on chairs, copying out the fates of mortals with reed brushes dipped in ink. Iris peers at the laden shelves curiously, her eyes darting over the records.

Hera spots Poseidon at the other end of the vast hall, bending over a table lit by a single clay lamp and reading avidly, Hermes at his shoulder. She sweeps towards him, barely glancing at Calliope, the muse of epic poetry, who is currently sorting a pile of scrolls that have just come in from the Fates, as she passes.

'And what do you think you are doing, Poseidon, here in the library at this hour?'

Poseidon gives a jolt of surprise. The papyrus snaps up from his hands and springs back into a roll. He attempts to seize it, but Hera is too quick for him.

'Well, well, well,' she says, snatching it and spreading it open to read the name inscribed upon it. 'Jason, son of Aeson. What were you hoping to find here, Poseidon?'

Poseidon glances over his shoulder for Hermes, as if hoping he would help, but Hermes is staring at Iris with an expression of intense dislike.

'I – well, I – I don't see why I should have to tell you.'

'Let's get to the matter at hand,' Iris says, turning from Hermes to Poseidon. 'Did you, or did you not, set that storm upon Jason and his crew?'

'And if I did? I'm the god of the sea, aren't I?'

As Iris grimaces in acknowledgement, Hera puts in, 'Jason always sacrifices plenty of oxen in your honour but, still, you thought—'

'It's not Jason,' Poseidon says. 'It's his mother. Alcimede.'

Hera is taken aback. 'His mother?' Her eyes narrow as she thinks back to Atalanta's mother, Clymene, and Zeus' admission of his seduction eighteen years before. 'It seems that the queens of Mount Pelion draw the gods of Olympus to them, like fish to bait.'

Poseidon is scowling so it is hard to see his eyes under the lowering eyebrows. 'She chose Zeus instead of me. Me!' He looks at Hermes, who shrugs and gives a noncommittal look of sympathy. 'There we were, in Pelias' bedchamber, not two days ago, and we told her we both wanted her and that she'd have to choose between us – and the fool chose Zeus!'

'I see,' Hera says. Her voice is so even that anyone who knows her will be in no doubt that she is in one of her deadliest, most dangerous furies. 'I see,' she says again, breathing deeply. 'So you decided to punish Jason for your stupidity in forcing his mother to choose between the two of you?'

'That's right,' says Poseidon. 'And now I want to know what's in store for Alcimede's brat. I want to punish her so that she knows she made the wrong decision. The death of her only son ought to do it, don't you think?'

Iris makes a small noise of disgust, but says nothing.

There is an awkward silence, in which nothing but the whispering of the Muses' robes across the floor and the sweeping of reed brushes can be heard.

'Well,' Hermes says, into the silence, 'this has all been very nice, Hera, but Poseidon and I should be going. If you had come with me and Apollo to Pieria straight away,' he adds to Poseidon in an undertone, 'and hadn't insisted on stopping here first, we wouldn't have had any of this in the first place.'

Poseidon opens his mouth to retort, and neither he nor Hermes notices as Iris slips a small crystal phial from her cloak and divides the contents – a black liquid – between two of the several goblets filled with nectar that are standing on a table, a few feet away from Poseidon.

166

'*Very well, then, Poseidon,*' Hera says, as Iris slips the phial back into the folds of her robes. '*I can see you will not be moved.*'

Poseidon turns from Hermes, his mouth still slightly open, clearly pleased and somewhat surprised at his victory.

'*Will you join Iris and me in a drink, at least? Before you go? And what is it you are planning to do, anyway?*' she asks Hermes, with a pleasant smile.

'*Nymphs,*' Hermes says, through a mouthful of ambrosia.

Iris raises an eyebrow.

'*Well, then, to nymphs, I suppose,*' Hera says, passing Hermes and Poseidon a goblet each, then handing one to Iris.

'*Nymphs,*' Poseidon repeats, chuckling into his goblet as he drinks, splashing nectar down the front of his robes.

There is a moment in which they all sip in silence. Hermes sets his goblet upon the table where, moments earlier, the scroll of Jason's fate had been laid, and glances towards it, then up at Iris with a flash of suspicion and alarm. He lifts it to his nose and sniffs, his eyes widening.

'*Poseidon—*'

'*Very . . . very good,*' Poseidon says, setting down his goblet beside Hermes', his speech a little slurred. '*But I think . . . I think before we . . . I think I'm feeling—*'

And with that, he and Hermes collapse together to the floor and begin to snore.

Betrayal

Colchis

The Hour of Prayer

The Seventh Day of the Month of the Grape Harvest

Later they would make epics of our travels. They would say that we met with Amazons, fought with terrible monsters and were abducted by nymphs. They would tell of Harpies that snatched the food of a blind man, and birds clothed in metal whose beaks were like darts.

Yet the harshest enemies we encountered on our voyage over the sea were our empty bellies, and I, who had always had plenty of stews and breads and sweet apples for the taking at home, learnt for the first time how hard an adversary hunger can be. Food supplies were running low, and our meals of stale bread and pickled olives were eaten now almost in silence. Spirits aboard the *Argo* were even lower, although at least, now that Myrtessa and I had come upon the plan to try to take the Fleece and protect the cities of Pelion from Jason, my old nightmares had abated and I was sleeping soundly again. Our legs were cramped from hours spent at the benches pulling against the adverse winds blowing into the prow, our arms and backs aching, the folds of our skin encrusted with salt from the sea air, our swords and arrows, which we had piled in the storage with such high hopes of adventure, sharpened and unused: for where were the enemies to fight atop the white surf of the waves?

We had left Kytoros many weeks before and had been skirting the edge of the ocean beyond the Bosphorus, keeping the land to our right and following the course of the stars due east. Hantawa had told us that the merchant sailors and travellers from the empire of the Hittites, whom he had questioned in Kytoros, had spoken of the land of Colchis, where the Golden Fleece was kept, and said it was reached by sailing towards the rising sun until the land curved back to meet the ship's prow. Others of the lords had heard this story also, and Theseus himself claimed he had sailed the northern reaches of the sea as a younger man. But as we rowed on and on and the days turned into weeks, the weeks into months and, though the sea-weather was unusually calm and the skies clear, no land appeared before us upon the horizon, and I began to fear we might never reach Colchis. We would row until we reached the very edge of the Ocean, and then . . .

'Land! I see land ahead!'

Laertes was leaning out over the prow, his hand held over his eyes. The words seemed strangely surreal after so many weeks spent imagining the phantom of land before us, telling ourselves that we were nearly there, closing our eyes at night with the thought, *Tomorrow . . . tomorrow we will sight land . . .*

At first none of us moved. I exchanged a look with Peleus, who was sitting beside me at the bench, his cheeks sallow from weeks of poor diet. His eyes darted up to the prow, then back to me. 'No,' he whispered. 'Can it be possible?'

As one, we banked our oars and jumped to our feet. I saw Hippomenes, Meleager, Theseus, Nestor, Jason – all the other lords – crowding forwards over the thwarts to where Laertes was standing. I felt my stomach flip with excitement and nerves. After all the risks Myrtessa and I had taken, after weeks spent upon the sea, voyaging towards the Fleece, could I be here at last?

My throat constricted.

And what happens now?

'Can you be sure, Laertes?' Jason called, over the slapping of the waves against the ship's hull. 'I want no mistakes.'

'See for yourself!' Laertes pointed to the north-east, a little to the left of the prow.

I narrowed my eyes and, with a thrill of anticipation, saw a dim grey outline upon the horizon, faint but growing ever clearer. I looked behind me, searching, and spotted the dark-haired figure of Myrtessa at the back of the crowd of slaves. She nodded to me, once, her eyes shining with excitement. *We are here*, she mouthed to me. *We have made it.*

After several hours more at the oars there was no mistaking the silhouette of land growing larger and larger, mountains soaring up to the sky in ridged and forested peaks topped with white snow, quite different from the rolling slopes of Pelion. As we drew nearer I saw the river the merchants had said was the Phasis, gushing out into the ocean, its wide mouth surrounded by lush, uncultivated meadows of reeds and grasses.

We navigated the currents of the river's mouth and rowed inland, the mountains towering at either side of us, throwing us into shadow. We were silent now, all of us, and the wind had quietened so that there were no sounds except for the splash of oars dipping into the clear water and the cries of birds of prey, circling overhead, their sharp beaks outlined against the bright sky.

'How much further?' Theseus asked, from two thwarts before mine, as we followed the meandering course of the river.

'I cannot be sure,' Argus called from the steering oar. 'There are few travellers who have made it as far even from the lands of Anatolia as this. Those Hantawa spoke with talked of a city on the slopes of the mountains, reached by a long and winding river, but I do not know how far inland it lies.'

We rowed on. Meleager was seated beside me at the bench now. He looked pale and wary, and we moved together in silence. He had not approached me since the gift of the cup in Kytoros, and I had not encouraged him. After Myrtessa's warnings I had attempted to put as much distance between him and myself as I could, and this was only the second time he had been my companion upon the thwart since we had departed Kytoros' harbour. I looked at him, wondering what he was thinking. His eyes were darting over the shore, perhaps searching for ambushes as his oar stroked the silent waters of the river.

Hippomenes voiced the same thought. 'It is too quiet. I do not like it.'

'You fear a surprise attack?'

He pulled another stroke at the oar. 'It would be an easy place to hide, upon those mountains,' he said, and directed his gaze up at the dense forests covering the darkened slopes. 'It is what I would do.'

The sun had slid behind the soaring peaks of the mountains and we were plunged into chilly shadow, our oars dripping upon the water, then splashing faintly as we dipped them into the river. The eagles were silent, no doubt sheltering for the night within their nests on the crags, and the water was turned a deep jet in the darkness, no longer clear and welcoming.

'Perhaps we should rest for the night.' Argus' voice broke into the silence from the stern. 'And continue tomorrow.'

Jason, seated upon the bench before me, shook his head. 'We go on,' he said. 'We can rest once we reach the city and know its position.'

Argus fell silent, and we rowed on.

'My lord,' Argus began, an hour or so later, 'I must speak. It is not wise—'

But Jason held up his hand to silence the steersman, and I saw at once what had made him do so. We had just turned another bend in the river, and ahead of us, on the sloping flanks of the mountain just before the river's banks, a city was blazing out of the shadows, torches flaring upon every rampart.

The slave beating the drum faltered and stopped. Jason pulled his oar out of the water and slid it across his lap. The rest of us followed.

I peered through the darkness. The city appeared to be built of grey stone, its battlements and gate-towers forbidding in the deep shadows cast by the mountains. A cluster of square towers reached up to the night sky from within its walls, all of different heights and some topped with stone ramparts of their own. Two outer gates were visible, both closed and made of wood, set before a ditch, which seemed to have been dug around the city walls. Guards patrolled the perimeter, bows and quivers filled with arrows, upon their backs.

'They do not appear to welcome visitors,' Hippomenes said, from his place at the thwart beside Jason, one hand moving to his sword's hilt.

Theseus looked up at the sky overhead, scattered with bright stars, pinpricks of light above the jagged peaks. 'We should wait until dawn,' he said.

Nestor's voice sounded through the darkness: 'Let us wait until daybreak, Jason. To attempt to beach and approach the city when we have no sense of the lie of the land would be foolish, to say the least.'

Jason considered for a moment. 'Very well,' he said, and I saw him tap his fingers against the smooth handle of his oar. 'Let us run the ship up on shore here, in this bay, where they cannot see us. We will approach the king with our requests in the morning.'

I could not hide my surprise. 'You plan to petition him for the Fleece? You do not intend to take it by force?'

Jason turned to smile at me, his teeth gleaming in the starlight. 'Why, we will begin with a request,' he said. 'We are Greeks, are we not? And if he does not accept it, then, well . . .' He left the threat hanging upon the air.

I glanced at Hippomenes. He still looked wary, but said nothing.

We drove the ship's keel up onto the sand and jumped down into the waters, then settled upon the beach to sleep, side by side for warmth. After a while lying upon my back, looking up through the branches of the fir overhead and unable to sleep, I sat up, drew my cloak over my shoulders and glanced around me. The sky above us was alive with stars scattering the darkness, like raindrops upon a still pool, and the sounds of the river lapping at the shore were soothing, accompanied by the humming of the cicadas in the pine trees. I gazed at the prone, sleeping figures of the men around me. My eyes fell upon Peleus, his sandy eyelashes sweeping his cheek in sleep, one arm flung out beside him. I smiled to myself. Peleus had been a friend from the very first: it was he who had welcomed me aboard the *Argo*, and who had aided me in the storm when none other would. Argus lay behind him, the only one of the heroes, aside from Peleus, who dared to stand up to Jason, his cloak tucked around his body, snoring gently. There was Hippomenes, broad-backed, a man of few words but with a strong sense of honour, his fingers interlaced over his chest, rising and falling with his breath; Meleager, bold, ardent and careless, rolled upon his side, long hair brushing his shoulders. These, I thought, were heroes indeed: men who fought hard for what they wanted, who lived on little and took pleasure in good wine and the strength of their hands. Men who had become my friends and my companions.

Will I be able to steal the Fleece from them, when the time comes? I hugged my knees tight into my chest. *I have spent so many weeks with them, shared my meals with them, laughed with them side by side and shared my grievances with them when we rowed too far.*

Will I be able to take from them what they have come so far to get?

And it was with that disconcerting thought that I was left, for many hours, to stare up into the moonless sky and wait for what tomorrow's embassy might bring.

As it turned out, the Colchians did not wait for our embassy.

I awoke the next morning on the sand of the river's shore, stiff with cold, my cloak over me wet with dew. None of the other lords or the slaves had woken yet, and I pushed myself to my elbows, rubbing my eyes.

Then I stopped.

I had heard hoof beats, gentle, unmistakable, on the dawn air. I turned slowly, searching the grassy meadow that extended up the bank behind the bay into a thicket of trees and up to the mountain slopes, looking for a sign of movement. All was still, hushed, the only sounds the rippling waves against the bank and the swishing of the pines in the faint breeze.

Suddenly an arrow hissed through the air. A thud and a cry of pain. One of the slaves upon the ground, Cedalion, a friend of Myrtessa, was groaning and shrieking, clutching at the arrow that was sticking from his thigh, dark blood leaking out over his tunic, his mouth gaping as he drew long, gasping breaths.

All at once, the camp was in pandemonium. Arrows were hailing through the air, the lords were staggering to their feet, clutching at weapons, slaves were running, screaming, in all directions.

'Over there!'

I pointed towards the thicket up ahead. At least fifty horsemen were thundering out of the cover of the trees towards us, appearing like phantoms through the early-morning mist rising up from the forest behind them, each carrying a bow with a quiver of arrows hanging at their side. They rode without bridles, and it was as if they and the horses were of one mind, the horses' manes flying out behind them as they galloped, like pennants in the wind, and still the arrows showered down upon us thick and fast as the archers shot down the slopes again and again.

As fast as I could, I leapt to my feet, snatched up my quiver from the ground and fastened my sword-belt around my waist. Heart pounding, I drew my bow, nocked an arrow and took aim, twisting to follow the course of an archer, then loosed it. It flew through the air and struck its target directly between the collarbones. The man choked and fell from his steed. He gave a shattering, unearthly scream as he hit the ground, his legs crumpling beneath him, the arrow snapping in two.

I stared at what I had done, my hand dropping to my side. The hail of arrows was still falling around me but I was unable to move – I could not have moved even if a horse had come galloping at full force directly towards me. It was as if my limbs were not mine any more, as if my mind had separated from my body at the realization of the terrible deed my hands had done. I had let my arrow fly with as little thought as when I was hunting an animal in the forest – but this was different. This was awful. The man was screaming and writhing. I could see his face, the whites of his eyes, his gaze as he searched for me, wordless. I could hear his gasping breath. I felt bile rise in my throat, my hands shaking.

Cold began to flood through me, the image of the man falling from his steed imprinted upon my eyes. My vision was clouding and spots flashed here and there. I stumbled a little, and my bow slid towards the ground.

Do you want to lose Myrtessa? a small voice inside my head said. I blinked, shivered. The words began to penetrate slowly through the fog obscuring my thoughts. *Meleager? Peleus? Hippomenes? Do you want to lose them all?*

I tightened my grip upon the bow until my knuckles whitened, and gradually my sight came back into focus.

You have to do it, to protect yourself and those you love.

I made myself turn back, repeating their names to myself one after another – *Myrtessa, Meleager, Peleus* – as I nocked more arrows and let them fly into the air, not allowing myself to think of anything but their names as I fought. Two more Colchians fell to the ground, my arrows piercing their thighs and shoulders, rolling over and over down the slope as their horses whinnied and reared in fright. Missiles were whistling past my ears, I could see Pollux and Laertes crouching beneath their shields, and behind them Hippomenes, weighing a spear in his hand, then hurling it at one of the archers' steeds, burying the bronze tip deep in the horse's haunch so that the beast screamed in pain and bucked its rider from its back before collapsing to the ground, eyes rolling. And now they were upon us. I drew Corythus' sword from my belt, the blade gleaming. A Colchian had leapt from his mount and approached me, a small dagger in his hand. I turned to face him, feinted to the left and he darted aside to miss the blow. Quick as wind I whirled around and lunged forwards, swiping my blade through the air, and felt it slice the man's sword-arm. He dropped his dagger, howling, clutching at the wound. Dust was rising in the air around us from the horses' hoofs and I could smell the iron tang of blood. War cries in a language I did not know mixed with shrieks of pain, whether from our enemies or the lords of Greece I did not know . . .

I swivelled on the ball of my foot, shivering, forcing myself not to think anything but the names of those I was trying to keep from harm – *Hippomenes, Phorbas, Laertes.* I spotted Peleus, mouth bleeding, duelling a broad-chested man with shoulder-length hair and thick eyebrows that were coated with sand and dust. As I watched, a second Colchian advanced upon Peleus from behind, and Peleus, who was busy blocking and parrying, his feet flashing over the sand, had not seen him—

Before the second attacker could so much as raise his sword I had fitted another arrow to my bow and sent it whistling towards him. There was a terrible splitting sound as the arrow tunnelled through the bone of his thigh, the shaft quivering from the impact, and he crumpled, screaming, his blade clattering to the ground beside him.

'My thanks to you, Telamon!' Peleus called, still parrying and thrusting. He forced his opponent to follow him, darting out of his way, and the man, not watching his feet, tripped on a large rock protruding from the ground. He fell forwards with a crash and Peleus drove his sword downwards into his back, leaning his weight on the hilt.

'Where—' I began, as another wave of nausea overcame me, searching desperately for Myrtessa's dark head amid the clouds of sand flying around us. But at that moment a Colchian thundered past me on his horse and leapt from the saddle, drawing his sword with a flash of bronze. I raised my blade to his and we began to duel, sweat flying from my face as I parried and blocked, ducked, feinted to the side to draw him towards me, then lunged forwards. He brought up a dagger with his second hand and managed to knock my blade aside – it sliced his upper arm, opening a deep gash in the muscles, splitting the veins and splattering me with blood. He dropped his sword, howling, and I turned away, trying with all my might to close my ears to the sound as he knelt on the ground, cradling the wound.

A Greek slave was behind me, crouched to the earth, holding his hands over his head and muttering prayers to the gods in a rapid torrent. I knelt down and recognized him as Melanthius, a slave of Nestor. 'Have you seen Dolius?'

He stared at me, eyes wide, mouth still moving in a stream of invocation. I took him roughly by the tunic. 'Have you seen Dolius?' I repeated, shouting over the tumult of the battle raging around us.

He nodded then, teeth chattering, and pointed towards the trees. 'Escaped – before they came,' he said. 'Other slaves – over there – taking shelter.'

I nodded briefly, taking in the stench of fear upon him. 'Come with me. You take this.' I snatched up the shield from the corpse of a Colchian nearby, an arrow sticking from his chest, struck by his own people in the hail of darts flying this way and that over the beach. I tried not to look at his open, glassy eyes. 'Hold it above your head,' I instructed Melanthius, showing him how to cover himself with the shield. 'Now – *move!*'

He did not need telling twice. He crept through the groups of duelling men, stepping over dead bodies with a shudder and keeping the shield raised close to his head. A spear clattered into it, denting the centre, and he whimpered but held fast. We proceeded together, I leading the way to the battle's edge, clearing our path with my sword, Melanthius crouching after me until, at last, sweating and covered with blood and sand, we reached the edge of the skirmish.

'*Go!*' I pushed him towards the trees some fifty paces distant, where the group of slaves could just be seen hidden within the shrouding darkness. He mouthed his thanks and ran, the shield held behind him, like a tortoise's shell upon his back.

Then, as I turned to move back into the fray, I felt a blinding, searing pain in my left shoulder. A blazing, shuddering scream of torment spread through me as I felt the muscle tear beneath the blade that had struck me, felt the blood spill and leak into the wool of my tunic, hot and sticky. My vision was clouding, I felt weak, dazed, apart from myself, and all I wanted was for this numbness to overtake me entirely, to separate me from the pain and from the body, which was tearing itself apart in agony. Time seemed to slow as I gazed down and, as if through a mist, saw the long, slim shaft sticking from my body and the white-feathered fletching upon the end.

'Ah,' I said. 'It was an arrow, after all.'

And then I collapsed to the ground.

'Telamon. Telamon.'

Someone was calling my name and slapping my face, cold fingers striking against my cheeks. But it was not my name, was it? Why should I answer them?

'Leave me be. Leave me!'

'Atalanta.' A softer voice, higher. And they had said my real name.

My eyes fluttered open.

Myrtessa came into focus, standing above me, her silhouette framed by the light of a lamp that was sputtering beside her, throwing shadows against the canvas of a tent. The features of her face were blurred in the dreary fog of lifting unconsciousness, but I could see her outline, the linen tunic she was wearing and her wide, frightened eyes.

I tried to sit up and an agonizing red-hot pain arrowed through my left shoulder. I put my hand to it and felt rough linen bandages there, smelt poppy extract, saffron and bitter rose root. The pain was so strong that I wanted to cry out with it, but I bit my lip, feeling the corners of my eyes burn. 'What happened?'

'You were hit by an arrow,' Myrtessa said. Her face was clearer now and I could see the tear-tracks running down her cheeks, her cut lip. She was trembling from head to foot. 'You were unconscious for hours, and I thought . . . I thought perhaps . . .'

I pushed myself onto one elbow, feeling sand shift beneath me, then looked at the small tent erected around us, draped over two oars buried in the sand and weighted at the edges with several large pebbles. 'Where are we?'

'We moved downriver after the battle. The Colchians fled,' Myrtessa said, and as she spoke she seemed to come to herself a little more, 'after it became clear that they were unable to hold; but it was too dangerous to stay so close to the city when they might send more raiders. We beached the ship here, in a cove. The other slaves and I made tents for the wounded from the old sail of the *Argo*.'

'And Meleager, Hippomenes, Melanthius, Phorbas?'

'Shaken, but alive.'

'Cedalion? Peleus?'

'Both wounded. Phorbas is attending to them now.'

I hesitated before asking the most important question of all. 'And did we – did we lose any?'

Myrtessa swallowed. 'We – we lost Castor,' she said in a small voice.

A chilling wave of grief crashed over me for Pollux, his brother and his twin, who had been closer to Castor than any brother I had ever seen. 'How is Pollux taking it?'

'Not well. But he will come to terms with it. And they will see each other again in the Underworld. They have a young sister at home, too, in Sparta – did you know that?'

I shook my head, then felt a shooting pain down my arm and stopped.

'Helen,' she said, 'that is her name, Pollux told me. And now Castor will never see her again.'

There was a long, grave silence between us. I leant back, and the pain in my shoulder ebbed a little. I glanced down, saw the bandage there, strips of linen tied and knotted over the ruptured skin. 'Did you . . .'

She nodded. 'I made sure to do it myself, and only here. No one saw anything. They do not know.'

I let out a breath. 'There is that, at least, then.' I closed my eyes.

'Shall I leave you?'

I nodded as much as I could without pain. 'I should probably get some rest.' I reached out to her and took her hand. 'My thanks to you, Myrtessa.'

She squeezed my hand and stood up. 'You would have done the same for me. Sleep well, soldier,' she said, with a faint, tear-stained smile, drew aside the canvas at the front of the makeshift tent and left, footsteps fading away over the sand.

It was some time later that I woke – when, I was not sure, but the lamps in the tent around me had gone out and it was dark. My shoulder was aching – no longer burning with pain as it had earlier, though when I moved it was bitterly uncomfortable. Perhaps it had been that which woke me.

I heard footsteps approaching. I tried to sit up, pushing myself up on one elbow.

'Myrtessa?'

A voice laughed. 'Who were you expecting? A lady friend, Telamon?'

A flint was struck close to the entrance to the tent, and an oil-lamp lit. Meleager was standing there, his face shadowed in the dim light, dark red grazes from the day's battle struck across his left cheek, his shoulder blackened with old blood.

'Meleager!' I gasped. 'Why – why are you here?'

He moved towards me, footsteps soft, and knelt down beside me. 'You ask why I am here . . .' He reached out a hand and ran his fingers through my hair, then suddenly gripped it and tugged so that I was pulled towards him, inhaling sharply with pain. 'I thought you had died,' he said, his voice very low, and now that I was close to him I could smell the fusty scent of rich wine on his breath.

'You have drunk too much,' I said, knocking his hand away and struggling to sit fully, pushing myself a little distance away from him but, still, I did not send him away.

'You are the most beddable boy I have ever seen, Telamon,' he said.

I started, felt the pulse begin to race in my veins.

I let the silence lengthen. 'You should not talk to me so,' I said at last, trying to keep my voice even. 'I accepted your gift, my lord, and I am grateful for your affection, but that is all. That is all there can ever be . . .'

'No,' he said. He reached out towards me and traced the line of my jaw from my chin to my ear, down the side of my neck and to the bandage over my wound. He pressed it, just a little, and I gasped. 'No, my Ganymede. There is more. Much, much more.' He continued tracing down my arm, past the crook of my elbow and over the soft skin of my forearm, making my skin tingle with pleasure, and he laughed, knowing the effect he was having.

'You fought bravely today, young Telamon.' He circled my palm with his fingertip, and I stared mesmerized at his lips in the lamplight, the fullness of them, the flickering depths of his hazel eyes. 'What is it the poets say?

> *'Don't caress me with words, your mind elsewhere,*
> *If you love me and your heart is true.*
> *Love me with a pure heart or renounce me,*
> *Start a fight, hate me openly.*

'Tell me you want it too, Telamon,' he said, his voice barely a thread of sound, his eyes fixed upon mine. 'Tell me you want me as much as I want you for, truly, I feel as if I will burn up for desiring you, for hating you, for needing you.'

I felt my desire rise in response to his, the tingling in my thighs and the pit of my belly. He moved towards me, very slowly, his eyes never leaving my face.

I made up my mind. As he came close to me, so close that I could feel the warmth of his breath upon my neck, and reached towards me to lift up my tunic, I struck out. Swift as I could and ignoring the pain in my shoulder I gripped his wrist with one hand, his elbow with another and twisted, pushing against him so that he fell, grimacing, face down upon the sand, then pinned him with one knee, still turning his wrist back behind him. He gave a moan of pain, then smiled up at me, panting, his pupils dilated in the darkness.

'I do desire you,' I said. 'But there is something you must know first,' and though my pulse was throbbing hard at my neck I held firm. I caught his gaze and held it. 'You must swear to me never to reveal it to anyone, upon the name of the sacred goddess Artemis. I must know I can trust you.'

'Trust . . .' he repeated. For the first time his voice slurred a little, and I realized he was even drunker than I had thought.

'Yes,' I said, pushing harder against his wrist so that he winced and his eyes smarted with tears.

There was a pause as he breathed, slow and ragged.

'You must swear to me,' I repeated, 'that you will not reveal what I shall tell you – that, if I ask you to, you will aid me, as you have aided Jason. Do you swear it, Meleager?' I twisted his wrist back further. He was flat against the sand now, trying to avoid the stabbing pain in the joint, eyes watering, face pale. 'Meleager?'

'I—'

He stopped mid-sentence. His head lolled slightly, as if he were about to pass out, and instinctively I let him go and bent forwards, pushed the hair back from his forehead.

'Meleager! Meleager, are you—'

With sudden swiftness he grabbed the shoulder of my tunic and tore it, fingers ripping at the material, revealing the bare skin of my shoulder and chest. I cried out, but he pushed me roughly onto my back upon the ground in the half-darkness, knocking the breath from my lungs, hands greedily groping at my hips, my belly, and though I writhed and twisted I could not move against the drink-emboldened strength of him. I could feel his arousal pressing hard against me – he was pinning me down against the sand, his hands pressing roughly upon my shoulders and making me cry out as my wound seared with pain, his hips bearing down upon mine, and then he bent to kiss me, forcing his tongue into my mouth, exploring me with rude familiarity, the stench of wine foul upon his breath . . .

A deep revulsion welled inside me. Mustering all my strength I wrenched my mouth from his and brought my head up, hard as I could, slamming my skull against his, trusting in the force of the drink to double the blow. He staggered backwards, and I took the only opportunity I had. Pushing myself to stand I thrust my knee, hard as I could, into his groin. His eyes bulged, his lips quivered, then he sank to the ground, coughing and spluttering, his face a nasty puce. I slapped him full across the face for good measure.

'How dare you?' I shouted at him, my voice trembling. 'You foul – you—'

He turned his face up towards me as I stood before him, his blood-shot eyes resting upon my bare breasts, and it was in that moment – that awful, heart-stopping moment – that I saw my tunic was hanging open, ripped from shoulder to belly, and, until that instant, blinded by drink and in the half-dark of the tent, he had not known.

But he did now.

His face was slowly, terribly, registering his comprehension.

'A – a woman,' he choked. He raised a shaking finger towards me, his eyes wide. 'You are – you are a *woman*?'

The blood drained from my face. 'Meleager,' I said, dropping to my knees beside him and laying a hand upon his arm. 'Meleager, please, you don't understand—'

But he was shaking his head from side to side. 'Do not touch me,' he spat, and he struggled to his feet. 'Don't even come *near* me!'

'No – please—'

He picked up the oil-lamp and dashed it upon the ground. The flame went out at once, extinguished in the wet sand. I groped around in the darkness for him, trying to feel my way, tears streaming down my face.

'Meleager—'

There was a breath of wind, then silence. He was gone.

In Exile

The River Phasis

The Hour of Daybreak

The Ninth Day of the Month of the Grape Harvest

I stood upon the shore next morning wearing a thin tunic, my shoulders hunched, chin trembling, feeling nothing but overwhelming shame and fear, and a vague dizziness from the shooting pain in my wounded shoulder. A faint mist from the rising dew still hung over the beach, and the sun was hidden behind the faceless, shadowed expanses of the cut-rock mountains, the sky pale overhead, the river colourless as it lapped against the beach. I shivered, feeling the hairs on my arms prickle against the chill. Myrtessa stood beside me, her whole body shaking, though whether from the cold or terror I could not tell. I reached out and clasped her hand, tight, though there was little comfort I could give. We had infringed every law of Greece – Myrtessa twice, since she was both a woman and a slave.

The best we could hope for was a clean death at Jason's sword.

And we knew it.

The lords were standing in a circle around us, all of them wearing cloaks fastened at the throat with silver clasps, their swords sheathed in leather belts at the waist. I felt the hostile stares of them all – Jason, Peleus, Laertes, Hippomenes, Pollux and Meleager – upon me; all the men with whom I had fought, slept and eaten for so many weeks as an equal.

And now I was nothing to them but a woman, and a liar.

I looked at the ground, my hands clenched at my sides, my eyes burning.

'In the name of Zeus, king of the gods and men, protector of the Greeks, I call this council of the nobles of Greece to bring to judgement the impostor Atalanta and her slave, Myrtessa, upon the testimony of the lord Meleager.' Jason's voice rang out clearly in the still, calm air of dawn.

The words broke through my shame and despair, registering slowly, my mind taking longer to process them in the faintness from my wound. *Impostor? He calls me an impostor?* I felt a small, defiant part of me rise up to his insult. *I may be shamed, but my courage is not all lost.*

'Do you deny that you intentionally deceived us?' Jason asked, his voice boring into me, like a sword slicing through rope.

I felt Myrtessa move slightly beside me and gripped her hand more tightly.

'I do not,' I said, taking a deep breath. I met his narrowed gaze, saw the features chiselled like pale marble and his cheeks flushed, refusing to take my eyes from his, 'but—'

'Do you deny,' he continued, his voice overriding mine, 'that, as Meleager has informed us, you impersonated a man, wearing the clothes and the armour of a lord of Greece, for which the penalty in the lands of the Greeks is death?'

'I do not,' I said, 'but—'

'And do you deny,' Jason finished, a vein pulsing at his temple, his lips thin, 'that you forced yourself upon this quest, knowing full well that the gods consider it ill luck to allow a woman to row at the oar – that you, in short, put my claim to the thrones of Iolcos and Pagasae in danger by your wilful spite?'

'I do not,' I said, and then, before he could say anything else, 'but you accepted me on the quest by my own merit, did you not? You saw me hunt, and fight, and row alongside the other lords, and you did not find me wanting! You trusted Telamon – why should Atalanta be any different?'

'Because you are a woman,' Jason said, his voice as icy as the snow cap of Mount Pelion in winter, 'a spawn of Pandora, and because all the laws of gods and men dictate that it is neither your place nor your right to fight, to sail or even to speak among us. I should have had you killed for your first disobedience, when you forced your way onto my ship, and again on the Propontis when you disobeyed my orders. You have lived too long upon my mercy.'

He jerked his thumb at Myrtessa, who was shivering and weeping silent tears. 'Atalanta, she said your name was – "the equal of all others".' There was a smattering of laughter from the lords, though there was no mirth in it. My nostrils were flaring with anger, and I longed to start forwards and slap him hard across the face, but I restrained myself. 'You were a fool to think you could ever be our equal. You will go down to the Underworld, proclaiming to all the spirits of the dead the folly of a woman who thought that she could be the equal of a man.'

In a single movement he unsheathed his sword and brought it up into the air, then sliced the point down, ripping through the front of the tunic I had stitched up the night before in the half-darkness, tearing through it and exposing my breasts. I gasped, horrified, and clutched my arms across my chest as Jason's sword flashed once more towards Myrtessa, tearing her tunic, too, from neck to navel, leaving us standing together, pale-skinned and bare-breasted before the ring of men surrounding us. Myrtessa screamed and tried desperately to cover herself, pulling the shreds of fabric back over herself. Jason let out a short, derisive laugh.

A rage such as I had never felt before boiled up inside me, heat flushing through my body, my fingers itching for my bow, and I reached instinctively behind me for an arrow, then remembered that they had taken my bow and quiver from me earlier, two tall slaves pinning my arms back as I had kicked and struggled. Jason had cleared the tent of my belongings before they dragged me out to the shore. As one, the lords drew their swords with a sharp scrape of metal and pointed them at Myrtessa and me, and Myrtessa whimpered with fear.

'Do not dare to challenge us, woman,' Jason said, and the lords nodded, their jaws set, faces grim. There was a glint of malice in Meleager's eyes, and I knew as he stared at me and tossed his sword slowly from hand to hand that he was thinking of the night before. Hippomenes' eyes were cast down to the ground and his brow was furrowed deeply; Peleus was looking away, his expression filled with disappointment. I thought fleetingly, for a moment, of dropping to my knees and begging Jason for mercy, in the name of the king. But then I recalled myself.

I will not beg. I will not weep. I had done nothing but use my skill, and if I had deceived them, why, it was just as much their folly for not recognizing it as it was my error for having done so. I felt my courage return a little, and raised my head higher.

The swords levelled at us glimmered palely, an encircling snare of death. I shifted slowly on the sand, my eyes upon the sharpened tips of the bronze, and took Myrtessa's hand again in mine.

'I propose we kill her for her insubordination, and the slave too,' Jason said. 'All those who favour disposing of the treacherous slatterns,' he extended his sword forward a little, so that the tip caught on the hem of my tunic and lifted it very slightly – some of the men jeered, Meleager among them – 'nod your agreement, and I will do away with them both myself this very moment.'

The heads of the lords bowed, and I felt a wave of panic, nauseating, unstoppable.

This is the end, then.

I am going to die here, at the very edge of the world, far from my family and my home.

Bitter tears welled in my eyes and overflowed down my cheeks as I thought of how I had failed them, at the very last – and I squeezed Myrtessa's hand as hard as I could, closing my eyelids, unable to watch my death approach on Jason's sword.

There was a swish of a blade through the air.

I felt nothing.

I opened my eyes, my whole body shaking. Hippomenes had lowered his sword.

'I ask for her life, my lord Jason,' he said. I was taking deep, steadying breaths, half gasps, half sobs, and Myrtessa was trembling at my side, like a leaf in a storm, but he looked directly past me, towards Jason. 'Not out of pity for her, but as an act of justice. She saved my life, my lords, and the gods punish anyone who disregards the repayment of a debt.'

'You would save her?' Jason's expression was incredulous. 'Though she wove her web of woman's lies about you, you would rescue her from death?'

'She did so for me, my lord,' he said, and he turned to me at last, and there was nothing but disappointment in his eyes. I looked away, unable to bear the shame, tears still spilling down my cheeks. 'My life for her life. She can live out the rest of her days in the wilderness of Colchis, far from the lands of the Greeks. Is that not punishment enough?'

Myrtessa was sobbing openly beside me, and though my tears would not cease, I felt my breathing become more even, the feeling returning to my hands and legs.

'But,' Nestor interjected, frowning slightly, 'if we ever see you or your slave again, we will kill you, and instantly, without remorse. You have broken the laws of Greece. You have transgressed against the gods. It is only the debt Hippomenes owes you that saves you now.'

There was a pause as Jason considered this. Then—

'Very well,' he said, though his irritation was plain in the twist of his mouth. He sheathed his sword. The other lords did so too, first Hippomenes, then Theseus and Bellerophon, Laertes and the rest, the bronze scraping against the scabbards and making the hairs on the back of my neck prickle. Myrtessa was gasping and shuddering beside me, one arm still clutched over her chest. 'You are exiled. You are banished from Greece for ever more. You will wander the forests and hills of Colchis, and if you do not survive it, then so much the better. May the bears and the wolves do for us the work that should have been done here today.'

'*No!*' I exclaimed.

'Atalanta,' Myrtessa gasped under her breath, 'you have been given your freedom. You should take—'

'No, I shall not!' I turned to Jason. The defiance in me was growing stronger, sharper, a blazing fire in my chest that would not be dampened. 'You say I have acted against the will of the gods, but tell me this: if the gods had not wanted a woman to have the skills of a man, then why would they have given them to me? You have seen my skill with the bow, you have watched me fight, you have seen me run faster than any man. Tell me, is it I who should be blamed if I can do these things?'

'That is blasphemy,' Nestor muttered. 'Will you take the gods down with you, too, though you have already shamed yourself with your deceit?'

'But I—'

'That is *enough*,' Jason said, and his gaze was as sharp and chilling as the blade of a sword. 'If you argue more, we will kill you. My lords? Do you agree?'

I looked around at the other lords and saw each man nod, one by one, slowly and deliberately, making sure that I could see.

I hesitated. Even Hippomenes had agreed – Hippomenes, who had invited me to eat with him upon the deck, who had walked with me through the streets of Kytoros and told me of his life in the country in Boeotia.

'Myrtessa, then,' I said, faltering, my throat constricting, 'may I at least take Myrtessa with me?'

Jason shrugged, then kicked Myrtessa in the small of her back so that she stumbled forwards and fell upon her knees. 'If you want another life upon your hands,' he said, with a sneer, 'for she will surely be killed in the wilds of this land, and here we should have done it for you.'

He stepped aside so there was a gap in the circle, and I saw the lords move around behind us, felt the pointed tips of their swords digging into the skin at my back, forcing me away into the wilderness of the mountains. They were consigning us to death. I would die, here, in these bleak mountains . . .

'Wait.' Hippomenes' voice rang out. 'We should give her something to hunt with, at the very least.'

'Hand her a weapon?' Jason scoffed. 'Have you lost your wits, Hippomenes?'

Hippomenes continued, his voice steady: 'To let her loose in the forests of this savage land without a weapon is not to save her life: it is merely to postpone her death.'

Silence fell. I held my breath, every muscle tensed, waiting, waiting for them to reply . . .

When no one said anything, I looked up to the skies overhead, my voice shaking slightly. 'My lords, I swear by all the great gods of Olympus, if you give me back my bow, I will not return here to harm you. I give you my most sacred oath.' I paused, and a single tear rolled down my cheek and fell upon the sand. 'Please, I beg of you. Give me back my bow.'

Hippomenes hesitated, then I heard him walk forwards, sandals crunching on the sand, and pick up my quiver from the ground. I felt a sudden dart of pain through my shoulder as he slung the strap roughly over my neck. A weak sense of relief flickered through me as I felt it upon my back, the wood of the bow's stave behind my head.

'You are not to touch it till you are out of our sight, or I shall not rest until I have sliced you *limb from limb*,' Jason said, his voice grating, and I felt the sword tips at my back press harder, cutting through the wool of the tunic and grazing my skin so that small beads of blood gathered there. 'Now go.'

'I—'

'*Go.*'

At last, shamed, despairing, with nothing left to ask for, I recognized my defeat. Slowly, Myrtessa by my side, my thoughts pounding with anger and humiliation, I walked out of the circle of lords who had once called me one of their own and made my way across the shore and up towards the dark overhanging forests above, one arm clutched across my bare chest, Myrtessa walking huddled and shaking beside me.

Wondering, with a dull ache within my heart, whether I would ever see Greece again.

A few days later we were walking across the lowlands of Colchis, wild goats cropping on the meadows, dark, marshy earth underfoot, mountain streams gushing over rocks. In the distance we could see the mountains forested with firs and broken by rocky canyons. It was a fine late summer's day, the warm air stirred by a slight breeze, the sun sparkling upon the tumbling water of the streams. Eagles soared overhead and cried echoing calls to each other, their feathered wings outlined against the sky. We had been moving from village to village, stopping only for the night, then travelling on – though Myrtessa had made sure we found a weaver-woman willing to lend us a needle with which to stitch up our torn clothes. Now we were striking out, without much hope, towards a small gathering of dwellings sending up curls of smoke into the air from their house-fires, nestled on the slope of the mountains and visible for several leagues from the valley beneath.

For I had determined my course almost as soon as I had left the Greek camp.

Jason could exile me from the quest, he could threaten me with death, but he could not stop me trying to rescue Pagasae and Kaladrosos from his rule.

The rich, earthy scent of the marshes and the sounds of the waters of the next mountain stream tumbling over rocks filled my senses as we stopped to eat at the middle of the day. I had caught a red fox – the wound on my shoulder was beginning to mend, thanks to Myrtessa's ministrations, and though it still twinged with pain I could handle my bow to hunt – and Myrtessa had lit a fire beside the river with piles of dry twigs and leaves gathered from the outskirts of the nearby forest. We busied ourselves skinning and spitting the carcass on a forked twig and roasting it over the flames, and it was not until we had eaten our fill that we settled down to talk.

'I have been thinking,' I said, cupping some water from the stream in my hands and sipping at it. 'We were almost killed by the lords, upon the shore of the river.' I gave her a frank stare. 'Why did you come with me? You did not know me. You had a life in Pagasae. You had Neda, Philoetius, Hora. What made you risk everything to journey beside a person you hardly knew?'

She tipped a bilberry into her mouth and smiled. 'I don't know.'

'I am serious, Myrtessa.'

She looked into my face, and the smile faded from her lips. 'I told you,' she said, and I saw her rub at the brand inside her right wrist. 'I disliked being a slave. You already know all there is to know.'

I shook my head. 'I do not think you wanted to leave Pagasae simply because of that. I think there is more.'

There was a long silence this time. At last she said, 'Trust me, Atalanta, you are better off not knowing.'

I almost laughed, but then I saw the look in her eyes, and my laughter died in my throat. 'If you do not want to say . . .'

But she was not listening. A glazed look of pain had come over her face. 'I was born in Lesbos,' she said, her gaze distant. 'The mainlanders raided the island when I was five years of age. Corythus was among them. He – he captured me, and took me among his prizes.'

She was talking in a flat voice, as if the painful memories were now nothing but dim recollections of sufferings past. I said nothing, but watched her. An eagle soared above us, calling into the lonely wilderness. 'I can hardly remember my parents, or my homeland. I hear the other slaves, sometimes, talking of an island whose valleys are carpeted with violets in spring and where coves shaded by pine trees curve around pale waters and white sands – but I do not remember it. Not much.'

She took a deep breath. 'In any case, Corythus enslaved me, along with several other young girls and a few of our women. We returned to Pagasae with him, ordered to tend his fires, scrub his floors – and, when we were older, we were summoned to his chambers, to bathe our master and to lie with him in his bed.'

Her eyes were bright with tears, and she swallowed, hard.

When she spoke again, her voice was slightly unsteady. 'After a few months of his summoning me to his bed almost nightly, I told him I was with child. He did not call for me again, and when it was time for the baby to come, I bore it in the pantry off the kitchens, with only Hora and the girls to tend me with a tub of cold water and some old cloths. He – he was a boy, a beautiful little baby boy, with –' she let out a sob and her voice shook '– with the – the sm–smallest fingers and a t–tiny dimpled chin and—' She was unable to continue. I moved to sit beside her and clasped her shoulders, holding her tightly as she wept. After a while the shaking in her body subsided. She sniffed a couple of times and wiped her eyes upon the back of her hand, then turned to me, her eyes red-rimmed.

'He had the baby taken away almost as soon as it was born,' she said, her voice barely a whisper. 'Where he was taken, I do not know. Exposed to die on the rocks above Makronita, most likely, though perhaps he was sold into slavery. And every day, there was the fear that Corythus might summon me again . . . that I might once again have to bear the pain of carrying his child within me, bringing it into this world, then letting him tear it away from me and send it to die.' Her voice broke as she said, 'I did not think I would have the strength to do it again.'

She dried her eyes on the corner of her tunic. A silence fell between us, broken only by the bubbling of the river nearby over the stones.

'A moving tale, is it not?' she asked at last, glancing back at me with the ghost of a smile.

I could hardly speak. I opened my mouth to say something, though

I knew not what, but Myrtessa held up a hand to stop me. 'Enough,' she said. 'It is done. I would rather you did not speak – Lady Hera knows I do not need consolation, not any more.'

'I would have said the same,' I said honestly, and I saw a flicker of gratitude in her eyes.

'Do you understand, now, why I had to leave?' she asked.

I nodded bleakly. There was nothing I could say to comfort her. But as we sat there, upon the plain of a foreign land, a lone eagle soaring overhead and the river gushing before us, I moved towards her and held her in my arms: two women alone in the world, unloved, unwanted.

Bound together by our abandonment and loss.

'Come,' I said at last, moving away from her and feeling the tears wet on my cheeks, the bandages on my injured shoulder damp where hers had fallen. I stood up. 'Come,' I said again, and held out a hand to her. 'We should be able to reach the village before dusk.'

It was nearing sunset when we finally arrived, for we had had to cross several rocky gorges, the branches of willow trees trailing from the banks. Our tunics were damp from wading across one particularly fast-flowing ravine, where the water ran in eddying currents over the rocks. Our feet and ankles were crusted with the mud of the marshes, our hair hanging lank beside our faces. I was hot, thirsty and harrowed by hunger, the palms of my hands cut from scrambling over the rocks, the wound at my left shoulder breaking open and bleeding as we climbed. My anger at Jason for his cruel and unjust sentence pulsed through me, urging me on, on, though my thighs ached and the gash at my shoulder throbbed.

We approached the village, which we later learnt was named Suzona, by a dirt track surrounded by marshy green plains lined with eucalyptus trees that released their heady scent into the air, accompanied by the tolling of goats' bells. The houses were dark and squat, clustered close together and built from whole tree trunks, with low, sloping roofs and small windows set high in the walls. A goatherd crossed our path with his flock, and stared at us with dark, unfathomable eyes, the ribbon tied around his forehead fluttering in the breeze. The dwellings were becoming more frequent now, and we could see women scattering grain to geese in the enclosures before the houses, children playing with sticks in the mud, men chopping wood beneath the shade of the forest with heavy-bladed axes. All of them stopped and stared at us as we passed, and I nodded and smiled at them, trying to ignore the cloud of suspicion that seemed to follow us.

I approached a woman who was scrubbing the doorstep at the threshold of her house. She had continued to work in spite of our presence and her expression seemed – though perhaps I was only imagining it so – a little less wary than those of the others. She straightened, wiping her hands on a coarse cloth tied around her waist and giving me an even stare.

I pointed at myself, then at Myrtessa. 'Greeks,' I said, slowly and clearly. 'Friends.'

The woman's eyebrows contracted very slightly. Footsteps behind her announced the arrival of a thick-set man with high cheekbones. She talked to him, very fast, in a language I did not know. I glanced at Myrtessa, who shrugged her shoulders.

'Greeks?' the man asked, pointing at me, his accent so strong that I hardly recognized the word.

I nodded, my heart pounding. 'Yes, Greeks. Do you know Greek? Can you speak it? Can we—'

But he pushed past the woman, unhooked a burning torch that was hanging on a bracket on the outside wall of the house, and started to walk up the beaten track, in the direction of the mountains. He stopped and turned to beckon us.

'I think he wants – he wants us to follow him,' Myrtessa said in a low voice.

I hesitated, my eyes on the broad sword hanging from the belt at the man's waist. 'Should we trust him?'

'Do we have a choice?'

'I suppose not.' I reached behind me to check the bow upon my back, taking comfort in the sturdy stave and the fletchings of the arrows. 'Very well.' I beckoned to Myrtessa and we started up the track after the man. Men and women wearing thick boots and patterned tunics over trousers, tied at the waist with belts, stood watching us as we passed, and goats tethered to doorposts bleated balefully into the silence. The light was fading fast, and I rubbed my arms, shivering, as the path climbed upwards and the trees grew denser, tall fragrant pines and firs with a thick underbrush of bilberries. Soon the dwellings had fallen away and we were crunching over leaves in the darkened forest upon the mountain slopes, the air thick with the damp, earthen smell of moss, large rocks protruding from the forest floor, like a giant's knuckles, shadowed in the flickering light of our guide's torch. Myrtessa was climbing in silence beside me, her shoulders hunched against the cold but her expression set, determined. I looked around warily, wondering where we were being taken, feeling the bow tapping upon the back of my head and waist as some small comfort in this dark, unknown place . . .

Then, at last, a single dwelling came into view, perched within the undergrowth, low-lying and of dark wood, like those down in the village. A fire must have been blazing inside, for the small, high windows were lit, and smoke was rising in a twisting spiral from a chimney set in the centre of the roof. A single column of stone shaped into the vague likeness of a human body stood before it, a ribbon of dark blue tied around it, a wreath of summer flowers set beneath it and a clay plate filled with offerings of fruits and grain. The man gestured to the door of the house, nodded once, then turned upon his heel and trudged away down the path, his footsteps, crunching upon the leaves, fading into the distance.

I exchanged a look with Myrtessa. She was pale but her eyes were bright in the flickering light from the windows. She nodded. 'Go on.'

I stepped forwards to the low wooden door and knocked, then clasped my arms around my body, waiting.

The door opened a crack, and an eye appeared behind it, dark like the eyes of the villagers, fringed with long lashes. Then the door was drawn open, and I felt a rush of warmth on my skin. A fire was indeed burning inside, on a circular stone hearth, its light obscured by the woman who stood before me, her skin creased and weather-beaten, her hair greying at the temples, a simple blue fringed robe thrown over her trousers and belted with a leather girdle. Beside the hearth another woman, younger, crouched before the fire, her arms encircling a little boy of no more than three, with nut-brown skin and dimpled cheeks. The flames cast leaping, dancing shadows over the walls, and I noticed woven carpets decorating the floors, simple, low furniture carved from wood and, towards the back of the room, a single bed-frame covered neatly with woven rugs. A pair of fish were frying in a flat-bottomed pan set over the fire, and the scent of strong oil and unfamiliar herbs – some of which were hanging from the roof-beams in neatly tied bunches – wafted past my nostrils, making my stomach growl with hunger.

The older woman's eyes swept over my short hair, the bandages on my shoulder, then down to my patched tunic and the bow and arrows hanging at my back.

'Well, well,' she said, in strongly accented Greek. The corners of her mouth flickered into a smile as my eyes widened to hear her speak my native tongue. 'I am sure you have quite a story to tell.' She stepped away from the door and beckoned us inside.

'I don't know . . .' I turned to Myrtessa, but she had already darted into the hut, her arms clutched around her, and was crouching at the fire.

'I will not harm you,' the woman said, with a half-smile. 'It is you who are entering my house with weapons, not I.'

I ran my thumb back and forth along the strap of my quiver, still uncertain. The fish smelt crisp and sweet, enough to make my mouth water, and the warmth of the fire was beckoning me. I felt a wave of fatigue wash over me and decided, for once, to fling caution to the winds. There would be time for watchfulness later, once I had eaten and warmed my cold limbs.

'How is it that you speak Greek?' I asked, stepping forwards as she closed the door behind us and slid a bolt into the bars. To judge from her appearance – the dark eyes, high cheekbones and hair drawn back from the temples – as well as her accent and dress, she was not a native Greek. And yet . . .

'How is it that you have come to Colchis?' she asked, throwing a bright glance in my direction before leaning over the fire and turning the fish in the spattering oil.

I looked up to see that she was smiling at me, her eyes sparkling in the firelight. 'Shall we eat first, before either of us asks another question?'

The fish was salted past my taste, but I was so famished I hardly cared. The flesh was tender and served with heavy bread, almost like the cake we baked for the gods on feast days in Kaladrosos. I looked over at Myrtessa, licking the tips of my fingers for the last of the oil, my belly warm with the satisfaction of a good meal, wanting to ask her how she liked the food. But her eyes were fixed elsewhere. I followed her gaze and saw that she was watching the child, who was being fed sips of watered wine from a tiny clay pot fitted with a spout by his mother, with an expression of such tenderness and longing that I felt as if I had intruded on some private grief that could not be put into words.

I turned quickly to address the older woman, hardly knowing what I would say, only that I wanted to appear as if I had not seen the pain upon Myrtessa's face, but she forestalled me, holding up her hand. 'You must dress before we talk,' she said. 'In this country a guest who has not been clothed in proper raiment is an offence to the gods.'

'It is so in our country also.'

She got to her feet from the stool upon which she was sitting, her movements surprisingly fluent and graceful for her age. 'Come,' our host said, and held out a hand to Myrtessa, who stood slowly, her eyes still drawn towards the child. She led us through a doorway into another room, fitted from floor to ceiling with wooden shelves loaded with clay pots, jars, rough-woven cloths and blankets. She plucked a couple of patterned tunics, trousers and boots from one of the shelves and handed them to us. After she closed the door behind us we changed, stripping the wet tunics from our skin and pulling on the scratchy woollen trousers and boots.

'You look like an Amazon,' Myrtessa said, appraising me as I twisted left and right, trying to get used to the curious sensation of the material around my legs. She snorted with laughter.

'And you look like a true-born Greek, do you?' Indeed, Myrtessa, with her dark hair, her belted tunic covered with striped patterns, her loose leggings and high cuffed boots, appeared so similar to the stories they told of trousered Amazons that I half expected her to draw an axe from her back.

I pushed open the door back to the main room, and found the old woman waiting there for us.

'Just a moment,' she said, placing a hand on Myrtessa's arm as she made to follow me. Myrtessa hung back as I went to the hearth, seating myself upon a wooden stool by the flames, and I heard the sound of their whispered voices over the spitting of the fire. A few moments later Myrtessa joined me, flushed, her eyes bright.

'What did she ask you?'

Myrtessa shrugged, lips pressed together, though a smile was lingering at the corners of her mouth. 'Nothing of consequence. I will tell you later.' She settled herself upon the carpets of the floor with the child upon her lap, as our host passed me a cup of heated water flavoured with sprigs of mint, and another to Myrtessa.

'You have honoured us as your guests,' I said, taking a sip of the drink, 'and it is owed to you by custom that you know the names of those to whom you give your hospitality. I am Atalanta, daughter of Iasus, king of Pagasae.' I was growing more accustomed to it, especially since I had seen Prince Lycon's medallion with my own eyes, yet still, it felt odd to say it aloud. 'This is Myrtessa, my companion and my friend.'

Myrtessa gave me a half-smile, her cheeks pink from the warmth of the fire, the child's little hand gripping one of her fingers.

I took a deep breath and decided – since I had nothing left to lose – to risk the truth.

I looked directly into our host's eyes, my heart beating rather fast. 'We are here to ask you of the fabled Golden Fleece, in the hope that someone may know where it is kept and how to win it. I do not,' I said quickly, seeing the shift in her expression, 'seek the Fleece for the riches that it brings, but to save my home and my people from a most cruel ruler, foretold as it is in prophecy.'

The old woman stood and lifted a poker from beside the fire, then rustled it in the ashes.

'My name,' she said at last, 'is Dedali.' She looked aside at me, her dark eyes glowing like coals, the blue edging of her tunic glimmering.

'I am the priestess of this village, and I travelled to the oracle at Delphi where I learnt to speak your language. And I advise you not to seek the Fleece.'

'So you know of it? You know of the Fleece?' I leant forwards, heart leaping.

The old woman surveyed me through heavy-lidded eyes. 'Yes,' she said. 'I know of the Fleece. Indeed, it is so well guarded, so impossible to reach, that King Aeëtes cares not if all of Colchis knows where it is kept. You cannot know how many lords and princes have come to this land, each dreaming of capturing the Fleece. And each has been killed by the king's guards, their armour stripped from their bodies and taken to the king's treasury, their corpses left as carrion for the birds.'

I opened my mouth to speak, but she said, 'You must understand me.' Her voice was serious, her expression grave, and as she spoke, with the twisting, curling smoke of the fire rising between us and the polished wooden beads at her ears shining in the soft light, it was as if her words were conjuring the very scene before my eyes. 'This is no mere tale. I have seen them, for as a priestess of Arinniti I am bidden to the temple of Zayu for the holy feasts each year. Corpses lining the valley, skeletons where the bones shine white in the summer heat and ravens circle overhead. This is the fate of all who attempt to steal the Fleece.' She eyed me. 'And if kings with battle-hardened armies have failed, how will you, a young girl with no armour, succeed?'

There is truth in what she says. I shuddered at the thought of the valley of death she had described. But I pressed on. 'I can only try, can I not?' I said, with an attempt at a smile. 'And I swear to you, I seek the Fleece only to protect my home. Surely that makes me different from the others who sought it only for their greed.'

She let out a breath, eyeing me beadily. In the silence the fire sputtered and the child shifted on Myrtessa's lap.

Time passed, but I held her gaze, hardly daring to breathe, willing her to tell me what she knew.

'Very well,' she said at last, throwing up her hands, making the beads at her ears rattle. 'The goddess knows I do not wish to see you killed like the rest, yet there is a god-given determination in you that I think will never let you rest till you recover the kingdom of which you speak.'

I bowed my head, and Myrtessa at my feet laughed and glanced up towards me, bouncing the little boy up and down upon her knees. 'That is true enough, is it not, Atalanta?'

The child giggled and clapped his hands. Dedali frowned as she plucked at her tunic and settled herself on a stool beside me. 'Well,' she said, her brows contracting again. 'What is it you would know?'

'Where to find the Fleece, and how best to journey there from here,' I said at once. 'And how it is guarded,' I added, 'if you are able to tell me.'

The old woman closed her eyes. 'The Fleece,' she said, and opened them with a sigh, as if she had told this story too many times with too much loss, 'is the sacred golden covering of the holy image of Zayu in the form of a ram, woven from ten thousand threads of gold, and of a worth that exceeds all the king's treasury and more. It is kept in the most sacred temple of Zayu, within the valley of a tributary of the Phasis river, a day's journey on horseback from here, hidden between the steepest cliffs. The passage to the temple from the Phasis' banks must be made on foot, for the way is too steep for a horse to traverse. Each year the priests of this land travel far and wide to the sanctuary to worship the gods, yet even I have not seen the Fleece, for it is kept in the innermost sanctuary of Zayu's temple, ringed by a hundred guards armed with swords and spears – the best in the land – and five hundred archers lie posted along the pass, hidden upon the crags above the temple where they may strike down within moments an intruder with their darts.' She leant forwards and placed a hand over mine. 'Go home,' she said softly. 'Leave the Fleece to others. You are too young to die.'

'Who says that I shall die?'

She gazed a while into my stubborn face. Then, to my surprise, she chuckled. 'Ah, the spirit of Atimite indeed runs strong in you,' she said. After a moment, she pressed her hands upon her knees and pushed herself to stand with a small groan. The younger woman ran towards her to help, but she shooed her away.

'Come,' she said, and she plucked a torch from the wall and lit it in the hearth, then led me to the front door and out towards the rear of the house. She disappeared around the back, towards a lean-to shed, and I made to follow her, when—

'Wait – Atalanta!'

It was Myrtessa. She hung at the corner of the hut, fingers scraping the rough walls, her feet crunching on the leaves scattered around the path.

'Think of what you are doing! Hippomenes said he would kill you if he ever saw you again! Can we not . . . can we not stay here, at least for a while? What do you owe to Pagasae and Kaladrosos?'

I gazed at her, watching the shadows from the fire within play across her features. 'Nothing,' I said, raising my eyebrows, 'except the lives of the family I love, and the freedom of all their people.'

Myrtessa paused, and I saw her expression shift. 'I – I wish to stay.'

The words hung on the cool night air. I stared at her. 'You wish to stay?' I repeated. 'Here?'

She shrugged one shoulder and walked towards me, taking my hand. 'This is your journey, Atalanta,' she said gently. 'Mine finishes here – I can feel it.'

She inclined her head, unwilling to meet my eye. 'Dedali said, when she whispered to me, that the goddess had told her I should remain. She asked me if I would be willing to serve the goddess as an initiate. And I have accepted.'

Her cheeks were still glowing from the fire's heat, and I sensed the determination in her, accompanied by a calm I had not noticed before. I knew suddenly, as she did, that she was meant to stay here, and that she would be happy.

'I do not wish to leave you alone,' she said, her words tumbling over one another, 'but in Pagasae I am not . . . Here, I can . . .' She gestured towards the brand upon her wrist, wordless. 'I am not a slave here,' she finished. 'I hope you can understand.'

I nodded. The memory of Myrtessa, dark-eyed, laughing and wilful, pulling me from the crowd in Pagasae those many months ago, rose to my mind, and I swallowed, wanting to tell her not to stay, to come with me . . . 'I shall miss you,' I said, a lump rising in my throat as I blinked the tears from my eyes. 'My dear friend.'

'I shall miss you too, Atalanta,' she said. She enveloped me in her arms and embraced me tightly.

Dedali appeared again around the corner of the house. 'Daughter of Iasus?'

We broke apart.

'May the gods be with you, Atalanta,' Myrtessa said softly. 'I shall pray for your safe return to Pagasae.'

I nodded, unable to speak, squeezed her hand, then turned away, my eyes blurred with tears, towards the bright halo of light that surrounded Dedali's torch. I glanced over my shoulder as we turned the corner to the back of the house, but Myrtessa was already gone.

Dedali led me, ducking, into a covered shed whose roof leant against the back of the main dwelling, where two high-necked horses were stabled. I shook my head to clear my eyes of tears, trying to ignore the hollowness in my chest and the dryness in my throat, and instead took a deep, steadying breath, inhaling the scent of warm hay – trying not to think of Myrtessa, settling down to start her new life within Dedali's hut.

You have to think of Pagasae and Kaladrosos, I reminded myself. *Think of Neda, Philoetius and Lycon – think of your family. Remember the justice Jason dealt to the slave you saw upon the street, and to Phorbas. You must remember them, too.*

And Myrtessa will be happy here.

'He is yours,' Dedali said, recalling me to the here and now, clicking her tongue to one of the two horses who stood before me, a fine chestnut that was stamping his hoofs and snorting in the night air. A simple woven rug and a leather bridle hung on a wooden peg upon the wall. 'But I would advise you to stay the night with us and leave for the pass at dawn. These forests are treacherous at night and the riding is rough.'

I turned to her, and the question was out of my lips before I had even thought it. 'Why are you helping me?' I asked. 'I mean,' I struggled to correct myself, 'you advised me against going after the Fleece. Why, now, are you assisting me?'

She smiled, the wrinkles at the corners of her eyes creasing. 'Perhaps it is because I see the spirit of the gods in you, or perhaps Arinniti herself is watching over you.' She raised one hand to the darkened sky. 'Who can tell the ways of the divine beings who live upon the Kaukasos peaks? But I ask you again: will you not stay the night?'

I shook my head and held out my hand to take hers, feeling a deep rush of gratitude to the stranger who had given my cherished friend a home, and who was aiding me now.

'I am indebted to you for your kindness, Dedali,' I said, and I meant it. I would be sad to leave this warm sanctuary upon the mountain slopes. 'And I pray the gods I may one day be able to return the favours you have done me. But I must leave now. I have not a moment to lose.'

An image swam into my mind of Jason and his crew sailing up the Phasis, storming the city of Colchis and demanding the location of the Fleece, rowing swiftly down the river towards the valley, oars dipping and pulling, perhaps even at this very moment . . .

I felt my pulse rise, and Dedali must have seen the colour in my cheeks because she smiled a little. I took the rug from her and threw it over the horse's back, then vaulted up into the seat and pulled up my tunic to sit above my trousers, securing my quiver upon my back. Dedali fixed the bridle straps, then threw me the reins, and I pulled my steed around to face the slopes of the mountain falling away towards the village below, its few dwellings lit with flickering torches, then into darkness. 'Which way to the valley of which you spoke?'

'Ride until you reach the river,' Dedali said, pointing down towards the plain, which was lit in silvers and greys by the bright-shining moon and the stars scattering the heavens, like the sun's rays glinting upon water. 'Then follow it east by the stars, until you find the tributary that runs from the north through a deep gorge edged with steep rocks at either side. Dismount there and follow the smaller river on foot. You will find the sanctuary beyond. Then only the gods can help you.'

'And what of the horse? How may I return him to you?'

She waved away the question. 'He will know his way back.'

I pulled on my steed's reins, wincing a little as the wound on my left shoulder strained, and he reared, his hoofs towering to the night sky.

'My thanks to you, Dedali,' I called to her. It felt glorious to be upon a horse again, for all the dull pain from my wound, and I kicked him forwards, longing to feel the wind through my hair, to gallop as hard and fast as I could. I began to race down the path towards the village, the clear beams of the moon edging the branches and trunks of the trees in silver. 'May the gods repay you for your kindness to me this night.'

And Lady Artemis, I muttered a prayer, turning my eyes to the heavens, *lady of the moon and the hunt, light my way.*

I dug my heels in harder, mud flying from the horse's hoofs. The trees flashed past as I galloped down the mountainside, focused on one thought and one thought alone: *Get to the pass before Jason.*

Poseidon Awakes

Mount Olympus

It has been nearly eighty days since Poseidon, god of the sea, and Hermes, god of thieving, fell asleep upon the floor in the Library of the Muses. Eighty days of perfect weather, Iris thinks, as she riffles through the pile of scrolls on the shelf before her. Eighty days of halcyon seas and clear blue skies. Eighty days of cloudless views upon the jewel-bright islands dotting the ocean, and the tiny ships with their fluttering white sails cruising in and out of port. She gives a little inward sigh, and searches on.

The night sky is dark as ink, visible through the open colonnade that faces one wall of the Hall of the Fates. Around the figure of Iris, bent forwards slightly as she pulls down, unfurls and reads one scroll after another, the Muses are walking to and fro holding lamps, some collecting scrolls of papyrus from the nightingales who have flown here from the caverns of the Fates in the Underworld, others copying them, their reed brushes swishing gently in the silence.

Iris glances up from her search to look at Poseidon and Hermes, who are still slumped face forward upon the marble floor in the corner. She has been sent here on Hera's orders, of course, commanded to be there when the two gods awake, to make sure the situation does not get out of hand.

But that does not mean she cannot do a little searching of her own.

And there is something in particular that Iris is looking for tonight. That she has been looking for, in fact, for quite some time.

It takes a little while for Poseidon to wake, then a little longer for him to realize where he is. Iris can almost see the dawning comprehension on his face as he looks around him, sees the stirring figure of Hermes prone at his side, and the events of a few months before slowly come back to him: how Alcimede, Jason's mother, chose Zeus instead of him; how he tried to destroy her son's

213

ship in a storm; how, when he failed, he came to the Library of the Muses, searching for Jason's fate; how meddlesome Hera and her irritating messenger had found him there and—

Poseidon's head snaps up.

'Worked it out at last, have you?' Iris asks him, stepping out of the shadows.

Poseidon almost knocks over the inlaid wooden chair set at the desk beside him as he leaps to his feet, and Hermes starts up at the noise, eyes wide, looking left and right.

'You!' Poseidon splutters. He picks up the goblet from the table and sniffs it, then throws it away. It clatters over the floor, bumping into the ankles of one of the Muses who picks it up and replaces it on a nearby table with a disapproving look. 'Waters of the Styx! I knew it! How long—'

Iris folds her arms. 'Nearly eighty days.'

'Eighty!' Poseidon's chest is heaving, his face turning a deep red. 'And Jason?'

'Arrived in Colchis.'

Poseidon gives a roar of rage, like the rumbling of thunder over the sea in a storm. 'You—' He starts forwards as if to pick Iris off the floor by her robes and slam her against one of the shelves of scrolls, but she darts to one side. Hermes scrambles to his feet as Poseidon, purple now with rage, balls his fist and punches at Iris, who ducks. His knuckles meet instead with a shelf of papyrus rolls, which totters gently and then, with a resounding crash, slides to the floor, sending scraps of mortal fates spilling out over the shiny marble. Poseidon swears and turns back to Iris, his palm raised, roaring with anger . . .

And across the ocean, from the furthest islands of the Hesperides all the way to where the shores of the Black Sea turn towards the north and the river Phasis pours its waters into the ocean, the still, calm surface of the sea begins to roil, surging and seething, though there is no breath of wind upon the air. Clouds – thick, dark storm clouds – roll across the land of Colchis and cast it in shadow, making the goatherds look up to the skies and mutter a prayer before they turn back towards their homes, driving their anxious flocks before them, the birds twittering from the tops of the pines. A rumble of thunder breaks over the sea, and then the wind begins to blow: a westerly wind, the Zephyr that drives ships away from Greece to the very ends of the earth; not *a springtime breeze, which rustles blades of grass beneath the feet of nymphs, but a howling, blistering gale, a roaring scream of wind that breaks the firs upon the mountains, sending them crashing to the forest floor, and whips the surface of the ocean into a furious swell that pounds the rocky shores of Colchis with foaming spray.*

Heavy clouds of rain billow down the mountain slopes, turning the sky dark as night, as Atalanta pushes her steed on through the dense forests, though her trousers are sticking to her skin and her fingers are slipping on the reins.

The Argonauts, stumbling back towards their ship, bow their heads against the water pouring from the skies and hug their arms around their soaking robes, slipping over rocks, wading through mountain streams, which have turned from dried-out creeks to torrents of foaming water, as lightning splits the sky overhead.

And Jason wonders what he has done to earn the enmity of the gods.

Not long after, Iris is to be found in Hera's lamplit bedchamber, the stars glittering down through the opening in the roof, following Hera with her eyes as she paces up and down the marble floors.

'The gods have taken their sides,' Iris announces, as her mistress rounds a corner and paces furiously back across the room. 'There is nothing we can do about it now. Zeus,' she says, and ticks the names off on her fingers, 'for Atalanta—'

Hera rounds on her. 'He promised me he would cease to interfere.'

Iris raises her eyebrows. 'And you trust him to keep that promise?'

Hera says nothing.

'You,' Iris continues, as Hera begins to pace once more, 'for Jason.' She holds up a finger on the other hand. 'And against Jason, Poseidon.'

'It is not Poseidon I care about!' Hera explodes at last. 'It is Jason, and his retrieval of the Fleece. And at the moment,' she looks down through the roiling grey clouds towards Colchis and glowers as darkly as the storm clouds, 'he and his Argonauts are in danger of being drowned before they even reach the sanctuary of Zeus.'

'Then you should do something about it,' Iris says. 'Part the waters, send a beautiful woman to his aid, or – or give him immortal strength.' She shrugs. 'The usual strategies.'

Hera stares at her. 'A beautiful woman,' she says, pausing, her head to one

215

side. 'I like that. We haven't done it for a while – not since Ariadne, anyway. Hmm. Perhaps we can persuade Aphrodite to send the cupids to visit the daughter of King Aeëtes, Medea . . .'

She seats herself upon the bed, deep in thought. Then she rounds on her messenger, eyes narrowed. 'If Poseidon remains angered, and the seas are rough and the winds blowing from the west, then they cannot sail, even if we help Jason retrieve the Fleece.'

Iris bows her head. 'That is true.'

'Then how are we to return Jason to his kingdoms in Greece?' Hera bursts out. 'We have guided him halfway across the world, given him fair winds and calm seas, led him to the very threshold of Colchis! Are we to be stopped now by a paltry water-god and that idiot messenger of his?'

Iris peers at her from beneath her eyelids. 'You would do well to show Hermes some respect,' she says softly. 'He may be only a messenger, but he is a dangerous enemy. And at the moment, I believe, he is throwing in his lot with Zeus.'

'Hermes and Zeus?' Hera snorts. 'What do I have to worry about from them?'

In Zeus' rooms on the other side of Olympus, the king of the gods is pacing up and down in a remarkable imitation of his wife, knocking aside jars filled with ambrosia and pushing over tables in his rage. Hermes is seated nearby on a stool, munching a mouthful of ambrosia with vigorous enthusiasm and sublimely unperturbed by the wreckage being created around him.

He finishes chewing, then swallows. 'Remind me again why you are taking such an interest in this sudden storm? I thought you didn't care for Jason.'

Zeus rounds upon him, blinking at Hermes. 'I don't!' he says.

'Ah,' says Hermes.

There is a pause.

'In that case,' Hermes plucks another bunch of ambrosia and pops it into his mouth, 'I may be being very slow, but why is it that you are upending everything within your chambers with, I might add, a considerable lack of aim?' He snatches the bowl out of Zeus' way just in time to save it from tumbling to the floor along with everything else. 'Just out of curiosity . . .'

Zeus begins pacing again, muttering, 'Atalanta was supposed to outride

216

Jason and the Argonauts to the pass, but with this blasted sea-storm turning all the rivers of Colchis to torrents and blocking the way into the gorge . . .'

Hermes is considering the king of the gods with mild interest, his hand suspended over the bowl. 'Atalanta? The girl from Pagasae? But I thought you promised Hera you would stop interfering in her cause – that, if I remember your words correctly, she would not get her kingdom?'

'Well, I lied, didn't I?' says Zeus, shortly.

'Ah,' Hermes says, a smile half forming upon his lips. 'That's interesting.'

Back in her chambers, the wife of Zeus is still railing against Poseidon. Iris leans against Hera's carved side table, absently tracing the grain of the wood with her fingertip, her mind also, like the king of the gods, on Atalanta and her return to Greece.

'. . . and then we won't have a chance upon the throne,' Hera finishes.

Iris looks up. She hasn't been listening for half an hour at least, but the wonderful thing about being Hera's messenger is that Hera rarely requires a reply: her disdain of her message-bearer's station prevents her giving any real weight to Iris's words.

Which gives Iris, cunning and resourceful as she is, plenty of time to form her own plans.

Now she straightens, plucks her golden apple from a fold in her robes and tosses it to the ceiling, then catches it deftly with one hand. She holds it up to the flickering light of the bronze oil-lamps so that the flames reflect from the surface, like a thousand dazzling stars. 'What if we distract them?'

Hera rounds on Iris. 'Distract them? How? And who's "them"?'

Iris takes the stalk of the apple between two fingers and twirls it around with her other hand, like a child playing with a top. 'Poseidon,' she says, spinning the apple. 'And Zeus. The two who are most likely to get in our way. And in the meantime I,' she gestures towards herself, 'can send Aphrodite's cupids to Medea, make her fall in love with Jason, and . . .' she gives the apple another twirl '. . . she will help him recover the Fleece. Think about it! That way no one will know what you're doing. You won't have to raise a finger to help Jason – Medea will do it all for you. And,' she glimmers a smile at Hera, 'best of all, you can keep the two of them busy so that the seas are clear for Jason's return.'

Hera's eyes are following the flashing apple. 'How will you do it?' she asks, her eyes narrowing.

'All we have to do is find the gods' greatest weakness and exploit it,' Iris says. 'And, luckily, the greatest weakness of the gods is so clear that even Tiresias, the blind prophet, would be able to see it.'

'And what is that?'

Iris shrugs. 'Vanity.'

Hera's eyes narrow further, so that they are slits in her face. 'Be careful whom you insult, Iris. There are other goddesses I could choose to be my messenger.'

'Very well. Have another run your errands. But there is no other way to stop Zeus and Poseidon than this.'

Hera considers her for a moment, her face filled with suspicion, as if she would discover whether Iris is telling the truth or merely bluffing. At last she says, in a voice stiff with disdain, 'What is it you would suggest?'

Iris tosses the apple into the air. It spins through the dim room and, as if by instinct, Hera stretches out her hands to catch it. She clutches it to her chest, then holds it up, watching the lamplight sparkle off its golden skin. 'Set up a contest,' Iris says. 'Announce a contest between you, Poseidon and Zeus, with the apple as a prize. The greatest god wins.' She grins. 'And while you three battle it out, I will fly over to Aphrodite and persuade her to give the king's daughter Medea a little puncture wound.'

Hera's eyes snap as she stares at the golden apple. When she speaks her voice is sharp, accusing. 'Where did you get this from?' She gestures towards the apple with a flick of her eyes.

'A gift,' Iris says. 'From—'

'The Muses.' Hera completes the sentence for her. 'Yes. I thought as much.'

The two goddesses exchange a look, Hera's dark eyes wary, darting, Iris's expression calm. The silence stretches between them.

'It is something I treasure,' Iris says, and she spreads her hands, 'but I am willing to give it up on your behalf, my lady.'

Hera is silent. Then: 'I suppose there is something to it,' she says at last. Iris feels a quiet surge of triumph: she has Hera in the palms of her hands, trapped between her ambition and her pride. 'I distract Zeus and Poseidon with the contest for the apple and, in the meantime, you and Aphrodite can set Medea to help Jason with the Fleece . . . Yes . . . Wait – what are you doing?'

Iris has picked up an ivory-headed hairpin from Hera's dressing-table.

Bending forwards, she sticks it into the apple's skin and inscribes upon it two words: ΤΩΙ ΝΙΚΩΝΤΙ.

'For the Winner,' she says, holding it up to the light to examine it. She shoots a smile towards Hera. 'I think that will pique their interest — don't you?'

PART III

ANATOLIA

1260 BC

. . . and Kytoros was theirs; they dwelt around Sesamos and built their beautiful homes near the river Parthenios, Kromna, Aigialos, and steep Erythinoi.

Homer

Defeat

Colchis

The Hour of Daybreak
The Thirteenth Day of the Month of the Grape Harvest

Rain was lashing my face, my cheeks, dripping from my soaking hair and pouring down the back of my neck: a sudden storm that had broken without warning. I had paused once to unstring my bow, looping the twisted ox-gut, wrapping it in an oiled cloth and pushing it into the quiver along with the linen strips, wool cloths and dagger I always carried, then fastening it shut to keep it dry. Apart from that I had not stopped. I was cold to my very bones, exhausted to the point of agony, my joints sore and my thighs rubbed raw against the horse's wet sides. My boots were sodden and filled with water. It was impossible to say if day had yet broken, though I thought, as I squinted through the pouring water, that there seemed to be some slight definition now to the black outlines of the trees around me that there had not been before, and perhaps a pale rim of yellow light just framing the silhouettes of the mountains.

I narrowed my eyes, thinking balefully of Myrtessa, sheltered and dry in Dedali's hut. Through the dark storm clouds that surrounded me, I could just make out the bends of the river Phasis in the valley below, its waters churning over the rocks, swollen and black as the sky above. I dug my heels into my horse's sides, pushing my hair from my face, blinking the water out of my eyelashes. A flash of lightning arrowed down from the sky, flooding the valley with light, and as the drum roll of thunder rumbled across the earth, I saw it at last, through

225

a clearing in the trees: a deep, narrow gorge lined with rocks, half hidden by a cluster of overgrown trees, through which a churning stream was gushing out into the Phasis.

'There!' I shouted, though there was no one to hear me. 'Down there!' I leant forwards and pushed, harder and faster, down the drenched slopes of the mountain, the horse's hoofs sliding over the soaked leaves, my eyes half closed against the driving rain. And now the trees were clearing and I was out into the valley, flying across the sodden ground. The pass, as Dedali had said, lay on the opposite side of the seething river, and as I galloped closer to the bank it became clear that any fording place there might have been had been swept away by the vicious storms squalling in from the ocean.

I wheeled my horse around at the bank, his hoofs stamping the drenched earth, looking across at the foaming waters and jagged rocks.

There was only one way.

He seemed to sense what I wanted to do. Rearing onto his hind legs he came down, hard, the rug slipping on his wet back so that I had to clutch at his mane to keep my seat, then leapt straight into the frothing waters, plunging first legs and then body into the deep water. Fresh and cold as an icy winter's day, it closed around my waist, so turbulent that it knocked the breath from my lungs. Quick as I could I slipped the quiver from my shoulders and held it above my head to save it from being soaked. The horse was holding his muzzle above the water, kicking and struggling against the current, and I knotted his mane around my other hand and gripped harder than ever with my thighs so that the muscles screamed with pain. The waters were swirling around us, pulling and tugging, and now we were in the very centre of the current, waves rolling over waves and crashing against the rocks with bursts of white spray. I felt the knife-sharp edges of a rock scrape past me and a burst of pain in my knee but I could not think about that: I could think only of going on. And then, at last, the waters were growing shallower, warmer, and the tug of the current, though still strong, was easier on my legs. I was lifted bodily out of the river, water streaming down my shoulders and sides, as we reached the shallows. The horse splashed across the pebbles, then climbed up onto the muddy, soft banks, shaking his head and sending spray slicing through the downpour.

I shook the water from my hair, feeling relief flood through me that we had made it to the other side and not been swept away, trying to ignore the chattering of my teeth and the trousers sticking to my thighs. It was certainly growing lighter now: I could see the leaves upon the trees, loaded with raindrops, and the rounded stones that lined the river's edge.

'*Hah!*' I kicked the horse forwards and rode ahead towards the pass, my heart thumping, one hand still holding my quiver and the other on the reins as we galloped. I was two hundred paces from the entrance to the pass . . . one hundred . . . fifty . . .

And then I heard a piercing, whinnying shriek that cut through the lashing rain and the rumbling thunder of the storm. *Another rider!* I froze with fear, but even as my numbed thoughts turned towards my bow my horse let out a cry of alarm and bucked in terror, then reared to the sky.

'No! No – no, no—' I clung to the reins but they slithered through my fingers, clutched at his mane, but the rug was slipping beneath me on his wet back and I had nothing to hold onto. With a desperate cry I fell, still searching for a grip, and was tossed onto my side in the thick, wet mud, my bow clattering as it fell out of the quiver upon the ground. At once I pushed myself to my feet, splattered with muck and drenched, bent to pick up my bow and fumbled in my quiver for my dagger.

'Tel— Atalanta!'

I heard the sound of two boots dropping to the ground a few paces away, though I could see nothing further than the tip of my dagger.

I turned, blade pointed straight ahead, fingers shaking. There was something familiar about that voice – and it was speaking Greek. *Who could know my name?*

'Who are you?' I demanded.

No reply.

'*Who are you?*' I repeated, into the pounding rain, keeping my arm tensed.

And then a figure appeared out of the mist and rain beside me, broad-shouldered, looming out of the darkness. I almost dropped my dagger in shock and gasped aloud, water pouring down my face. *'Hippomenes?'*

He was gasping too and soaking wet, his hair plastered to his head, his face and arms shining with rain, the tunic and cloak sticking tight to his large frame.

'Are you alone?' I shouted, keeping the blade pointed directly at his forehead. He nodded. 'Armed?' He gestured to the sword hanging at his waist then showed his hands, which held the reins of both our horses.

'I mean you no harm,' he bellowed, through the storm. 'Let us – seek shelter – before we talk more.'

I hesitated, still wary.

'You first,' I called, and followed him, keeping my weapon raised, along the edge of the Phasis and up to a small copse at the base of the mountain slopes that offered some shelter from the pouring rain.

Hippomenes tied up the horses to the trunk of a nearby fir, then turned to me. He raised his eyebrows at the sharp knife still pointing between his eyes, then unsheathed his sword and tossed it to the ground. 'There. I am unarmed. Will you lower your dagger now?'

Very slowly, keeping my hand still tight upon the hilt, I let it fall a little. 'Why are you here?' I asked. 'What happened to Jason and the other Argonauts?' I doubled my grip on my weapon. 'Where is the Fleece?'

As I looked into his eyes the memory came back to me of the last time I had seen him, begging for my life upon the shore of the Phasis river. My voice broke a little as I said, 'Why should I even trust you?'

He held up a hand. 'We have not much time,' he said. 'I will tell you all I know, and then you can decide whether to trust me or not. Is that fair?'

I weighed him up, and his brown eyes stared frankly back into mine. 'I would not trust a man who had sent me to exile without a chance to explain myself either,' he said, his voice low. 'But I ask you, please – *trust me now.*'

'Very well,' I said, though I did not lower my blade any further. 'Go on.'

He began to pace. 'Jason has the Fleece,' he said, ignoring my barely suppressed intake of breath. 'He stole it, with the help of Medea, princess of the Colchians. She led us to the sanctuary along a hidden path from the other side of the pass two nights ago, left us outside and went in with Jason alone. They came out together with the Fleece. Jason is even now riding with the others as fast as he can, back towards the *Argo*, which we left at the bay we fled to after the battle.'

He turned to me. 'When I thought of returning to Greece without you . . . My acquiescence to Jason's sentence dishonoured me. Leaving you behind . . . I have been imagining you wandering through the forests, hunting deer and sleeping upon the hard earth, wondering where you were, if you were still alive . . . I swear to you, I have come to regret deeply the punishment we gave you. To exile you from Greece . . .' he pushed the hair back from his forehead '. . . it is worse than death, and you, with your courage, your determination . . .' He looked away from me. He was having difficulty expressing himself. 'You deserved no such thing. I have been waiting for you here for many hours, as long as I dared.' A smile was just visible at the corners of his lips. 'I thought that, knowing you, you might find your way to the pass – to the Fleece. And you came.'

He took a deep breath. 'It is a lot to ask of you, I know, but,' he placed a hand upon the bridle of my horse, 'if we are to overtake Jason and board the *Argo* back to Greece, we have not a moment to lose. Will you trust me? I vouch,' he said, bowing his head, 'for your safety among the Argonauts. They will not harm you if I promise to protect you.'

He gestured towards me, holding out the reins, his eyes upon mine. 'Ride with me, Atalanta.'

I looked up at the sound of my name as the rain hissed down upon the leaves above us and the river tumbled out upon the plain beyond.

But then I remembered what I had come for, and what I was set to lose.

What, perhaps, I had already lost.

'Why,' I said at last, my voice shaking with emotion, 'would I return to the *Argo* after all they have done to me? When your leader threatened to kill me, and beat me with his own hands when I attempted to protect a slave? When one of your number tried, brutally and cruelly, to take me by force? When he betrayed me, then brought me and my friend before all of you to see us insulted, threatened, and finally exiled as if we were worse than slaves – though you had treated me as an equal before?'

I swallowed the bitterness in my voice. 'I thank you for your concern for me, Hippomenes, but I have no need of your help,' I said, biting back tears. I thrust the dagger back into my quiver and retied the straps upon the lid. 'And now, if you please, I will have my horse.' I snatched the reins from him; swung myself up onto the horse's back. '*Go!*' I shouted at my mount, and kicked him hard in the flanks, whipping at the reins.

'But, Atalanta—'

I galloped off, my head bent against the storm, heading as fast as I could back down along the muck-mired banks of the Phasis.

I rode for many hours, pushing my horse as fast as he would go and taking as few breaks for rest as I could, until the sweat was foaming white upon his flanks. Rain sliced through the air to either side of me, like silver needles, while thunder crashed overhead, and though I rode hidden beneath the cover of the trees, following the winding course of the Phasis down the valley, the storm did not abate, lowering thunder-clouds rolling overhead as if an endless storm had settled itself over the land of mortals and was raining upon us the never-ceasing displeasure of the gods.

And, still, there was no sign of Jason.

As the darkness deepened around me and day slid into evening, I reached at last the woods just above the cove where I had awoken many days before, wounded, upon the shore – where Jason had summoned the lords and sent me into exile. I slowed to a halt, dismounted and secured my horse to a tree, stroking his nose as he snorted into the damp air. Raindrops splashed upon the leaves and thunder rumbled in the distance over the foaming of the swollen river, and the scent of moss filled the air. The light was fading fast, the outlines of the trees darkening, and I shivered, the hairs on my arms standing on end. The clothes Dedali had given me were soaked and clinging to my skin, yet there was no time to warm myself.

I began to run, slipping over the uneven branches and rocks of the forest floor, barely able to see, breath coming quickly, down towards the riverbank and to the bay with its stretch of sand. The edge of the forest was ahead – I could see the dark-blue twilit sky flashing between the trunks of the trees . . .

And then the branches cleared, and the open ground began to slope away towards the river, scattered with grass and rushes towards the wide, curving beach.

It was empty.

A single trough, cut deep into the sand and running down to the water, showed where the keel of a boat had been.

I collapsed upon my knees by the river's edge. I was cold to my bones and pushed to the very edge of exhaustion, after a full night and day of riding in gales and chilling rain. Far worse was the knowledge that I had, at the very last, been defeated. That Jason had won, where I had not.

That I had failed to recover the Fleece, after all that I had done and tried to do.

I do not know how long I knelt upon that shore, sobbing, the tears upon my cheeks mixing with the deluge of rain from the skies. The desolation and loneliness were beyond any I had ever felt before. I was a thousand leagues and more from my home. I had been defeated, outstripped by Jason at the very last. I had lost the only chance I had ever had to prove my worth.

And worst, worst of all, I had failed my family, my friend and my gods.

They trusted me to aid their city – my city. And I have failed them.

I have failed them all.

I never should have left.

I clenched my fists, the nails digging into my palms, weeping freely, great sobs that caught in my throat and made my chest heave.

That was a dark night indeed.

At last, shaking with cold and grief, the tears and the rain dripping from the end of my nose, my tunic sticking to my skin, I seemed to come to myself. I needed to find shelter if I was not to perish, here and now, from the chill damp that was pervading my body. I pushed myself, trembling, to my feet, felt the raw ache in my thighs and back from the ride, the bruising soreness in my hips, and started, slowly, limping, to make my way back up to the thicket where my horse waited.

Then I stopped.

The sound of hoof beats was echoing along the valley, just audible over the splattering rain: the dull thud of hoofs in mud. Ignoring the pain in my legs, I broke into a run, fast as I could, making for the shelter of the trees. My horse was cropping moss and raised his head, ears pricked. He gave a soft whinny as I ran towards him.

'Hush, hush,' I whispered, taking his reins in my hand and gently stroking his nose, trying to silence my ragged breathing.

The hoof beats were growing louder now, so loud they must be almost upon us. Very quietly, as softly as I could, I backed deeper into the cover of the trees, pulling at my steed's reins, trying not to make a sound upon the fallen leaves and twigs, silently drawing my bow from behind me and nocking an arrow . . .

And then the hoof beats stopped, quite abruptly, and there was the sound of boots landing in mud and the scraping of a sword in its scabbard. I peered through the low branches of the pines, string pulled taut, the wood of the arrow's shaft smooth against my cheek.

'*Hippomenes!*' I hissed, stepping out from behind the trees. He turned at the sound of my voice, his eyes sweeping the dark pillars of the tree trunks until he found the two glinting pinpricks of my eyes. I moved towards him, lowering my bow. 'What in Hades' name are you doing here?'

He did not answer, but drew his sword and searched the glade. When he seemed satisfied we were not being watched, he turned back to me and sheathed his blade.

'The bay is empty,' he said, his voice tight, teeth gritted. He swore and thumped the palm of his hand upon the trunk of a nearby tree. 'The *Argo* is gone. I assume,' he shot towards me, 'you were too late to board it and beg passage back to Greece.'

I stared at him. 'If you think that is why I came,' I began, tightening my grip upon my bow.

'Is it not?'

I looked aside, refusing to answer. Now that my frustration had subsided a little I was thinking more clearly, and there were far more pressing matters ahead.

'The mark in the sand from the keel is fresh,' I muttered to myself. I looked up at the sky through the trees. It was fast darkening now beneath the veil of night. 'The *Argo* cannot be far out to sea yet, and in this weather . . .'

The beginnings of a plan were forming in my mind. *With such a storm the progress of the* Argo *must be slow, at least at first . . . and if they are forced to stop once more, as we were in Kytoros . . .*

'If I change horses often,' I said, 'I could cover ten or fifteen leagues each day. Following the coastline back to Pagasae would be easy . . . and . . . yes . . .'

It might just be possible to reach Pagasae before Jason. And if I do . . . I realized the full implications of what lay before me, and felt the same determination that had driven me for so many weeks rise up within me again. *I will stand upon the shore and challenge him to a duel to the death.*

He will have to accept upon his honour before the heroes.

The Fleece will go to the winner, and with it, the kingship of the towns of Pelion.

I looked at Dedali's horse, the reins slack in my hands, and though my thighs ached at the thought I knew, instinctively, that it was my only hope. I hesitated at the prospect of taking the horse further, when I had promised to set him free; then vowed I would send him back as soon as I could get a change of mount.

I glanced at last towards Hippomenes, his face shadowed in the darkness, and saw the intensity of his gaze upon me. 'Are you saying what I think you are?' he asked at last, breaking the silence. 'That you are planning to ride back to Greece – alone?'

There was no way I could deny it. 'Yes.'

He took a step forwards, as if to lay a hand upon my arm, but I moved away. 'That is impossible. You know enough of the wilds of our journey here to be sure that you would never survive it alone.'

'I thank you,' I said, moving to untie the reins of my horse, 'for your conjectures upon my survival, but,' I tugged at the knot, 'I believe I am perfectly capable of looking after myself.' The knot was proving harder than I had thought to loosen. I frowned and cleared my throat, determined not to let Hippomenes see my discomfort. 'And I do not need the assistance – of a companion of Jason and Meleager.'

At the last word, the reins slipped free and hung limply in my hands. I turned to face him.

'I have no doubt as to that,' he said, and his stare – open and frank – unsettled me; it would have been easier if he had mocked me. I tried to keep my features arranged in what I hoped was a defiant look. 'But you will not be safe from Jason and the other lords if I am not there to answer for you. And in any case . . .' he moved to his horse and, with one swift movement – exceptionally graceful, I thought, for a man so broad about the shoulders and so tall – he swung a leg over the animal's back to mount '. . . I must return to Greece myself.'

'What are you doing?'

'What does it look like? I am coming with you.'

'You are not.'

I laid a hand on my horse's neck and pulled myself up to sit on the rug, then wrapped the reins around each hand. As I tugged on the bridle he tossed his forelock back and snorted gently, as if in anticipation of the journey ahead.

Hippomenes flicked his reins beside me, his steed stepping nervously from side to side and shaking its mane. 'Yes,' he said, 'I am. I would not let even a man do that journey alone.'

'Well, I am not a man,' I said, digging my heels in and starting forwards at a walk towards the river's bank, away from the dank, mossy darkness of the forest. 'And I do not need help, especially from you.'

And with that, I turned downriver, and galloped out from under the shelter of the trees into the night, towards the plains of Anatolia, and back to Greece.

The Return

The River Phasis

The Hour of the Stars

The Thirteenth Day of the Month of the Grape Harvest

It was deep night, so dark that I could hardly see when I pulled up to rest later, my skin freezing from the rain, my horse's flanks shining with sweat and water. I had followed the turbulent river all the way to where it emptied into the sea. By the flashes of lightning, which occasionally set the sky alight, I could make out the meadows surrounding the river's mouth, which we had seen when we first touched land. The long grass was now flattened with rain and the reed beds turned into swampy marshes. The ocean was seething, roaring waves plunging into the coast and sending spray shooting up towards the sky, the wind howling about my ears. I moved to take shelter beneath a copse of beeches not far from the shore, their leaves dripping rain and their branches swaying in the tempest. I dismounted, limbs riddled with pain, and reached behind me for my bow, hands slipping on the oiled cloth as I unwrapped the ox-gut and strung it. *There must be some game to be had here*, I thought, and my stomach rumbled as if in answer. I could barely remember when I had eaten last.

As I began to tie my horse to a bough of the nearest tree, however, I was stopped short by the sound of hoof beats over the marshes, splashing in the rain.

I turned. Hippomenes was approaching, his hair streaming water, his cloak gathered around him. For all his bedraggled appearance, he

237

was smiling. 'You are a fast rider,' he called to me. 'I almost thought I would lose you.'

Irritation rose within me, prickling in my belly. 'What are you doing here?'

He dismounted without a word, landing upon the sodden grass, and led his steed over to me, head bowed. He tethered it, then ducked out again from beneath the shelter of the leaves, back into the rain and towards the woods that lined the meadow's edge.

When he returned, it was with handfuls of sour berries, roots and a few wild mushrooms, gasping for breath in the cold. I was sitting beside one of the trees, wet, hungry and bad-tempered, my bow safely returned to my quiver upon my back, my knees tucked into my chest, trying to rub some warmth into my arms.

'It is too damp for a fire,' he said. 'Here.' He handed me a cluster of berries and a long-stemmed mushroom.

'I – I don't— Thank you,' I said stiffly, too hungry to refuse. I bit into the mushroom, relishing its sweet, earthy taste. Rainwater trickled down my chin, and I wiped it away with my forearm. 'Though I could have gone myself.'

'I know.'

There was silence for a moment, except for the drumming of the rain upon the earth, the pounding and crashing of the waves.

Then Hippomenes turned to me. 'Atalanta—'

But I had flung my berries to the ground and covered his mouth with my hand.

He pulled me off. 'What—'

'Armed riders,' I hissed, my voice barely a whisper. 'Over there. In the forest.'

I pointed across the meadow. A flash of lightning illuminated the sky, lining the leaves of the distant trees with silver and silhouetting a small group of men mounted upon horses and carrying short, sharp-tipped spears. They were emerging from beneath the branches at the wood's edge. A second lightning flash showed them cantering towards us. I could see the leader not fifty paces away, the distance closing every moment. He was leaning back and had one hand upon the reins.

I barely had time to scramble to my feet, and ran for my horse as Hippomenes picked up his spear. I had just swung myself up when the leader approached us, swaying slightly in the saddle. His eyes were on the bow upon my back and the sword at Hippomenes' waist, and he snarled something at us in his own language. The other men closed around him, spears held aloft. As another burst of lightning illuminated the razor-sharp tips, I swallowed, my mouth dry.

'We are friends,' Hippomenes said, walking slowly towards the leader, drawing his sword from his scabbard and laying it on the drenched grass. 'Friends,' he repeated, holding up his bare palms in the rain. 'If you let us go,' he pointed at our horses, 'we will not harm you.'

He gestured towards his sword, then back towards the bandit leader.

As the leader turned and held a muttered conversation with his companions, I leant towards Hippomenes. 'They want our arms and our mounts,' I hissed in his ear. 'We should have fled when we first saw them.'

Hippomenes held up a hand to silence me and I bit my lip, annoyed almost beyond bearing that he was there, that I was not doing this alone. 'Wait for a moment,' he said. 'If we keep our heads, we may be able to avoid a fight.'

My eyes were drawn to the leader, his profile revealed in the lightning that sparked upon the horizon. His long hair was loose over his shoulders, and he wore a cap and trousers of leather, and a wide war-belt about his tunic, made of animal skin and fitted with hooks from which hung all manner of deadly swords and daggers. A double-headed axe swung from his right hip, a small curved bow and open quiver from a loop on his left. He was gesturing to our weapons, then to Hippomenes, then to our horses. The tone of his voice did not seem to suggest reconciliation.

Then, out of nowhere, an arrow grazed my cheek, the blade whistling over my skin, and buried itself into the tree behind me. I cried out, one hand raised to my stinging face, and stared through the darkness. Shadows were materializing in the distance behind the riders, looming larger, mounted upon steeds, their bows raised . . .

'There are more of them!' I shouted. 'Hippomenes, watch—'

Hippomenes turned at my cry, and behind him I saw the leader leap from his horse, long sword drawn and held before him in both hands.

'*Hippomenes!*'

Just in time, Hippomenes whirled around, bent to pick up his sword and parried the bandit's blow from beneath, bronze shrieking on bronze, the blades glimmering in another brilliant flare of lightning branding the sky overhead. My heart was thumping loudly in my chest, desperately unsure what to do as I watched the leader bring his sword down again through the rain with enough speed to split Hippomenes' skull. I gasped: Hippomenes had rolled swiftly to one side, bringing his sword around, and then he was springing to his feet and thrusting the blade forwards, his whole strength in the blow, burying it deep in the man's chest. A piercing shriek of agony from the leader rent the air as he sank to the ground. Blood was pouring from the wound into the earth, and the whites of his eyes shone in the darkness. Hippomenes wrenched his sword out with a terrible wet squelch and a final scream of pain, followed by a roar of rage from the other bandits.

'Move! We have to *move!*'

Arrows were hailing down upon us now through the darkness, coming from nowhere and thudding into the sodden ground. Hippomenes was already vaulting onto his horse as I turned away, half blinded by panic, head down, whipping the reins and screaming at my horse to move. Behind me I could hear the thunder of Hippomenes' hoofs, and close behind that the pounding of the riders, yelling and cursing, chasing us. Lightning split the air ahead, exploding the landscape into a sudden burst of light, thunder rumbling so loudly that it made the bones of my ribs tremble.

I twisted in my saddle, my hair flying out in the screaming wind and rain, and saw the bandits closing upon us, galloping across the sodden, marshy terrain. I pushed my horse on, kicking harder, slapping at his neck, but he was struggling in the clinging damp earth and it was slowing him. Hippomenes was directly beside me now, his steed kicking up large clods of soil, its mouth open, nostrils flared as the rain poured down its nose, flanks heaving.

A spear hissed past my right ear.

'Down! Get your head down!' Hippomenes shouted, and I ducked close to the horse's neck, barely able to see anything, my head jolting up and down as we galloped over the rough terrain.

'If we can reach the woods ahead, we have a chance of losing them!' he bellowed, as another spear shot overhead, followed by a storm of arrows.

I leant forwards, squinting through the rain, scanning the outline of the forest three hundred paces distant, which curved down to meet the sea, bordering the grassy plains of the river mouth. The trees seemed to grow thickly together, branches knotted into each other, tall tips reaching to the lowering sky.

'Can we reach it in time?'

He twisted to peer over his shoulder. The bandits were galloping at full speed not forty paces behind, and in another burst of light I saw three who still had their spears holding them high at their shoulders, aiming towards us. 'Can you use your bow while you ride?'

I stared at him. I could aim an arrow from horseback on the tracks of Mount Pelion, but in the darkness, and with a wet string? 'I'll have to get closer to them,' I shouted. 'And I will need to follow you.'

He did not answer but spurred ahead, his horse's hoofs tearing up the dark, muddy earth. Mine shook his head a little, whinnying, and set his course after Hippomenes. I took a deep, shuddering breath, willing myself to focus harder than I ever had before, to ignore the chill in my body and the rain pouring down, and to feel only the rhythm of the horse's body beneath me as my own. Gripping hard with my thighs, I let the reins go slack, felt my hips rise and fall, rise and fall, as if my mount and I were one, galloping over the plains . . .

I turned, pulled my bow from the quiver, set an arrow to the string. Every thought upon the rolling gait of my steed below me and the flint tip of the arrow ahead, I twisted around, drew the string tight away from my body and aimed into the darkness, waiting, waiting, every sinew tensed . . .

A flash of lightning silhouetted a rider behind me in silver and black. Quick as a thought, I let the dart fly. The string was damp from the rain and the darkness closed in almost instantly, but I heard a scream of pain to tell me my aim was true, a shrieking cry from the horse, and the whinnying, cursing and splashing as the bandit's steed crumpled beneath him.

'Again!' Hippomenes shouted, and I reached back, eyes straining to seek out the barely visible shapes behind me, letting loose one arrow after another through the night as I thundered along. I heard cries and shrieks as some made impact. I paused to look ahead, heart pounding at my throat. Another pillar of light showed the trees at a hundred paces now and nearing, towering ahead of us into the sky. As I summoned the last of my strength and twisted around to draw again I saw one of the two remaining brigands lean his body back on his steed, then hurl his spear towards us.

'Watch out!' I cried to Hippomenes and, still holding my bow in one hand, I tugged at the reins and veered to the left, narrowly missing the spinning spear shaft, which flew past me and buried itself with a splitting *thud* in the trunk of a tree ahead. *Fifty paces to go . . . twenty-five . . .*

And then there was a sudden screech from my horse. He reared, then tumbled, toppling to the earth. I screamed and let go of the reins as I was tossed sideways through the air and slammed into the sodden soil, sending spray and mud streaming up into the air.

I stared up into the rain splattering down upon my face. I was fighting as hard as I could against passing out. It felt as if one of my ribs had broken and I was gasping and choking for air. Dedali's horse was sprawling in the marsh, an arrow sticking from its hindquarters.

I saw Hippomenes running towards me, watched him bend and pull the arrow from the horse. It struggled immediately to its feet, and, limping slightly but roused by fear, bolted for the forest. I felt Hippomenes' warmth through my sodden tunic as he knelt beside me, and struggled not to close my eyes against the pain and the water pouring down my face.

'Here,' he said, and placed my elbow around his neck. 'Hold still.' He took me in his arms and lifted me as easily as a child, and I moved instinctively towards the heat of him. As he turned into the rain, I saw, through a mist of pain, the two remaining bandits riding towards us, nearing, and one still held his spear . . .

Hippomenes stooped suddenly low, pulling me against him so I winced, and the bronze spear hissed overhead into the forest, crashing through the branches. He ducked and ran, holding me close, towards his horse; I could hear it snorting, smell its musky scent. I felt my feet touch the ground, then his hands around my waist as he lifted me onto its back. I threw one leg over, gasping at the sharp stab that darted through my side as Hippomenes vaulted up behind me, placed his arms around me and tugged at the reins.

'*Go!*' he shouted, kicking hard, and it began to gallop, mane flying in the wind before my face. Though I could not see behind me I thought I could no longer make out the sounds of the bandits pursuing us, and Hippomenes' arms were tight around me, his chest pressing against me, his thighs steady and strong, guiding the horse forwards toward the trees ahead . . .

And then darkness, deeper even than that upon the river's plain, submerged us with the sudden silence of a deep, cold pool, and the branches of the trees stretched up, tall and menacing, outlined like spiders' webs against the lightning-filled sky.

'On! On!' Hippomenes shouted, and we cantered onwards, and I could see nothing but Hippomenes' hands beside me upon the reins, turning us this way and that, and the thick, twisted trunks of the trees flying past us at either side. We made our way further into the forest, winding left and right and left again until I could not have told where we were, even if I had not been half unconscious with pain, or whether we had not turned in a complete circle and were back again to the meadow's plain. But there was no sound of hoofs behind us, and finally Hippomenes allowed his steed to slow to a trot, and I felt it flicking its head back and forth, its warm breath sending mist into the air. Hippomenes turned and looked behind him, his left thigh pressing into my back.

'I think we have lost them,' he said, in a low voice.

I tried to move and felt a sharp, shooting pain in my ribs. I gave a little moan.

'Hold still,' he said, laying his hand upon my shoulder so gently that his fingertips barely brushed the skin of my neck. 'We will stop soon, and then I can find you a place to rest.'

*

I awoke later – how much later I did not know – from a fretful sleep in which odd, disjointed visions of the smoking ruins of Kaladrosos floated across my dreams. At once I felt the pain in my chest, my breathing coming short and shallow. I was chilled through and exhausted. Every part of my body seemed bruised, and my eyes were still heavy with fatigue. I blinked a little, getting my bearings on my surroundings. Then, clutching my ribs, I tried to push myself to sit.

As I looked around it became clear we were in a cave, the dark walls hollowed out of the rock, the ground scattered with lichen-covered pebbles. A fire was crackling and spitting a few paces away, flames leaping to the cave roof and sending patterned shadows dancing over the stone, bathing my skin in a delicious warmth. I looked down, with a sudden premonition, and saw, with relief, that I was still dressed in Dedali's tunic and trousers. Hippomenes' cloak lay tucked over me. It was still damp, but he had tried to wring out the water – he must have covered me while I was asleep. I looked around, and spotted him seated on the other side of the fire towards the back of the cave. He was propped against the wall in his woollen tunic and boots, one hand across his knee as he cleaned his sword with a cloth, entirely absorbed. I watched him for a few moments, following the sure, steady move-ments of his hands, wondering why he had chosen to stop for me, out upon the plain.

'My thanks to you.'

He started and dropped the cloth. The firelight was playing shadows across his face, highlighting the curves and contours of his cheeks and the break on the bridge of his nose. He leant forwards, picked it up and started polishing the blade once more. 'What for?'

'For saving me.' I indicated the fracture in my ribs, where the skin was swelling painfully beneath my sodden tunic.

He rubbed at a stain upon the bronze, saying nothing. A few sparks shot from the embers and caught the uplift of the smoke, swirling to the cave's ceiling and into darkness. 'You are welcome,' he said at last.

We lapsed into silence.

'I – I apologize. For the things I said before.'

'I deserved them.' He smiled, and his eyes sparkled in the light of the fire. 'Well, some of them, at least. You certainly have a temper.'

I scowled at him, and he grinned, discomfiting me. His refusal to be drawn was so steadfast, so irritating, so . . . The flames rustled and cracked.

'While we are making apologies,' he said, and stroked the cloth again along the sword blade, 'I did you wrong on the shores of Colchis. You were angry with me earlier, and you had every right to be. But I wanted to tell you – I underestimated you, Atalanta, and I am sorry for it.'

I tossed a stick into the fire and looked up at him. His eyes were hooded in the darkness, but I could sense the frankness of their gaze: comforting, trustworthy, so different from Meleager's. 'Is this an apology? Is Hippomenes, son of Megareus, lord of Onchestos, apologizing to a woman?'

He bowed his head. 'He is,' he said awkwardly, and I could sense the resentment in his tone of a proud man who was being forced to admit that he was wrong; and suddenly I realized I did not need to hear it.

'Enough,' I said, and smiled across the fire at him. 'I accept your apology.'

'But I—'

'Enough,' I said again, and threw another stick at him, this time meeting my mark. It clattered off his shoulder and onto the ground. 'Have I not said? It is forgotten.'

He gazed at me, his lips curving into a smile, too. 'Very well, then.'

We lapsed into silence again. An ember flew from the fire and sparked upon a pile of dry leaves near my feet. I tried to get to my feet to stamp it out, but pain lanced through me and I slipped. In an instant, Hippomenes was at my side and caught me before I fell to the ground, and lowered me gently to his cloak. 'Take care,' he said. 'This is not a time for heroic feats. You need rest, and food, and water.'

He passed me a gourd, which it seemed he had fashioned from a piece of birch bark, filled with rainwater. As I took it from him our eyes met.

'I – thank you,' I said, and I took a draught, the gourd dripping a little. He was close to me, so close that I could have brushed his chest with my fingertip if I had stretched out my hand, and I could smell his scent, a mixture of horse sweat, grass and leather.

When I had finished drinking he took the cup back from me without a word and knelt upon the floor, one knee tucked into his chest, staring into the fire.

'When can we ride again?' I asked, gingerly propping myself against the cave wall and gathering Hippomenes' cloak around my shoulders.

Hippomenes turned towards me with a half-smile. 'We?'

'I only meant—' To my dismay, I was beginning to blush, the heat creeping up my neck to my ears. 'If you want to come, that is no concern of mine.'

He made no reply, but his gaze was fixed on mine, silent, with an intensity as palpable as heat. Without a word he moved towards me. I felt my breath catch in my throat. His hand was behind my head, then his lips were upon mine, kissing me fiercely, so strong that he would almost bruise me. I felt myself respond to him, my broken rib forgotten in the urgency of that moment, my hands running through his damp hair, lightly at first and then more passionate, down the ridged muscles of his back and along his broad shoulders. Desire was coursing through me stronger than I had ever felt it before, so strong that I longed for nothing more than that he would lift me onto him and have me, hold me close to him and never let me go . . .

We broke apart, breathing hard.

'I have wanted you from the very moment I first saw you,' he said to me, his eyes gazing into mine, the softness in his voice sending a thrill down my spine. 'As a young man on the hunt, when you pierced the boar with your arrow, then at Kytoros, when you tore my heart out in your desire for Meleager, then as a woman on the shore of Colchis.' He shook his head. 'The fire in your eyes that day I shall never forget.' He stroked a lock of hair back from my face with his finger and kissed me again on the lips, tenderly this time, his mouth brushing mine, making my skin tingle. 'You are the most desirable woman I have ever seen.'

I took a deep breath, then choked as a stab of pain seared through my ribs, tears starting to my eyes.

I realized at once – too late – that it sounded as if I had laughed. Hippomenes' forehead was creasing in a frown, his eyes darkening, his jaw clenched tight.

I held up a hand. 'No – no, I am sorry,' and I coughed, trying to recover myself.

But the moment was gone.

He turned aside and reached into my quiver, pulled out a strip of linen, dipped it in the gourd of water and then handed it to me without speaking. 'Press the cloth to the swelling and make sure it is kept cool,' he said shortly, standing up and moving towards the fire, settling himself beside it and closing his eyes, his back to me. 'You should rest.'

I passed the cloth under my tunic, still wheezing, and held it there, half closing my eyes at the cool sensation on the bruised and swollen skin.

We sat in silence for a long while, broken only by my shallow breathing and occasional coughs.

'We must stop here a few more days only,' I said, once I regained my voice, glad to have something to say. 'Then I must return, whether I am well or not – for I must reach Pagasae before Ja—' I stopped short.

'Before Jason?'

I cursed silently at my mistake: no one except Myrtessa could know what I planned to do. I glanced over towards the back of the cave, and saw that Hippomenes had recovered Dedali's steed and had cleaned and bandaged it across the hindquarters; the two horses were lying side by side, legs tucked beneath them for warmth. I bit my lip, feeling a fresh wave of guilt. 'We will have to change horses soon,' I said, wincing as I adjusted the cloth upon my ribs. 'My steed is not mine to take and, besides, we will have need of several changes of horse to return to Greece, if we are to make good time. Do you have silver with you?'

He gestured towards a leather pouch hanging from his belt, beside his dagger.

'If we retrace our steps back to the river and ride due west along the ocean shore we should be able to follow the route we came by, for we were never far from sight of land.' I spoke quickly, the journey ahead unfolding in my mind. 'Once we have passed through the lands of the Hittites, if we can cross the strait of the Bosphorus we can ride through Thrace and down to Pagasae from the north.'

'You are not one to rest from planning, are you?'

'If you knew what was at stake upon my return, perhaps you would take as much trouble as I,' I shot back at him.

'It is not for want of asking.'

I felt disgruntled and irritated with him once again, and after further silence in which the horses in the corner snorted and the fire spat, I curled up under Hippomenes' cloak, my face turned towards the cave wall, and tried to sleep. But it was a long time before I was able to fall into a fretful doze, and even then my sleep was filled with confused dreams, where Hippomenes lifted me onto his hips and took me against the rough rock of the cave, my arms wrapped around his broad shoulders, his lips biting into mine and his sweat upon my skin – and in my dream he used my name, my real name, Atalanta . . .

When I woke, the fire had burnt down to a dark pile of glowing embers.

And Hippomenes was gone.

Golden Apple

Mount Olympus

A few hours later, in the skies above and many hundreds of miles to the west, dawn is breaking. Iris and Hermes are seated on the rocky outcrops of one of Olympus' lower peaks, the summer snow glittering and sparkling around them in the first rosy rays of the sun. The air is fresh and clear, and the dark outlines of the trees to the south are just tinged with gold. Hermes is sitting with his arms folded across his chest, staring at Iris with a distinct expression of mistrust as she idly tosses a golden-skinned apple from one hand to the other.

'They may not even come.'

'They will come.'

Silence falls again, except for the rustling of the early-morning breeze upon the snow, blowing it up into eddying circles of glittering ice, and the twittering of the swallows circling overhead, forked tails twisting this way and that as they soar and dive.

Iris turns to her left and glances down towards the Aegean, its waters storm-tossed, and then past the Hellespont, the Propontis and the Bosphorus to the vast, roiling, tempestuous expanse of the Black Sea. Poseidon's wrath is still playing itself out upon the ocean, all the way from the rocky shores of Mount Pelion to the wide sandy mouth of the river Phasis, twenty-foot waves of ink-black water crashing upon the beaches from Greece to Colchis, ships rocking and keeling in the blistering winds. And as she looks, her eyes are drawn, inevitably, inexorably, to one ship above all: the wide-bellied, white-sailed Argo. *Its oars are flailing in the roiling waters just beyond the Phasis' mouth, its prow plunging into the sea, then emerging, surrounded by salt spray, to soar for a moment before hitting the tempestuous waters once more . . .*

Iris's eyes snap away. The Golden Fleece is upon that ship, hidden in a leather sack and kept locked within the hold. She had been irritated beyond belief, last night, to discover that Jason had captured the Fleece – which she had never intended, for all that she had told Hera.

Atalanta was supposed to do that.

She taps her foot against the rock in annoyance. The worst of it all, she thinks, gazing up into the arch of the sky, which is slowly turning now from dark blue to the palest pink and gold, is that Medea, daughter of King Aeëtes, fell for Jason of her own accord! The princess had succumbed to him like a hare captured in the claws of an eagle, and aided him in capturing the Fleece, as docile as if the arrows of the cupids really had struck her in the breast. Yes, yes, of course Iris had suggested sending Aphrodite to the princess of the Colchians to make her fall in love with Jason – but she hadn't actually done so. Aphrodite had been left untroubled to do whatever she did of an evening in that rose-filled chamber of hers, and Iris had had a full night to herself to plot and scheme for Atalanta's return.

There is a moment in which Iris contemplates the strangeness of the workings of Fate – that the mortal Medea should have chosen, of her own free will, unwittingly to follow the course set for her by a pair of scheming gods . . .

And then she lifts a hand to hide her smile as a sudden, inspired idea begins to form in her mind.

Perhaps things may go her way, after all.

Hermes interrupts her train of thought, peering down the slopes of the mountain, covered with loose scree and, further down, a layer of bright-green brush. 'I bet they won't —'

'They will,' Iris says again.

Hermes uncrosses his arms, crosses them again, then stands up, his shadow long over the ridges of the mountain in the dawn light. 'I don't trust you, Iris. First you put Poseidon and me to sleep and ruin a perfectly harmless evening of—'

'Ravishing innocent nymphs, yes, I know.'

'And now there's this golden apple,' Hermes continues, ignoring her, 'you and Hera suddenly all keen for a contest – I don't like it. What schemes have you two been hatching in her boudoir?'

'Iris?'

Iris springs to her feet, tossing the apple into the air one last time and catching it, clasped, between her pale hands. 'Hera.'

Hera, dressed as always in robes of white and wearing her golden crown of oak leaves, gleams a smile at her as she approaches her herald, then looks at Hermes. Her eyes narrow slightly. 'Messenger boy.'

'Hera,' Hermes says, with easy nonchalance. 'Well, at least one of you is here. I was placing bets with Iris that none of you would respond to the summons, but then, I suppose, we all know who is the master and who runs to Iris's every command—'

'Silence,' Hera snaps.

'Hermes is a fool, Hera – a court jester engaged to humour Zeus,' Iris says, and she gives Hermes a look of contempt, wrinkling her nose as if she has a bad taste in her mouth. 'You should ignore him.'

'I always try to,' Hermes says cheerfully.

Hera turns to Iris. 'How are things progressing?' she asks, lowering her voice.

Iris glances around, then draws her mistress to sit on an outcrop of snow-clad rock on the other side of the mountain's face, well out of Hermes' earshot. The sun's rays have not yet reached here and it is cold and dark, shadowed – a good place in which to plot.

'Jason?' Hera asks, without preamble.

'On the Argo,' Iris replies, her voice low. 'They departed the Phasis as night fell.'

'With the Fleece?'

Iris nods, disguising her twitch of annoyance.

'Medea aided them, as we planned?'

She nods again, noting the 'we' with bitter amusement.

Hera relaxes, her shoulders falling. 'You have done well,' she says, and Iris bows her head, not meeting Hera's eye.

'Now, then, it is time,' Hera continues, rising to stand and brushing the snow from her robes, 'that we distract Poseidon from the storm, and Zeus from Atalanta. You have the apple?'

Iris takes it from her robes and shows it to the queen of the gods. Hera nods, once, and turns away. 'Oh – and you have not seen the girl since she was exiled, have you?' She looks back over her shoulder at Iris.

Iris shakes her head, schooling her expression. 'No, my lady. I have not seen her at all.'

Hera walks to the other side of the peak, Iris following her, just in time to see Zeus and his brother Poseidon striding up the steep mountainside, their footsteps kicking up a fine veil of snow as they go. Zeus' expression is merely curious, but Poseidon is glowering with fury, his teeth gritted, clearly determined to beat the queen of the gods hands down in the contest as vengeance for the incident in the Library of the Muses.

'Hera,' Zeus calls. 'What's this I hear about a golden apple?'

'I have it here,' Iris says, stepping out of the shade of the peak and holding it up to the light. The sun's rays — so much clearer and warmer up here on the peak of Mount Olympus — sparkle off the apple's golden skin, splitting into a thousand tiny dots of glimmering light that shimmer over the jagged rocks surrounding the gods. Upon its surface are the two words, inscribed in her own long, slanting writing: ΤΩΙ ΝΙΚΩΝΤΙ.

'The winner of the contest earns this,' Iris says, into the sudden silence, enjoying the power of knowing that the three gods' eyes are fixed upon the apple in her hands, that she has them completely in her grasp.

She holds the apple, spinning it around its stem, and in the golden light of dawn a thousand fine threads of light sparkle from its skin, spiralling out, then joining into an intricate pattern, lacing over each other, forming images, shapes, figures. She can almost see three scenes forming themselves in the air: a mirage of the beholders' deepest desires.

For Poseidon, to win means to reign alone: a mountain, gold-tipped and showered in golden snow-dust, upon which he alone is the ruler, without his brother Zeus, the entirety of earth spread out beneath him in intricate, gold-laced detail, his to command.

For Zeus, it means to hold his rule: a throne, surrounded by gods who love and respect him and a wife who congratulates and supports him in his command, the mortals all at peace below, sacrificing golden calves whose smoke wreathes heaven in flaxen spirals.

And for Hera: a garden lined with pebble paths where she and Zeus walk together arm in arm, gold blossom falling upon them from the apple trees, as Zeus whispers a word in her ear. Hera looks away as the vision fades.

Each of them dreaming of winning.

Each of them dreaming of what winning this contest — then the next struggle, and the next conflict, in the fight that has been going on and will go on for all eternity — might bring them.

The silence is so deep that Iris can almost hear the storm clouds in faraway Colchis receding, the thunder rumbling itself into nothing, the air clearing as the sun's light penetrates the mists and reflects from the flooding plains. Hera's plan is working. Poseidon is entirely engrossed, his eyes fixed upon the shining outlines of the letters upon the apple's flesh.

'The first god to fell both of his—'

'Or her,' interrupts Hera.

'Or her opponents,' Iris bows to Hera, 'wins the apple.'

She moves down the mountain slope a little to a level plateau that stretches out in a scree-covered basin below the peak. As the three gods take their positions for the contest over the plateau, Iris moves to seat herself upon a jutting crag with a full view of the battleground, acting as judge. She can sense Hermes behind her, still seated upon the peak, his arms and legs crossed.

'Choose your weapons, gods,' she says, and in spite of herself her heart starts to beat a little faster with excitement as she holds her rod high into the air.

It is a marvel to watch, even for Iris, goddess of the rainbow, who has seen the gods shape the elements to their whims so many times before. The air above Zeus, god of thunder, is thickening, growing dark, as if a cloud has opened above him, and flashes spark above his head as lightning crystallizes and forms itself in the god's outstretched hands. Hera's robes are rustling in a wind that has whipped up around her, blowing the locks of her hair, the loose stones of the slope swirling in snake-like circles around her figure. Poseidon is holding his cupped hands before him, and in them water is swelling, rising, surging, forming itself into a roiling sphere of blue, growing larger with every moment . . .

'Fight!' Iris calls, bringing her rod down to her side with a swish of gold.

It is Hera who attacks first. Pursing her lips she blows, and the wind whistles from her in a fierce gale and blasts into the sphere of water in Poseidon's hands, sending it crashing over its maker in a wave of flashing droplets. Poseidon stumbles, water spilling out of his palms, and Zeus seizes the advantage to send a thunderbolt sparking across the battleground towards Hera. She parries it with a swirl of wind that sends it arrowing towards Poseidon, who deflects it with a wall of water that quenches its flames with a hiss of steam . . .

Iris watches with fascination as Poseidon rolls his palms around the water, *letting it grow larger and larger until it curls over on itself into an enormous, swirling ball. Then, with a single swipe of his hands, he sends it rolling towards Zeus. The father of the gods tries to reach for another bolt but, before he can hurl it towards his assailant, the water has engulfed him, crashing over him, with Zeus held in the centre, like a fish flailing in the midst of a raging sea-storm. She feels Zeus concentrate on the thunderbolt in his hand, the current running through him with a powerful, vital force, crackling with blue light; watches as he brings the strength of the bolt into himself, then sends it rushing out through his skin. With an explosion of fire the water collapses outwards, wave upon wave crashing down over the plateau, and with a blast of wind from beneath, Hera lifts the waves up, up, up into the sky, then lets them drop, the force of a waterfall breaking over the two gods, soaking their robes. She moves forwards, gales howling about her figure, and Poseidon and Zeus can barely move for the force of the hurricane that is driving them backwards, their beards flying out behind them . . .*

With the effort of a Titan, Zeus fights the wind to crouch to the ground and, his shoulder muscles taut with exertion, hurls a thunderbolt through the gale to strike at Hera's ankles. The flaming bolt catches her robes and, with a roar of bright orange fire, they are set alight. Hera's figure is a pillar of flame, sending burning black smoke up into the sky, and she is shrieking to Poseidon for water, but the two gods are fighting each other with vindictive fury, Zeus sending a thunderbolt crackling in a wave of white light, Poseidon summoning his waters into a wall that slams into Zeus' chest and sends him stumbling backwards. Through the column of flame that surrounds her, Hera whirls the winds to her and summons the waters, wave breaking over wave, until they crash down upon her and the fires are extinguished in a column of spiralling grey-blue smoke.

The battle rages until the sun has risen fully out of the sea to the east and is burning into a sapphire-blue sky, heating the rocks of Mount Olympus and warming the air so that eagles glide by the gods, wings outstretched, and still Zeus is hurling balls of fire at his adversaries, Poseidon is shaping water into darts that arrow through the fireballs, and Hera is blowing wind that blasts water into tiny slivers flying through the air, and none of them has fallen . . .

At last Iris holds up her rod.

The three gods are panting, chests heaving with effort. This could go on for all eternity – in truth, Iris thinks, it already has, for these three have been fighting each other ever since they were first created.

'A draw!' Iris calls.

She holds the apple up to the skies, its pale gold skin shimmering in the morning sun, and takes a deep breath.

'For the Winner!' she calls, and then, with all the strength she can muster, she tosses the apple up, up, up into the air, as if towards the gods who have battled for the trophy. The three gods and Hermes turn their faces towards it – she sees them stretch their arms high as the apple curves on its arc – but it hurtles past their outstretched fingertips, tumbling through the sky, out through the clear, sharp air, over the slopes of the mountain and the sparkling jewel-bright sea towards the mass of land towards the east, down, down through the treetops and into the very depths of the forest where the gods will never be able to find it . . .

'What did you do that for?' Zeus explodes at Iris, turning an irate, bedraggled, sweat-covered face towards her.

'Sorry,' she says, her expression guileless. 'Missed.'

And yet, while Iris deals with the angry rebukes of Zeus, Poseidon and Hermes, and Hera secretly congratulates herself on having distracted the sea god from his vengeance upon Jason, the queen of the gods would not be amused to know that Apollo is, at that very moment, on his way to earth on Poseidon's orders.

That Poseidon has seen through her scheme and has already taken measures to ensure he can have his revenge on Jason while Hera's back is turned. While she thinks she is tricking him, he is, in fact, planning to do to Jason the very worst he can imagine, aside from sinking his ship in a storm.

He is going to steal the Fleece.

Apollo's journey to earth is uneventful. He's a little sleepy, as it is earlier than he usually likes to wake up, but Poseidon promised him several seanymphs in return for what he's doing now, so he is bearing it with as good a grace as a child bribed to attend his lessons.

Not much, in other words.

He lands upon the Argo light as a seabird skimming over the waves and looks around him. The ship has made its way out of the storms that have plagued it since it left Colchis and is floating upon the now-calm, pink-tinged *sea, rather the worse for wear. He takes an inventory of the damage: torn sail, several wounded sailors, countless sacks of grain split open or sodden and ruined, a broken prow, a shattered steering oar and at least five oars split . . . That will take quite some time to repair.*

He tries to commit the details to memory, and grins as he surveys the extent of the destruction. Poseidon will like to hear how much damage his storm has wreaked on Jason's ship.

The mortals have laid anchor – they clearly did so as soon as the winds abated – and are draped over their rowing benches and the ship's edge, fast asleep after an exhausting night battling the storm. He spots Jason, slumped forwards, his head on his hands, beside a slim, black-haired woman, who is lying on her back alongside him and has rather lovely—

Focus, he tells himself. Focus. Get the Fleece.

Remember the nymphs.

It is not hard to find, for mortals always mark their most treasured possessions by hiding them away; and sure enough, a blast of wind from Apollo's pursed lips is enough to blow open the locked storage. He steps over the prone figure of Peleus, passes Meleager, then stoops to look into the dark hold beneath the stern deck. A leather sack is hidden there, tied tight with two thongs that unravel as he gazes upon them. The bag falls open. Apollo draws it closer and peers inside.

A shimmering golden cloth is folded carefully within, woven from ten thousand golden threads, the early-morning light sparkling on its glimmering surface. Apollo recognizes it at once, with a jolt of surprise.

It is a shawl.

Aphrodite's shawl.

Hadn't she dropped it, a while ago, when she and Ares were getting it on in the Caucasus Mountains? Yes, he thinks, leaning closer – he even remembers Ares telling him it happened. Hadn't she snagged it on the peak of Mount Elbrus, and hadn't Ares, hot with passion and keen on doing the deed, tossed it away, saying she was too desirable to wear clothes?

He chuckles to himself.

Only the mortals, he thinks, could turn the abandoned raiment of a divine hussy into an immortal manifestation of the king of the gods.

He reaches in and runs the material over his hands, the threads, no doubt woven by those consummate spinners, the Fates, shimmering through his fingers like liquid gold. At least Aphrodite will be glad to have it back.

He strokes the material, fine as a woman's hair.

Maybe she'll even confer a favour in repayment for the return of her shawl . . .

A slow grin broadens on his face.

Three nymphs promised to him, Aphrodite too, he thinks, and the sun hasn't even risen over the horizon.

He is so busy imagining the compensation Aphrodite might provide as he backs out of the hold that, as he straightens and turns, he catches the corner of the shawl upon the bolt of the door. He pulls it free, fumbles and takes a few steps to the side, trying to avoid the sleeping figure of Meleager. As he does so the shawl, slippery as silk, glides through his fingers and over the side of the ship.

It floats down through the air, light as a spider's web.

With a faint 'plop', it settles on the surface of the sea, and slowly, ever so slowly, the threads discolouring in the water, it is submerged. And then it is gone.

Apollo looks at the place where the gold shawl disappeared, watching the rings upon the water growing smaller.

Then he shrugs his shoulders. 'Oh, well,' he says. 'He wanted it gone, didn't he?'

And, unaware of the enormous significance of what he has done, he turns and, leaving the crew of the Argo *still sleeping, makes his way across the calm surface of the sea back towards Olympus.*

Before Greece

The River Phasis

The Hour of the Rising Sun
The Thirteenth Day of the Month of the Grape Harvest

Footsteps over the wet leaves beyond the cave awoke me shortly after dawn broke. My thoughts flew instantly to the riders from the day before, and I tried to push myself to stand, my fingers fumbling over the dirt and leaves of the cave floor for my quiver. My breathing was easier but my side was still swollen, a large bruise blossoming over the skin, and I forced myself to move, though the pain was making my eyes smart.

Then the footsteps grew louder, and Hippomenes appeared at the mouth of the cave, silhouetted in the pale pink light, his head bowed, a young deer slung over his shoulders.

'Where have you *been*?' I accosted him, my momentary terror at being left alone and wounded turning instantly to anger. I was angry, too, with myself that I should have cared whether he had left or not. He ducked to enter and flung the carcass down beside the ashes of last night's fire. I tried to move towards him, but he was too far from me and I could not go any further for the pain in my side. I collapsed upon the ground. 'I thought you had gone! I thought you had left!'

He shot a glance at me as he knelt beside the remnants of the fire and began to try to light the branches he had gathered from the forest. 'Would it have mattered if I had?'

I did not answer. 'Well, in any case,' I said, discountenanced, and I shifted to remove his cloak from beneath me and threw it to him, for he was bare-armed, 'you should have woken me to tell me.'

He shrugged the cloak off. 'I do not need it,' he said, and as he gestured to his woollen tunic I noticed for the first time another pouch that had not been there before, hanging from his belt beside his money bag, something round inside it creating a soft bulge against the leather. Hippomenes saw me looking at it, and covered it with one hand, pushing it around so that it was hidden, tucked beneath his sword. I opened my mouth to ask him about it, but he continued, as if nothing had happened: 'I am hardened to the cold after winters in Onchestos, cutting wood and tending the farmers' vines – and in any case, you have need of it, with your wound.' He passed the cloak back to me.

I hesitated, then took it from him and wrapped it around my shoulders.

The following day I was well enough recovered to ride – or, at least, so I said to Hippomenes, and in truth, though the bruise over my ribs was tinged with blue and green, the pain had lessened to a bearable degree. I insisted, despite his remonstrations, that we should depart immediately for Greece. Dedali's horse, though well mended in the hindquarters, was not yet fit enough to ride, so Hippomenes redressed the surface wound with fresh linen from my quiver before we left. I watched his hands, gentle and strong, upon the horse, listened as he whispered in its ear to comfort it. He turned and saw me staring. 'Are you ready?'

I started. 'I – yes.' I turned and bent to retrieve my quiver from where it leant against the cave wall, then swung it onto my back, trying not to grimace. Hippomenes picked up his sword, kicked at the ashes of the fire to disguise our presence in case anyone tried to follow us, then led out the two horses by the reins, their large eyes blinking in the morning sunlight now pouring down from a pale sky.

'The gods be thanked,' he said, looking up to the heavens. 'The rain has cleared at last.'

He held out his hand to halt me, and gazed around, shoulders tensed, as if listening for any sounds of riders, any sense that we were being watched; but after a few moments of silence, he nodded. We were alone.

I moved to Dedali's horse and stroked his soft nose. He snorted a little, then snuffled at the crook of my elbow.

'Thank you, my friend,' I said in a low voice into his ear. 'Return home safe to Myrtessa.'

He gave a low whinny and pawed at the ground, flicking his tail.

I stepped back.

'Very well,' I said, with a sigh. Hippomenes threw the rug Dedali had given me upon the horse's back, then slapped him on his uninjured hindquarter. He started at a trot, then began to canter, through the dappled light of the forest, tossing his mane a little, back towards the mountains of Suzona. I watched him go, thinking of the house upon the edge of the darkened woods, and Myrtessa, wondering what she was doing now.

'Here.' Hippomenes turned to me and placed his hands upon my waist.

I started, like a nervous colt. 'What do you think you're doing?'

His eyebrows rose. 'Do you think you can mount alone?'

I looked towards his bay horse, stamping the ground beside us, his withers just above the height of my shoulders.

'Yes, thank you,' I said, chin held high, picking up the horse's reins and leading him over to the moss-covered stump of a tree nearby. I scrambled onto it, one hand clutching my injured rib, and managed to push myself to stand. But as I placed my hands on the horse's withers and tried to leap up, I felt a searing, blistering pain in my side.

I winced, clutched at my chest, slipped and lost my balance.

'Steady.' Hippomenes was there in a moment, one large hand upon my back, the other at my hip, bracing me.

I held onto his shoulder, tears smarting in my eyes. 'I think, perhaps, after all . . .'

He smiled a little as he lifted me, as easily and swiftly as he had done before, and placed me upon the horse, then vaulted up behind me. The mysterious pouch he had picked up in the forest pressed against my hip, and as he slid it quickly behind his belt I wondered once more what was inside it.

'To Greece, then?' he asked, reaching around me so that I felt the warmth of his chest against my back, and flicking the reins to bring his steed around. There was something comforting about his steady strength. Perhaps, I thought, it was that he, too, had grown up on the land as I had, on the Boeotian plains.

I smiled a little and nodded, gathering his cloak around me. 'Yes,' I said. 'To Greece.'

Over the next weeks we passed through many settlements as we rode towards the west: fortressed cities set upon windy hilltops, villages nestling in wooded bays, and market towns upon the plain, where we were able to mix with traders and purchase new clothes – a wool cloak and new boots for me, a tunic for Hippomenes – and fresh horses for us both, once I was able to ride alone. My shoulder was almost fully healed with a clean silver scar, and though there was still a bruise across my ribs I could breathe without pain. Hippomenes would not call me Telamon – 'Since I know the truth I can hardly pretend otherwise with good conscience,' he had said – and as I refused to pretend to be his slave, we had agreed after much argument to be a voyaging merchant and his wife. How else could we explain to the Greek traders we met upon our journey that I, a freeborn woman, was travelling alone with a man to whom she was not married? Although I acknowledged that this guise had its merits, I baulked particularly at having to hand my quiver to Hippomenes at every settlement we passed. He had argued that a true merchant's wife would never be seen carrying a bow, let alone using it – and I, recognizing the truth of this, had at last, though with an ill grace, given way.

The country became less mountainous as we rode further west, rolling into grass-covered plains dotted with olive trees and watered by broad shallow rivers. Hippomenes did not ask why I pressed on towards Greece with such haste, and I did not tell him – neither about the Fleece, nor that I was racing towards Pelion to challenge Jason before he reached the palace – so we rode in companionable silence through lands inhabited by farmers who worked the black earth for barley and emmer wheat. They were a peaceful people, whose fields bordered with the warlike Hittites to the south. As we neared the Bosphorus, we began to meet more of the Kaskaean merchants who sailed the ocean in galleys, trading with Troy and the cities of the Anatolian coast. Many spoke Greek, and we ate and slept in their homes, laughing with them as we told tales of our adventures, exchanging horses at the traders' stables and moving on.

That evening we stopped in Kromna, a small town set back from the sea just down the coast from Kytoros. We were making good time – it was twenty-three days since we had left the shores of Colchis. Dedali's house, the valley of the Fleece and the armed bandits felt so long ago, almost as if they had never happened. We arrived at dusk, our horses' hoofs kicking up dust as we approached the gathering of mud-brick dwellings. A few fishermen were returning home for the night, sacks filled with shellfish, mullet and sturgeon slung over their backs, and when we signalled to them and they heard our language, they pointed us towards a hut on the outskirts of the settlement.

The trader, Illa, who lived there with his wife, sister and five children, welcomed us in fluent Greek as we offered our coins and gave our story. Hippomenes was a merchant, Daikrates, and I his young wife Galatia; we had been turned out of our homes in Sparta by raiders from the Taygetus Mountains and were now travelling the coast of Anatolia to persuade our former partners in trade to support us in recovering our estate. Illa was a native Kaskaean who, it turned out, conducted frequent business with the wine merchants from Lesbos; he accepted us without question, apologizing for the inadequacy of his home and its lack of stables. We tethered our horses instead to posts in the meadow behind, where they joined a flock of grazing goats and sheep. The hut was dark and stiflingly warm as we entered, with few windows. Chattering children were playing on the packed-earth floor while two women worked at clattering looms in the corner.

'In here.' Illa gestured us to a chamber at the back of the hut, divided from the main room by an ill-fitting wooden door. It was tiny, with one pallet bed laid upon the floor covered with a thin blanket, a single chair and a plain clay bathtub filling the rest of the space. A single window in the wall opened over the meadows behind, a welcoming breeze blowing in and lifting the hair on the back of my neck, cooling my hot skin. 'We normally sleep here, Mala and I, but,' he held up his hands, ignoring our protests, 'it is yours for the night. You are young and newly married, and,' he winked, 'it's clear enough you both have other things on your mind than sleeping.' He grinned and pointed his thumb to the door. 'Mala and I can sleep out there with the children.'

I glanced at Hippomenes, the memory of his urgent, passionate kiss in the forests of Colchis flooding my mind, his lips pressing hard into mine, his hands pulling me to him . . . Hippomenes was flushing around the neck, his ears reddening, avoiding my eye. I stammered our thanks, and Illa left, bowing himself out of the room.

'Oh, and another thing,' Illa said, pushing the door open and poking his head in. 'We don't have slaves, not being a family of means, but I'll set my sister to heating up some water over the fire for you to bathe.' With that, he closed the door.

Illa's sister, Sarpa, found us sitting in silence when she knocked and entered, holding a cauldron filled with hot water by a sturdy wooden handle. She was a plump, round woman without much Greek, but she smiled as she poured the steaming water into the tub, returning two or three times until the bath was full, then gestured to a pile of towels and stoppered clay jars filled with olive oil, which she had placed beside it upon the floor. We nodded our thanks, and she left us alone again.

'You should—'

We began together, and stopped, embarrassed.

'You should bathe first,' Hippomenes said at last, breaking the silence. He picked up the chair and turned it so that it faced the wall, then sat upon it, looking determinedly away. I grinned, wondering whether to protest at his foolish gallantry, but I was covered with sand, dust and dried mud from several days' riding, my hair matted with sweat and dirt, and the water, steaming in the homely clay tub, looked inviting.

I stood carefully and pulled off my boots, sighing as I felt the earth on my feet, then undid my belt, slipped out of my trousers and pulled my tunic over my head. The material rippled down to the floor, and then I was standing naked behind Hippomenes, his eyes still fixed upon the plain mud-brick wall, feet planted slightly apart upon the floor. It felt odd to be so close to him, only a few paces away, and so vulnerable, trusting him not to ill-treat me as I had thought, after Meleager, never to trust a man again. I drew my arms protectively across myself, though I knew he could not see me, then walked towards the tub and lowered myself with a soft sigh into the water.

Once I had washed, oiled, dried and dressed myself again, I touched Hippomenes gently on the arm. 'You can turn around now.'

His shoulders relaxed. 'Thank the gods,' was all he said, and he stood. Without waiting for me to leave, he untied the fastenings of his tunic. I bent to pick up a flask of oil for him, and when I straightened and turned I found him directly before me, not an arm's length between us, his tunic unfastened to his waist.

My eyes were drawn to him, irresistibly, like a crab drawn into the deep sea by the tide. His shoulders were ridged with muscle, the skin of his broad torso a light olive colour, paler than his tanned arms, and soft curls of brown hair covered the tight muscles on his chest and belly; the heavy-set, work-honed body of a farmer and a warrior, not the slim athletic figure of a noble.

I bit my lip and looked down, trying not to inhale the scent of him – that heady mixture of horse, leather and sweat.

'Your – your oil,' I said, and pressed the flask into his hands, feeling his gaze bearing down on me, his chin so close to the top of my head that we were almost touching. I held his stare for a moment, and felt my heart beat faster, in spite of myself.

Then I turned and fled out of the chamber.

Hippomenes found me later, seated in the meadow behind the hut with the horses, which were cropping the long grass, my arms clasped around my knees. I tried not to look at him as he settled beside me, one leg outstretched, his long damp hair framing his broad cheekbones and jaw. I became suddenly very aware of the pulse at my throat and the dryness of my lips.

Remember why you are here, I told myself firmly.

You let down your guard once with Meleager, and see how much good it did you.

I plucked a stem of grass and peeled it between my fingers.

It is the Fleece you are pursuing, nothing else.

I looked at the nearby stream, which trickled through the meadow, trying to distract myself. The water was leaping lightly over rocks, and swifts skittered overhead, catching insects on the summer air. If I had not known better, I should have thought we were already in Greece, for there was a warm familiarity about the olive trees scattered over the field, the rocky outcrops of the hills in the distance and the line of the sea upon the horizon, shimmering gold in the setting sun. Even the clanking of goat bells and the scent of the sea salt mixed with thyme upon the warm air felt like a summons from my home. My stomach flipped. *Pray the gods I will be in time to get there before Jason . . .*

Hippomenes shifted beside me and stood slowly, rubbing the small of his back, then stretching his arms to the sky, deepening from yellow to a pale turquoise.

'I have been too long on horseback these past days,' he said. 'I am growing stiff as an old man.' He glanced around him. 'Would you care to race? Say, from here to that young oak? I would give anything to stretch my legs after all the riding we have done.'

I let out a laugh. 'You wish to race me?'

'Why not?'

I plucked another grass stem and squinted up at him, smiling into the evening sunlight. 'Because you will not win.'

Now it was his turn to laugh. I raised my hands in indignation, and he subsided into a chuckle. 'I am sorry, Atalanta,' he said, still grinning, 'but you know that that cannot be true. I am a head taller than you and stronger by far.'

I frowned. A part of me did not want to rise to the provocation, but another part – the part that, I supposed, had sent me sailing across the world in the guise of a man – was determined to show Hippomenes that he was wrong.

I placed my hands on the grass beside me and pushed myself to stand. 'Very well, then,' I said, and I bent down to loosen the ties on first one, then the other of my boots, shaking them off so that I could feel the soft meadow beneath the soles of my feet. I straightened to look up at him, raising my eyebrows and cocking my head with a smile. 'If you wish to lose, it is no care of mine.'

We drew the finish line between two young oaks, around two hundred paces distant. The winner was to pass between the trees before the other. I bent down to the grass, kneeling, my fingertips pressing into the earth, my toes curling into the warm blades beneath me, every muscle tensed, my eyes fixed ahead upon the trunk of one of the oaks, its leaves waving slightly in the breeze. The sun's rays slanted down over the field, turning everything a deep, pinkish gold, and somewhere above, in the deep blue heavens, a swallow sang and the nearby river gushed over the stones.

'Now!' Hippomenes shouted.

I leapt forwards.

The air flew past me. Like one of my arrows, I felt myself fly, straight and true. The ground seemed hardly to touch my feet, and I could feel a strength in me I had never felt before, new-found after days spent pulling at the oar and sweating beneath the heat of the sun: a hardiness, a suppleness to my muscles that added strength to my speed. I felt alive, more alive than I had for a long time, and behind me Hippomenes was pounding the earth while I flew ahead. This was effortless – this was where I was meant to be: to feel my bare feet upon the grass and the beating of my heart. My tunic was clinging to my skin as I ran, the air deliciously cool upon my face. For a moment I closed my eyes, and when I opened them, the hills on the horizon were nearing, the green-grey leaves of the trees so close I could almost hear them rustling in the wind . . .

And then I was past them, my hair flying out behind me, turning to watch Hippomenes hurtle in, red-faced and panting, several paces behind.

I grinned as he bent over to rest his hands on his knees and catch his breath.

'Another?'

Later that night, as the pale circle of Artemis' moon rose through the window in Illa's chamber, Hippomenes and I were lying to rest – I, at Hippomenes' insistence, alone upon the pallet bed, and he on the earth floor beside me, his cloak spread beneath him. Illa, Mala, Sarpa and the children were already asleep, their muffled snores and grunts just audible from the room beyond. The single window in the back wall let a slant of moonlight down into the tiny room, casting the rickety wooden chair and clay tub into relief and lining the profile of Hippomenes' face with silver. The scent of olive oil from our bath was still upon the air, mixed with the tang of evening dew from the meadow beyond, and I shifted a little upon the prickly straw of my pallet bed, trying to get comfortable.

Hippomenes was lying upon his back, his hands folded behind his head. 'Atalanta?' he said softly.

'Hmm?'

'I have been thinking – I have been riding with you for weeks now and yet I know nothing about you.'

I sat up and patted the straw down beneath my back, trying to smooth it. 'You know my name.'

He chuckled. 'Gods be praised, I know your name.' He sat up and turned towards me, propping his head upon his hand. 'I was thinking of other things besides – your parents, say. Where you come from. How,' he grinned, 'you happened to be hunting with us upon Mount Pelion, disguised as a Cretan nobleman.'

I bit my lip.

'You can tell me the name of your father, at least?' he pressed me.

I let out a breath. *That is the one thing I cannot tell you.* 'I – I cannot tell you all,' I said.

He shrugged in the darkness. 'Then say what you can.'

I wondered how much to tell him; whether I should tell him anything at all.

'You have nothing to fear from me,' Hippomenes said gently into the silence.

Slowly, I lay down, looking up at the darkened wooden beams of the ceiling so as to avoid the sense that he was watching me. 'What is it you would know?' I asked.

'Tell me where you come from.'

An owl hooted softly outside the window, somewhere across the meadows.

I took a breath. 'I come from Pagasae,' I said, my voice halting. 'I – I am a mainlander. Not a Cretan.'

I heard his cloak stir beside me as Hippomenes nodded. 'And your family?'

I swallowed. I had never told anyone this, except Myrtessa. And yet . . .

And yet I sensed that I could trust him.

'My father abandoned me when I was born.'

Hippomenes became very still.

'I was the firstborn of two children,' I went on, the words coming more easily now that I had begun and – though I did not know why – I did not want to stop them. 'The second was a boy. My father, a nobleman by the name of . . .' I searched for a name '. . . Tegeas, had no use for a girl, for he needed a firstborn son, an heir who could oversee his estates. And so he . . .' I swallowed, my throat tight '. . . he gave me up.' Silent tears were running down my cheeks, and I let them fall unheeded upon the straw. 'He abandoned me upon the peak of Mount Pelion in the depths of winter, wrapped only in a swaddling cloth, and left me there to die.'

The chirping of the cicadas in the olive trees outside the window filled the silence that followed.

I raised the back of my hand to wipe the tears from my face. 'I was found by a woodcutter who dwelt in Kaladrosos, on the slopes of Pelion,' I continued, my voice unsteady, hardly knowing if Hippomenes was still listening, yet I wanted to go on. Indeed, though it was painful, it was almost a relief to tell someone after so long. 'He brought me up with his family, never told me who I was, how he had rescued me from my fate. He taught me how to use a bow, and I learnt to hunt, to run upon the mountain slopes.' The corners of my mouth lifted a little, and I let the sunlit memories pass before my eyes.

'But then my father told me I was not his, that I had been found upon the mountain with the symbol of Tegeas woven upon my swaddling cloth,' I moved my hand unconsciously to the cord of the medallion at my neck, felt the metal against my fingertips, 'and I journeyed to Pagasae to find my family. When I discovered . . .' The corners of my eyes were stinging once more: I took a deep breath and collected myself. 'When I discovered from Tegeas' slaves that he had cast his daughter out upon the mountain, that he had purposefully, cruelly consigned me to death for the crime of being a woman, I realized the truth. That I had never been wanted. That I had been left to die by my own father, simply for who I was.'

Hippomenes stirred beside me, as if he would say something, but I continued, ignoring him, the words pressing tightly against my chest as if they had to be spoken.

'And so when I heard of Jason's journey for the Fleece, I determined that I would accompany him too – as a noble. As an equal. I was determined that I would return to my city, to my father, and show him that I was worthy to be his heir, though he had thought I was not. I was determined I would prove myself the equal of a man, so that he would know what he lost when he cast me out because I was a girl.'

I turned to the dark outline of Hippomenes, lying upon the floor beside me. His eyes shone in the moonlight and I felt a strange sensation of warmth, of something like safety, in the pit of my belly as his gaze met mine. 'Do you understand now?' I asked.

He was silent for a long time. Then, at last, he said, 'I did not know.'

'I did not tell you.'

'I would not have—'

'You need not apologize. It is done and, as you say, you did not know. Most of the women I have met, all they do is spin and sleep and take care of their husband's children. You could not have known I would be so—'

'Different.' He finished the sentence for me with a laugh. 'No, that I could not.'

Silence fell again between us, so long that I thought Hippomenes must have fallen asleep. I settled down upon the bed, pulling the fleece over myself against the faint breeze blowing in through the window, listening to the snuffling of the horses outside and the humming of the cicadas. I felt my eyes grow heavy with sleep after the long day's ride, the bath, the bread and stew we had shared earlier with Illa and his family. I heard Hippomenes stir on the floor beside me.

'Atalanta?'

I shifted onto my side to look at him, his eyes reflecting the dim light of the moon slanting through the slatted window. 'Yes?'

'Do not misunderstand this.'

'Very well.'

'Whoever left you to die on that mountain was a fool.'

I turned onto my back and smiled up into the darkness of the hut. 'My thanks to you for that, son of Megareus,' I said. I brought the blanket up over my shoulders and closed my eyes, still smiling, to sleep.

PART IV

GREECE

1260 BC

For you rule over a wide, broad plain,
upon which clover thickly grows, rushes,
wheat and rye and pale broad-eared barley . . .

Homer

Farewells and Greetings

Pagasae

The Hour of the Middle of the Day
The Thirtieth Day of the Month of Ploughing

We rode another four weeks from Kromna, stopping only to change horses, find food and sleep at night. Summer turned gradually to autumn and the breezes grew cooler, the evening light slanting gold over the plains, and the rows of grapevines hanging heavy with black fruit. We passed over the rolling hills of Anatolia and forded the narrow neck of the Bosphorus, where the torches of Lygos blazed upon the shores of the Propontis and the water lapped softly against the hulls of the trading ships. As we entered the valleys edged by the vast dark mountains of Thrace, I could feel my fear rising, steady as the waves upon the sea, that Jason might have reached Pagasae before me . . .

That he might already have given the Fleece to the king . . .

That fear spurred me on so that we left our horses at each trading post, flanks gleaming with sweat, legs encrusted with mud, only to leap onto our new mounts and fly again across the grassy plains, scorched yellow after the heat of the summer, scattered with olive trees and wild thyme and sage that sent their woody fragrance into the air.

We approached the bay of Pagasae from the north towards the very end of the Month of Ploughing, skirting along the flanks of Mount Olympus and down through the valley edged by Ossa to the south, past the city of Meliboea and then across the flat plain towards Iolcos and Pagasae. Tears sprang to my eyes as, with a painful rush of joy, I saw the achingly familiar outline of Mount Pelion rising ahead, shrouded in

281

mist and carpeted in verdant green, the promontory curving round to protect the sea, the still waters of the bay of Pagasae shimmering upon the horizon. *Kaladrosos lies just behind there, just over the ridge of the mountain* . . . A day's ride away, perhaps, my family were going about their everyday tasks, chopping wood, feeding the goat, not knowing I was here . . . My heart beat hard in anticipation as I galloped side by side with Hippomenes across the grass-covered plains, following the course of the dried-up river, my hair flying behind me in the wind, the midday sun beating down upon my head and making my temples throb, and all I could think was: *Am I in time?*

Am I in time to intercept Jason before he finds the king, and takes the rule of Pagasae?

At last, when we reached the stretch of plain below the city, I brought my horse to a trot, then drew him up, Hippomenes beside me. We stood beneath the shade of a pine tree, gazing up at the fortified walls of the city and the distant figures of the guards striding along the ramparts, just as I had seen them so many months before. Goats wandered around us, their bells clanking softly in the afternoon heat, and rows of cultivated vines heavy with grapes spread before us, like the waves of the wine-dark sea.

'This is where I leave you.'

I found I could not look at Hippomenes as I spoke, and let my gaze instead follow one of the goats as it wandered over the rocks, glad for a distraction. After so many weeks together upon the Anatolian tracks, eating together, laughing and sharing our stories, racing each other on the dusty roads and making up tales about our merchant disguise, I was exerting all my strength against begging him to stay.

But I have to. I have to do this alone.

He was silent for a moment. 'What will you do?' he asked at last, and the coolness in his voice made me long to grasp his hand and tell him to come with me, but I could not allow myself to do so.

Remember, Atalanta, I said to myself. *Remember what happened last time you tried to confide in a man.*

What you owe to Myrtessa – to your family – is worth more than that.

And, in any case, he probably does not care for you at all.

I brushed the hair out of my eyes and gazed over the sea lapping against the harbour, willing my voice not to waver, to sound offhand. 'Go to the house of Tegeas, I suppose,' I said. 'Give him these,' I pointed to a pouch at my side, which contained a set of Anatolian hunting knives I had been given as a guest-gift by a wealthy merchant with whom we had stayed, 'and hope that he accepts me, that I have proved to him my worth.' I turned to him in spite of myself. 'And you?'

My stomach lurched at the clear, hard look he was giving me, the set line of his jaw, all gentleness and humour gone. 'I shall ride back to Boeotia,' he said, and as he spoke his horse moved slightly and pawed at the dust, as if he was already in a hurry to be gone. 'It is only a few days' journey, and I have been gone long enough – my father will be wanting me.'

'You – you will not stay to see Jason return?'

He shook his head. 'I owe him nothing. I did not join the expedition for him.' He glanced towards me, and his expression softened, though still he did not smile. 'Will you be safe, by yourself?'

I almost smiled, as the bittersweet memory of the words he had spoken at the pass in Colchis, all those many weeks ago, rose up in my mind. I bent to pat my horse's neck to avoid looking at him. *How different it would all have been, if I had not let him come.* It shook its head to rid itself of the flies that buzzed in the warm air. 'You need not worry for me, Hippomenes. I can take care of myself. And I work better alone.'

'That much I know.'

Silence fell between us as my eyes rested on the bay, the sun's light reflected on the waters of the Pagasean harbour where I could see several fishing boats drawn up – though no sign of the *Argo*.

Because they have not yet arrived?

Or because they have left Jason in Pagasae and moored elsewhere?

A cry made me look up: a lone falcon was soaring overhead, its wings stretched to catch the breeze. I shivered as a chill wind blew past me, presaging the approach of winter – or perhaps a sense of what lay ahead.

'I must leave,' I said at last, as much to myself as to him, looping the horse's reins around my hands. I knew the time had come for me to go, yet I did not want to say farewell to Hippomenes, to know that I would never see him again. *But if I delay I risk everything.* 'You have several days' journey to Boeotia. You should ride on to make distance before nightfall.'

He bowed his head. 'Atalanta—'

'I bid you farewell,' I said, my voice a little harsher than I had intended. I could not allow myself to hear him in case my self-control broke. 'And I wish you a safe journey back to your own city.'

He reached out, then, and clasped my hand briefly. I felt the warmth of his fingers enclosing my own. I looked up, and our eyes met. Heat spread through my body under his gaze, caressing my chest and making every part of my skin tingle, as if I were standing bare-skinned beneath the sun in full summer. With an effort that took all my will, I pulled my hand from his and flicked the reins, avoiding his eye. 'Travel well, son of Megareus,' I said, and, kicking my heels into my horse's flanks, cantered away down the slope of the hill towards the harbour.

I turned then – I could not help it – to look over my shoulder. Hippomenes sat there, motionless, his cloak across one shoulder, the sunlight picking out the golden threads in his hair and glinting off the handle of the sword at his waist. 'May the gods be with you, Hippomenes,' I whispered, my voice catching in my throat.

And then I turned back towards the city and galloped down the hill, furiously brushing the tears from my eyes, and thinking: *I will never see him again.*

I rode as hard as I could towards the harbour, forcing my thoughts to focus upon the only thing that mattered now, the only thing that had to matter, after all those months' voyaging upon land and sea to the ends of the earth and back.

The Golden Fleece, and rescuing my family from Jason's tyranny.

I galloped across the plain, my horse's hoofs kicking up dark clods of earth, and as the walls of the town grew larger on the hill above me and I could begin to make out the figures of townspeople streaming up the track through the gates and oxen pulling carts, the memory of my conversation with Myrtessa in Kytoros suddenly rose, unbidden, in my mind. Her voice was clear in my memory, laughing: *It truly was a day blessed by Zeus when you broke through the gates of Pagasae, Atalanta . . . We shall recover Pagasae from Jason and free Neda and Philoetius, Hora, Opis and your family, from his rule!*

As I raced beneath the high walls of the city, the memories crowded into my mind: how Myrtessa and I had walked the ramparts, popping honeyed apricots into our mouths; the nights spent in the taverns, talking with Sagaris and his son the carpenter; the crowded kitchens of Corythus' house, where Philoetius, Neda and Hora were working even now. I frowned, pressed my lips together and spurred my mount on faster.

I would not let Jason rule as a tyrant over all of this.

I approached the harbour at a full gallop, kicking up dust along the path and showering a pair of traders, who were seated nearby sharing some bread and a jug of wine. The road was quiet, with only a few merchants carrying their wares up and down from the ships. The bustle and clamour of the town drifted faintly towards me on the breeze from the hill above. I leapt from my horse onto the dry grass, tied him to one of the olive trees, then ran, the wind whipping through my hair, down the rocks that sloped towards the bay. My heart was hammering against my ribs in anticipation as I scanned the sweeping shore from headland to headland, past the pier and out to the swelling silver-blue sea, searching, searching for the gilded eagle at the prow of the *Argo* and the spreading white sail . . .

But it was as I had seen from upon the plain: only a couple of fishing boats and a trading ship floating low on the water, weighed down with goods.

I raced across the shore, the soles of my boots pressing against the pebbles, towards a group of fishermen taking their midday meal around a couple of wooden crates draped with netting. Seagulls dipped and cawed overhead, searching for crumbs, and I pushed my hair back from my face as I approached. The men turned to stare at me, taking in my strange Anatolian dress, and I lifted my chin a little higher: I would not let them think they could discomfit me.

One, with weather-beaten skin and a knobbly nose, like the withies of an olive tree, considered me for a moment longer, then spat onto the stones at my feet. 'What do you want?'

'The *Argo*,' I said. 'Has it come yet? Have you seen it?'

The fisherman took a swig from a clay jar. 'And who wants to know?'

'A – a slave of Jason's,' I said, pressing my right wrist close to my side and sending a prayer up to the gods that they did not see I had no slave's brand.

His eyes roved over the bow and quiver hanging from my back, Corythus' sword at my waist, and he raised his eyebrows.

'These belong to Jason,' I explained quickly. 'I brought them for him. I wanted to know if he has yet returned.'

The three men's expressions took on a look of interest. 'One of Jason's girls, eh?' said a younger man, his dark hair crusted with sea salt. He leered. 'A little flat of chest, but otherwise—'

'I am not here for your appraisal. I am here to learn of the *Argo*,' I said, and heard my voice take on a bite of impatience.

The older man shrugged. 'It's not here,' he said. 'I heard a couple of traders, come from Sithonia not too long ago, said the ship had stopped there – you spoke with them, did you not, Naios?'

Naios, a middle-aged man with a receding hairline and a pouch of a belly, nodded. 'Told me as they'd had a spot of trouble with a storm, up in the Hellespont by Troy. They were staying in Olynthos for repairs, the traders said – sold them a few ropes and such.'

'And when was this?' I asked, a little breathless.

Naios tore a chunk of bread from the loaf and bit into it. 'Oh, a few days ago, I'd say.'

My mind began to race. Olynthos was maybe thirty leagues from Pagasae. That meant, with fair winds and a calm sea, the *Argo* could be here in, perhaps, a couple of days . . . But how long had they stopped to mend the ship? 'My thanks to you,' I said, turning to leave.

'Join us, won't you?' the younger of the three called out to me, patting the pebbles beside him.

I shook my head, though my stomach growled. I would not risk even the promise of food for the chance that the men might discover who I was. 'I thank you, no,' I replied, over my shoulder, and, before they could say more, I ran away from the shore to where my horse stood tethered, to wait.

*

I hid in the boughs of an olive tree, masked by the leaves and the dappled shadows, my horse cropping the grass and flicking his ears to rid himself of the summer flies. The sun dipped down from its peak to set over the western mountains, and the stars flickered into being in the dark night sky. Day dawned again behind Mount Pelion in a burst of pink and gold, and still there was no sign of the *Argo*. I had nothing to eat except the fruit upon the trees, and little water to drink. My eyes were sore from straining out over the sea, my limbs stiff, the hard leather of my quiver pressing into my back, yet I could not sleep. My thoughts were treading the same path again and again, feverish, determined, preparing myself for the moment when the *Argo* came: *challenge Jason to a duel.*

Challenge him to a duel for the Fleece.

It was as twilight neared again, and I was draining the last few drops of water from my pouch, that I saw it out of the corner of my eye – a solitary speck of white – a sail, on the horizon . . .

I sat up so quickly that I dropped the pouch to the earth.

I had seen it.

The *Argo*.

I climbed higher, careful to keep my head hidden, squinting, my heart racing. It had to be the *Argo*. It had to be . . .

The sail was growing larger, the ship slowly coming into view as it approached the harbour. I almost laughed aloud as I spotted the golden wings of the eagle at the prow, gleaming in the evening sun. For a moment – one wild moment – I longed to jump down and run to the shore to greet it: to see Peleus again, and Lycon, Phorbas, Laertes, Argus, all of the men I had come to see as comrades-in-arms, friends, even.

But then I thought of Meleager, and of Jason, and my breathing steadied, my gaze focused.

Not all of them would welcome you.

The *Argo* was within the headlands of the harbour now; I could see the letters of her name upon the hull, the blades of the oars dipping in and out of the sea and swirling the water into a white froth. I checked the strap of the quiver over my shoulder and slipped to the ground, landing in silence on the dry grass beneath. I watched as the oars were drawn onto the deck of the ship, as the thrust of the last stroke carried the *Argo* forward, as she ploughed up onto the shore, prow first, keel cutting into the pebbles.

Figures began to leap down into the water and lay their shoulders to the stern, pushing the ship ashore, as we had so many times when we had taken her in to land for the night.

I took a deep breath.

Now is the moment.

There was a clatter as the yard was dropped from the mast and the sail furled. Slaves were calling and leaping down from the ship – some I recognized, others I did not. I could hear Jason shouting orders, his voice unmistakable even amid the noise: breastplates, shields and spears were being thrown onto the shore with a great clanking and clattering and cries of triumph from the men aboard. The traders and fishermen whose boats were tethered along the pier were gathering at the beach, welcoming the heroes home, offering them leather pouches from which I could see several figures drinking.

I wrapped my hand around the hilt of my sword, fingers shaking.

But just as I was preparing to step out from my hiding place, to run down and challenge Jason to a duel, I heard raised voices from the beach below, coming closer. I edged back under the canopy of the leaves, straining to hear, one hand still at my waist.

'. . . tell Iasus?' That was Laertes, I was sure of it.

'What do you expect I shall say?' Jason snarled back. 'That I lost the Fleece?'

Laertes was panting slightly as he spoke. 'But if you tell the king it was stolen – that you retrieved it, that it was taken from you – surely that would be enough.'

I did not hear Jason's retort. I stood, fixed to the spot, the dappled evening light filtering through the olive leaves shimmering on my skin, my back pressed against the knotted trunk.

He has lost the Fleece?

A shiver ran through me. I shook my head, unable to believe what I had just heard. And then the significance of Jason's words began to sink in.

He cannot fulfil the prophecy!

Heat was flooding through me now as the blood pulsed hard in my veins.

He cannot fulfil the prophecy, I thought again, repeating it over and over. *He cannot fulfil it.*

He will not become king.

The towns of Pelion are saved.

I could hear the indistinct sounds of Jason's muttered curses and accusations as he strode up the path to the city, not a hundred paces from where I stood. A branch moved in the breeze, and I caught sight of him, jaw set, hair flying behind him, striding along the track and pushing his way past the pedlars and hawkers who had gathered to see the *Argo*'s return. I pressed myself against the tree trunk, my spine digging into the bark, keeping my whole body perfectly, absolutely still, barely even breathing, as I watched the rest of the men and their slaves, arms filled with weapons, following Jason towards the city. As the last of the slaves – Melanthius, Nestor's steward – disappeared behind the trees, I let out a breath and closed my eyes, allowing, for the first time, a small sense of hope to suffuse me.

Now that Jason does not have the Fleece, we are equals once more.

My fingertips moved slowly to the medallion around my neck.

In fact, I thought, I might even have something that he did not.

I waited a while before following Jason and the lords back up to Pagasae: long enough to ensure I would not run into them, but not so long that entry to the city would be barred to me for the night. I untied my horse and left him grazing among the olive trees upon the shore, swung my cloak over my shoulders to cover the bow and arrows on my back, and slipped in through the gates with a couple of goose-girls bringing their flock back for the night. A tavern near the walls drew my eye, a discreet place with a small shuttered shopfront offering wine from a stone-built counter. I used the pouch with my mother's coins – almost entirely emptied now – to pay the innkeeper, a plump man with a shiny bald head that he wiped continually with a dirty cloth. He raised his eyebrows as I handed him the money for my room and board, small eyes squinting at my patterned tunic and trousers, the gleaming sword at my waist.

'And another coin,' I said, reaching to the bottom of the purse, 'for your silence.'

I climbed the ladder to the chambers above, a slave following with a platter of meat, bread and wine, and emerged into a narrow corridor. I pushed open the door of the nearest chamber and gestured the slave to place the food and wine upon the table beside the low pallet bed, then thanked him as he turned and left, closing the door behind him. I slung off my bow and quiver and lay down, arms resting behind my head, gazing up at the timbered ceiling. The evening sunlight poured through the open window behind me and turned the floating dust motes to specks of gold. The floor had been scattered with bay leaves, the scent of sweat and herbs mixing upon the air, and the noise from the kitchen below mingled with the chattering of birds.

I bit my lip, thinking. By now Jason would be at the palace. Yet what I truly needed was a change of clothes and a bath: I had not bathed properly for what seemed like weeks, and if I arrived at the palace smelling and looking like an Anatolian peasant, I would have little chance of convincing the king . . .

A knot of mixed fear and excitement twisted in my belly as I thought of what would happen the next day when I told them all, at last, before the whole court, who I was. It was likely – more likely than anything, I thought, remembering how Jason had sent me to exile from the shores of Colchis merely for being a woman – that, without the Fleece, without any proof of my worth except the medallion I wore, the king would throw me from the palace and force me to return to Kaladrosos. Yet I had heard Laertes suggest to Jason that the king might accept his claim. I could not risk King Iasus choosing to make Jason king of Pagasae, though neither he nor I had the Fleece . . .

I had not let myself think about what would happen if I did not win the Fleece. Indeed, the days with Hippomenes on our way from Colchis had been so filled with talk and laughter that I had thought less and less of what would happen upon our return as we rode . . .

At once, I pushed Hippomenes from my mind and forced myself to face the hard truth.

What if all this has been for nothing?

What if the king casts me off once more, and makes Jason king?

What then?

I frowned. *No,* I thought. *No. I have waited too long, risked too much, to give up now.*

All I can do is make the choice to try.

I picked up the bell that lay upon the table beside me and rang it, as if to set the seal upon my determination. A young slave appeared at the door, his face smut-stained. I stood and reached for my money-pouch. 'What is your name?'

He swallowed. 'Battus, my lady.'

'Battus,' I said, 'I need to bathe.' I passed him a coin. 'A pitcher of hot water, a wash basin and some oil will do. And a man's clothing – something fit for a noble lord, if you can find it.' Battus' eyes widened a little. I lifted the pouch and tipped half of what little I had left into my hand and held it out towards him, seeing his eyes widen even further as they fixed upon the glittering metal. 'And not a word to anyone – do you understand?'

The boy nodded, his eyes never leaving my hand.

'My thanks to you,' I said, and dropped the coins into his outstretched palms. 'I want you back within the hour if you are to earn the rest.'

Freshly washed and rubbed down with rosemary-scented oil, I felt more myself. I had cut my hair again to my shoulders and was dressed in a fine brown tunic embroidered with blue thread, a dark-blue cloak, a leather girdle and new sandals – the best my money could buy, Battus had assured me. Night had fallen in earnest by this time, and a clay oil-lamp was burning merrily on my table, casting leaping shadows over the wooden walls. Battus had brought back news from the marketplace that the king was planning to summon a council of the lords the following day to welcome Jason on his return.

'Will that be all?' he asked, at the door. I noticed his eyes lingering upon my tunic, the bow, quiver and sword lying on the floor, his face an unspoken question.

I nodded and bent to reach into my quiver, producing one of the Anatolian hunting knives from the journey. I passed it to him. He took it with both hands, staring at the bronze and the intricate scenes inlaid upon the blade. 'For your services to me this night. Who knows? It may even purchase you your freedom.' I smiled a little, thinking of Myrtessa. 'But remember,' I said, my tone suddenly serious, and I laid a hand upon his arm, 'not a word to anyone.'

He was turning the knife over and over in his hands. 'I – I – my thanks to you, my—' he stammered, then stopped in confusion, unsure what to call me.

'You may call me Atalanta,' I said, with a smile.

He grinned, then edged out of the door, holding the knife in both hands as if it were made of the finest ivory.

I lay back upon the pallet, listening to the creaking of the floorboards as he crossed the corridor, then the fading sound of his footsteps down the ladder to the level below. I blew out the lamp and stared up into the darkness, hearing the grunts and snores of the other inhabitants of the tavern. It was not until the birds were singing in the cypress trees behind the inn, and the walls of my chamber were coloured pale pink and gold with the light of the rising sun that, at last, I drifted into a dream-filled sleep.

Iris's Last Message

Mount Olympus

Day is breaking upon Earth, and to the east of Mount Olympus, Dawn is spreading her rosy fingers over the horizon, inching her pink-tinged visage into the sky. The view from the spacious arena of the gods' council upon the mountain top is spectacular. Beneath, the gentle hills and valleys of Olympus' slopes lead down towards the villages and towns of the mainland – Meliboea, Iolcos, Pagasae, Onchestos – still shrouded in darkness nestled upon their hilltops. In the distance, the sea, swathed in mist now, reflects the rays of the sun in a rainbow of colours. Above, the deep-blue arch of the sky is lit by the fading white curve of the moon and the fiery pinpoint of the Morning Star, while, closer to earth, the constellations of black swallows spiral in and out of the tips of Olympus' pines, tinged golden by the light of morning.

Iris makes her way light-footed from the Library of the Muses, her robes rippling behind her in hues of pale pink, green and blue, a papyrus scroll held loosely in her hand. The fountains of the many gardens of Olympus tinkle softly into the silence of dawn, and the dew on the grass beneath her feet is cool. She smiles a little, and walks on, quickening her pace.

As she reaches the council, with its empty ranks of thrones facing the gap in the clouds that opens to Earth, she spies Hera and Zeus sitting side by side upon their thrones as she knew they would be, leaning forwards, gazing down through the gap in the clouds towards the light-tinted ramparts of the city of Pagasae. They are waiting, she knows. They are waiting for the day to begin – waiting to see who has won this contest for the throne of Pagasae, so many months in the making: Hera's contender, the handsome prince of Iolcos, or Zeus' rival, the unwanted daughter of the king. Even as Iris sweeps into the council area and past the rows of vacant thrones placed in serried ranks upon the clouds, she sees, through the pool of clear blue sky ahead, the

295

crowning walls of the city of Pagasae, the columned outbuildings of the palace fringed with oaks, and the small dark tavern by the gates where Atalanta sleeps . . .

Iris gives a cough, and Zeus looks around. 'Ah,' he says, and rubs his hands. 'Daughter of Thaumas. Have you come to summon us to our breakfast?'

Iris grits her teeth at the insult and seats herself beside Zeus. 'I must talk with you,' she says, in a low voice.

Zeus notices the scroll of thick, woven papyrus clutched in her hand. 'A message for me?' he says, reaching out for it, but she snatches it away.

'For both of you,' she says. 'In fact, I had expected Poseidon to be here too . . . But perhaps it's better so.'

Hera barely moves; only the faint contraction of her eyebrows shows that she is listening.

Iris draws a deep breath. 'I went to the Library of the Muses last night,' she says, into the silence, broken only by the twittering of the swallows around the pines. 'To the Hall of the Fates. There was a matter – a riddle, in fact – I wanted to solve, and it turns out . . . well, it turns out I was right.' She pauses. 'But I also found something else – something I think will be of great interest to you both.' She holds out the papyrus and, in spite of themselves, Hera's and Zeus' eyes flick towards the scroll.

'I have long considered you mistaken in thinking Atalanta was your own,' she plunges on, addressing Zeus. 'And what I have found,' she brandishes the scroll, 'confirms my suspicions. Your assumptions were unfounded. Atalanta is a mortal.'

She turns to look Zeus directly in the eye. 'She is not your daughter.'

There is a long silence, broken only by the twittering of the birds and the faint sound of the breeze moving through the pine needles on the slopes below. Zeus' lips have parted in surprise behind his ringleted beard, his eyes widening as he ponders what she has said. Hera's eyebrows are knitted, her eyes darting from the scroll in Iris's hand to Zeus and back again.

'Not – not my daughter?'

'No,' Iris repeats, unrolling it to produce two scrolls of papyrus folded into each other, written in the neat copy of the Muses, and spreading them upon Zeus' lap. The first is titled, 'Atalanta, Daughter of Iasus,' the second, 'Lycon, Son of Zeus'.

'She's Iasus',' Iris says, pointing to the flowing script. 'Lycon, the boy, is yours.'

Zeus stretches out a hand to take the scrolls and bends down to examine them, but Hera is too quick for him. She snatches them from his hands and scans them quickly, then rolls them up and taps them against her knee in irritation. 'Why did you not come to me straight away?' she says. 'I am your mistress, Iris. You owe your loyalty to me!'

'I am a god, my lady, and I owe my loyalty to no one but myself,' Iris replies, in a steady voice. 'Yet, as you see, I did indeed come. You are the first to know. I have told none other.'

Zeus turns to Iris, ignoring his wife, who has opened her mouth to retort. 'Lycon?' he says, furrowing his brows. 'Who is this Lycon?'

'The prince and heir of Pagasae,' Iris replies. 'The king's son and Atalanta's twin, though born of a different father, and a poet at heart, not a warrior, though the king would wish him otherwise.'

'What – that foppish blond boy?' Zeus asks, pointing down to the palace, where Lycon is even now lying asleep upon his cushioned bed, one arm loosely flung over the edge of the frame.

Iris bows her head. 'The very one.'

'But he looks nothing like me!'

The words, so typically vain, so misguided, escape from Zeus' lips so fast that even he realizes their stupidity by the time they reach his ears. 'I mean to say,' he mumbles, 'I am the god of lightning, the patron of cities, destroyer of empires. I cannot have fathered a – a—' his tongue seems to labour over the words '— a poet,' he finishes, his face wrinkled in a perfect expression of distaste.

'And Atalanta's skills,' Hera adds, 'what of those? Her speed, her skill with the bow – no mortal can aim an arrow or run as fast as she does by pure skill alone. It is impossible, Iris. You must have made some mistake. Atalanta is as clearly the child of a god as Lycon is not.' Her tone is so final, the wave of her hand so regal, that Iris can tell Zeus is halfway to being convinced already.

'And yet it is the truth,' Iris says, forcing herself to be patient. 'By the very words of the Fates themselves, Atalanta is the daughter of a mortal. Her prowess with the bow, her swift-footedness – they are her own abilities, achieved by her own merit, her own labour.' She hears a faint note of pride in her voice and almost smiles as she turns to Zeus. 'I tell you, it is true. Lycon is your son.'

She waits for this news to sink in, watches the rage creep over Hera's face, like the red glow of sunrise, the vague disappointment clouding Zeus' eyes as he sees he has been playing the game with the wrong dice.

It is Hera who breaks the silence first. 'You are here to tell me,' she asks, her voice as soft as the coat of a Scythian mare, 'that I have been putting all my efforts into stopping her for nothing?' Iris winces in expectation of the familiar blast of rage, but it is directed at Zeus instead of herself. 'She's not even your bastard?' Hera shrieks at her husband, voice rising now, dark eyes sparking. 'You are telling me that all this has been – for nothing?'

'Not for nothing, Hera dear,' Zeus says, avoiding her eye. 'You have still won Jason his throne, or as good as. That's something, is it not? Though . . .' he peers down again to Earth and the blond-haired prince, 'I suppose it is not too late to put forward my own contender.'

'Don't you dare – don't you dare even think about putting Lycon on the throne of Pagasae!' Hera shouts, anticipating him. 'I have been behind Jason from the very beginning – it was your fault that you backed the wrong challenger.'

'I was as much in the dark as you were, Hera, my dear, and, really, I do think it's fair that I have my own candidate for the throne.'

'Not a chance.'

'It's only right—'

'– married a trickster and a swindler—'

'– that my son should sit upon the throne of Pagasae—'

The shouts of the two gods merge, indiscriminate words and threats knocking around the council of the gods.

Iris stands and moves before them, her back to the gap in the clouds. 'When you've quite finished,' she says.

Zeus and Hera turn to her, their cheeks red with exertion, their expressions revealing that they have forgotten she is there.

'What?'

'You have not asked me why I went to the Library of the Muses in the first place.'

'Why should we care?' Hera asks, her lip curling. 'Do you think we have nothing better to do than to worry about your whereabouts, Iris? You should remember who you are and where you came from.'

Iris flinches a little at the casual slight so easily handed out. Then she opens *her mouth, ready to deliver her final blow. 'I came from the loins of a god, Hera, as did you,' she says. 'And I went to find out who would get the kingdom.'*

Iris watches as Hera's indignation wrestles with her outrage at Iris's presumption in entering the Library of the Muses to discover the will of the Fates – which, as every god knows from their earliest birth, is one of the deepest and most primal secrets, held from the gods except, on occasion, from Zeus alone. For a god to seek the twisting and turning of the thread of Fate, without the express permission of the three old crones who spin its fibrous web, is unthinkable. A contravention of the only and most sacred law that ever bound the gods.

A law that the gods break almost daily.

'You – you can't do that!' Zeus stammers, in a feeble attempt to uphold the law and order he personifies. 'It's – it's against the rules! The sacred laws of the gods and . . . so on.'

'Never mind that.' Hera waves aside her husband's objection, as if it were a troublesome fly. She turns to Iris. 'Did you find it? The prophecy of Pagasae's kingship?'

There is something in the emphasis on 'you' in Hera's question that makes Iris raise her eyebrows and has Zeus looking from the messenger to the queen as he puts the pieces together.

'You've already looked, haven't you?' he says at last, turning to his wife with an indignant expression. 'You searched for the fate of Pagasae!'

Hera scoffs at him. 'As if you did not try to do the same.'

Zeus hesitates. 'Oh, very well. But you didn't find out, did you?'

Hera ignores him. 'You've got it, then,' she says to Iris. 'What does the scroll say?' Her eyes are glittering. 'Whom does it name as the new king of Pagasae?'

Iris gleams a smile at her. 'No one.'

'No one?' Hera's barely suppressed expression of delight fuses instantly into confusion and anger.

Zeus groans. 'Oh, no, it isn't time for that wretched "rule of the people" yet, is it?'

Iris shakes her head. 'No – no, it's not that. The scroll says simply . . .' she draws a deep breath '. . . that it has already been decided who will take the throne of Pagasae. But it is not the Fates who have determined it.'

There is a moment of silence. Then Hera waves a hand impatiently. 'What does that mean? The Fates decide everything.'

'The scroll says that it has been decided by a power higher even than the Fates.'

'That cannot be,' Zeus says. 'Everyone knows that we are the most power-ful beings in the world, and that we bow only to the Fates . . . If there were something more powerful than the Fates, then,' he glances at his wife, 'what would we be?'

'We are gods,' Hera says, her eyes narrowed as she turns to observe her messenger. 'There is no one and nothing more powerful than us. You are betraying yourself and your kind, Iris, by suggesting otherwise.'

'I do not suggest so,' Iris says. 'I am merely repeating the words of the Fates, as written in the scroll I found last night.'

'You are lying!'

'I am not.'

There is a silence.

Then: 'Well?' Hera snaps her fingers. 'Are we to be told what power it is you are speaking of – if indeed it exists at all – or are you simply going to stand there gawping at us like a fool?'

Iris swallows her anger. Her moment is coming – and soon. She has only a little longer to wait. 'Choice,' she says simply.

'What?' Hera is looking scornful, Zeus bemused.

'Choice is the power that overcomes Fate,' Iris says, her voice strengthening as she goes on. 'The choice to believe that Fate does not determine destiny. The choice to make the world your own – not because the Fates have decreed it, not because the gods have willed it, but because you, yourself, decide.'

'What rubbish is this?' Hera scoffs.

'Don't you see?' Iris asks, and, in spite of herself, she takes a step forwards, her breath coming rather fast. 'It means that it's not about Fate, or forcing the mortals to do our will, as we thought. It is about the choices mortals make – a world of freedom, where our destiny is our own, and not determined for us.' Her eyes shine like twin stars.

'You sound as if you will become a mortal at any moment,' Hera observes drily.

'I would, if I could,' Iris retorts. 'There are mortals living upon the earth who are ten, twenty times the gods that we are here.'

300

Hera starts forwards upon her throne, her expression murderous, but — *unexpectedly, as if from nowhere — Zeus lays a hand upon her arm and draws* *her down to sit again. 'Sit, Hera. Hear the child out.'*

Iris glances towards him. Zeus is looking at her, a curious expression on his *face — as if he is remembering some long-forgotten dream from many nights* *ago, now buried in the mists of memory.*

'We are gods, and gods we will remain. That much I know,' Iris continues. *'But we do not have to meddle. We do not have to intervene, like a tiresome* *puppet-master pulling the strings upon his dolls. All we have to do is to* *observe the laws of chance — to watch the unfolding of the possibilities that are* *predicated on the choices that we know mortals will make, because we know* *their characters. The laws they live their lives by. The people they love.'*

Hera's face is a picture of scepticism and anger. Her mouth is a thin line, *and her eyes are flashing dangerously.*

'It's logic,' Iris presses on, hardly pausing to breathe — she is getting to it, *now. Any moment . . . 'What will Iasus do when he finds out Atalanta is his* *daughter? What will Jason say to persuade him to his suit? How will Lycon* *try to evade the throne, and how can Iasus force him to do his bidding? Don't* *you see?'*

Hera's eyes are narrowed to slits. 'You are speaking in riddles, Iris, and you *know I cannot stand slanted speaking. What does all this mean?'*

'I may be a mere messenger, and I may not know what is fated, but I know *the mortals in a way you, Hera, who always interfere to get your way and* *never stop to listen to what the mortals themselves may choose to do,* *never have.'*

Iris turns on her heel and walks back past the rows and rows of empty seats *to the entrance to the council, her robes swishing at her ankles. Then she looks* *over her shoulder, straight-backed, her eyes gleaming in the light of the rising* *sun, smiling a triumphant smile. 'I already know who will win the throne.'*

Return to the Palace

Pagasae

The Hour of Music
The Second Day of the Month of Rains

The following morning I stood before the gates of the upper city, my hair washed, oiled and scented with rosemary, my new cloak thrown over one shoulder, my quiver upon my back. I passed well enough for a man, Battus had told me, and when I gave the name Telamon, son of Deucalion, and said that I was to attend the king for his morning audience, the spear-carrying guards ushered me through the gates without comment. I reached up and ran my thumb nervously over the leather cord around my neck, as the squire led me, along the same labyrinthine passage I had walked many months before, to the Great Hall where the king was holding court.

He pushed open the painted double doors that led into it and stepped aside, ushering me forwards. The large chamber greeted me, the same as it had been before, with its towering red-painted columns, polished stone floors and vaulted ceilings, but now the hearth was empty and the pale light of day was filtering down through high-set windows. Nobles and courtiers were grouped around the hall, talking loudly to each other, some clutching clay tablets for petition to the king, others pouches filled with money for redress. All, it seemed, were awaiting their turn to consult with the king, who was once more upon his fleece-lined throne against the far wall, his long fingers tapping its arm, his brow furrowed. I elbowed my way through the crowds, some of them scowling and complaining, others raising their eyebrows and muttering to each other. I caught snatched words as I passed – 'Where he comes from . . .', 'By his dress he's a lord at least . . .', 'A stranger to the court?' – but I ignored them all.

At last, I reached the foot of the king's throne, and bent myself low to one knee, my head bowed, my heart throbbing so that the medallion leapt against my collarbone. My stomach was filled with a fluttering sensation, and though I opened my lips to speak my mouth was dry and I could say nothing.

I am here – after all this time.

How should I begin? How can I tell him I am his daughter?

I felt the herald's stare upon me, heard the intake of breath that was intended to dismiss me, to bid me wait my turn among the crowds of nobles come to petition the king's justice, when King Iasus' voice broke across him.

'Let him speak, Copreus.' I felt a slight stirring of the air past my face as the king moved aside his cloak and leant forwards to address me. 'What is it that you want?'

I swallowed. Then, as I had anticipated for so long, I looked up, directly into my father's eyes, and parted my lips to speak. 'I am no man, my king,' I said, my voice clear, ringing through the hall. 'I am a woman, and your daughter.'

For a moment, there was utter silence in the hall as the king stared at me, his eyes as brown and piercing as an eagle's. Then, as if by command, everyone began to speak at once – at first a low buzz, then mounting to a swarming, hissing swell of gossip, accusation, speculation. But I was gazing only at the king. He was seated still as a hawk poised to swoop upon a hare, his lips drawn together in a thin line.

'Throw her from the palace,' he said, his eyes not moving from mine, 'and have her whipped within a hair's breadth of her life for her insolence.'

The herald bent forwards, grabbed a handful of my tunic and pulled me roughly to my feet.

But I would not give up, not now that I was here. I balled my fist and drove it with all of my strength, with the desperate force of someone who had everything to lose, into the herald's belly. He doubled over, wheezing and gasping, and I felt the tension loosen at the neck of my tunic as he released his grip on me.

'There!' I shouted, my fingers closing over the medallion, ripping it from my neck so that the clasp broke and throwing it towards the king. The thin golden disc clattered on the stone at his feet, and as I ducked away from the herald, darting sideways to avoid two slaves who were approaching to apprehend me, I saw the king bend to pick it up, saw his fingertips brush the medallion and the dawning comprehension on his face.

'Stop!' he commanded.

The slaves backed away at once, their heads bowed low. 'Come here,' he said, beckoning to me.

I stood before him, my hands shaking a little at my sides.

'Do you have any idea,' he said, his voice a thread of sound that made me shiver with the menace of it, 'what manner of thing you have here?' He twisted the disc between his fingers so that its tiny embossed figures caught the light and glinted, as if moving.

I drew my chin up, squaring my shoulders.

'Your life is already forfeit,' he said, tapping his fingers again upon the arm of his throne, as if he were bored with me and wished to have me dealt with then and there. 'You will tell us whence you stole this medallion, and save yourself the pain of a death even more agonizing than that you are already destined to suffer.'

I felt my temper rise at the threat, and my voice returned. 'I did not steal it,' I said. 'It is mine by right.'

'But of course she is lying!' one of the lords interjected from behind me.

'It is mine,' I repeated, ignoring him. 'It was found with me upon the slopes of Mount Pelion by my father, a woodworker from Kaladrosos, who delivered me from the mountain's peak when he came upon me there, abandoned, in the dead of winter.'

I saw King Iasus' face pale, but his eyes were still hard as gimlets.

'I came here under the guise of Telamon, son of Deucalion. I excelled at the hunt by Jason's side. I voyaged to Colchis to win the Golden Fleece and prove myself to you as your daughter and your heir,' I pressed on, my eyes never leaving the king's. As I spoke I could feel my courage rising, and a tiny spark of pride ignited in my chest. 'I have done everything you could have hoped for from a son, and more.'

Silence fell between us. The nobles around the hall were hushed now, as if straining to hear every word of the conversation.

'And what of the Fleece?' he asked at last.

'It transpires – I found— That is to say, I was too late.' I gritted my teeth. 'But,' I looked around the group of lords and nobles, searching for Jason, who did not seem to have appeared in the hall yet, 'you should know that Jason was unable to keep it either. I swear to you, my king, I did everything within my power to bring it back to you and to prove to you my worth.'

To my surprise, the king laughed aloud and clapped his hands. The sound of merriment echoed hollowly around the silent hall.

'But of course! A woman's excuses,' he said, and the courtiers around him began to laugh, as if all tension had been released. 'You went on the quest for the Fleece, you say?' His voice snapped, as cold as a winter frost. 'Tell me, my lady, what fearsome monsters did you fight upon your quest? What mighty heroes did you slay?' He pretended to wipe tears of mirth from his eyes upon his cloak.

The herald was grinning, and echoing howls of laughter assailed me on all sides. I felt anger blooming, and my fingers itched to reach behind me for my bow. But then there was a crash of the doors to the hall behind me, and I heard the sound of many booted footfalls ringing out over the stone floor.

I turned slowly upon my heel. Jason, accompanied by a dark-haired woman with hooded eyes, and followed by all the lords from the *Argo* – my brother Lycon, Meleager, Nestor, Pollux, Laertes, Orpheus, Theseus, Peleus, Bellerophon, all except Hippomenes, I noticed, with a sinking feeling – was striding into the hall, his cloak flying out behind him.

Our eyes met.

'*You!* What by Hades—'

In a flash of metal his sword was drawn before him, the long blade glinting in the midst of the crowded hall like a pillar of lightning, and as one the nobles around him drew back. My hand flew to the sword at my waist.

'My king, this – this *woman*, she is no better than a treasonous liar and a whore,' Jason snarled, advancing upon me. I drew my sword, the bronze scraping upon the scabbard, and held it high before me, smiling.

'Oh, yes?' I replied. 'You might wish to ask the king about the medallion he is holding, Jason, before you go any further, and perhaps,' I gestured with the gleaming tip of my sword towards Meleager, 'the lord Meleager will tell you how he tried to force himself upon me, before you accuse me of being a whore.'

Jason's eyes flickered towards Meleager, and in that pause I struck, knocking away his blade and slicing through the shoulder of his tunic with my sword point, the blade nicking the skin. Jason roared with anger, holding his hand up to the wound, which was pricking with blood.

'You see, Uncle?' he bellowed, raising his sword higher and advancing towards me. 'You see her insolence? This nobody – this daughter of a pig-farmer – threatens my inheritance, which is mine by right!'

Jason began to attack in earnest, slicing and thrusting, the bronze of his blade flashing through the air. I parried his blows. Around us, the lords circled, muttering, whispering, some shouting words of encouragement, others jeering – and I felt the king's eyes upon me, like the beady stare of an eagle.

Jason lunged, and as he did so, I twisted to one side, drawing my dagger from my belt with my left hand, thrust forwards with my sword against his blade so that it was driven up towards the hall's high roof, then raised my dagger and brought it down, hard, to the floor, knocking the weapon from his hand. I sheathed my dagger, bent to pick up his sword and tossed it into the air, catching it by the embossed hilt.

'I would that you know me at last for who I am, Jason, son of Aeson,' I said, and I heard my voice echo around the silent throne room.

This is the moment.

This is it.

Slowly I turned to face him, one sword held lightly in each hand, my heart beating hard against my chest. The sunlight slanted down from the high windows of the hall and reflected from the polished tiles of the floor, gilding the surrounding lords in light. I raised myself a little taller.

'My name is Atalanta, daughter of Iasus, and I challenge you to the throne of Pagasae.'

There was a moment's silence as Jason and I stared at each other. Jason's eyes were bulging with rage – he was struggling for words, opening and closing his mouth.

'That is *enough*!'

The king's command rang through the Great Hall, echoing from the vaulted ceiling. We turned, both of us, eyes narrowed, Jason's hand clutched to the wound on his shoulder. I sheathed my sword and turned Jason's, point down, to the floor, then leant upon it.

'There are, quite plainly,' King Iasus said, as if he would ensure that the whole court heard him, 'some matters that need to be clarified. First, I wish to announce to the court that Jason did, in fact, capture the Golden Fleece – though, as he informed me last night upon his return, it was stolen from him in an unfortunate incident upon his voyage back to Pagasae. Yet he captured it, my lords, and brought it with him from Colchis. Is that not what the prophecy required? There was no mention,' he said, his teeth gleaming, 'of returning the Fleece to Pagasae. Jason has, in my eyes and in the eyes of the gods, fulfilled the prophecy.'

The men around me glanced at each other, their expressions registering their astonishment at this piece of news. Some bowed to mutter in their neighbours' ears. My eyes did not leave the king's face, which was impassive, unreadable.

'Yet,' King Iasus continued, 'should there be any doubt as to whether Jason is Pagasae's intended king, the Fates have been even more gracious. Indeed,' he said, his eyes flickering towards me, his voice as smooth as first-pressed oil, 'they have presented us with something of a solution.'

'There can *be* no solution!' Jason screamed, ripping his hand away from his shoulder and starting towards the king, hands outstretched, almost as if he would throttle him. I flinched and stepped back: his face was red and contorted with anger, a vein throbbing upon his temple. 'It is my inheritance! *I will not lose my inheritance!*'

'No, no, nephew – you misunderstand me,' the king said, holding up a hand. 'You will still have your kingdom.'

Jason faltered, breathing like a warrior winded in battle. I stared at the king – *what does that mean?* – my heart drumming so insistently at my ribs that I was sure the whole hall would hear it. The king's expression was as inscrutable as ever, and the thin-lipped smile he turned to the crowd glimmered like a mirage on a hot day upon the plains, threatening to disappear at any moment.

'We have this very day received my long-lost daughter at this court.' Iasus gestured to me, holding up the leather cord to the crowd so that the medallion circled, flashing, in the sunlight. 'After examination of the medallion, which I presented to her as a birth-gift, I have decided to uphold her claim. I recognize her as my daughter.'

He held out his arm, still bearing the medallion with his seal-stamp upon it. 'My daughter, Atalanta, is returned!'

There was a brief smattering of applause, followed by a chorus of low mutterings, growing louder every moment. Jason's expression was as dark as a storm cloud, the vein upon his temple pulsing once more. I saw Lycon staring at me, his mouth open.

I felt my face pale as the medallion flashed in my father's hand.

He is recognizing me?

He is recognizing me, in truth, before all the court, as his daughter?

My hands faltered upon Jason's sword.

'And what better way to welcome her to the palace than with her betrothal?' the king continued. 'Atalanta, you will wed Jason.' He held up his hands to the skies. 'The captor of the Golden Fleece in marriage to my daughter – the heir to the kingdom both prophesied and tied to Pagasae by the bonds of the marriage bed!'

The young woman with the hooded eyes behind Jason moved, and her lips parted as her eyes flickered towards me. The gathered nobles were shouting now, a vague noise above the ringing in my ears, whether of rejoicing or confusion I could not tell, and Jason's expression was transforming into a slowly breaking smile of triumph.

I felt my hands shake with anger. The storm of shouting around me was silenced by the blood rushing through my body. I was fixed to the floor with shock and filled with a terrible, burning rage – that after all

I had done, all I had been through, this was to be my end! The king had acknowledged me, only to barter me off as a pawn to a man who threatened to kill those I loved, who had beaten me with his own hands and left me to die in the wilderness? He had calculated his losses after Jason's failure to retrieve the Fleece – the cold set of his eyes was telling me so. He had determined in that moment to accept me, whether I was his daughter or not, as a chattel to be bargained in marriage, to bring Jason to the throne should anyone doubt his fulfilment of the prophecy.

My temper burnt higher, blazing within me until I could bear it no longer. '*No!*'

King Iasus' eyes narrowed. The entire court fell silent, the hush sweeping over them, like wind through a glade of trees.

'What did you say to me?' Once more the king's voice was filled with menace.

'I said no,' I repeated, growing bolder. 'I have done everything to serve you, to prove my worth. You cannot do this! I do not wish to marry – and there is no man in the world I would wish to marry less than *him*!' This last word I spat across the hall at Jason. I lowered my voice. 'I have felt the harshness of his justice, seen his cold heart in his treatment of both his equals and his slaves. He would not be a good king to this kingdom.'

'You presume to know better than I the qualities that Pagasae's kings should possess?'

'I— No, I merely—'

But then a voice cut across my own. 'Is it not the case that the daughter of the king is entitled to a contest for her hand, by the laws of this city?'

I turned. Lycon's face was a little pale, as if he was nervous to be speaking before so many people, but his jaw was set in determination.

'And what do *you* know of the laws of this city?' King Iasus said, his mouth turning down in a sneer. 'It was my impression that you preferred poetry to the tablets of the laws.'

Lycon held his ground. 'I have spent many evenings in conversation with the lawgivers of this land, father, and the laws of the city are inscribed upon stone by the temple of Zeus, beside this very palace.' He recited in a ringing voice: "'Any man who wishes to wed the daughter of the king must prove his suit by contest, and the winner shall gain her as his wife, and the inheritance of the kingdom of Pagasae.'"

I turned to mouth my thanks to Lycon, and he nodded to me, smiling a little. The king turned towards a group of ten aged men, seated along the wall to his right, who, from their white beards and the ceremonial strip of embroidered wool upon their tunics, I took to be members of his council. 'Is this so?' he asked.

One of the old men pushed himself to stand from his seat, leaning upon a wooden stick. 'The lawgiver commands it,' he said, in a quavering voice. He nodded to Lycon and repeated: "'Any man who wishes to wed the daughter of the king must prove his suit by contest." It is the law. It must be done.'

A storm of muttering broke out through the hall.

'Very well, then,' the king announced, nursing the seal-ring at his finger as the old councillor sat back upon his stool. 'If we must do it in the traditional way, I announce a contest in three days' time for Atalanta's hand.' He turned to me, his yellowing teeth bared in a grin. 'Lord Jason is as much a contender as any other noble.'

'But he will win, won't he?' I said. 'You will ensure it.'

Jason started towards me, his hand raised as if he would strike me across the face.

'That is *enough*,' the king thundered, and Jason stopped where he was. King Iasus turned to me, his eyes as hard as a frozen lake in winter. 'As my daughter, Atalanta, you should remember you are my property, to do with as I wish. You should be thanking the gods on bended knee to have such a loving father who cares for you so well.'

I could feel the panic rising in my throat. I had meant to return as a victor, to prove myself to them in my own right. And now I was being taken as the property of the king, to be married off at his will, an object with which to pass the kingdom to a tyrant . . .

'At least,' I said, thinking quickly, raising my voice so that it carried well across the hall, 'at least, then, Father, allow me this. Allow me to determine the nature of the contest for myself.'

The king raised his eyebrows, a flicker of amusement crossing his face. 'If you think we will hold a spinning contest for your hand . . .'

There was a titter of appreciative laughter from the crowd.

I gritted my teeth and continued: 'If I must marry, then let it be to a man who is my equal. If a man can win against me in a footrace, then I will be his. But,' I said, gazing around the room so that every noble and courtier witnessed what I said, 'if I win, then I gain my freedom, and will be no man's wife.' I paused. 'I do not beg for the kingdom. Only my liberty.'

And then I shall return to Kaladrosos and protect my family, I thought. *The father who truly loves me, as you never did.*

The king gazed at me for a while, his eyes flicking from Jason, taller than I and with lean, well-muscled legs, to my slight calves and slim frame, as if he were a gambler at dice weighing the odds. I knew that he was summing me up, judging that I could never outpace Jason.

At last, he looked around the waiting crowd and, very slowly, he smiled, the deliberate, goading smile of a man who has laid a bet he already knows he will win.

'Very well,' he said. 'A race. Let it be known that the contest for Atalanta's hand will be held in three days' time, on the fifth day of this month. Any noble of high birth who wishes to contend for her hand may try.'

He spread his hands wide. 'I swear to you all here and now, by Zeus, protector of kings and lord of the gods of Olympus, the man . . .' King Iasus' eyes darted towards Jason for the briefest of moments, and the corners of his mouth curved into a smile '. . . who wins the race will gain my daughter's hand, and this kingdom.'

The Race

Pagasae

The Hour of the Middle of the Day
The Fifth Day of the Month of Rains

I was kneeling, crouched in the sand, beads of sweat trickling down my forehead. I could hear the cicadas singing in the cypress trees and the soft beating of waves against the cliffs nearby. I could feel the rubbing of sand against one knee as it pressed into the ground, the warmth between my bare toes. Blood was pounding in my ears, my heartbeat racing, preparing for the burst of speed that was about to come, my thighs tensed and ready, like a spring about to snap.

But none of that mattered. Because I was straining to hear a single sound. One sound, which would begin the race that would determine my destiny. I had to win.

Before all else, I have to win.

To my right, the herald raised his sceptre. His long white robes billowed out around his arm, like a flag. The sound of my heartbeat in my ears was deafening, and my eyes were fixed on the finish line drawn in chalk in the dust, far in the distance, shimmering in the midday heat.

The line of suitors stretched out to my right. *The kingdom of Pagasae is a prize worth winning*, I thought as I looked around. *Twenty men would surely not turn out for my hand alone.* Some I did not know, though I could see several of the crew of the *Argo*, Peleus among them, Pollux too. Jason stood beside Theseus, the two of them talking. Jason's entire manner exuded arrogance, and I wondered, with a small flutter of fear, what scheme he and my father had in place to wrong-foot me. And then I saw the flash of gold as Jason took Theseus' hand in his, as if to wish him luck, saw the leather pouch hanging at Theseus' belt – indeed, there was one at the belts of all the other suitors, I saw, as I scanned the line – filled to the brim with coins; and I realized.

All of the men had been bribed by my father not to outrun Jason.

I exhaled slowly.

That I, in turn, might outrun Jason had clearly not crossed either of their minds; for who could imagine that a woman might outpace a man?

But then, I thought, pressing the tips of my fingers deeper into the sand, *they do not know how fast I am.*

A movement behind me. Another suitor was arriving late, slipping into line beside me.

I turned. My mouth opened in a soundless exclamation.

It was Hippomenes.

A surge of emotion flooded through me, my heart lighter than it had been in days to see him once more, when I had thought never to see him again: the familiar broken line of his nose, the broad set of his shoulders, the strong line of his jaw. And then I remembered where I was, what I was about to do – that he should have come now, at this moment, at the most important moment of all . . .

I took a deep breath. *You have to calm yourself*, I told myself. *Steady, and sure, and fast. You cannot lose your focus.*

'What are you *doing* here?' I hissed under my breath, not looking at him. 'I thought you had returned to Boeotia!'

He unfastened the cloak from around his neck and untied his sandals. 'What do you think I am doing?'

I could not help myself: I turned to stare at him, suddenly very aware of my pulse racing. *He cannot mean what I think he means.*

'Don't be a fool.'

He shook his head and knelt beside me, fingertips pressing into the sand so that the muscles of his arms and shoulders stood rigid, gleaming with sweat. 'I have never been more serious in all my life.'

I bit my lip, trying not to smile as the memory of our race in the fields of Anatolia floated into my mind. 'You know you cannot beat me!'

He shrugged his shoulders, smiling a little, too, as he glanced over at me, his brown eyes clear in the sunlight. 'Even so.'

'*On your marks!*'

The herald's cry rent the air, and at once I felt my body tense. The suitors around me bent low to the ground, some kneeling, others standing with one foot weighted before the other, sweat dripping from their foreheads to the ground in the heat of the day.

'*Prepare yourselves!*'

I pressed the ball of my foot into the sand, felt it give a little beneath my bare skin.

'*Run!*' The herald brought his sceptre swishing down to his side with a shout, but I was already gone before the word had finished echoing on the air.

My feet were flashing across the golden sand, so fast that the trees around me were mere blurs of green and grey. My heels barely touched the ground before they were off again; I was a whirl of colour and sound. I was faster than a darting bird, faster than a lion in pursuit of its prey. I was Atalanta, the fastest runner in the world.

And they would never outrun me.

I glanced back at my competitors. Most were already hidden in the cloud of dust kicked up by my heels. Pollux seemed to have got a thorn in his foot and was limping and cursing the gods. Theseus was breathing hard, neck on neck with Peleus, who tripped and fell behind. Even Jason and Hippomenes, both of whom were leading the group of suitors, were still more than ten paces behind, their lungs heaving with the effort to keep up.

I leapt forwards, even faster than before. The wind was rushing past me, so fast now it felt as if I were racing Zephyr himself, the god of the west wind, and my toes were so light on the sand I could barely feel the ground beneath me. I could see the finish line coming ever closer, the line of my freedom drawn across the track. And then I heard a curse yelled to the heavens, a thud and then more oaths. I glanced over my shoulder to see Jason sprawled upon his belly on the earth, and beside him Laertes and Theseus, groaning and clutching at their bruised sides where they had tripped and fallen upon the track.

I laughed aloud and ran on.

I am going to win. I will show them that a daughter can be as good as a son, that I am strong enough to beat men at their own game as I have done all my life. They will see me, at last, for who I am.

Their equal.

I sprinted faster, darting quick glances behind me. Hippomenes had overtaken Jason, who had stumbled to his feet again and was roaring threats and imprecations at him. I could hear Hippomenes' footsteps thundering down the track behind me, and when I glimpsed over my shoulder again I saw him ten paces behind, his face streaming with sweat. Jason was nothing but a diminutive, red-faced figure far behind him in the dust. The blood was pumping in my veins, the determination that I would show the world, the king most of all, what I could do. Nothing could go wrong now. The finish line was only forty paces away.

I am about to make my destiny.

I am about to win.

And then, out of the corner of my eye, something caught my attention.

A glint of gold.

I turned my head to see it, even as I ran. It was an apple, a beautiful, perfectly round, golden apple, rolling at a tremendous speed along the track past me and then ahead, bumping on the uneven earth. For a moment, something flashed across its surface: a message. It disappeared, then reappeared as the apple rolled and bounced over the ground. I quickened my pace, squinting to make it out.

And then I read it. Inscribed in curling letters across the apple's golden flesh were two words.

ΤΩΙ ΝΙΚΩΝΤΙ.

For the Winner.

There was the sound of footsteps behind me, and I looked round again, my heart beating painfully hard with – was it fear? Or anticipation? Hippomenes was charging down the track towards me, sweat flying off his body, the dust kicked up by my heels sticking to his skin. He was only a few paces behind me and the gap was narrowing with every moment. I looked forwards, panicking, to the finish line thirty paces ahead, then at the apple, which was gathering speed now, flashing as it tumbled down the slope of the track and then, inevitably, inexorably, starting to curve away to the side of the cliff and the sea. In a moment it would roll over the edge of the rocks and then it would be lost for ever in the pounding surf.

I stared at the apple, my eyes following the bouncing sphere of gold. As if from a great distance, Myrtessa's words from so many months before, when we had stood upon the walls of Pagasae, sounded in my head:

> *Bring back the treasure gold in legends twin,*
> *That's at the black earth's furthest ends concealed;*
> *Or else hope not the city's crown to win,*
> *And see your city to destruction yield.*

And what had she said then?

They say there are only two treasures of legend to which the prophecy could refer – the Golden Fleece of Colchis, in the lands furthest to the east where the sun rises, or the apples of the Hesperides, at the very edge of the world where the summer sun never sets.

The apples of the Hesperides.

I looked back and forth, frantic, between the shimmering finish line and the glittering apple, rolling towards the cliff . . .

Two prizes, one ahead of me and one beside.

The race, which would set me free but see Jason become king, or the apple, which would make me wed, but which would proclaim me the kingdom's rightful queen.

Two ambitions fighting each other.

Two desperate desires.

And I had only moments to decide which I would choose.

In a heartbeat I veered to the right and ran, faster than I had ever run, chasing the golden apple as it glinted in the sun, bounced and rolled, like a pebble flung from heaven by the gods, towards the sea. I could smell the salt on the air – I was only a few paces away from plunging over the sheer cliffs into the sea. The apple bounced over a stone and spiralled up, up into the air in a graceful arc . . .

I threw myself forwards, face down on the ground, my hand

stretched out over the cliff edge to catch it, tight, in my palm.

Another moment, and it would have been lost to the waves for ever.

I pushed myself to my feet, the apple clenched in my hand, and spun around in time to see Hippomenes launching himself towards the end of the track, every muscle in his body tensed, driving him onwards, Jason following in the dust kicked up by Hippomenes' heels . . . ten paces . . . five paces . . .

And then he crossed the line, and he was on his knees in the dirt, and the herald was shouting to the skies that Hippomenes, son of Megareus, had won the race and Atalanta's hand.

'How did you know I would choose it?'

We were lying together many weeks later upon our marriage bed in our quarters in the palace of Pagasae, Hippomenes propped up on the pillows with his arms behind his head, I on my belly upon the soft woollen covers, my chin resting on my hands. I thought back over the last few hours and closed my eyes, my skin tingling at the memory of how Hippomenes had lifted me in his arms and taken me into the bridal chamber; how he had laid me down upon the bed and then, with strength but such tenderness, had run his hands along my body, wondering at my nakedness, planting kisses on my ears, my neck, my breasts . . . and then how, when I was moaning for his touch, he had taken me, and we had moved together, both of us as one, gasping for breath in the pleasure of our closeness . . .

The breeze played across my back and set the curtains billowing at the window, wafting the warm, tangy scent of the box hedges from the courtyard beyond. We had been married that morning: a small ceremony in the palace's private shrine, I in a red tunic with a posy of myrtle and white rose blossoms in my hands, Hippomenes wearing a dark-green cloak thrown over one shoulder, his sword hanging in a bronze sheath from his waist. The race upon the sandy cliffs of Pagasae's shore seemed as remote as the islands of the Hesperides, a distant memory – yet I had to know.

'Choose what?' he asked me, as if he did not know.

'The apple,' I said. The mottled light of the sun through the windows, scattered by the leaves of the trees in the garden, shone on his dark hair and turned it a burnished red-gold. 'How did you know I would choose it? That I would not run on and win the race?'

He turned towards me, shifting onto his side. 'Before I answer that, tell me first: why *did* you choose it?'

I gleamed a smile at him and pushed myself off the piles of fleeces and rugs to stand, then wandered over to the open window and reached through to pluck an apple from the tree beyond. It was a blushing pink-red, firm to the touch. I tossed it towards him. 'I'd hate to destroy any illusions you might have had.'

He grinned back at me as he caught it, entirely undismayed. 'After several weeks spent together upon the roads from Colchis, I doubt I have any left.'

I arched an eyebrow at him, then let out a laugh. 'Well, then.' I plucked another apple from the branch and bit into it, the sweet juice filling my mouth. 'If you must know, I recognized the apple as the golden treasure spoken of in the prophecy.'

I felt a shiver run down my spine. *The prophecy* . . . It had sent me to the ends of the world and back, had determined the outcome of the race, my marriage – and the rule of the kingdoms of Pelion, even. Myrtessa would most likely have said that the gods had foretold everything, I thought – and I smiled as the image of my friend's face, bright-eyed and grinning, rose before my mind's eye.

But, Myrtessa, what you do not see is that the gods might have thrown the apple – and I might have chosen not to follow it.

It was I who determined my fate: by choosing to go after it.

I wiped my mouth on the back of my arm and settled at the end of the bed. I frowned as I recalled the moment I had seen the golden apple speeding down the track before me in the dust. 'I knew that, if I took it, I would fulfil the prophecy and win the city on my own terms, as its rightful heir,' I continued. 'And if it also meant taking you as my husband into the bargain,' I said, looking up at last and giving him a smile, 'well, I thought I would be able to endure it.'

He chuckled. 'I see. And what would you have said if I told you that I knew you would choose the apple and the kingdom, and that that was the only way I could ever persuade you to have me?'

I moved forwards upon the bed to lie beside him, my body ever so slightly turned towards his, my lips brushing his ear. 'I knew you knew it,' I said softly. 'And I would have said that you were the only man worthy of my hand, because you were the only one who knew me, and respected me, for who I was.'

'Ah,' he said. 'I see. Then that makes us equals, Atalanta, does it not?'

I considered him for a moment, a smile playing at the corners of my mouth.

'Yes,' I said at last, lying back upon the covers, gazing up at the canopy over the bed where a single golden apple had been embroidered – a wedding gift from Hippomenes. I turned to him and smiled, intertwining my fingers with his. 'Yes, I suppose it does.'

Epilogue

A year or so later, a woman is standing upon the walls of the citadel of Pagasae, watching. It is a habit she is trying to break, watching things from above; but, as the poets say, not even the gods fight necessity, and she cannot resist it.

Not today.

Not now.

The view spread beneath her is indeed spectacular. The citadel is thronged with colour as nobles, citizens and slaves mill about the forecourt of the palace, women wearing flounced dresses of red, blue and gold, children playing hoop-and-stick, vendors selling handfuls of honeyed nuts, grapes, and sweet mead flavoured with juicy cut lemons. A circle of young men watches the fire-breathers exhaling flame to the skies, and in the very centre of the forecourt, surrounded by a ring of townspeople, a dark-skinned acrobat wearing a loin-cloth vaults over the gilded horns of a huge, roaring bull, his muscles girded in sweat as he twists and turns and somersaults into the air.

And then there she is, emerging from the temple of Zeus with the high priest, her forehead wreathed in dark-green laurels, resplendent in flowing skirts of white and gold, a gold-threaded cloak over her shoulders and the sceptre of the ruler of Pagasae in her hand, treading lightly, but her head held high and her mouth set with determination. It is Atalanta.

The woman on the walls watches with a smile upon her lips as the new queen glances back to her husband, the king, and he lays a reassuring hand on her shoulder. Atalanta exchanges a last smile with her parents from Kaladrosos, Tyro and Eurymedon, who stand to her left beaming with pride, their eyes filled with tears. She draws a deep breath, clasps Hippomenes' fingers briefly, then moves forwards to address the swarming crowds.

They break into cheers and applause as their queen climbs the few steps to the dais that stands beside Zeus' temple, a broad platform of polished limestone guarded on either side by twin images of the god. The watcher smiles a little to see the heavily built form of the king of the gods sculpted here, his arms encircling the crowned battlements of the city of Pagasae.

As Atalanta begins to address the crowd, her voice high and clear, the woman on the wall turns aside and gazes over the plain to the north of Pagasae, across the sparkling waters of the bay, its white-sailed ships like seagulls floating upon the waves, towards the forested green slopes of Mount Pelion and then beyond, to where the majestic peaks of Olympus thrust from the rocky plains of Pieria into the cornflower-blue sky to be wreathed in wispy clouds.

With a smile, Iris turns her back upon the mountain of the gods and walks over to join in the festivities.

Author's Note

The legend of Jason and the Argonauts is one of the oldest in Greek myth, predating even Homer's *Iliad* and *Odyssey*. It tells of the quest of Jason, the son of Aeson, and the band of Argonauts (or 'sailors of the *Argo*') for the legendary Golden Fleece in the land of Colchis. It is as fabulously rich as it is implausible, relating remarkable tales of centaurs, dragons and metallic birds; narrow escapes from clashing rocks and fire-breathing bulls; terrifying man-killing women, seductive Sirens, and shrieking, half-bird half-female Harpies.

To summarize briefly the major points of the myth, as they occur in the texts in which they have been handed down (and it is important to remember that myth is famously fluid, constantly altered and adapted as it suited the various poets and historians through the ages, so not all versions will agree): when Jason arrived from the slopes of Mount Pelion, where he had been kept under the tutelage of the centaur Chiron, and demanded the kingdom of Iolcos as the rightful son of King Aeson, Pelias, Aeson's brother and usurper to the throne, retaliated by setting Jason a task: the retrieval of the Golden Fleece, which was kept in the land of Colchis (modern Georgia) on the very edge of the known world, guarded by a serpent that never slept. Jason assembled a crew of the greatest heroes in Greece – among them Atalanta[1]

---

1 Atalanta's participation in the quest for the Golden Fleece is disputed by some ancient authors. Pseudo-Apollodorus includes her on the list of the Argonauts (*Bibliotheca* 1.9.16), but Apollonius of Rhodes mentions in his epic *The Argonautica* that Atalanta 'eagerly desired to follow on that quest; but [Jason] of his own accord prevented the maid, for he feared bitter strife on account of her love for Meleager' (transl. E. V. Rieu, *Argonautica* 1.769–771).

– and set sail for Colchis on the *Argo*, encountering many adventures and obstacles along the way (including, among others and perhaps most famously, the Clashing Rocks or 'Symplegades', which Jason navigated with the help of the seer Phineus, sending a dove ahead to fly between the moving rocks).

When he at last arrived in Colchis, he was required to complete yet further feats to prove his worth upon the orders of King Aeëtes, legendary king of Colchis, son of the sun-god Helios and father of Medea. With a pair of fire-breathing bulls, Jason was commanded to plough and sow a field with dragon's teeth, which then transformed into fearsome warriors, completing the tasks with the help of the infamous Medea, who fell in love with him and who aided him with her (supposed) sorcery. The Argonauts then took the Fleece and returned to Greece, where Jason claimed the throne of Iolcos.

The legend of the Argonauts was related and retold in many of the central texts of ancient Greek and Roman literature, from Homer's *Odyssey* to Hesiod's *Theogony*, Pindar's Pythian Ode 4 to Valerius Flaccus' Roman (first century CE) *Argonautica*; but perhaps its most famous incarnation was in one of the great (and underrated) epics of the ancient world, Apollonius' *Argonautica*. The *Argonautica*, named for the sailors of the *Argo*, Jason's famous ship, was written in the third century BCE in Greek by a scholar–poet and librarian of Alexandria called Apollonius, and remains the only surviving Hellenistic (that is, post-classical) epic – an extraordinary achievement and testimony to the flourishing literary culture of Alexandria.

Yet, to many critics, Jason in the *Argonautica* is depicted as a rather cold, repellent character, very different from the larger-than-life heroes of the Homeric epics – and it isn't until the entrance of Medea, their passionate love affair and escape from Colchis, along with, of course, the myth (not related in the *Argonautica*, most famously given in Euripides' tragedy) of Medea's horrific revenge upon Jason after his abandonment of her in Corinth, that the story starts to become really interesting. But Medea – rather like Helen of Troy – is difficult to get a hold on. More and more scholars are now acknowledging that Euripides' depiction of her, for example, tells us far more about classical Greek (fifth century BCE) male fantasies and fears towards women than the actual realities of being a woman in the Bronze Age Mediterranean. Medea, as we know her, is a figment of a deeply patriarchal imagination, a terrifying projection of a male-dominated society's deepest fears and anxieties.

So, when I turned to the myth of Jason and the Argonauts, I looked instead to the story of a woman who has tended, in spite of her brilliance, her courage and her determination, to be ignored. I decided to tell the story of Atalanta, to focus on the struggles of a woman and a warrior trying to make her way in the world, to prove herself the equal of a man. The only woman to participate in the quest for the Golden Fleece, Atalanta carves out a niche for herself in a mythical tradition that is singularly hostile to female characters (the Lemnian women, Sirens, Harpies, and, of course, Medea). Yet there is much more to Atalanta than simply her participation in the voyage with the Argonauts. Her story, handed down to us in the works of the Greek and Roman authors who write of the tale of Jason and the Golden Fleece, is as varied and hard to piece together as the woman herself. The fundamentals of the mythical tale are represented in this book: Atalanta's birth to King Iasus and Queen Clymene; Iasus' wish for a son and heir, and his disappointment at the birth of a girl; Atalanta's exposure upon the mountain and her rearing by a foster-parent (in the myth, a she-bear); her involvement in the famous Calydonian boar hunt along with the heroes Jason, Meleager and many of the other crew of the *Argo*, in which she was the first to wound the boar; Meleager's subsequent infatuation with Atalanta (the subject of a lost tragedy by Euripides); her participation in the heroic quest for the Golden Fleece with Jason and the Argonauts; her eventual discovery by her father, his demand of her marriage and her imposition of the condition that she would marry only in the event that a suitor could outrun her in a footrace (which she knew was impossible as she was 'far faster than swift-footed men', to quote the Roman poet Ovid); and her eventual defeat by Hippomenes when he rolled a golden apple in her path. I have attempted, in retelling the story of Jason and the Argonauts, to nod to the many alternative versions of the myth (from Euripides' vengeful Medea to Apollonius' humorous and domestic gods),[2] while keeping the fantastical elements – mythical beasts and clashing rocks among them – at a minimum to privilege Atalanta's very human story. Where I have departed from the myth is in giving Atalanta a voice: allowing her to tell her own story, in her own way. And part of telling her own story meant responding to the assumptions that were made about her in myths – often created by and for men, then rewritten and reworked by male poets and playwrights until the 'real' Atalanta became entirely lost from view.

This made me think about the reasons Atalanta might have had for one of her most famous so-called 'mistakes': her distraction by the golden apple during the race for her hand, and her subsequent defeat. What really happened in the footrace – and why did Atalanta stop instead of winning as she knew she could? I began to wonder if there wasn't another story here to be told: one that explained Atalanta's decision to go after the golden apple instead of continuing to win the race, one that motivated her extraordinary achievements as both a hunter and a warrior, that earned her a place on the *Argo*, among legendary heroes like Jason, Theseus and Perseus, and that carried her from Greece to the ends of the earth and back again. It was from this starting point that I began to reimagine Atalanta's motives for taking part in the quest for the Golden Fleece: the prophecy of the golden treasure, and her fight with Jason to claim the throne of Pagasae.

So what of the places and peoples mentioned here – and did they really exist? Although no remains of ancient Pagasae are left to us, it is named in the ancient Greek texts as a town around the bay from Mount Pelion – a mountainous region in the north-east of Greece, close to the modern city of Volos – and its harbour is mentioned in Apollonius as the starting point for Jason's voyage. (Its name continues on in the modern Greek name for the Gulf of Pagasae, Pagasitikos.) The Bronze Age settlement of Iolcos (modern Volos) has, as recently as 1997, yielded some important archaeological remains – a Bronze Age palace in the suburb of Dimini, thought to be Jason's Iolcos, as well as tombs and

2 One of the most striking contrasts between Apollonius' epic and those of Homer is in Apollonius' depiction of the gods, who become even more realistic, ordinary, almost domestic in the *Argonautica* – in Book 3, for example, we see Aphrodite at her dressing-table combing her hair, quarrelling with her son Cupid, and then – as a bribe – buying him a ball to keep him happy.

dwelling-places in the city proper. I have used as much as I can of the textual and archaeological evidence – from the stone and mud-brick houses of Dimini to the description of the harbour of Pagasae in Apollonius – to assist in the reconstruction of this important coastal area of Thessaly and to bring it to life, from the slopes of Pelion to the streets of Pagasae. And, of course, Mount Pelion itself is a beautiful and remarkably unspoilt area of Greece, situated on a promontory around the Pagasetic Gulf, which you can still visit today.

The towns and cities mentioned on the journey of the Argonauts are as close to the descriptions given in the ancient texts and to the landscapes as we have them today as I could make them. Thus, for example, the harbour town of Kytoros, visited by Atalanta and the Argonauts on their journey towards Colchis, is mentioned in both Homer's *Iliad* and Apollonius' *Argonautica*, as well as Strabo's *Geography* and Virgil's *Georgics*, and can be found today at modern Gideros in Turkey – complete with the enclosing headlands of the harbour and steep cliffs covered with boxwood, just as Apollonius and Virgil described it. You can find more details on the individual locations of the towns, cities, mountains and so on of Atalanta's voyage, as well as the sources on which I drew for them, in the Glossary of Places (see page 343).

The kingdom of Colchis deserves a special mention. On the one hand, it seems that the Greeks did at some point pin down a geographical location for the Golden Fleece on the shores of the Black Sea around the Phasis river (modern Rioni); as Richard Hunter observes, 'At least as early as the seventh century BC the kingdom [of the Golden Fleece] was identified with Colchis in modern Georgia, where the river Phasis formed the traditional eastern boundary of the known world.' However, even though the archaeological record shows an independent Bronze Age culture in Colchis, no Mycenean Greek (i.e. Late Bronze Age) artefacts have been discovered in the area – therefore making it likely that there was no significant contact between the Greeks and the kingdom of Colchis during this period (c. 1600–c. 1100 BCE). It has been suggested instead that, in the light of later Greek settlements of the Black Sea coast in the seventh and sixth centuries BCE, the myth of Jason and the Argonauts was retrospectively attached to an area that, at the later period, was undergoing increasing exploration and trade with thriving cultural centres like that of Vani. I have attempted to infuse as much of the native Colchian Bronze Age culture into my descriptions of Colchis as I could: both in the details of the building of Dedali's home and the implements she would have used, all of which come from the archaeological discoveries from Bronze Age Colchis as given in Otar Lordkipanidse's *Archäologie in Georgien*.

As for the legendary Golden Fleece, theories abound as to what it might have been, from an allegorical symbol of royal power and divinity to recent suggestions that it was perhaps a historical representation of local methods of panning for gold. As with the richest myths, the Golden Fleece seems to symbolize both the wealth, and the impenetrability, of legend.

If you are interested in finding out more about the world of Atalanta and the Argonauts, take a look at the suggestions for further reading (see page 335), and visit my website, www.emilyhauser.com.

Suggestions for Further Reading

Apollonius' *Argonautica*
Translations from the ancient Greek

Green, Peter. 1997. *The Argonautika: The Story of Jason and the Quest for the Golden Fleece, by Apollonios Rhodios*. Berkeley: University of California Press.

Hunter, Richard. 1993. *Apollonius of Rhodes: Jason and the Golden Fleece (The Argonautica)*. Oxford: Clarendon.

Rieu, E. V. 1959. *Apollonius of Rhodes: The Voyage of Argo*. Harmondsworth: Penguin.

Secondary readings

Gutzwiller, Kathryn J. 2007. *A Guide to Hellenistic Literature*. Malden, MA: Blackwell, 74–84.

Hunter, Richard. 1993. *The Argonautica of Apollonius: Literary Studies*. Cambridge: Cambridge University Press.

— 1996. 'Apollonius Rhodius'. In *The Oxford Classical Dictionary*, edited by Simon Hornblower and Antony Spawforth. Oxford: Oxford University Press, 124–6.

The myth of Jason, the Argonauts and the Golden Fleece

Colavito, Jason. 2014. *Jason and the Argonauts through the Ages*. Jefferson NC: McFarland.

Lordkipanidse, Otar. 2001. 'The Golden Fleece: Myth, Euhemeristic Explanation and Archaeology'. *Oxford Journal of Archaeology* 20 (1): 1–38.

Okrostsvaridze, A., N. Gagnidze, and K. Akimidze. 2014. 'A modern field investigation of the mythical "gold sands" of the ancient Colchis Kingdom and "Golden Fleece" phenomena'. *Quaternary International*, 20 November 2014.

Wood, Michael. 2005. *In Search of Myths and Heroes: Jason and the Golden Fleece*. Dir. Sean Smith. TV Series: BBC 4/PBS.

Atalanta

Barringer, Judith M. 1996. 'Atalanta as Model: The Hunter and the Hunted'. *Classical Antiquity* 15 (1): 48–76.

Harder, Ruth, and Anne Ley. 2016. 'Atalante'. In *Brill's New Pauly*, edited by Hubert Cancik and Helmuth Schneider. Brill Online, 2016.

Mayor, Adrienne. 2014. 'Atalanta, the Greek Amazon'. In *The Amazons: Lives and Legends of Warrior Women across the Ancient World*. Princeton: Princeton University Press, 1–16.

Bronze Age Greece

Adrymi-Sismani, Vassiliki. 2007. 'Iolkos: Myth, Archaeology and History'. *Phasis* 10 (1): 20–32.

Chadwick, John. 1976. *The Mycenaean World*. Cambridge: Cambridge University Press.

Vermeule, Emily. 1964. *Greece in the Bronze Age*. Chicago: Chicago University Press.

Bronze Age Colchis and its connection to Greece

Braund, David. 1994. *Georgia in Antiquity*. Oxford: Oxford University Press, 8–39.

Hughes, Bettany. 2015. *Caucasian Roots: Episode 1*. Presented on BBC Radio 3, 22 March 2015, available at http://www.bbc.co.uk/programmes/b05mqhb3.

Licheli, Vakhtang. 2007. 'New discoveries in Colchis and an interpretative version'. *Phasis* 10 (1): 111–17.

Lordkipanidse, Otar. 1991. *Archäologie in Georgien: Von der Altsteinzeit zum Mittelalter*. Weinheim: VCH, Acta Humaniora, 93–145.

Bronze Age Calendar

The evidence from ancient Mycenaean Greek tablets for the calendar is fragmentary and difficult to piece together, but various different words have been found that seem to apply to months of the year. Thus we have *wodewijo* – the 'month of roses'; *emesijo* – the 'month of wheat'; *metuwo newo* – the 'month of new wine'; *ploistos* – the 'sailing month'; and so on. Although we have no further clues as to which months these referred to, by matching them to the farming calendar in Hesiod's *Works and Days*, as well as the seasonal growth of plants and crops in Greece, I have amassed the following Bronze Age calendar, which is followed throughout the text:

dios	The Month of Zeus	January
metuwo newo	The Month of New Wine	February
deukijo	The Month of Deukios (?)	March
ploistos	The Month of Sailing	April
amakoto(s)	The Month of the Harvest	May
wodewijo	The Month of Roses	June
emesijo	The Month of Threshing Wheat	July
amakoto(s)	The Month of the Grape Harvest	August
. . .	The Month of Ploughing	September
lapatos	The Month of Rains	October
karaerijo	. . .	November
diwijo	The Month of the Goddess	December

The ancient Greeks of the later period split the hours of daylight into twelve, no matter the time of year – meaning that these so-called 'hours' were longer in summer and shorter in winter. Each hour was named after one of the twelve *Horai*, goddesses of time. Taking the hours of daylight on the summer solstice at the site of Iolcos, modern Volos (14.7 hours), I have divided them into twelve to create an approximation of the hours of the *Horai* below:

Augé	The Hour of Daybreak	06:02
Anatolé	The Hour of the Rising Sun	07:16
Mousiké	The Hour of Music	08:30
Gymnastiké	The Hour of Athletics	09:44
Nymphé	The Hour of the Bath	10:58
Mesémbria	The Hour of the Middle of the Day	12.12
Spondé	The Hour of Offerings	13:26
Életé	The Hour of Prayer	14:40
Akté	The Hour of the Evening Meal	15:54
Hesperis	The Hour of Evening	17:08
Dusis	The Hour of the Setting Sun	18:22
Arktos	The Hour of the Stars	19:36
. . .	The Hours of Night	20:50 until dawn

Glossary of Characters

Most of the characters in this book come from the real myths, legends and literature of the ancient Greeks. Mortals are indicated in **bold**, and immortals in ***bold italics***. Characters I have invented for the purposes of this story are marked with a star *.

Aeëtes – Mythical king of the kingdom of Colchis, home of the Golden Fleece, and father of the legendary Medea.

Aeson – Father of Jason and rightful king of Iolcos, before he was usurped by his half-brother Pelias.

Alcimede – Wife of Aeson and mother of Jason.

Aphrodite – Goddess of love and sex.

Apollo – God of archery, medicine, the sun and poetry.

Ares – God of war.

Argus – Builder of the *Argo* (the ship was named after him) and one of the Argonauts.

Artemis – Goddess of hunting, the moon, childbirth and virginity; twin sister of Apollo.

Atalanta – The narrator of the story, Atalanta is the daughter of Iasus, king of Pagasae, and one of the Argonauts.

Athena – Goddess of wisdom and war.

Bellerophon – A hero from ancient Corinth, and one of the Argonauts.

Castor – Mortal twin brother of Pollux (and half-brother of Helen of Troy), the son of Tyndareus of Sparta; one of the Argonauts.

Clymene – Wife of King Iasus of Pagasae and mother of Atalanta and Lycon.

*Corycia – Atalanta's foster-sister in Kaladrosos, daughter of Tyro and Eurymedon.

*Corythus – Nobleman of Pagasae and Myrtessa's master.

*Dedali – The priestess of Suzona; the name is taken from the Zan (the language of the ancient Colchians) word for 'mother, woman'.

Deucalion – Son of the mythical King Minos of Crete.

Dolius – The name Myrtessa takes when she disguises herself as a slave.

*Eurymedon – Atalanta's foster-father in Kaladrosos.

Fates, the – Three goddesses whose task it is to spin the thread of human life.

*Hantawa – An Anatolian slave, steward of Bellerophon.

Hera – Queen of the gods and wife of Zeus; goddess of marriage and childbirth.

Hermes – The son of Zeus and Maia, Hermes is the messenger god, and god of tricks and thievery.

Hesperides, the – Daughters of the evening, these three nymphs dwelt in their garden at the edge of the world tending the mythical golden apples.

Hippomenes – Sometimes also known as Melanion, Hippomenes is the son of Megareus from Onchestos in Boeotia, and joins Jason as one of the Argonauts.

*Hora – One of the slaves in Corythus' house.

Iasus – King of Pagasae, husband of Clymene and father of Atalanta.

*Illa – The trader with whom Atalanta and Hippomenes stay on their return from Colchis. The name is testified in Anatolian texts.

Iris – Messenger goddess for Hera and goddess of the rainbow; daughter of the sea god Thaumas and the nymph Electra.

Jason – Son of Aeson and heir to the throne of Iolcos, Jason is sent by the usurper Pelias to recover the Golden Fleece and thus leads the voyage of the Argonauts.

Laertes – King of Ithaca (father of Odysseus) and one of the Argonauts.

*Leon – Atalanta's foster-brother in Kaladrosos, son of Tyro and Eurymedon.

Lycon – Son of King Iasus and Queen Clymene of Pagasae, and one of the Argonauts.

*Maia – Atalanta's foster-sister in Kaladrosos, daughter of Tyro and Eurymedon.

*Mala – The wife of the trader with whom Atalanta and Hippomenes stay on their return from Colchis. The name is testified in Anatolian texts.

Medea – The mythical daughter of King Aeëtes of Colchis, who falls in love with Jason and accompanies him back to Greece, only to exact her revenge upon him when he deserts her for another woman.

Meleager – Son of Oeneus, king of Calydon, and one of the Argonauts.

Muses, the – The nine goddesses of poetry and song, daughters of Apollo and the goddess Memory.

*Myrtessa – Slave of Corythus, companion and friend of Atalanta.

*Neda – One of the slaves in Corythus' house.

Nestor – A Greek noble and lord of Pylos; one of the Argonauts.

*Opis – One of the slaves in Corythus' house.

Orpheus – A Greek lord from Pieria in the north of Greece (and one of the Argonauts), Orpheus' song was said to be so enchanting that he could summon the birds and the beasts to him whenever he played.

Peleus – The lord of Phthia in Thessaly and one of the Argonauts; also the father of the legendary Achilles.

Pelias – The half-brother of Aeson and usurper to the throne of Iolcos.

*Philoetius – One of the slaves in Corythus' house.

*Phorbas – A steward of Peleus.

Pollux – Immortal twin brother of Castor (and brother of Helen of Troy), the son of Zeus and Leda; one of the Argonauts.

Poseidon – God of the ocean and brother of Zeus.

*Sarpa – The sister of the trader with whom Atalanta and Hippomenes stay on their return from Colchis. The name is testified in Anatolian texts.

*Telamon – A noble of Crete, son of Deucalion (and thus grandson of the legendary king Minos); the name Atalanta gives as her disguise aboard the *Argo*.

Theseus – Legendary king of Athens in Attica and one of the Argonauts; also famous for defeating the Minotaur in Crete with the help of Ariadne.

*Tyro – Atalanta's foster-mother in Kaladrosos.

Zeus – King of the gods, Zeus is the god of thunder and husband of Hera.

Glossary of Places

Many of the locations visited by Atalanta and the Argonauts in this book are real sites which you can still visit today; most are also described in the myths, legends and literature of the ancient Greeks. Places I have invented for the purposes of this story are marked with a star*.

Achaea – A city state in the north of the Peloponnese in Greece. Its principal city in the Bronze Age was Mycenae, home of Atreus, father of Agamemnon (later commander of the Greeks against Troy) and Menelaus.

Aegean (Sea), the – The part of the Mediterranean Sea that separates the mainland of Greece from what is now the mainland of Turkey.

Aetolia – A city state on the northern coast of the Gulf of Corinth in Greece.

Anatolia – The region later known as Asia Minor, encompassing all of modern Turkey and some of modern Syria and Iraq, bordered on the west by the Aegean Sea and to the east by the Euphrates River, to the north by the Black Sea and to the south by the Mediterranean. It was peopled in the thirteenth century BCE (late Bronze Age) by a number of different groups, from the Masians and Kaskaeans in the north to the vast Hittite Empire that spread across the Anatolian Plateau, to the Trojans, Mysians, Maeonians and Lycians on the western and south-western coast of the Aegean.

Anauros, the – The river running from Mount Pelion past ancient Iolcos.

*Aphussos – A small village on the bay of Pagasae; based on modern Áfissos.

Argos – A city state on the north-east of the Peloponnese in Greece, ruled by Diomedes. The ruins of Argos can still be visited today.

Athens – The major city of Attica, a city state on the Attic peninsula; settled in the Bronze Age and legendary home of Theseus, but not the centre of democracy until the fifth century BCE.

Black Sea, the – The large, subsidiary sea of the Mediterranean, to which it is connected via the strait of the Bosphorus, which divides south-eastern Europe and western Asia. It was bordered in the Bronze Age by Thrace (to the west; modern Turkey and Bulgaria); Anatolia (to the south; modern Turkey); and Colchis (to the east; modern Georgia).

Boeotia – A region in the south-eastern part of central Greece, flanked either side by the Gulf of Euboea and the Gulf of Corinth, in which the cities of Thebes, Orchomenos and Onchestos, among others, were located. Its broad, fertile plains, watered by Lake Copais and several others, meant that it was renowned for its farmland (wheat in particular), and its inhabitants were caricatured in antiquity as stolid, simple farming folk.

Bosphorus, the – The strait lying between the Propontis and the Black Sea, separating the kingdom of Thrace to the west and Anatolia to the east.

Calydon – A city in ancient Anatolia. The Calydonian boar hunt, in which Atalanta was the first to strike the boar, was said to have taken place here; it was the city of the hero Meleager.

Caucasus Mountains, the – See **Kaukasos**.

Colchis – An ancient region located on the eastern coast of the Black Sea in modern Georgia, bordered to the north by the Caucasus Mountains and to the south by the Meskheti Range. Colchis was the mythical site of the kingdom of King Aeëtes and the location of the Golden Fleece. Bronze Age remains have been located throughout the area, and Greek settlements from the seventh century BCE onwards have been discovered in the region, particularly at Vani.

Copais, Lake – The large lake in Boeotia, Greece, on the shores of which the town of Onchestos was built. The lake has now dried up, but the plain, Kopaida, still bears its name.

Corinth – Ancient city on the Gulf of Corinth with ruins well worth visiting, near modern Néa Kórinthos, in the northern Peloponnese; city of the hero Bellerophon.

Crete – The largest of the Greek islands and home to a flourishing Bronze Age Greek culture, most famously at Knossos (the site of which was excavated by Sir Arthur Evans; impressive, if vastly reconstructed, ruins can still be visited today).

Delphi – Said by the Greeks to be the 'belly button of the world', Delphi is still an imposing and beautiful site.

Greece – Homeland of the Greeks, comprising the city states of Achaea, Aetolia, Argos, Attica, Laconia and Thessaly, among others.

Hades – Both the god of the Underworld and the name of the Underworld itself, where the ancients believed that the spirits of the dead went to spend eternity. It was reached by crossing the River Styx in a boat ferried by a man called Charon. There were several different parts to the Underworld: Tartarus, where the wicked were punished, the Elysian Fields, where the heroes went, and the Isles of the Blessed, the ultimate destination and eternal paradise.

Hellespont, the – The narrow strait opposite the ancient city of Troy, now called the Dardanelles.

Hittite Empire, the – One of the largest empires of the Bronze Age, the Hittite Empire reached its zenith in the mid-fourteenth century BCE. It endured until its sudden collapse in around 1200 BCE, around the same time as the destruction of the Bronze Age kingdoms in Greece and the fall of Troy. Its capital was at Hattusa (modern Boğazköy in Turkey).

Imbros – An island, now called Gökçeada, just off the western coast of modern north-west Turkey near the Dardanelles (ancient Hellespont).

Iolcos – Modern Volos, the city of Aeson and, later, his son Jason. Iolcos is mentioned by Homer in the *Iliad*, by Hesiod, Pindar, and many other ancient Greek poets. A Mycenaen town from the fourteenth and thirteenth centuries BCE has recently been excavated in the area of Dimini, including several houses, a central road, a palace and a couple of tombs, suggesting that this may be the site of ancient Iolcos.

Ithaca – A rocky island to the west of mainland Greece ruled by Odysseus.

*Kaladrosos – The village where Atalanta grew up, on the eastern slopes of Mount Pelion (modern Kalamaki).

Kaska – A region of Anatolia, bordering the Black Sea, inhabited by the Kaskaeans, a semi-nomadic tribe who lived at the edge of the Hittite Empire.

Kaukasos, the – The Greek spelling of the Caucasus, the region containing the great mountain system of the same name that spans the Black Sea and the Caspian Sea.

Kissos, the – One of the streams on Mount Pelion.

Kromna – Also spelt Cromna, located at modern Tekkeönü on the Black Sea coast of Turkey; mentioned by Homer in the *Iliad*.

Kytoros – Also spelt Cytorus, this city on the southern shore of the Black Sea (the northern coast of modern Turkey) is mentioned in Homer's *Iliad* and Apollonius' *Argonautica*. The harbour, with its boxwood-covered cliffs, is located at modern-day Gideros in Turkey.

Laconia – The ancient city state in the south-east of the Peloponnese (also known as Lacedaimon or Lacedaimonia), of which Sparta was the major city; home of Tyndareus, father of Castor, Pollux and Helen (later Helen of Troy).

*Lechonia – A town inland from Kaladrosos, towards Iolcos and Pagasae.

Lemnos – An Aegean island to the west of Troy.

Lesbos – A large Aegean island to the south-west of the Troad; later the birthplace of the poet Sappho.

*Makronita – A spring of natural water on the slopes of Mount Pelion above Pagasae.

Masa – A region to the north of the Hittite Empire, adjoining the shores of the Propontis (modern Sea of Marmara).

Meliboea – A town on the eastern coast of Thessaly (modern Melivoia).

Mycenae – A city in the Peloponnese, one of the largest in the ancient Greek Bronze Age world. It was ruled by King Agamemnon and was rediscovered by Heinrich Schliemann in 1876. The ruins of the impressive palace can be seen today. Mycenae was famous for its gold: Homer calls it 'rich in gold'.

Ocean, the – The ancient Greeks believed that the Ocean encircled the whole world like a river around a flat disc of land. The sun and moon were thought to rise and set from the waters of the Ocean.

Olympus, Mount – A mountain in northern Greece and the home of the Olympian gods.

Olynthos – A Bronze Age city in northern Greece, on the modern peninsula of Chalkidiki located near the modern city of the same name.

Onchestos – A Bronze Age city, mentioned in Homer, in the region of Boeotia in mainland Greece. It was located in the territory of Haliartus (modern Aliartos), and was probably located around five kilometres to the east of modern Aliartos, near the basin of Lake Copais – which has now dried up, but is still recognized in the name of the plain where it was located, Kopaida.

Ossa, Mount – A mountain in northern Greece (modern Kissavos), located between Mount Olympus and Mount Pelion. The myth tells that the giants, when they rebelled against the Olympian gods in the Gigantomachy, attempted to pile Mount Pelion on top of Mount Ossa in their attempt to reach the home of the gods.

Pagasae – An ancient coastal harbour city in Thessaly. The name is recorded in Apollonius as the starting point for the Argonauts' voyage, and it is still retained in the modern name of the Pagasetic Gulf, or Pagasitikos in Greek. Pagasae is the home of Atalanta in this book.

Pelion, Mount – A mountain in the south-eastern part of Thessaly in Greece (Pilio in modern Greek), which forms a peninsula around the Pagasetic Gulf. Mythical home of the centaur Chiron and the mountain upon which Atalanta was exposed.

Peparethos – The ancient name for the island of Skopelos, one of the Sporades in the north-west Aegean.

Phasis, the – The river, which either bordered the southern edge of Colchis or ran through its centre, according to various different ancient writers; the modern river Rioni in Georgia.

Phthia – A city state in the north of Greece, in the southernmost part of Thessaly, and home to Peleus (father of Achilles).

Pieria – A region in the north of Greece, beyond Mount Olympus; said to be the home of Orpheus and the Muses.

Propontis, the – The ancient Greek name for the Sea of Marmara, the inland sea that connects the Aegean to the west and the Black Sea to the east. The straits to its south-western end were called the Hellespont (modern Dardanelles), and to the north-east, the Bosphorus.

Pylos – The ancient kingdom of Nestor in the south-west of the Peloponnese; impressive ruins of a Bronze Age palace were discovered nearby, at modern Ano Englianos, and you can still visit them today.

Sesamos – A city on the northern Anatolian coast of the Black Sea (modern Turkey), mentioned by Homer.

Skiathos – The small island just off the tip of the promontory of Mount Pelion.

Sparta – A city in the south of the Peloponnese, ruled at Atalanta's time by Tyndareus; later the home of Menelaus and Helen of Troy.

Styx, the – The river that formed the boundary between Earth and the Underworld; to enter the Underworld the ferryman Charon had to be paid to take the dead across. It was seen as sacred by the gods: they would often swear oaths by the River Styx. Its waters were thought to confer immortality, and it is into the River Styx that Thetis dips her son Achilles in the hope of making him immortal.

*Suzona – A village in the mountains of Colchis. The name is taken from the Zan (ancient Colchian) toponym, *Sužona–.

Thessaly – A large region to the north of Greece, incorporating Mount Olympus, Mount Ossa and Mount Pelion, as well as the cities of Pagasae and Iolcos.

Thrace – The mountainous region to the north of Thessaly in Greece.

Troy – The ancient city of King Priam, situated at the north-western coast of modern Turkey beside the Hellespont (modern Dardanelles), which was besieged by the Greek forces of King Agamemnon around the twelfth century BCE. It was rediscovered by Heinrich Schliemann in 1871 on the hill of Hisarlık in north-western Turkey, and its ruins can be visited today.

Underworld, the – Also called Hades, this was where the ancients believed that the spirits of the dead went to spend eternity. It was reached by crossing the River Styx in a boat ferried by Charon. There were several different parts to the Underworld: Tartarus, where the wicked were punished, the Elysian Fields, where the heroes went, and the Isles of the Blessed, the eternal paradise.

About the Author

Born in Brighton and brought up in Suffolk, **Emily Hauser** studied Classics at Cambridge, where she was taught by Mary Beard, and completed a PhD at Yale University. She is now a Junior Fellow at Harvard University. *For the Most Beautiful* – the first book in the Golden Apple trilogy – was her debut novel and retells the story of the siege of Troy. Her second, *For the Winner*, is a brilliant reimagining of the myth of Atalanta and the legend of Jason, the Argonauts and the search for the Golden Fleece.

To find out more, visit her website: www.emilyhauser.com